# APRIL'S GRAVE
*and*
# CALL IN THE NIGHT

# SUSAN HOWATCH

# APRIL'S GRAVE
## AND
## CALL IN
## THE NIGHT

STEIN AND DAY / *Publishers* / New York

# APRIL'S GRAVE

# ONE

## I

Marney had not thought about the Conway twins for a long time. He knew that Karen, the elder twin, was working in New York and that she had neither sought a divorce from his friend Neville nor even acknowledged Neville's maintenance payments by so much as a Christmas card, but Karen had seemed remote, part of a buried past which had no relation at all to the present, and it had never occurred to Marney until he was standing by the window of his hotel room and staring out over Central Park that Karen was the only person he knew in the entire city.

He had just concluded a successful working-holiday, lecturing at five Canadian universities, and had visited a friend at Harvard before flying south to New York. He was booked to sail back to England the next day, but meanwhile he was faced with an evening in Manhattan and was beginning to wish he had stayed overnight in Boston instead. He could have caught an early shuttle flight and still have had plenty of time to reach the docks and board the liner in comfort. Boston would at least have been cooler. Beyond the window and the labored hum of the air-conditioner, the Park shimmered in the heat-haze of a summer evening. Even the trees, Marney noticed with professional interest, were beginning to look as burnt as the worn, parched grass.

Marney always noticed trees. Trees were his business. Sometimes it seemed to him that the world of trees and natural vegetation was a world preferable to the scrabbling ant-heaps

of humanity in which he was forced to live and work daily.
Marney did not like cities, did not like New York. America
had always made him uneasy. It was just as he was trying to
imagine what it could be like to live and work in New York
that he thought of Karen.

He thought of her twin sister April Conway almost simultaneously but so immediate was his rejection of the memory
that the thought was little more than a brief tremor of the
muscles, a small shallow breath, a flicker of some nebulous
emotion in the furthest recesses of his mind. He turned aside
and picked up the phone by the bed.

"May I help you?" said a voice a moment later.

When he had obtained Room Service he ordered a whisky,
and then, remembering that he was a foreigner using incorrect
vocabulary in a foreign language, he amended the order to a
scotch on the rocks. Really, he thought, America was very
exhausting. He sat down on the edge of the bed, an Englishman a long way from home, and thought of the solitary peace
of his flat by the river at St. George's Square, the mellow comfort of his office near Birdcage Walk, the pub where he and
Neville would go for a sandwich at lunchtime . . . It was
three years now since Karen had left Neville and returned to
America. She had written to Neville's lawyers to inform them
of her address and give instructions that maintenance payments were not necessary as she had returned to her former
job on the staff of one of the huge magazines dedicated to the
young career woman. Neville had made the alimony payments
just the same. Neville would, thought Marney. It would be
intolerable for Neville to realize that Karen could exist inde-
pendently of him and that he could give her nothing whatsoever, not even money. He would rather pay her the unwanted
money than face the fact that there was no longer anything
she required of him.

The waiter arrived with the scotch.

Later, after he had finished the drink, Marney stood up
restlessly and went back to the window to look at the trees.
He supposed he should have dinner. The Americans, he knew,
dined early, but unfortunately his stomach, trained as it was

on English eating habits, was not hungry. He decided to order another drink.

He meditated for a long time over his second scotch and wondered what he should do. He knew all the signs by this time and was far too intelligent not to admit his state of mind to himself. If he stayed in the room much longer he would remain there the whole evening and get very drunk. He always got drunk when he thought of the Conway twins. He must go out, he told himself, go out, find a good restaurant, perhaps meet a charming companion . . . The scotch was already making him unrealistic. He was in his forties, but looked older and had none of Neville's dark good looks or tailored elegance. "Charming companions," such as he envisaged them, were not acquired in the course of a single evening by the crook of a little finger.

He suddenly realized that he was appallingly lonely. On the strength of this realization he ordered another drink, and then in a moment of panic at his weakness he fumbled with the Manhattan telephone directory by his bedside and began to search among the columns for Karen's phone number.

He could not find it, and then as his third scotch arrived and he began to sip it, he wondered if Karen had reverted to her maiden name on returning to New York. He began to search through the Conways, and suddenly he saw her name and the eastside address in the seventies. He stood staring at her name for a moment while his memories clouded his mind and sought to overwhelm him, and presently he found he was not thinking of the Conway twins at all, but of his own friend, Karen's estranged husband, Neville Bennett.

He thought of Neville for a long time.

At last he picked up the receiver and asked the reception desk to dial Karen's number.

The line began to ring, and he listened to the loud long buzz, so different from the soft purr of an English phone. It rang three times before she picked up the receiver, and he heard again the low attractive voice he remembered so well. Her voice was exactly the same as April's, the only identical feature shared by unidentical twins.

"Hello?"

"Karen?" He pronounced her name with the long English "a," the pronunciation she had used in England, and knew at once from her sharp intake of breath that he had already given himself away. "Karen, this is Marney."

There was a short absolute silence. Then she said slowly: "Marney!" but he could not tell whether she was pleased or sorry.

He heard himself stammer some explanation about his lecture tour and how he was sailing back to England on the next day. "I—I was wondering . . . Just on the off-chance, of course—well, are you doing anything tonight? I thought perhaps we might have dinner . . . Of course, I realize it's very short notice, but—"

"No," she said. "I'm not doing anything tonight."

"Then—perhaps—" He could feel himself reddening as he spoke. "Would you care to have dinner with me?"

"That would be very nice," she said, her voice still charming, but as carefully expressionless as the clichés she selected to accept his invitation. "Thank you."

"I'll call for you at your flat, then," he said, and conscientiously correcting himself added: "Your apartment, I mean. Would it be too soon if I came in half an hour's time?"

"No, I can be ready by then." He heard a slight change in her voice and caught his first glimpse of her astonishment at the unexpectedness of his call. "This—this is such a surprise, Marney, please forgive me if I sound a little dazed. How is everyone in England?"

"Oh, fine." He was sure she was going to ask about Neville. He was so sure that when her question came it took him by surprise.

"How's April?" she said.

There was a silence.

The phone would have slipped in his clammy hands but he was holding the receiver so tightly that his knuckles hurt.

"April?" he said after a long while.

"Isn't she still in England?"

"April?" he said. "In England?" He tried to pull himself together. "You mean she isn't back in America?"

There was a pause. Then: "I haven't seen her since the day

I left Neville," Karen said. "I assumed she had stayed on in England."

"We all thought she'd gone back to America."

"You mean no one's seen her or heard of her for the past three years?"

"Haven't you?"

"No, of course not! I guessed—" She stopped. Then: "But that's extraordinary, Marney! Where on earth can she be?"

And it was only then, more than three years after her disappearance, that it was first realized April Conway was missing.

## II

Karen had been trying not to think about her twin sister April since the day she had decided to try not to think of Neville Bennett any more. Now, as she replaced the receiver after speaking to Marney, she discovered that her memories of both of them were scarcely less painful even now after three years. The realization was so vivid and so unpleasant that for a long moment she merely remained exactly where she was in the still room, but at last she left the couch and went to look for a cigarette.

Of course, she had thought of April from time to time and had never been foolish enough to suppose that she would not. One could not simply forget a sister, let alone a twin sister. But she had made up her mind that she had no wish to see her again. She had left April in England; let her stay there, she had thought at the time. What did it matter? She was past caring what April did and wanted only to get away, to try to pick up the threads of her old life which she had abandoned so readily when she had first met Neville Bennett.

But she would not think of Neville. Not just yet. It was painful enough to think of April, to think and remember . . .

She found a cigarette, lit it, and tried to focus her thoughts on the present. She must be ready when Marney arrived in

half an hour's time. It was kind of him to have called. Marney
had always been kind. In the old days she had been rather
fond of him.

Moving quickly into her bedroom, she selected an outfit to
wear for the evening, shed her working clothes, and took off
her make-up to reapply it afresh. There really wasn't much
time. She worked quickly and deftly, and the concentration
on the familiar motions helped to still her confused thoughts.
In the end she was ready on time and Marney was late, so she
lit another cigarette and in spite of all her will-power, allowed
herself to think of Neville.

Neville Bennett. She could still remember her amused
astonishment when they had met for the first time. There had
been a party in a chic apartment near Washington Square; a
friend of hers had married a lecturer at the University.
"Darling," the friend had screeched to her above the roar of
the cocktails, "a wonderful man . . . *must* meet him . . .
English professor—botanical science, darling—devoted to trees
. . . *so* sweet . . ." And Karen had turned, expecting to see a
whitehaired, stooping scholar, and had come face to face with
all six feet of the charm and grace and frank sexual interest
which emanated from Neville Bennett.

He was thirty-eight and a widower. His wife had died in a
road accident two years earlier shortly after the birth of their
son, and because Neville seldom referred to her, Karen had
assumed that it still hurt him to be reminded of his loss. In
fact, as she discovered later, his silence stemmed not from
grief but from guilt. He had become bored with his shy, quiet,
self-effacing wife whom he had married in the belief that an
attraction of opposites was likely to prove long-lasting, and
although he had done his best to conceal his boredom he had
found it increasingly difficult to do so. He had, it was true,
made great efforts to be a satisfactory husband, and to some
extent he had been rewarded for his efforts when his son was
born; somewhat to his surprise he had been fascinated by the
baby, so intrigued by its newness and helplessness that he had
automatically responded with more warmth towards its
mother, but before he had had the chance to attempt a new
beginning with his wife she had been knocked down while

crossing a London street and had died before reaching hospital. This abrupt termination of his marriage was distressing enough, but what was even more distressing was that he now felt guiltier than ever about his secret boredom before the arrival of the baby. It was as if fate had deprived him of the opportunity to turn over a new leaf and had left him instead with a handful of useless good intentions. As the months passed, he spoke about his wife less and less until, by the time he had met Karen, he so seldom mentioned his marriage that for a long while she had thought he was a bachelor.

He had certainly behaved like a bachelor. It had not taken her long to realize that Neville was enjoying his new life as a single man so much by then that to persuade him to change his status a second time would be very difficult. However, she was sufficiently mature to know how to play her cards correctly and at last, after many anxious moments, several exasperating delays, and more than one occasion when she had wished they had never met, she flew to England for the wedding.

They were married in London at the Savoy Chapel, and Marney was best man. Neville's unmarried sister Leonie, who had been keeping house for him in Cambridge since his first wife's death, welcomed Karen politely, and the child, who was still little more than a baby, accepted her with enthusiasm. As for April, she hadn't even bothered to send a telegram. She was still in Hollywood at that time, still concentrating on being photographed at premières and dating "useful" people. The only member of Karen's family who had been present at the wedding had been Karen's brother Thomas, then living in Paris. Thomas was considered the black sheep of the family by his brothers who had all settled down on Minnesota farms and married local girls; he spent his time seeing the world and working as an actor or film extra to finance his travels.

I wonder, thought Karen, as she waited for Marney that evening, whether Thomas has heard from April during the last three years. It was unlikely, since both April and Thomas had long been in the habit of disappearing for long stretches of time, and neither of them were in touch with the family in Minnesota, let alone with each other, but it was still possible. Since they were both on the fringes of show business, Thomas might have heard some whisper of gossip on the grapevine.

By chance she had his current address. He had sent her a birthday card a week ago from Rome.

"Filming a hokum epic here," he had scribbled. "They've dug up a bible story again. What would scriptwriters do without that book? I've got a part in an orgy scene, Sodom-and-Gomorrah style. I have to sprawl on a couch, toy with a leg of chicken and leer at an Italian slave-girl. Very good pay, and the slave-girl's not bad either. I'll be here till the 20th—mail me a line or two if you get the chance."

Thomas had never liked Neville. She remembered Thomas's arrival in England for the wedding and his first meeting with his new brother-in-law.

"Rather a rolling stone," said Neville afterwards. His voice was carefully devoid of contempt, but she knew nonetheless that he was contemptuous. Neville, who had been a success all his life, had no patience with people who were by his standards failures.

"Kind of a smooth operator," said Thomas to her in private. He took pains to sound casual and unconcerned, so that there was no risk of her taking offense. "More like a business tycoon than a professor. Are you happy?"

Half-annoyed, she assured him that she was. Neville had, by this time, left academic life and had begun working for the government in London. He had bought a beautiful house at Richmond and Karen had been busy both with her new home and with her small step-son who was then two-and-a-half years old. The child was still very small and it was easy to believe that at birth he had been so minute that his father had described him as being no bigger than a pinch of snuff. The comment had not been forgotten; even after his christening the nickname had lingered on.

It was just after Snuff's fourth birthday when April had come to England. Karen had already been worrying about her marriage for some months, but had managed to convince herself that she was worrying unnecessarily; although it had certainly seemed to her that Neville was now taking greater

pleasure than usual in talking to attractive women at the
parties they went to, she told herself that her imagination was
too vivid and it was foolish to suspect when there was no
cause for suspicion. And then, suddenly, April had arrived,
and her suspicions had grown to such monstrous proportions
that finally there had been nothing else left to do but to prove
the suspicions justified.

"The bitch!" Thomas had commented with his customary
frankness, but not everyone had held the same views on the
subject. Neville, for example, had liked April at once; she was
a suitably admiring audience, and Neville, like most men,
loved to be admired. Marney had been reserved and withdrawn; April's unabashed femininity had made him shy, although Karen had suspected at the time that he admired
April more than he cared to admit. Neville's sister Leonie had
been frankly disapproving. Within a short time, Karen had
begun to realize dimly that her relationship with her husband
was deteriorating much more rapidly than before.

The buzzer rang in the kitchen. Recalled with a painful
wrench to the present, she went to answer it and heard the
doorman say from the lobby: "A Dr. West is here to see you,
ma'am."

"Tell him to come up."

She had not seen Marney since before she had left Neville.
She wondered how much he had changed.

The doorbell rang and, after glancing at herself quickly in
the mirror, she went to open the door.

He was there, looking just the same. And it was the sight
of Marney which made all her old longing for Neville surge
within her again, and she realized with mingled horror and
hopelessness that she still loved him.

III

They dined at the Tower Suite and went on afterwards to
the Plaza for drinks. They had talked of Neville, of Neville's

sister Leonie, of the child. Leonie was apparently acting again
as Neville's housekeeper as well as looking after Snuff.
"Neville's taken a lease on a carriage house, very charming,
off Kensington High Street." They had talked of Marney's
work, reminding each other of the coincidence which had led
years ago to himself and Neville working in an advisory
capacity for the same government-owned concern. "I still have
affiliations with the Varsity and often wish I'd never left
teaching, but Neville's in his element. He's better in this job
than he was with the students." They talked of Karen's job, of
New York and London, of current events, of other people
they knew, and finally when there was no one and nothing
else left to talk about, Karen said:

"It's very odd about April."

It seemed almost as if he had been waiting for her to introduce the subject; she saw his features relax and guessed he
was glad she had spoken of April again without reticence.

"Haven't your parents heard anything of her during the past
three years?"

"I'm sure they haven't heard a word. I've been back every
year for Thanksgiving and April was never mentioned. She
hurt them a lot, you know, by voluntarily cutting herself off
from them. And my brothers—the ones who live in Minnesota—
never mentioned her."

"What about your brother Thomas?"

"I thought I would write and ask him if he's heard anything.
There's just a possibility that he may have some idea where
she is."

"Haven't you asked him before if he knew where she was?"

"I haven't seen him since the business with April three years
ago, and he's a bad correspondent. I've spoken to him a couple
of times on the phone, but each time it was long-distance and
we didn't have time to do more than confirm that neither of
us had any sensational news of her. I knew the affair with
Neville had come to nothing because Neville wrote and told
me it was finished, but I didn't know where she'd gone afterwards. To be honest I didn't want to know. I didn't even
want to talk about her with Thomas."

There was a pause. Marney took another sip of his Benedictine.

Karen said casually: "Neville mentioned in his letter that she didn't stay at the farm long after I left."

He did not look at her. "She left the same day."

"Was Neville much upset?"

"I think Neville had had quite enough by that time," said Marney soberly. "When he found her clothes were gone from the farm and that she had walked out, I think he was more relieved than sorry."

Karen was aware of bewilderment. "But when did she leave?"

"No one was quite sure. I suppose it must have been some time while you were lost and Neville was searching for you. April would have been alone at the farm then, if you remember." He paused delicately. "After Neville left the farm to look for you, April must have packed her bags, rowed across the lake and thumbed a lift from a passing car. One of the two boats was found on the other side of the lake afterwards, so that would seem to confirm the theory."

Karen was silent. She had no wish to recall the past, but against her will she was remembering each event which had led up to the ultimate disaster; she saw again April in London, April flirting with Neville at the house in Richmond, her brother Thomas arriving unexpectedly from abroad and trying to warn her what was happening—as if she were blind and could not see it for herself! Poor Thomas, he had been so upset. Then had come the discovery that April's plane ticket for a weekend in Paris was in fact a train reservation to Scotland where Neville had important business in the Highlands. She remembered how she had followed April north a few hours later, and how, unknown to her, Thomas had done the same thing, remembered their meeting at the little hotel at Kildoun, the tortuous journey in the hired rowing boat across the lake to the small farm where Neville stayed whenever he was in Scotland on business. He had been there with April. The shock of that confrontation had been so great, despite the fact that she had known what she was going to find, that Karen had barely paused to speak to them. She had rushed out over the

moors, not knowing or caring where she was going, until
eventually she had lost herself in the forestry plantation, in
the dark silent acres of Plantation Q, and when Neville had
found her three hours later she had insisted on being taken
to the foresters' lodge where she had phoned Thomas in
Kildoun and asked him to come at once to take her away. He
came; they left together, and after that she had never seen
either Neville or April again.

"I'm sorry," Marney was saying awkwardly, "perhaps we
should talk about something else."

"No, I don't mind talking about it now after all this time."
She lit a cigarette with a steady hand. "I was just puzzled that
April had left the farm—and Neville—so suddenly and vanished
into the blue. It seems odd somehow, unlike her."

"Well, now you come to mention it," said Marney, "I suppose it was. But at the time I don't think it occurred to any of
us that there was a mystery involved. We were all too glad
to be rid of her, and were too upset by all that had taken
place. I suppose that's why we merely accepted her departure
and didn't stop to question it in any way."

"Yes, yes, I can understand that. I guess Neville hasn't
heard any word from her since?"

He hesitated. "I doubt it."

She wondered for a moment to what extent Neville would
have confided in him.

It had always seemed odd to her that Neville and Marney
were such friends. Marney had appeared to her to be a typical
bachelor, ascetic, scholarly and self-contained, whereas
Neville . . .

"I'm surprised Neville hasn't wanted to get a divorce and
remarry," she heard herself say before she could stop herself,
and then immediately regretted the remark. The champagne
at dinner followed by the liqueurs seemed to have loosened
her tongue.

"Really?" said Marney. "One might almost say the same
thing about you, my dear." And she was just realizing with
relief that the liquor had made him even less reserved than
she was when he added: "Why haven't you married again?

A woman like you ought to be married. Didn't you ever think of getting a divorce from Neville?"

"Yes, I thought of it."

"And decided to stay married to him?"

"There was no one else I wanted to marry. And I couldn't face the prospect of putting the divorce wheels in motion."

"Hope you're not still in love with him," said Marney, finishing his Benedictine. She saw now that he was much more inebriated than she had supposed earlier. "Women always fall for Neville. It's such a mistake. At least he's fond of the child. That's something, I suppose. I'm glad he's fond of the child."

"Yes, Neville was devoted to Snuff—and so was I!" She sighed. "How I'd love to see Snuff again! I've thought of him so often."

"I'm sure you have." He hesitated before adding: "Another drink?"

"No, really, Marney, no more. It's been a lovely evening, and I've enjoyed seeing you again."

He saw her back to her apartment. She half-wondered if she should ask him in for coffee, but he solved the problem for her by taking her hand in his and thanking her for making the evening so successful. "I hope I'll see you again one day before too long," he said, and much to her astonishment leant over and kissed her clumsily on the cheek. "Goodbye, Karen. God bless you."

And he was gone, his footsteps receding towards the elevator, and she was left alone in the solitude of her apartment.

She undressed, went to bed, and lay awake for a long while. At length when it became patently obvious to her that sleep was out of the question, she got up and wrote two letters, the first to her brother Thomas in Rome, and the second to her friend and former room-mate Melissa Fleming who now lived in London. She wanted to ask Melissa if she could stay with her during any possible future visit to England.

## IV

Melissa Fleming was English but had worked in New York for two years and had met Karen there before Karen had met Neville. The two of them had shared an apartment in the Gramercy Park area for a year; they had not been close friends, but Karen was the kind of person who could get on well with nearly everyone, and Melissa, who needed a room-mate for economic reasons, was quick to realize that Karen was one of the few women whom she might just possibly be able to live with. On the whole, Melissa did not find her own sex congenial companions. As Karen was then a stranger to New York she knew few people; she was prepared to like Melissa and Melissa was prepared to like her. The friendship proceeded cautiously for several months while both of them continued to lead their separate lives as far as possible, and only began to founder when Neville arrived on the scene and Melissa realized that Karen attracted him more than she did.

Melissa prided herself on her sex-appeal; the idea of playing second fiddle to Karen was definitely not appealing.

However, before the friendship dissolved amidst the destructive atmosphere of jealousy, first Neville and then Karen left for England and Melissa resigned herself to the fact that Neville was completely out of her reach. Having been salvaged so unexpectedly, the friendship flourished again by letter as Melissa remained in New York and Karen settled down as Neville's wife four thousand miles away. Later Melissa inherited a sizeable legacy which induced her to return to England and start up a business there, but by that time Karen had left Neville and had returned to America so that the width of the Atlantic Ocean still lay between them. Gradually their letters to one another became more infrequent and their friendship more nominal. In the end Melissa, immersed in her new business, no longer bothered to write.

Melissa was a designer. She had worked in fashion houses, had some flair and a considerable amount of business acumen. The providential legacy was used to open a boutique off Knightsbridge, and because Melissa was prepared to cultivate the right people and had certain valuable contacts dating from the days when she had been to the right schools, she soon had the right clientele. The boutique had been highly successful now for nearly two years and Melissa lived above the shop in a modern, sophisticated and expensive flat.

She was not married. Her one and only venture into matrimony had been an adolescent mistake and she preferred not to talk about it.

When the letter from Karen came, she was first conscious of a slight feeling of guilt because she had not written to Karen for many months and had more or less decided to lose touch with her. After all, thought Melissa practically, one couldn't keep in touch with *everybody;* besides, Karen seemed to belong to the past now, and Melissa was much too interested in the present and the future to have time for sentimental memories.

She opened the letter and was conscious of a shock. It had never crossed her mind that Karen would come back to London to see the child, and yet, Melissa had to admit, it was a perfectly logical thing to do. Karen had always been exceptionally fond of her small step-son, particularly since she had had no child of her own.

She glanced back at the letter. Karen was frank in asking if she could stay at the flat. That could be very awkward. Well, perhaps awkward was too strong a word, but the situation might possibly prove embarrassing.

Still frowning slightly, Melissa picked up the white telephone receiver and began to make a call to Neville Bennett with whom she happened, at that moment, to be having an affair.

## V

Leonie Bennett, who now acted as Neville's housekeeper, was only two years older than her brother but looked and behaved as if she were very much the elder sister entrusted with a brother who needed all the care and attention she could give him. Her parents had left her a large amount of money at their deaths, so she had never had to work for a living but had instead passed her time either by zealously pursuing her favorite outdoor activities, gardening and golf, or else playing endless rubbers of bridge at the club to which she belonged in London. Except for the eighteen months during which Neville had been married to Karen, she had been obliged to look after her nephew since soon after his arrival in the world, and this had resulted in the number of her social activities being reduced. However, the acquisition of a Swiss nanny while the child was still very young had helped the situation, and now that he was at school she was once more free to do as she pleased. As for the house, she enjoyed running it and gained great pleasure from looking after her brother as lavishly as possible, but she did miss having a garden; window boxes were a poor substitute and nothing interesting would flourish in the little backyard of the carriage house, although she had tried several times to grow roses in tubs. But in spite of this disadvantage she was content. She was very fond of her brother, and no doubt it was because of Neville that Leonie had become so fond of the child, for she had never been greatly interested in children before and had certainly never shared Karen's absorption in Neville's son.

She was reminded of Karen with an unexpected jolt when not merely one but two American letters appeared on the mat after Neville had left for the office that morning. The mail had been arriving progressively later all that week and she had just returned to the house from taking Snuff to school when the mailman pushed the letters through the front-door slat on to the floor below.

She went to pick them up and saw the American stamps at once.

One letter was for Neville, the other for the child.

Leonie paused, consumed with curiosity. She knew very well that Karen had not written to Neville since leaving him three years ago. What would she be writing about now? Leonie seriously debated whether to steam Neville's letter open and then reseal it, but finally decided against this idea as she felt sure Neville would somehow find her out. Neville was so clever. After simmering with curiosity for another unbearable half hour, she had a brainwave. The child would never know. She would open the letter to Snuff.

Five minutes later, the letter in her hand, she was dialing the number of Neville's office with trembling fingers.

VI

The child attended school at a French Lycée near his home and had been there just long enough to have a confused but increasing grasp of the French language. He had already decided that the nickname Snuff was the kind of adult absurdity that would make his life difficult among other children, and had rechristened himself with an extravagantly French name which he had learnt from his former Swiss nanny. He did not like to use his own name, which was Neville. Neville was a special name with special connotations, much too sacred for his own everyday use.

That afternoon his Aunt Leonie met him after school as usual and took him home under her personal supervision. He was already beginning to regard this as yet another embarrassing example of adult absurdity, but experience had taught him that his aunt was easily upset and he knew better than to provoke a new emotional crisis.

"Good afternoon, Aunt," he said politely as they met outside the school, and remembered to smile. If he did not smile she would assume he was unhappy and would start to worry about him.

Aunt worried about everything. Given half a chance she would worry if there was nothing to worry about.

"Snuff darling . . ." To his profound distaste she even embraced him within sight of his schoolfriends. He disentangled himself very firmly and hoped no one had noticed.

Aunt was tall, too tall for a woman, and rather thin with no curves, and had a dark bony face with teeth and a nose.

"Darling, I've got some very unexpected news for you. You mustn't be too worried or upset. It's really very exciting." Her voice was a shade higher than usual; he looked at her with extreme suspicion.

"It's about your step-mother—about Aunt Karen."

"Oh yes?"

She was twisting her gloves nervously. "You know she went abroad three years ago."

"Yes, of course. She's living in New York." He looked at her with astonishment. Surely she remembered that Aunt Karen wrote to him and sent him beautiful presents on his birthday and at Christmas? For a long time now he had been able to read the letters all by himself.

Aunt said in a rush: "She's just written a letter to Daddy— and there's a letter for you as well which I opened ready to read to you as soon as you came home." And then as Snuff opened his mouth to protest that he liked to open all his letters himself, she said rapidly: "She's going to come and stay in London for a while."

The news was so surprising that he even forgot to be angry. "Really?" he said with interest. "You mean Aunt Karen's coming to London soon?"

"She wants to see you again, darling."

Snuff failed to see anything odd about this. "Does Daddy know yet that she's coming to London? Did he get the letter yet?"

"I telephoned him at the office but he was out. I had to leave a message."

"With Uncle Marney?"

Aunt looked taken-aback. She often telephoned the office and asked to speak to Neville even when she knew Neville wasn't there. Snuff had noticed this long before he started school, but he supposed Aunt had not realized he had noticed. He always wondered why she didn't ask for Marney directly if she wanted to talk to him so much.

"Well, that's all right, isn't it?" he said defensively. "Uncle Marney will give Daddy the message."

"Oh yes," said Aunt. She sounded a little absent-minded. "Marney will tell him."

## VII

Neville had had a long business lunch at the Athenaeum with a Scottish land-owner interested in forestry techniques. By the time he returned to his office it was nearly three o'clock. As he had been out most of the morning he was not altogether surprised at the long list of telephone calls which had accumulated since his departure.

"Your sister called twice," said his secretary. "The first time I switched her to Dr. West's office and the second time she just left a message for you to phone her. Dr. West also wanted to speak to you, by the way. Then Miss Fleming called twice, first this morning and then again just now . . ."

Melissa. He wondered what she wanted. He hoped she did not intend to be difficult or create undignified feminine scenes. He was gradually easing himself out of his relationship with her, and with great tact and a large amount of diplomatic skill was stealthily cutting each of the emotional bonds which had once linked them together. She had appeared to accept this so undemurringly that he had assumed the wish to terminate their affair was mutual, but it was hard to be entirely sure; perhaps it was safer to assume that she would enjoy an emotional scene if the opportunity for one arose.

"Get Marney for me, would you?" he said absent-mindedly to his secretary. He would leave the chore of answering

Melissa's calls till later. Taking off his raincoat, he shook the
water from his umbrella into the elegant Adam fireplace and
adjusted his dark tie in the old-fashioned Victorian mirror.

Vanity, thought his secretary.

"Dr. West? One moment, please, I have Professor Bennett
for you."

Neville took the receiver from her. "Thanks . . . Marney?"

The room was still and peaceful, the silence broken only by
the rain slewing against the pane and blurring the view into
St. James's Park. His secretary was moving out of the room.
The door closed softly behind her but he did not hear it.

Suddenly he did not even hear the rain on the window any
more. His eyes still watched the trees swaying in the park beyond, but he did not see them. He was in another land altogether, in another time long ago, and there were lamps
glowing in a room of a small Highland farm and long shadows
veiling a face he thought he would never see again, and outside the sky was still light with the afterglow and the lake had
the opaque, mysterious quality of darkened glass.

"I'll talk to you later, Marney. I see a call's come through on
my other line."

He slammed down the receiver and held it there for a long
moment. Then with great deliberation he put on his raincoat
again, picked up his umbrella and walked out of his office
without even telling his secretary that he would not be back
that day.

## VIII

In a hotel in Rome not far from the Via Veneto, a letter with
an American stamp was handed to the young American actor
who was staying there. Letters from home were a rare luxury
for Thomas Conway. He put it in his pocket, strolled to the
nearest outdoor cafe and then at a table bathed in sunshine
and with his cup of capuccino before him he opened the en-

velope and read the letter inside. Ten minutes later he was back in his hotel and writing a reply.

Thanks for the letter. It was good hearing from you again—too bad I didn't understand a word you said! What's all this about April? I couldn't make you out at all. Do I think something's happened to her, you say? Sure I think something's happened to her! She's Sheik Whoosis' nine hundredth wife or she's entertaining sailors in Rio de Janeiro or she's decorating some fancy whorehouse in Bel-Air. So who cares? I wish to God you'd quit worrying about her and let her take her own primrose path to wherever she wants to go. You say it sounds as if she treated Neville badly. Good! It was about time someone did. I think it's a great idea for you to make a trip to Europe to see the kid, and with any luck I can fix things so that I'll be in England to see you. Be sure and let me know when you plan to come. Incidentally, I don't know whether you're planning on a reconciliation with Neville, but I wouldn't get too sold on that idea, if I were you. It's none of my business, of course, but all I can say is that any man who leaves you for a flirtation with April deserves all he gets, and I wouldn't like to think that all he gets includes a reconciliation. You look after yourself and don't get taken for a ride by a lot of smooth talk, or what the English so politely call charm. And stop worrying about that sister of ours. What does it matter if no one's seen her for three years? I haven't noticed anyone weeping and beating their breasts in lamentation.

Seeya!

LOVE, THOMAS

# TWO

## I

When Neville left the office he walked through St. James's Park to Buckingham Palace and then across the Mall and through Green Park to Piccadilly. The rain had stopped and the evening was not unpleasant; St. James's Park was a mass of summer blooms, and the beauty of the lush grass and thick-leaved trees soothed his mind and made him feel more relaxed. He reached the Ritz, drank two double whiskies and felt almost normal. Finally he found a cab and within a quarter of an hour was unlocking the front door of his house in Adam and Eve Mews.

The letter with the American stamp lay waiting for him on the hall table.

Leonie came out of the kitchen. "Neville—"

"Yes, yes, there's a letter from Karen. I saw it." He knew he sounded irritable, but this was not unusual as he found his sister an irritating woman and had long ago decided not to feel guilty about it. If it had not been for the child he would never have consented to her acting as his housekeeper, but he wanted more than anything for Snuff to have some semblance of a normal home even though Neville had—by his own stupidity—deprived him of Karen.

"Snuff took the news very well," Leonie was saying. "Very well indeed."

"Why shouldn't he?" He escaped into the drawing-room, his fingers tearing the envelope apart. "Forgive me if I sound abrupt, but I've had a tiresome sort of day."

"Oh, of course, dear—I quite understand."

"Is dinner ready?"

That got rid of her. She went into the kitchen, and he closed the drawing-room door and opened out the sheet of thin air-mail paper.

Dear Neville,

I've decided to take my vacation in Europe this year and hope to spend a few days in London with Melissa. My flight is booked for the 18th, and I'm looking forward to the chance of seeing Snuff again. I'll be in touch with you when I arrive.

KAREN

He stood there, not feeling bitter or angry or unhappy, but merely conscious of disappointment. Finally he tore the letter into tiny fragments, and to be certain that Leonie would not be able to piece them together, he set a match to them in the ash-tray.

He was just watching them burn when the telephone rang.

He picked up the receiver. "Hello?"

"Neville—"

Melissa. His mouth felt dry suddenly.

"Melissa, I can't talk to you now. I'll phone you back later."

He put down the receiver and turned away in relief but the phone immediately rang again. He grabbed the receiver in exasperation.

"Look, Melissa—"

"Must you," she said coldly, "be quite so childish?"

He would have hung up on her but he could never endure to suffer criticism and then deprive himself of the chance to answer back.

"It's not a question of being childish!" he said, much irritated. "I'm sorry I was so short with you just now, but—"

"Short!" she said. "Short! I'd call it by a much stronger word than that! I think it's about time you realized, Neville, that I—"

He sighed. He saw the pattern then, the remorseless inevitability of conciliation, pleading, flattering and finally succeeding, and felt jaded. Not so long ago he had found her attractive, a passable attempt to replace someone irreplaceable, but now all magic was gone and his interest was dwindling into indifference.

"I'm absolutely sick and tired of the way you treat me at times—I've often wondered if I mean anything to you at all."

He had heard it all before. He did not even bother to smother a yawn, but then his boredom drifted into a shaft of pain as he remembered Karen. How could he ever have looked upon Melissa as a replacement for her? He must have been demented. Anyone less suited to replace Karen would have been hard to imagine.

"Thank God you were never in a position to marry me!" she was saying. "At least I was spared that mistake."

He had heard that before too. It meant that somewhere and at some time during the course of their relationship, Melissa had secretly hoped for marriage even though she had always protested just the opposite.

"I don't recall that I ever proposed to you," he said very coolly.

"You often hinted you would get a divorce—"

"Well, I did think about it—"

"—and that when you were free—"

"I never said anything of the kind."

"You implied—"

"You chose to read an implication into my remarks."

She called him a name and hung up.

He shrugged. She would ring back in half an hour. She always did. Even having a lover who infuriated her was better than having no lover at all.

He thought of Karen again. The memory was so clear then that he winced with the pain of it. "I wish I hadn't married you," she had said. "You're clearly unsuited for marriage." And she had gone. He had thought at once, carelessly, not worrying too much: she'll come back. She's bound to come back. She'll calm down and realize that even having an erring husband is better than having no husband at all.

But she had not come back. She had walked on a plane to America and he had never seen her again.

He had a vivid memory then of the horror of it all, the shame of having to admit he had treated his beautiful charming wife so badly that she even refused to have any communication with him, the demoralizing embarrassment of failure in his private life, and worst of all the pain, the emotions he had never experienced or anticipated, the dreadful nagging ache of loss. How he had missed her! He could not sleep, eat, or work for the pain. He was desolate and miserable. It was brought home to him then with shaming clarity that he had never ever known what love was until he had suddenly found himself without the one he loved. In the end he had swallowed his pride—he, Neville Bennett, who had never had to humble himself to any woman!—and written to her, begging her to come home. It had taken him six hours and five drafts to complete, and although he still wasn't satisfied with it he had sent if off and waited hopefully for an encouraging response.

She had never replied.

He had tried to harden himself then, attempted to adjust. He had lost her and made a mess of his personal life—and hers —but it would be foolish and unrealistic to go on hoping for a miracle that would never happen. He had decided to re-organize his life and bring about such changes that there would be as little as possible to remind him of the past. He sold the house at Richmond where they had lived since he had re-signed his teaching position and begun to work for the gov-ernment on forestry projects. He did not want to live at Rich-mond any more. Instead he had taken a lease of the house in Adam and Eve Mews, made arrangements with Leonie for her to renew her role as housekeeper, tried to meet other women to take his mind off what had happened . . .

And all the time there was the child, asking why Karen had gone, asking when she would be coming back, reminding Neville of how much he had lost despite all his futile efforts to forget.

The door opened.

"Daddy?" It was Snuff's bed-time and he was in pajamas, his face scrubbed, his hair standing up in front in an aggressive tuft. "Aunt Karen wrote a letter specially for me even though it's not Christmas or my birthday." He waved a grubby scrap

of paper. "She's coming next week and she'll take me to the zoo
and Madame Tussaud's and buy me a bicycle at Harrods—"

"May I see?"

The child handed it over, beaming up at him happily. "Isn't
it nice?"

> Darling Snuff,
>
> I'm going to come and see you very soon, the Wednes-
> day after you receive this letter, and I'm so looking
> forward to seeing you again that I can hardly wait to fly
> across to London. Be sure and think of all the places you'd
> like to go and visit—I remember you told me in that letter
> which Aunt helped you write last Christmas that you like
> the zoo and Madame Tussaud's, so maybe we could go
> there again, if you wanted to. Do you still want that cycle?
> If you do we can go to Harrods or some other store to-
> gether and you can choose the one you like best. Longing
> to see you, darling, lots of love . . .

"Isn't it nice?" repeated the child, still beaming up at him.
Neville made an effort. "Very nice!" He smiled at his son
and patted the child on the head. "I didn't know you wanted
a bicycle. Why didn't you tell me? I'd have taken you to Harrods myself and bought you the best bicycle in London if I'd
known."

After pondering the diplomatic reply to this, Snuff suggested
that Neville and Karen could both go to Harrods to choose him
the best bicycle. "Because then it would be twice as good," he
explained, "since it would be a present from two people instead of one. Would you go to Harrods with Aunt Karen,
Daddy?"

"Perhaps. Yes, if you like." He smiled at Snuff again, but his
thoughts were already wandering back to his marriage and he
was conscious, as he had been conscious so often before, of that
insidious sense of failure. The memory of his recent quarrel
with Melissa added to his depression. As Snuff trailed off to
bed Neville had a longing to see Marney, his friend of a quarter
of a century, the one person who was always the same and
who never changed. They had met as freshmen at Cambridge

when they were eighteen and even though Neville had always outshone his friend socially and academically they had still remained friends.

Leonie called from the dining-room that dinner was on the table.

It was a pity, thought Neville as he went into the other room, that Leonie had not married Marney, but then Marney had always regarded women so warily that it was not surprising that he had remained a bachelor. Marney had seen straight through April from the beginning. Neville could remember him saying: "Leave her alone, let her be, she's not for you—Karen's worth ten Aprils—a hundred." Marney had made every effort to turn Neville's interest away from April, but Neville hadn't listened.

"I suppose Karen wants to come back to you," said Leonie tight-lipped over the roast beef and Yorkshire pudding. "I suppose she's had enough of living alone."

"I doubt it." He saw she was already worrying about the possibility of being usurped. If the usurper had been Neville's well-bred, very English first wife then no doubt Leonie would have relinquished her prized position in the household with grudging good grace, but the idea of being usurped by Karen would be most upsetting. Leonie, always distrustful of foreigners, had never fully accepted Karen as part of the family, and had never fully recovered from her original belief that Karen was a pretty adventuress who had skillfully and shamelessly manipulated Neville to the altar.

"Well, I suppose we should be grateful that she's bothering to come and see Snuff," she observed acidly. "He was so upset when she left, poor lamb. I always thought it was disgraceful the way she went off to America without considering the child's feelings in any way."

"He isn't her child."

"Yes, but she behaved toward him as if she were his mother!" Leonie had bitter memories of how Snuff had turned from her and accepted Karen with such ease. "She confused him, poor child. It wasn't fair."

"I'm sure the hardest part of her decision to leave England three years ago," said Neville deliberately, "was the fact that she had to say goodbye to Snuff. But once she had made up her mind to leave me she had no choice but to leave him, too. She had no claim on him. She couldn't take him with her."

"I should think not indeed!" Leonie exclaimed, and with an unmistakable edge to her voice she added: "You're always so ready to stand up for her—you're too generous in forgiving, Neville. After all, when it all boils down to it, what happened? She left you on the spur of the moment, abandoned all her responsibilities and caused you endless embarrassment among your friends. I always did say that Americans were much less scrupulous about the marriage ties than we are. And I'm sure they're more immoral than we are too, and much more prone to affairs."

The memory of the episode with April and its disastrous conclusion jerked instantly back into Neville's mind against his will; without warning he seemed to hear April's voice once more, the words which she had spoken during that last terrible weekend when she had followed him to Scotland, to the farm and Plantation Q.

"Poor Karen!" she had said mockingly after Karen had discovered them together and stumbled blindly out of the farm to escape from her discovery. "What a shock for her to find out she can't be lucky all the time. Why, Neville, where are you going? What are you doing? Oh Neville, please—don't go after her! Leave her alone—it serves her right! Why should you run after her when you don't care about her any more?" And when he had said nothing she had rushed at him in a frenzy of rage and shouted that she wouldn't let him leave, that she was pleased his marriage was finished, glad that Karen had lost him. "Glad!" she had screamed at him. "Glad, do you hear? Glad!" He could hear her voice still, ringing in his ears, shrieking through his nightmares. "I'm glad . . . glad . . . GLAD!"

He felt ice-cold suddenly. His body shivered.

Leonie was just about to continue her dissertation on Americans when the telephone rang again and Neville escaped in relief to answer it.

"Neville, I'm sorry I was so bitchy earlier—"

It was Melissa, just as he had anticipated. She was exactly the same as so many other women. Karen was the one who was different.

## II

When Karen arrived in London it was late at night and she felt tired after the long tedious hours in the plane. The journey through the Customs and Immigration Department seemed agonizingly slow. At last when she was free to leave, she found a cab, gave the driver Melissa's address in Knightsbridge, and sank back thankfully against the ancient leather upholstery.

She was back.

Her mind had been so filled with thoughts of Neville and the child during the past few days that now when she was at last within a few miles of them she was unable to think of them at all. She was aware of a curious numbness muffling all poignancy and longing and rendering her detached, almost careless. I'm back, she kept telling herself. I'm back. But the thought was difficult to assimilate, for the new road into Central London was as modern as any American freeway and the darkness hid the English green of the countryside from her eyes. And then surprisingly quickly the countryside was gone and the suburbs began and there were signboards with English names so that her presence in this foreign land seemed at last to be a reality. Acton, Shepherd's Bush, Hammersmith, Richmond . . .

Richmond was where she had lived with Neville after he had left Cambridge and had begun to work for the government in London. Richmond was just a few miles away across the Thames. I'm back, she thought again, I'm back. And the past came rushing up to meet her, almost drowning her in wave after wave of memory, but the memories were happy and she strained to grasp each one and savor it again. She realized to her surprise that in America she had tended to remember only her unhappiness, but now, here in London, the unhappiness seemed as remote and as far away as Scotland and that terrible weekend when she had followed Neville and April north to Plantation Q.

Her mind closed automatically, obliterating the train of

thought before it reached the memory of her sister at Neville's in Scotland. That was all over, closed; she was back in London and remembering happier times, and if the memories were tinged with sadness because they belonged to the past they were also tinged with excitement because she was closer now to the past than she had been for three years.

The cab reached the entrance of Melissa's flat. The cabbie took her suitcases up to the front door, and suddenly there was Melissa, very smart in that same cool indolent way which men found so attractive, and beyond Melissa were soft lights and comfort and the end of the journey.

"Why, Melissa, you haven't changed at all!"

"Darling, how devastating! You mean to say I haven't even improved slightly during the last few years?"

The cabbie was waiting to be paid, and the English money confused her unexpectedly so that she gave him a bigger tip than she had intended. Three years of handling cents and dollars had blurred her memory of pounds, shillings, and pence.

"You must be quite exhausted," Melissa was saying. "Let me make you some coffee."

"Well . . ." Melissa's spare room was small but elegant. There were flowers on the dressing-table, English roses, and a couple of fashion magazines placed unobtrusively near the bed. Karen abandoned her suitcases without unpacking them and within five minutes was relaxing on the living-room couch while Melissa brought in the coffee.

"I really appreciate you having me to stay like this," she said to Melissa presently. "I thought of staying at a hotel, but—"

"Darling, what on earth for? It's lovely to see you again! Now tell me all about New York and your job and all the people I used to know."

Time passed. Both cups of coffee were filled, emptied and replenished more than once. Finally Melissa gathered together the coffee cups and turned to take them out to the kitchen. Then: "What are your plans for tomorrow?" Karen heard her say casually.

"I expect I'll go shopping in the morning and call Leonie to find out if I can see Snuff after he finishes school in the afternoon. Apparently his term doesn't end till the day after tomorrow so I won't be able to see him tomorrow morning. I guess I shall have to phone Neville and make arrangements with him."

"You're not expecting any difficulty about getting Neville's permission to see the child?"

"Oh no, Neville wrote back in reply to my letter and said I could see Snuff whenever I wished—Neville's not vindictive, and besides I've been in touch with Snuff ever since I left. It's not as if I were returning to him as a stranger whom he had already forgotten."

"Hm-hm." Melissa was in the kitchen. "You're not looking forward to seeing Neville again?"

"Not particularly." She was amazed at how colorless her voice sounded when her heart was bumping so uncomfortably and her hands were tightly clasped with tension.

"I was wondering if you were hoping for a reconciliation."

"I came to see Snuff, not Neville."

"I see. Yes, of course." Melissa was rinsing the cups and saucers under the tap.

"Have you seen anything of Neville recently, Melissa?"

The tap was turned off. There was a slight pause. Then: "Well, as a matter of fact, darling, yes. Rather a lot." She was moving around in the kitchen; Karen heard her open a cupboard door and close it. "After you left we became quite friendly. Well, not *directly* after you left. Perhaps a year or two afterwards. Over the past twelve months or so I've been seeing him frequently."

There was another pause. Karen, the first wave of shock subsiding, was aware of mounting tension. Her limbs began to ache unbearably.

"Actually, darling, you came back just at the right moment. I've been trying to break off with Neville tactfully for some time, but . . . well, you know Neville! It's all been rather awkward really. I was so glad when I heard you were coming back because I hoped—well, I hoped Neville would be diverted, if you see what I mean . . ."

Karen tried to speak but could not. Amidst all her confused emotions she was conscious first of anger for letting herself imagine Neville would have spent the past three years in

celibacy to mourn her departure, then of anger that she should
care how he had spent the past three years, and finally of anger
that she should feel angry. Whatever happened she must not
let Melissa see that she cared in any way for Neville or was
hurt by what Melissa had just told her. That would be too
humiliating. Besides it was obviously all as embarrassing for
Melissa as it was for her.

". . . never any question of marriage, of course," Melissa
was saying carelessly. "Neville never even thought of getting a
divorce. He just used to come here now and again."

There was an ache in Karen's throat suddenly, tears in her
eyes. She turned, pulled back the curtain, forced herself to
stare out at the London skyline beyond, and tried not to think
of Melissa here with Neville, Melissa eating, drinking, sleeping
with Neville, laughing with him, enjoying life, savoring his
nearness to the full . . .

"Honestly, darling, it was nothing much really. We had a
holiday once in Italy, a couple of weekends in Paris, but it
didn't *mean* anything. How could it? You know Neville."

The words were like knives, tearing and wrenching the
fabric of happy memories Karen had woven for herself since
her arrival in England. Pain blinded her eyes, drummed in
her ears.

"I wouldn't have done it, of course, if I hadn't taken for
granted that you were going to divorce him. I held out against
him for the longest time, and then, well, I thought, 'Karen
never writes to him, obviously he means nothing to her any
more. Perhaps she's even found someone else.' And I did find
him attractive. And charming. And . . . well, darling, you
know."

Karen did know. She stared out into the darkness and in her
mind she was picturing Neville as she had last seen him in Scotland, and wondering if she would ever be able to endure seeing him again.

"Darling, I hope I haven't upset you," Melissa was saying
from the doorway. "I wouldn't have told you, but really I've
nothing to hide and from my point of view the affair is quite
finished so I thought it best to make a clean breast of it before
someone else told you out of spite. I'm sure Leonie will
manage to drop a hint or two when you see her tomorrow. Poor

woman, she's so—well, *soured*. Rather sad really. Neville told me she's still secretly in love with Marney. Talking of Marney, I suppose when you met him in New York he didn't mention that Neville and I—"

"No, he didn't say a word about it."

"Dear Marney—always such a gentleman! But I should imagine he knew what was going on—he and Neville are such close friends."

Marney had warned her against a reconciliation, Karen thought. Perhaps he had spoken with Melissa's involvement with Neville in mind.

"Now," said Melissa, abandoning her vague, abstracted tone and changing the subject briskly, "are you quite sure you have everything you want in your room? A glass of water, perhaps—"

Karen assured her that there was nothing else she needed.

"Then I'll say goodnight," said Melissa, turning to open the door of her own bedroom. "I do hope you sleep well. Oh incidentally, I knew there was something I was meaning to ask you! Did you manage to find out what had happened to April? You told me you were writing to Thomas—"

"Thomas knew nothing and neither did my family in Minnesota."

"How extraordinary! Then she really has disappeared?"

"I guess so. If she hadn't been in the habit of disappearing for long spells at a time maybe we'd have realized it sooner, but I was the only one she kept in touch with, and after that time in Scotland . . . well, I wasn't surprised not to hear from her afterwards." Karen was wondering as she spoke why Melissa should be so interested in April. "However, Thomas wrote and said he would try to get to London to meet me, so that was good news. I hope he makes it—I haven't seen him for such a long time."

"Of course, he went to Scotland with you when April and Neville—"

"Yes," said Karen, "he did. Goodnight, Melissa, and many thanks."

But it wasn't until she was leaning back against the spare room door and letting the tears stain her cheeks that she asked herself in irony why she should thank Melissa for making her so unhappy.

## III

She managed to sleep for about five hours and woke the next morning feeling less tired but still depressed. Pulling herself together with an effort she had a bath and dressed with care before going into the kitchen to make herself some coffee and toast. Melissa had already gone downstairs to the boutique after telling Karen to make herself at home and eat whatever she liked from the refrigerator and pantry. The morning papers lay on the kitchen table, the first "Telegraph" and "Express" that Karen had seen for years. She read them leisurely in an attempt to keep her mind from dwelling on her conversation with Melissa the previous evening, and then at last when she was too tense and nervous to sit still any longer she went over to the phone to call Leonie.

The conversation proved easier than Karen had anticipated; Leonie, formal but polite, told her that Snuff finished school at three-thirty that afternoon. Perhaps Karen would like to take him out to tea at four? Karen had, of course, spoken with Neville. She hadn't? Well, in that case . . . Leonie sounded faintly scandalized.

"I'm going to phone Neville now," said Karen. "But if you don't hear from me again, I'll see you at four this afternoon at your house. Thank you, Leonie."

She put down the receiver in relief and then, suddenly feeling unequal to the task of phoning Neville at that moment, she found her handbag and moved impulsively out of the house into Knightsbridge. At Harrods she bought a woolly giraffe and a snakes-and-ladders set for Snuff and lingered longingly among the fur coats before eating a snack lunch and returning to Melissa's flat. Back in her room, she paused. Melissa was out, lunching with a client, and Karen was alone. She had been shopping. There was no more unpacking left to do. The time had come when she could no longer put off making the phone call to Neville, but even as she realized this, she decided to have a cup of coffee and put off the moment a little longer. Just as she went into the kitchen the phone began to ring.

She picked it up cautiously. "Hello?"

A pause, very slight. Her scalp tingled in a flash of comprehension. "Hello?" she said again rapidly. "Who's this, please?"

"How are you, Karen?" said Neville, his voice very smooth and charming. If it had not been for that small pause she would have thought his manner completely effortless. "Welcome back to England. Snuff's much looking forward to seeing you."

"I was just about to call you." Her fingers were gripping the receiver so tightly that they hurt. She was vaguely amazed at how cool and composed she sounded. "I spoke to Leonie this morning and we thought that perhaps I might call for Snuff at four and take him out to tea. I hope that's all right with you."

"Yes, of course. His school breaks up tomorrow for the summer holidays, you know, so you'll have plenty of time to see him after that."

"Yes, you mentioned that in your letter." Neville's acknowledgment of Karen's letter had been as brief as her announcement of her visit.

There was another small pause.

"How long will you be here for?" said Neville presently.

"Between two or three weeks, I think. I've got a tentative reservation for the fifth."

"I see."

"How's Marney?"

"Marney? Oh, well enough, I think. Well, look, Karen, I won't hold you up now as I'm sure you're very busy, but I hope all goes well this afternoon—I shan't be home by four, of course, but Leonie will be there and I know Snuff is impatient to see you . . . I'll be in touch with you."

"Fine," said Karen. "Thank you, Neville."

She put down the receiver with trembling fingers and reached for a cigarette. The flame ignited, flared, died as she struck a match and blew it out. After a while she began to wonder what he was doing, what his reaction had been. Had he too reached for a cigarette and lit it unsteadily? Or had he stared out across Birdcage Walk to St. James's Park just as she

was now staring across the roofs of Knightsbridge? Probably
not. Probably he had merely summoned his secretary and dic-
tated a memo on Plantation Q, or busied himself in writing
some report. Or perhaps he had strolled down the corridor to
Marney's office to tell Marney casually that he had just spoken
to Karen. What did it matter anyway? Surely what mattered
was that she was left with her dread enhanced at the thought
of meeting him again. If his voice could succeed in shattering
her composure so completely it was certain that his presence
would reduce her to new emotional depths which she had no
wish to experience. It would be foolish to betray that she still
cared in any way for Neville when there was no future in caring. To Neville she would seem merely part of the past; he
would be more interested in Melissa than in her.

Turning very slowly she went to her room to rest for a while
before it was time for her to leave Knightsbridge and set out
for Adam and Eve Mews.

IV

The child was excited. He skipped along the pavements and
danced around each tree planted by the roadside, and all the
world was as bright to him as the afternoon sunshine. His Aunt
Leonie, who had collected him from school, followed at a more
sedate pace, her lips pursed with misgivings as she thought of
the meeting to come. As usual she was worrying. What effect
would this have on the child? Was he suffering even now from
the separation of his father and step-mother? Would he suffer
in the future? Would it be better if Karen had never come?
But Karen was here in London and would soon be at the house.
The meeting was unavoidable now.

Snuff knew his aunt was worried, but as she was always
worrying about something he was not concerned. He danced
down the steps and when he saw his step-mother waiting by
the front door he danced right up to her and into her arms. She
was exactly as he remembered her, and he thought with de-

light how nice she looked and how pleasant she smelt and how prettily she spoke English. He had specially remembered her accent. "I knew you'd come back one day!" he said with shining eyes, and began to wonder idly if she had brought him a present.

The woolly giraffe was a great success. Snuff knew he was really too old for soft toys, and had to pretend not to like it as much as he did, but secretly he was very pleased. The game looked promising too. He looked at his step-mother with renewed interest and wondered if she would buy him "dame blanche" for tea.

"What's that?" she said later when they were in the tea shop, and he discovered with amazement that she knew no French. He had thought everyone all over the world learnt French, particularly French food names like "dame blanche" which was white ice cream with hot chocolate sauce. A few minutes later, covered with chocolate sauce from ear to ear, he scraped his spoon furiously against the bottom of the cup so that not a drop should be wasted, and told her all about his life at his French Lycée.

She listened and ordered him another "dame blanche." It was then that he first realized what a good time he was having, and he wondered vaguely if she would come to England more often. She was much more "sympathique" than Aunt Leonie.

"Why do you live in America?" he asked presently.

She seemed to take a long time answering. In the end she said: "It's my country—where I was born and brought up. I work there."

"But you lived here once."

"Yes."

He was dimly aware of feeling confused. "Because you were married to Daddy?"

"Yes."

He felt he wanted to ask questions, but he could not put the questions into words. He was only aware of shadowy puzzles in his mind, of bewilderment which it was beyond his power to express.

"Will you live here again one day?"

"Perhaps."

Her eyes were watching her plate. He could only see her long black lashes. He glanced at her plate too, but there was nothing there.

"With Daddy?"

"I don't know."

He groped in his mind for words. "Doesn't he like you?"

She glanced up at him then and he saw to his horror that her eyes were brilliant with tears. Every muscle in his body went rigid. He pushed back his chair. "Can we go now?"

She nodded without speaking, fumbling in her purse for change. Moving very quickly he slid past her and edged his way through the shop to the door. While she paid the bill at the cash desk he stared through the glass and watched a policeman directing the traffic.

They went outside together.

"I guess it's time for us to go home," she said, and she sounded so calm and composed that he stole a glance at her. Her eyes were quite dry too, he noticed with relief. He felt himself relax a little. "Your aunt will be wondering what's happened to you."

She stretched out her arm to take his hand in hers but he pretended he didn't see it and skipped on ahead through the rush-hour crowds, careful never to be out of her sight but equally careful not to be near enough to enable her to talk to him. He had enjoyed his tea with her, but now he had had enough and wanted to go home. Her air of mystery frightened him and he was afraid to talk to her again at that time for fear she might tell him what terrible secret had brought the tears to her eyes. He was afraid of the unknown, yet afraid of knowing too much, and in all his confusion he only knew that he must not mention his father to her again.

They reached the house and Snuff stood on tiptoe to ring the doorbell. His step-mother was lingering behind, he noticed puzzled, and he wondered if she was frightened; she was carrying her gloves and twisting them over and over again between her fingers.

"Honey, I think I'd better say goodbye now—I'll come and see you again tomorrow . . ." Her voice trailed off as the door opened, and she stood very still, her eyes looking straight over his head to the doorway beyond.

The child swung round.

"Hello Snuff," said his father. "I deduce from your faint chocolate moustache that someone has been indulging you in 'dame blanche' again. Did you enjoy your tea?"

Snuff opened his mouth but closed it uncertainly as he saw that his father was already looking past him to the woman beyond. And as the child watched, an onlooker at a scene he did not understand, he saw his father smile slowly and hold out his hand as if he were offering her something which was both mystical and yet real.

"Won't you come in for a moment, Karen?" said Neville Bennett to his wife.

## V

They dined at Quaglinos and Neville ordered a bottle of her favorite vintage white Burgundy to go with the Dover sole she chose from the menu. First they had chilled cucumber soup and freshly-baked soft rolls, and then after the entrees, Karen chose the sherry trifle while Neville selected baked Alaska. The coffee, when it came, was strong and aromatic and flavorful. Neville ordered two glasses of Grand Marnier to accompany it, and then offered her a cigarette.

"How are you feeling?"

She smiled at him. "Still dazed, I think!" She looked very composed, he noticed, but not relaxed. He himself felt better now. The wine had lulled his tension and brought a genuine relaxation to him, but he still felt oddly vulnerable. He wanted her very much. Three years had changed nothing, least of all her power to attract him, and he wondered with a vague feeling of incredulity how he could ever have looked at another woman. The memory of April seemed like some nightmare, remote and unreal and even a little fantastic. As for Melissa, he had completely forgotten her. Melissa had ceased to exist, even

as a memory. In fact his memory was capable of recalling
nothing at that moment save for his past with Karen, just as his
mind was capable of focusing on nothing except the immediate present and his pleasure in being with her.

"Well," he said. "We seemed to have talked a great deal
about a great many subjects, but there's still a certain amount
left unspoken."

"Sometimes it's better to leave things unspoken."

"Sometimes," he said, "but not always." The waiter brought
the liqueurs and departed. Neville took a sip from his glass and
the Grand Marnier caressed his palate with its distinctive flavor.
"About April, for example," he said deliberately, not looking
at her. "We have to mention her name sooner or later or else it
will continue to lie between us like some monstrous skeleton
in the cupboard. You must know that I regard the incident with
April as one of the most foolish, contemptible things I've ever
done. If I could somehow obliterate the incident from my past
I would do so at once, but of course that's not possible, so I
just try to obliterate it from my mind. I treated you very
badly, I know. If I hadn't met April—"

"If you hadn't met April, it would have been someone else,"
said Karen, her voice cool and dispassionate. "You wanted an
affair, Neville. Since we're being so frank with one another,
perhaps I can remind you of how you began to behave at
parties, how often you used to hurt me even before April came
to London—"

"All right," he said, "I'll admit it. I admitted it in that letter
I wrote to you and I'll admit it again now. I treated you badly
and behaved even worse—but I didn't realize how much I
loved you until you were gone, Karen, and by that time it was
too late to make amends. As far as April was concerned, at
least I wasn't wholly to blame. I made no rendezvous with her,
you know; our meeting at the farm wasn't pre-arranged. I
went there on business and she chased after me as soon as she
heard you weren't going to be there. I know that when you arrived and found us together you thought you could see exactly
what was going on, but it wasn't as you supposed. You didn't
know that Leonie was on holiday at the farm at the time—that

April had misjudged the situation and that I wasn't alone after all—"

"Yes, you explained in your letter."

"I admit that if Leonie hadn't been there—"

"Yes."

"But there was no rendezvous. I had no part in bringing April there—it was her fault she was there, and her fault alone. Don't put all the blame on me and forget April altogether."

"I hadn't forgotten April and I never shall." She ground out her cigarette. "Have you heard from her since?"

"Not a word. After you—discovered us together that morning I quarreled with her and rushed out after you. That left April alone at the farm, since Leonie had left earlier to walk over to the foresters' lodge at Plantation Q to see Marney. By the time I eventually got back several hours had passed and April had gone. I looked around, saw her clothes and suitcases had vanished and then discovered that one of the boats was gone from the jetty. So she must have packed after I ran out after you, rowed herself across the lake and managed to get a lift from a passing car."

"But how odd that she should have left so suddenly!"

"I don't think so. We'd quarreled. I'd told her to go." He took a gulp of liqueur and fidgeted with his glass. "She must have left soon after I did," he repeated. "Leonie came back from the lodge at about eleven, she told me later, and April wasn't there then. I'm not sure what time I left to look for you but it must have been around nine-thirty. So some time between half-past nine and eleven o'clock that morning—"

"April disappeared into the blue."

"Well, if you want to put it that way, yes, I suppose she did. More coffee?"

"Please."

"Frankly I was too upset to think much about it at the time. I was only too glad to be rid of her."

"You had quarreled with her finally, then?"

"Irrevocably." He was still fidgeting with his glass. "She—but it's much too unpleasant to talk about in detail. Let's just say that she suddenly showed her true colors to me during the

quarrel, and I was horrified. You knew—realized—" He hesitated unexpectedly.

"What?"

"She was—unbalanced. You must have known that."

"Isn't that rather a strong word? She had her problems, certainly, but—"

He laughed. "What an American way of putting it!" Then,
serious again: "You always used to defend her, didn't you?
You were always prepared to make excuses for her, and now I
see you still are. Why's that, I wonder?"

"I—I don't know. I've never been sure—it's hard to explain—"

"It sounds as if you too have your problems!"

"Haven't we all!"

They laughed. Neville, sensing that the moment was pro-
pitious, tightened his grip on his liqueur glass.

"Karen, I didn't mention it to you before but I'm supposed
to be going to Scotland to Plantation Q on business on Monday. I could put it off to spend more time with you and Snuff
in London, but I don't want to do that. I want you to come
with me to Scotland and we can have a week by ourselves
at the farm and give ourselves a second honeymoon. Won't
you come? I want you back more than anything I've ever
wanted in all my life. I know you'll be reluctant to go back to
the farm and Plantation Q, but I'm a great believer in facing
unpleasant memories and not letting them haunt you, and
there are no ghosts there, Karen, I know for I've been back
often. It's still the beautiful secluded place it always was, and
it would take more than April's viciousness to destroy its
beauty and its peace. Come and see for yourself. I can promise
you I'd be a damned sight better husband to you this time than
I ever was before—I've learnt my lesson and I've learnt it in a
way I'll never forget. I love you and that's the truth, I promise.
I love you a thousand times more deeply than I ever did before."

Her hand moved involuntarily. He was aware of her beautiful fingers, of the rings he had given her nearly five years ago,
and he glanced up searchingly into her face, but her lashes
veiled her eyes and her expression was hidden from him. He
waited in an agony of suspense, every nerve strained for her

response, and still she did not answer. In the end he said desperately: "I know it must be hard for you to trust me after the way I treated you—"

And she said, interrupting him: "That's true certainly, but there are other factors which make me hesitate."

"Such as?" The liqueur glass slipped in his hot palm; a drop of Grand Marnier scarred the white cloth. "Look," he heard himself say with a clumsiness which was foreign to him. "I haven't been faithful to you during the past three years. I think you know me better than to suppose that I could be celibate for that length of time, and besides, when you didn't reply to my letter I decided it would be better to try and forget you—"

"You needn't make excuses," she said. "I understand."

The sweat was prickling at the back of his collar. His mouth was dry. "I had an affair with Melissa," he said. "Perhaps she told you—yes, I can see she did! That's typical! I suppose you were wondering when and if I was going to mention her. Well, there's little to say except that she was my mistress on and off for about a year and that I started to lose interest in her about three months ago after rather a disastrous weekend in Paris when she became much too emotional and dramatic for my peace of mind. As far as I'm concerned the affair is finished and was finished even before you wrote to tell me you were coming to England. I never loved her, but there were times when I enjoyed her company and felt reasonably fond of her. You'll notice that I use the past tense. At the moment I find her more irritating than anything else."

There was a silence. Around them the restaurant was alive with a low turmoil of sound; the hum of conversation, the ring of cutlery, the dull clink of plates.

"I see," said Karen.

"I suppose Melissa painted the situation a little differently."

"A little."

"She's bound to make some sort of scene if she believes there's a chance of our being reconciled. I'd advise you not to confide in her and pretend there's no question of a reconciliation."

"Uh-huh." She was fingering her rings.

He leant forward. "What are you thinking, Karen?"

She raised her eyes to his. He felt his heart turn over and the longing ache in his throat because she was so beautiful. He wondered if she could tell from his expression how much he wanted her.

"It's very difficult," she said at last. "I shall have to think it over for a while."

"Yes," he said automatically, his reflexes masking his disappointment and anguish. "Yes, of course." So much for his plans for them to spend the night together at the Dorchester. He had thought in such detail about his first night with her for three years that the realization that it was to be postponed was indeed a bitter pill to swallow. "Perhaps we can have dinner again tomorrow?" he said levelly. "What are your plans?"

"Snuff finishes school at noon and I wanted to take him out to lunch and then to the zoo or Madame Tussaud's. I had no plans for the evening."

"Then you'll dine with me?"

"I'd love to." She smiled at him, and the blood seemed to tingle through his veins.

He took a taxi with her to Knightsbridge but stopped some way from Melissa's apartment in order to avoid any risk of Melissa witnessing their parting. There was an unlighted shop window, a darkened doorway, and he drew her into the shadows to kiss her as he had dreamed of kissing her all through the evening. She felt light in his arms, but that was probably because there was so much strength in him, for her hands were firm enough as they clasped behind his neck, and her mouth was hard and passionate beneath his own.

"The hell with you 'thinking it over,'" he said unevenly at last. "The hell with that. Let's get a taxi—there'll be a room at the Dorchester—"

But she was withdrawing, elusive as ever, and her face was shadowed and hidden from him by the darkness. "I must think," he heard her say, her voice low and indistinct. "Please, Neville. Give me a chance to think it over." And then even as he shrugged his shoulders in a gesture of resignation she had turned aside from him and was walking away down Knightsbridge to the door of Melissa's apartment.

## VI

"Darling," said Melissa, rising to her feet with a smooth fluent motion of her body. "I hardly expected you back to-night! What happened? Did something go wrong?"

The last thing Karen wanted to do at that moment was to talk to Melissa. "Nothing happened," she said shortly, retreating to her bedroom. "We had dinner and talked for a while. What were you expecting to happen? I told you that I had no intentions of a reconciliation."

"Oh, I know you had no intentions, but you know Neville." She was in the doorway, poised and unashamedly curious. "Didn't he suggest—"

"I thought Neville's business was no longer yours, Melissa," Karen interrupted, and then added hastily: "I'm sorry, I don't mean to be rude, but—"

"Darling, of course not! I understand. I was only wondering, that's all. I'm glad you had a nice evening." But still she hovered in the doorway.

"As it happens," said Karen, "Neville's due to go to Plantation Q on Monday, so I doubt if I'll see much more of him on my trip."

"Really?" Melissa's voice was sharp. "Well, it's just as well you don't want a reconciliation, isn't it, or he might suggest taking you back there! I should think that must be the last place on earth you would want to go to."

Karen said, unthinking: "He said there were no ghosts there—" And then nearly bit off her tongue as she realized she had given away the fact that Neville had spoken of a return to Scotland together.

But to her amazement, Melissa did not seem to notice. "So he said there were no ghosts, did he?" she murmured. "I wonder." And she turned and moved indolently back into the living-room.

Karen followed her. "What do you mean?"

"Oh nothing." She lit a cigarette and shook out the light

with a languid flick of the wrist. Then: "Karen, what do *you* think happened to April?"

Karen stared. "Why, I don't know! I guess she's found some man somewhere, and . . . well, what do you think happened to her?"

"Oh Lord!" said Melissa. "How should I know? I wasn't at Plantation Q on the day she—disappeared. I've just listened to various people reminiscing—how can I judge? It merely occurred to me how strange it was that she apparently vanished so suddenly into thin air."

"The general opinion seems to be that she rowed herself across the lake and hitched a ride to—"

"But darling!" said Melissa deprecatingly, "imagine it! I've been to the farm—I stayed there for a week last summer actually, while Neville had business on the plantation—and quite frankly I just can't see a girl like April rowing across the lake to the road. Hell, darling, that's a long way to row! *I* certainly couldn't have done it! A tough, sporty spinster like Leonie—well, yes. I can see her making light of it, but a fragile slip of a girl like April who couldn't have had any rowing experience since her childhood by the Minnesota lakes—"

"Then how else could she have got away from the farm?"

"Well, that's just it, darling," said Melissa. "I rather wonder if she ever did get away."

# THREE

## I

"That's preposterous!" said Neville furiously. "Quite preposterous! I hardly thought Melissa would stoop so low, even if she were jealous of you, but it's clear she has no scruples at all."

He was dining with Karen again the following evening. Earlier in the day Karen had taken an enthralled Snuff to the zoo and to Madame Tussaud's and had then met Neville at eight. Now an hour later she had hesitantly told him of Melissa's theory that April had met her death by accident, and was in spite of herself astonished at the violence of his reaction.

"It's too much!" he added enraged. "That, I swear it, is the last night you stay under her roof! I'll not have you stay with her a moment longer—it's obvious that she's full of malice and jealousy and is determined to pay me back for terminating the affair—"

"But Neville," said Karen, half-amused by his vehemence, half-bewildered by the force of his anger, "anyone would think that Melissa suggested you murdered April! All she suggested was—"

"She suggested to you that April never left the farm, didn't she?"

"Yes, but—"

"If April had had an accident—suppose, for example, that she had fallen in the lake—how would that account for the fact that her suitcases disappeared with her? Besides, corpses resulting from accidental death seldom disappear without trace.

They don't bury themselves—or tie weights to their limbs so that they stay on the floor of a lake. If April met her death by accident, then where's her body? Why hasn't it been discovered? There's nothing whatsoever to suggest that April had an accident and never left the farm—or the lake."

"That's what I said to Melissa, but she merely shrugged her shoulders and said she thought it was all very suspicious."

"The devil she did! She was trying to make you think I'd killed her, that's all! She's so damned eager to prevent a reconciliation between us that she decided to try to tell you I murdered your sister—"

"Don't you think," said Karen, "that that's just a little too melodramatic?" She was certainly not going to admit that she had lain awake half the night wondering if Melissa had meant to do this and whether it was at all possible that April might somehow have met her death three years ago in Scotland. The possibility of an accident did seem unlikely, particularly since no body had been discovered. But if she had not died by accident . . .

"Melissa *is* melodramatic," said Neville. "It's just the kind of trick she would employ to try to make sure you don't agree to a reconciliation."

"But Neville, she must know I would never believe you killed April—"

"Precisely," he said. "Because April was never killed in the first place. Only it pleases Melissa for reasons of her own to invent this monstrous story—"

"Well, she never actually said—"

"She implied it, though! My God, I can see through her even if you can't! The trouble with you, my dearest, is that you simply won't hear a word against anyone, even your worst enemies—in fact you take great pains to speak up in their defense even after they've stabbed you in the back! But I see through Melissa all right, and I'm damned if I'll let you go back to her flat either tonight or any other night. You can stay at the house, if you like—we haven't a spare bedroom, but I can easily sleep on the sofa in the living-room. And since I'm off to Scotland on Monday it'll only be for a couple of days anyway."

There was a silence. The waiter flitted past and paused long enough to refill their coffee cups.

"If you prefer," said Neville, "I would pay for a hotel for you."

"I—" She hesitated, not knowing what to do. The thought of staying on at Melissa's was certainly distasteful, but the thought of staying under Leonie's critical eye was little better.

"I think you should move to a hotel," said Neville, making up her mind for her. He glanced at his watch. "I'll come with you back to Melissa's, collect your luggage, and then take you to the Dorchester."

She knew quite well what would happen at the Dorchester. She paused, toying with her cup, her eyes watching the steaming black coffee, and suddenly she was remembering a thousand small things, the stiff pace of her job in New York, the loneliness of her Manhattan apartment, the men for whom she cared nothing, the meaninglessness of her life beneath the rush and confusion of her daily living. And it seemed to her suddenly that for three years she had been living in shadow and here at last was another chance to walk back into the light.

She looked up at Neville. He was very still, but she saw how his knuckles gleamed white as he rested his hand on the table, noticed the strained set to his mouth.

"Well?" he said lightly. "What do you say? Do you think that's the best thing to do in the circumstances?"

Still she hesitated. Then finally after a long while she heard herself say: "Yes . . . yes, I think it is. Thank you, Neville."

II

Mercifully, Melissa was not at home when they returned to pick up Karen's luggage. Karen spent a full ten minutes trying to write her a note while Neville casually helped himself to a whisky and soda in the living-room, but the ultimate result of her attempts seemed worse than inadequate; however, the circumstances were so awkward that any attempt at a written explanation would inevitably be fraught with difficulties. In the end she wrote: "It seems I underestimated the possibility of a reconciliation! I shall probably be going up to Plantation Q with Neville on Monday and will give you a call before I go—if you should want to contact me I'll be at the Dorchester through Sunday. Meanwhile many thanks again for your hospitality and please excuse this sudden departure."

Leaving the note propped up on Melissa's dressing-table, she went back into the living-room.

"All right?" said Neville abruptly.

She nodded. "I hope so."

"Then let's go."

Karen could hardly wait to leave the apartment. It occurred to her how embarrassing it would be if Melissa arrived home at that moment, but fortunately their departure was without incident. Karen gave a sigh of relief. She had no wish to see her friend's face when Melissa read the note and learned of the pending reconciliation.

The Dorchester was aglow with soft lights, the epitome of peace and comfort and luxury. In the room on the fourth floor which overlooked the park, Neville tipped the porter who had brought up the luggage, and asked Karen if she wanted a drink.

"Perhaps some coffee."

The coffee arrived soon afterwards. Relaxing on the sofa Karen savored the coffee's warmth as she looked out through the window to the lights of Park Lane and the dark trees beyond.

"Karen." He was beside her, his fingers touching the nape of her neck, gently taking the coffee cup from her hands and putting it on the table. "Karen."

After a while he said: "I'll put off going to Scotland. We'll go somewhere else for a week—perhaps Paris—"

"No," she said instinctively. "Not Paris."

"Where would you like to go?"

Later, long afterwards, she wondered why she did not say Madeira—Greece—Capri—anywhere where there would be no long shadows from the past, no mocking memories. Perhaps it was some obscure response to a challenge. Or perhaps it was because she knew at heart she had been running away for the past three years and now if she was to stand and face her future squarely she knew she must overcome all weakness and be so strong that nothing, not even the most violent memory from the past could hurt her any more.

April has interfered quite enough in my life, she was aware of thinking with resolution, but she won't interfere any longer. Am I to say no to a trip to Scotland every time Neville is obliged to visit Plantation Q?

"I'm not afraid of going back to Scotland," she said firmly to Neville. "And I want to exorcise April's ghost finally and forever. Let me come with you to the plantation."

For a moment she fancied she saw a shadow in his eyes, a slight tightening of his fine mouth, and then he shrugged his shoulders with a smile and the moment of uneasiness was gone.

"As you wish," he said, and leant forward to take her in his arms.

## III

Melissa returned to her apartment shortly before midnight after visiting an old schoolfriend who lived in Surrey, and found Karen's note at once. She read it once carelessly, a second time in incredulous comprehension, and a third time to make sure her eyes were not deceiving her. Then she went to the living-room, mixed herself a stiff scotch and soda and sat down very calmly.

It was ridiculous to get upset. Ridiculous—and undignified. And humiliating. And a dozen other things which did not bear thinking about.

Melissa took a mouthful of scotch meticulously, much as a child would take abhorred medicine, and reached for a cigarette.

After all, she thought more levelly, it had only been an af-

fair. She always took scrupulous care not to become too involved with the men in her life, and why should Neville
Bennett have been different from any of the others whom she
had handled with such adroit competence? The answer came
flashing into her mind with a most unwelcome clarity. Because, she thought, it was not she who had handled Neville;
Neville had handled her. And she had been clay in his hands.

The wave of humiliation was so deep and so excruciating
that she nearly crushed the glass in her hands to fragments.
She had run after Neville like an adolescent; she had behaved
in a manner which for a grown woman had been incredible.
Her cheeks flamed as she looked back, remembering incident
after incident, how she had schemed to get him, schemed to
keep him, schemed—even schemed to marry him. Well thank
God nothing had come of that. It was incredible to think that
she could ever have been so foolish over a man. Incredible,
and unbearable.

The fury was edging the humiliation from her mind as she
got up and began to pace up and down the room. He had
taken her, used her for a year and then casually discarded her
—as if she were some tramp who had served her purpose!
Karen had only to crook her little finger, and . . . What did
Neville see in that woman anyway? She was pretty certainly,
but much too reserved and quiet. Deep, thought Melissa, seizing on the word. Yes, that was it! Deep. Still waters never ran
deeper . . . All that talk about there being no possibility of a
reconciliation! No doubt she had planned it all along.

Melissa finished her drink and ground her cigarette to dust
in the ash tray.

It was a pity, she thought, that Karen hadn't confided in
her. Melissa could have told her a thing or two about Neville
Bennett.

But perhaps Karen was so infatuated that she would have
refused to hear anything against Neville. Perhaps—and perhaps not. April was, after all, Karen's sister.

She considered the idea of an anonymous letter and then
rejected it instantly. That would be too obvious, too lacking
in subtlety, too—what was the word?—too crass. There were
surely better ways of pointing out to Karen what a fool she

was to go back to that man. Imagine going back to Scotland with him as well! Melissa's eyes narrowed in scorn. She felt cooler now, more composed. The anger was still with her but now it was an ice-cold controlled anger, infinitely more virulent than the first rush of rage. After a while she lit another cigarette and went to her files of correspondence which she kept in connection with the running of the boutique. She had always planned to do more research on the prices and suppliers of genuine Scottish tweeds. Tweeds always sold well, particularly to American tourists who thought such material was a typically British product. Perhaps in the autumn of next year she could bring out a comprehensive line embodying new styles of tweed, but if she decided to go ahead with such a project she would have to make a business trip to Scotland.

Pulling out her map of the British Isles she studied the section devoted to Scotland and began to calculate which was the nearest tweed mill to Plantation Q.

## IV

Leonie waited up for Neville till midnight and then went to bed with reluctance. She was, of course, accustomed to Neville's nights away from home and had long since learnt never to question him or even to make observations to him about them. Nonetheless she often worried in case he had had an accident in his car (most unlikely, for Neville was an excellent driver) and, in any event, she was always conscious of a faint but unmistakable disapproval when she was reminded of this discreet but recurring aspect of Neville's private life. Her father, she thought, would not have approved at all. Their parents were long since dead, but Leonie often thought of them, particularly of her father who had been a quiet, scholarly man with no recreations outside his archaeological studies except a round of golf on Sundays and an hour's gardening from time to time. He had been ascetic, almost monastic in his way of life, very different from his witty, gay, and much too attractive wife who had been occasionally unfaithful but had never quite made the effort to leave him.

Leonie sighed in irritation, turned out the light and lay back on her pillows in the darkness.

Sleep was impossible, of course; she might have guessed as much. At two o'clock she got up, went down to the kitchen and made herself a cup of tea. In spite of herself she could not stop wondering where Neville was, which was foolish because she knew very well that he had taken Karen out to dinner and it was obvious he was set on effecting a reconciliation. No doubt by this time they were at some hotel.

Leonie closed her mind resolutely, washed up her cup and saucer and rinsed out the teapot.

Not for the first time she wondered why such antipathy existed between herself and Karen. Leonie had never liked Americans. Nasty noisy people, she thought with distaste, brash, tasteless and inexpressibly vulgar. It made no difference that Karen was quiet, charming and had excellent taste. She was one of Them. Even the accent set Leonie on edge. And she thought of Karen's brother Thomas with a shudder, Thomas with his bold, cynical, baby-blue eyes, and that appalling drawl and that indescribably awful slang—and his clothes! Thank God that at least Karen looked respectable and was fit to be presented in the circles in which Neville moved. It would have been too dreadful if Neville had married a female equivalent of Thomas. April, for instance.

Leonie allowed herself one long shudder and moved briskly upstairs. Now was not the moment to begin remembering the past. If she started thinking about that terrible weekend at the farm she would be awake all night.

Which she was. Even her sleeping pills had no effect. She tossed and turned, read a few pages of her library book, and tossed and turned again. She was thinking of Marney now, remembering times long ago and comparing them to the present, her mind full of regrets, bitterness and a useless but persistent welling of self-pity.

At five o'clock in the morning she got up and began to move about the room in an agony of restlessness. This is all Karen's fault, she thought dry-eyed; if she hadn't come back I wouldn't have started to think of the past. The past was closed and forgotten—as far as one can ever forget—and yet now she comes back to remind me, to stir up all the old memories, the pain, the shock, the horror, the humiliation.

She was crying. Tears scorched her cheeks but she made no effort to check them. I shall be pushed aside now, she was aware of thinking bitterly, just as I was when he married Karen and brought her back to his house at Cambridge. I shall have to go away and live on my own, just as I did then—and after I've found somewhere to live, what then? I shall be a middle-aged spinster, discarded, redundant, and useless. And once I leave Neville's house I know perfectly well that I shall no longer have the chance to see Marney so often; there will be no more opportunities to speak to him on the phone.

And all because Karen had come back to London. And Neville wanted her back.

But perhaps it wouldn't last. Perhaps they would quarrel again and Karen would go back to America.

Leonie drew back the curtains to watch the dawn breaking over London. Her tears had stopped; she was calmer now, resolute and determined. She would not be usurped, she told herself tight-lipped. She would not be cast aside, discarded as valueless. She had her own life to lead, didn't she? She would show Karen that it would not be easy to push her out of the way; Karen would be surprised when she found out how awkward Leonie could make the situation.

Dawn had broken; the sun was rising. Suddenly exhausted, Leonie lay down again on the bed, and this time, all her anger spent, she slept until the child bounced into her room at seven o'clock to ask her where his father was.

V

Marney did not usually go to the office on Saturdays, but this time was an exception. His superior, a very senior gentle-

man in the current government, was expecting a report from
him on an industrial concern in the north which was experi-
menting with a certain type of lumber; there was a debate
in the House next week and the Minister must, absolutely
must, have the report by Monday morning. Marney had
sighed in resignation, wondered for the twentieth time why
he had left the peace of academic life, and buckled down to
his duties as a civil servant. He had just finished the last page
of the report and was relaxing in relief when there was a
knock on his door and Neville walked in.

Marney raised his eyebrows. Here was a different Neville,
vibrant yet relaxed, as sleek and content as a well-fed tomcat.
Marney felt his mouth twist ironically in the second before
the shock made his heart miss a beat.

"So there you are!" said Neville lightly. "I thought I remembered you saying you would be working this morning. I just
dropped in to collect my file on Plantation Q. We're off to
Scotland on Monday."

"We?"

"Karen and I."

The paper clip between Marney's fingers bent into a con-
torted fantasy and broke. Marney smiled. "Congratulations,"
he said pleasantly.

Neville grinned like a schoolboy, tossed back the lock of
dark hair which had fallen over his forehead and flung himself
down in the chair by the desk. "Surprised?"

"A little. But not unduly."

"I thought I'd phone Symons and tell him I'm taking five
days' leave. That means I can have a complete week with
Karen alone at the farm before I have to bother to go over to
the lodge on Plantation Q and do business with Kelleher. The
business isn't urgent, after all. I've been putting it off for the
last month so it won't hurt to put it off a week longer."

"True. In that case, why not go somewhere else for a week?"

"Karen decided against that."

"Oh?"

"Well, first of all I thought I would make a business trip of
it from start to finish, and then when Karen said she didn't

mind coming I thought I would postpone the business for a few days."

"I see."

"I've just been talking to Leonie about it, actually. We both wanted Snuff to come with us, but then decided it might be better if he joined us when I began my business at the plantation. Karen and I'll have a few days together first. Fortunately Leonie's volunteered to bring Snuff up to the farm herself so we don't have to worry about how he's going to get there."

"That was good of her."

"Well, it wasn't exactly what I had in mind, but it's certainly the best way of getting Snuff up to the farm since he's too young to travel so far on his own. Besides, I couldn't tell Leonie not to come because in fact, if you remember, the farm does belong to her. When I bought it I gave it to her by deed of gift as a tax dodge, and of course in the end she did go there often before Karen and I were married—she used to spend about two months of the year there, and even now she goes up for visits during the summer."

"I would have thought it an asset to have her at the farm when you begin work at the plantation," Marney said without emphasis. "It'll be lonely for Karen on her own there during the day."

"Well, yes, there is that to it, I suppose, but they've never got on too well, unfortunately . . . What really worries me is what I'm to say to Leonie when we come back from Plantation Q. I think it would be fatal if she continued to live with us, especially since she can't or won't get on with Karen, but so far she hasn't volunteered to look for a flat of her own. I can foresee an awkward situation developing."

"Tedious for you," said Marney.

"Very. Still . . ." He rose to his feet lithely and wandered back to the door. "There's no sense in worrying about it now, I suppose. I'll see you in about a fortnight's time, Marney. Phone me if an emergency crops up on any of my projects, but I'm not expecting any trouble at the moment."

"All right. Give my regards to Karen, won't you? Tell her I'm delighted everything's ended happily."

"Ended?" laughed Neville. "It's just beginning!"

"I suppose so. Goodbye, Neville."

"'Bye." The door slammed. Footsteps sauntered off down the passage.

Marney took a deep breath.

He stood up, conscientiously reminding himself that Neville was his oldest friend, but he still felt indignant. Beyond the window lay the lush green of the lawns and trees of St. James's Park, the glint of water glimpsed through the trees, the strolling Londoners relaxing on their day off. Marney turned back to his desk, collected the sheaf of papers which constituted his report and clipped the pages together. His hand, he noticed to his astonishment, was shaking. How extraordinary! He had known for twenty-five years that Neville was the type of man who always got what he wanted, so why should Marney now of all times feel so indignant because Neville had achieved the desired reconciliation with his wife and was frank enough to admit he now found his sister redundant? Neville was only conforming to his usual pattern of behavior. Why should Marney feel so angry?

It was because of Karen, of course. Marney admired Karen and was fond of her. He had admired her even more when she had done what no woman had ever done before, when she had walked out on Neville Bennett and refused to go back to him. The fact that she had consented so willingly now to a reconciliation was somehow an immense disappointment; Marney felt disillusioned. Perhaps Karen was the same as any other woman after all and he had overestimated her when he had considered her unique in relation to Neville.

He put on his raincoat, opened the door abruptly and stepped out into the corridor. He still felt angry, he realized, and what was worse he was aware of a contempt mingled with disgust which was somehow directed against his friend. Moving downstairs quickly he went outside and crossed the road into the park, but the feeling persisted, shamefully identifiable and profoundly uncomfortable.

He reached the bridge over the long lake and paused half-way across to look east at the fairytale skyline which was one of the most celebrated views of any city. The sun was shining; the sky was blue. And before him above the lake and the fringes of trees rose the towers and minarets of Horseguards, eastern, mysterious, cosmopolitan.

Be honest, he told himself, admit it. You're jealous of Neville, you always were and you always will be. Admit it and live with it and laugh it off but don't, for God's sake, let it fester and seethe and corrupt.

It was three years since he had had to reason with himself like this. Three long years. He had thought he had purged himself of all jealousy, cauterized himself of all hatred and resentment. He had thought that never again would he even feel the desire to let his emotions govern his civilized self-control or lose his grip on his sense of proportion, yet now here he was again, dizzy with the corrosive emotion he despised, willing himself to be sensible and realistic while the old scars he thought healed broke open and scorched his memory with their poison.

But he must not think of April. She was part of the past. It was foolish now to think of her and remember the part she had played in his life.

He turned blindly and walked off the bridge. None of this would have happened, he thought, if Karen had remained in America. Three years of peace, of learning to forget, and now this.

At least, he thought in relief as he reached the Mall and began to walk towards Trafalgar Square, at least this time he wouldn't be at Plantation Q.

## VI

Six days passed.

It was the following Friday at four in the afternoon when Thomas Conway reached Paris, installed himself in a modest but comfortable hotel, and placed a phone call to Melissa's apartment where he thought his sister was staying. Melissa, home early from her boutique, answered the phone.

"Hi Melissa—how are you?" In common with numerous

Americans he never bothered to announce who he was at the beginning of a telephone conversation. The curious part was that most of the people he telephoned seemed to have no trouble in identifying him unaided.

"Thomas, I presume," enquired Melissa, running true to form.

"In person. I'm calling from Paris and hope to fix a free plane ride to London tomorrow . . . Is Karen there?"

"No," said Melissa, very cool. "She left a week ago."

"What!" shouted Thomas. "You mean she went home so soon? Why the hell did she do that?"

"No, she hasn't gone home actually." Melissa sounded crisply composed. "She's gone to Scotland, to Plantation Q."

There was a silence. Then: "You have to be kidding," said Thomas at last. "You have to be."

"No, I'm perfectly serious. They went there a week ago."

"You mean she and Neville—"

"Yes, they had a reconciliation."

"My God," said Thomas.

"They were reconciled last Friday—exactly a week ago, in fact. Then on Saturday Karen called to tell me she and Neville would be in Scotland for a fortnight or so—Neville had business at the Plantation but they planned a few days alone together at the farm first. Leonie's flying up to Inverness tomorrow with the child to join them."

"But Scotland!" said Thomas appalled. "That god-damned Plantation!"

"I suppose she wanted to prove to herself that she could go back there again."

"She's nuts."

Melissa sounded slightly amused. "Perhaps."

"Look, can I stop by at your place when I get to London tomorrow?"

"That depends when you're arriving. I'm setting off for Scotland myself tomorrow, and I plan to leave at nine-thirty."

"Yeah?" He was interested. "Vacation?"

"Business. I want to visit a tweed mill near Fort William."

"Fort William? Isn't that near—hey, want a co-driver?"

He really was a confirmed sponger, Melissa observed dispassionately. Unless she was careful she would be paying his overnight hotel bill as well as providing him with a free ride to see his sister.

"Well, I must say," she said, affecting relief mingled with pleasure. "I would appreciate someone to help with the driving—have you ever driven a Fiat 600 before—and of course I'd appreciate your help with the petrol expenses too. That would be wonderful, Thomas."

If he was disappointed at her hint, he gave no sign of it. "I'll get a night flight tonight," he said. "I'll call the airport right now. Maybe I could come direct to your apartment when I arrive? If Karen's not there maybe I could use your spare room to save all the trouble of finding a hotel. You wouldn't mind, would you?"

Melissa did mind, very much. "Well—"

"That's all right," said Thomas comfortably. "I won't ask for anything I shouldn't."

Melissa, who had fended off a couple of routine attempts at seduction by Thomas when they had first met several years ago in New York, was not so sure.

"You think it over," he said winningly. "You've got my guarantee of good behavior. With luck I'll see you before midnight. 'Bye now."

The line clicked as he replaced the receiver. Melissa stared at the telephone in distaste and then shrugged her shoulders philosophically. Perhaps after all the situation could be turned to her advantage.

## VII

At about the same time in the office on Birdcage Walk, Marney was closing a file and looking forward to a pleasantly peaceful weekend. He was still looking forward to the weekend when the door opened and his superior walked into the room.

"Dr. West, something's come up in relation to Plantation
Q . . ."

". . . just received a call from Kelleher at the foresters'
lodge . . ."

His muscles slowly tightened.

". . . Neville Bennett's up there right now, of course, but he
doesn't have any of the files on the syndrome, nor is he particularly well-acquainted with them since they are, after all,
your project—"

Horror made the room blur before his eyes. A very polite
voice which he dimly recognized as his own was saying: "Sir,
is it really necessary for me to go? I'm very tied up at the moment with the White Paper. Perhaps Wilkins—"

"Wilkins is in Scandinavia. No, it'll have to be you, I'm
afraid. But it won't be for long. Let's see, if you flew up tomorrow you could be at the lodge in the evening—I'll send a
wire to Kelleher to have one of the men meet you at Inverness
airport. A couple of days should put matters right."

Marney listened, acquiesced, noted down his instructions
with meticulous precision. Then when he was alone at last
he sat for a long while at his desk before standing up, putting
on his raincoat and stowing into his briefcase the files necessary
for his unexpected, unwanted visit to Plantation Q.

# FOUR

## I

The lake was in the remote regions of the Western Highlands near the sea-loch of Hourn and bordering the vast territories of Lochiel. It was a little lake, small and peaceful, and the road wound all along one side of it from Kildoun to the junction of the road to Kyle of Lochalsh many miles away. The converted farm which Neville had bought and given to his sister some years ago lay on the opposite side of the lake to the road; decades earlier the lake had been fordable, but the modern age with its hydro-electric schemes had put an end to that and now a boat was necessary to cross the lake from the farm to the road; Neville kept two rowing boats for convenience's sake, and the farm had a small jetty and boathouse. Leonie had tended the small patch of ground nearby with great patience, and now a few hardy flowers flourished spasmodically in the beds beneath the windows. However, her pride and joy was the rockery which she had built some yards from the house, and it was here that her gardening talents had been most successful.

From behind the farm, a rough track climbed sharply up the mountainside and eventually surmounted the ridge to lead down into the next valley to the foresters' lodge at Plantation Q. The Q stood for Question-mark, for it was an experimental plantation, and Neville was often obliged to visit it to see how the trees were growing and to supervise the implementing of new schemes. From the lodge at the plantation, an estate road

ran a winding four-mile course to join the main road to Fort
William and a hint of civilization.

Neville and Karen had arrived at Inverness airport without
incident the previous Monday and had been met in person
by Kelleher, who was in charge at the foresters' lodge. A
trained forester with years of experience in Canada and Nor-
way, he drove an ancient, but aristocratic, Rolls Royce on all
expeditions away from the plantation, and it was in this griz-
zled old motor car that Neville and Karen were taken to Plantation Q. Here they had dinner with Kelleher and the foresters
and botanists who staffed the lodge, and then Neville borrowed one of the fleet of jeeps to drive over the mountains
to the little lake and the converted farm.

"Everything's ready for you," Kelleher told them. "As soon
as your wire came on Saturday, I contacted Mrs. MacLeod
and she and her daughter went over and aired the house and
saw that everything was in order. I drove over yesterday with
a supply of food and the place looked all right to me. If you
need anything more just give us a ring and I'll send one of the
boys over in a jeep."

But everything was perfect. They had set off in the jeep
from the lodge and Karen, who had privately dreaded the arrival at the farm, found that the drive was so breathtaking
that even her fears were eclipsed. They reached the boundary
of the plantation, surmounted the pass, and then Neville
stopped the jeep for a moment to look at the view. There
was a full moon. White light steamed across the bare moorland
of the valley before them: far below was the long slender
gleam of the lake. Everywhere was quite still, absolutely at
peace, and Karen caught her breath and felt the unexpected
tears prick her eyes because it was so beautiful.

"I'm glad we came back," she said.

He found her hand and held it tightly for a second before
they drove on.

The farm at first appeared to be set by the water's edge and
it was only when they drew nearer that it became apparent
that it was set more than a hundred yards back from the lake
on rising ground. The walls were whitewashed, and in the
darkness it was impossible to tell which were the original walls

of the one-room cottage and which were the walls which had been added when the building had been enlarged. Nearby, the cascading white waters of the creek roared downhill to meet the lake. After Neville had parked the jeep, Karen followed him across the wooden bridge, passed Leonie's rockery and so came at last to the back door of the cottage.

Neville lit a lamp and then went back for the remaining suit-cases, but Karen took the lamp and walked through the kitchen, through the small dining-room into the living-room. Everywhere looked just the same. She tried for a moment to picture April there, but to her surprise could not. Neville was right, she thought to herself. There were no ghosts.

And she was conscious of a great relief as all the tensions ebbed at last from her mind.

She went upstairs to the main bedroom, took off her coat and removed the counterpane from the bed. The sheets looked crisp and inviting. Slipping off her shoes she lay down and closed her eyes and so complete was her relaxation that she drifted into sleep almost at once and did not even hear Neville bring the suitcases upstairs. The next thing she knew was that he was beside her, his lips seeking hers, his arms pressing her closer to him, and it seemed to her for one bizarre moment that the past three years had been a dream and that she had just awoken after a long sleep; perhaps April had never come to the farm, perhaps none of the terrible scenes of three years ago had ever happened . . .

"Happy?" she heard Neville murmur at last.

"Mmmm . . ." And she was. Tonight for the first time the reconciliation seemed a reality.

Later he said: "Tonight at last you seemed to love me with-out reservations."

The match flared as he lit a cigarette; she saw his face for a moment in the darkness, but as the match died there was only the moonlight streaming through the uncurtained window, the tranquility, the peace.

"It wasn't easy at the hotel."

"I know."

"I felt more like your mistress than your wife."

"I should have waited till we got here—"

"I was impatient too, don't forget!"

They laughed. He leant over and kissed her. After a long while he said: "This marks the new beginning, then. A new life together, new happiness, new everything. Children too, if you wish. And the past is never, never going to come between us again."

But the past was there all the same. In the daylight the memories seemed sharper. She went down to the jetty the next morning and the boats reminded her of how Thomas had rowed her across the lake three years ago; she walked a short way up the track past the rockery behind the house and found herself remembering the morning when she had escaped from Neville and April at the farm and rushed blindly up the track towards Plantation Q. And most horrible of all, she went into the tumbled-down, deserted cottage further down the lakeside, and the atmosphere of crumbling decay reminded her unreasonably of Melissa's wild insinuations, the suggestion that April was still somewhere near the farm despite everyone's assumption that she had gone away. Karen shivered violently. She glanced around her again, but there was nothing there, only the moist walls of the cottage, the soft earthen floor littered with weeds and rubble, the sightless windows which faced the calm waters of the lake. But the next moment she was running, the breath tearing at her lungs, and when she met Neville at the door of the cottage she clung to him in relief even as she laughed at her ridiculous state of panic.

The days passed uneventfully. The weather was moderately good; it rained a little every day, but there was some sunshine too, usually in the afternoons, and the evening sunsets were magnificent, a blaze of scarlet and pink behind the mountain peaks. Neville took her boating and fishing, to the hotel at Kildoun for a drink and dinner, to Fort William to shop for provisions. They went for long walks up the stream or by the lake, explored the vast tracts of moors, discovered old paths in the heather. When it was wet they relaxed by the peat fire in the living-room, played records on the ancient gramophone which had to be wound by hand, or listened to the transistor radio.

But the past was still there. Despite herself, Karen was con-

scious of it, and although she sought to rationalize her aware-
ness of memory she wasn't altogether successful. After all, it
was impossible that she should remember nothing of what had
happened three years ago, she told herself sensibly. One
couldn't expect a convenient amnesia. Some memory was in-
evitable, but what was important was that it shouldn't matter,
shouldn't upset her in any way.

Yet the sense of discomfort persisted and grew.

It was more a sense of anticipation than anything else, an
intuitive core of dread lodged at the back of her mind. As the
week drew to a close she diverted herself by thinking that
Leonie would be there presently with Snuff and the arrival
would shift the past further out of sight, but even as she
thought this another part of her mind was saying: Leonie was
here three years ago. To some extent her presence will re-
create the horror of that other weekend.

Then came the news of Marney's pending arrival, and her
dread deepened.

"He'll be staying at the lodge, of course," said Neville carelessly, as if he guessed the cause of her anxiety, but his words
held no comfort for her.

Marney had stayed at the lodge last time.

She tried to pull herself together, told herself that it was absurd to see any relationship between the coming weekend and
the weekend that had ended her marriage three years ago.
Neville made arrangements by phone for Leonie to hire a car
which would meet her at the airport when she arrived with
Snuff, and Karen busied herself determinedly about the house,
dusting, cleaning and cooking in readiness for the visitors. By
the time they arrived she was well in command of herself, and
seeing the child again took her mind away from her worries.

Marney reached Plantation Q that evening and telephoned
Neville from the lodge, but this made little impression on her.

And then without any warning, Melissa and Thomas arrived
on Sunday night at Kildoun.

## II

Marney had driven over for dinner that evening, and it was
he who answered the phone when the call came through.
Leonie was in the kitchen making coffee and Karen had just
taken Snuff up to bed. Neville was sitting in the armchair by
the fire, his legs stretched out before the hearth, his hands
clasped behind his head as he yawned, while Marney was
changing the needle on the antique gramophone.

The bell rang.

"I'll get it," said Marney. "It's probably Kelleher." He picked
up the extension receiver. "Hello? Dr. West speaking."

"Hi Marney," said Thomas amiably. "How are you? Karen
around?"

"Thomas? Well, this is a surprise! Just a moment, please."
He put down the receiver.

"Who?" exclaimed Neville incredulously.

"A male American accent asking for Karen."

"Good God!" He was on his feet, moving over to the phone
while Marney went out of the room to fetch Karen. "Thomas?
Neville. Where are you phoning from?"

"Just across the lake." Neville heard him turn aside to speak
to someone else. "What's the name of this place, honey? I never
could remember . . . Kildoun. I had a lucky break and got a
lift all the way from London. Do you remember a friend of
Karen's called Melissa Fleming?"

Karen was right behind him. "What's the matter, Neville?"

Neville said disbelievingly: "Thomas is at Kildoun with
Melissa."

Karen stared at him. There was a silence. Presently the receiver began to shout at them in a little faraway voice: "Neville? Hey, what's happened! Neville, are you there? Neville—"

Karen took the receiver. "Calm down, Thomas, and stop
having hysterics. How are you, and how did you get here?
What a wonderful surprise!"

Thomas, slightly mollified, settled down to explain. He had gone to London, found Melissa was about to depart on a business trip to a mill near Fort William and had managed to persuade her to drive a few miles further north so that he could be delivered almost to the door.

"Wasn't that nice of her? Hey, Karen, why don't we come on over? Is there a boat this side we could use?"

"Let me check with Neville." She muffled the receiver against her breast. "They want to come over."

"Both of them?"

"Apparently."

"Good God—"

"I suppose Melissa hasn't told him anything at all. Neville, I can't refuse him—I haven't seen him for three years—"

"Of course. Let me talk to him." He took the receiver. "Thomas, I'll row over myself and pick you up—expect me in about fifteen minutes' time. Incidentally, I'm afraid we can't invite you and Melissa to stay as Leonie and Snuff are here and there's no room—would it be all right if you stayed at the hotel in Kildoun?"

"I guess that shouldn't be any problem."

"Good. In that case I don't suppose Melissa wants to be bothered with coming over, does she? Perhaps some time tomorrow—"

"You want to come, Melissa? They've no room for us to stay . . . You do? Okay. Neville? Yes, Melissa says she'll come over for the ride. See you in fifteen minutes then. Thanks a lot."

The line went dead.

"God damn that woman," said Neville, slamming the receiver back into its cradle, his face scarlet with rage. "God damn her."

"Is she coming?"

"Of course she's coming! Do you think she'd miss the opportunity to play the role of Woman Scorned? She's enjoying every minute of her petty little vendetta!"

"Well, don't give her the pleasure of seeing she's upset you," said Karen levelly. "Pretend you're amused, if anything. Make out that you don't give a damn." Neville's fury had the effect of making her calmer than she would otherwise have been, but when he left the room a moment later to get a sweater

and change his shoes, she felt the panic edge down her spine.
Thomas, Marney, Neville and Leonie were back once more
with her in Scotland; only Melissa had had no part in that
weekend of three years ago.

The child called from upstairs and she pulled herself together and went back to him. It was foolish to become neurotic
over what was merely an unfortunate coincidence.

Neville set off, still looking angry, and presently when Karen
had returned downstairs to the living-room Leonie brought in
the coffee. Half an hour passed. Marney was just putting more
fuel on the fire when they heard the sound of voices outside
and the next moment the front door was opening and Neville
was leading the way into the living-room.

"Karen!" shouted Thomas in delight, and embraced his sister
with a fervor which made the English spectators stare in surprise. He stepped back a pace admiringly. "You look great!"

He himself looked better than would most travelers who
had spent a week gravitating from one side of Europe to the
other. He was immaculately dressed; clothes looked well on
Thomas and he wasn't ashamed of looking smart and fashion-
able. He spent a great deal of money on his wardrobe, but considered it money well invested since in his profession it was
important to keep up appearances. He wasn't tall, but he was
tall enough to be able to describe himself as five foot eleven
and be believed. He had a vague air of being in excellent physical condition; his dark hair was short but not crew-cut and
curled in exactly the right places, his mouth was slightly
crooked, and his nose, broken in adolescence, had healed at-
tractively. He had a scar on his left cheek of which he was
proud, but apart from this idiosyncrasy he was not unduly
vain.

"I smell coffee," he said, sniffing like a dog. "Just what I
need! Have you eaten yet, by the way? I'm starved."

"Thomas," said Melissa, almost but not quite embarrassed,
"you're entirely shameless."

"I'll go and get you something, Thomas," said Karen.
"Melissa, would you—"

"Just coffee, darling. We had sandwiches at the hotel just
now but Thomas seems to have forgotten about them."

"I'm going to have a drink," said Neville. "What about you, Marney? Will you have a whisky with me?"

Karen escaped to the kitchen and heard footsteps padding along behind her.

"Where's the light-switch?" muttered Thomas, feeling the wall in the darkness. Then, as memory returned: "My God, you mean to say they've still got no electricity here? Isn't that hydro-electric scheme finished yet?"

"Neville didn't bother to have electricity put in. He figured it wasn't worth it as he didn't live here permanently." She lit a lamp and turned up the wick so that the kitchen was illuminated with a gloomy brightness. "How about some cold ham or chicken with salad?"

"Delicious." He watched, sharp-eyed as a lynx, as she began to move about the kitchen. "Well, well," he said at last. "Who would ever have thought that we'd meet again here? Who would have thought three years ago that here we'd all be again three years later—"

"I suppose you're surprised I agreed to come back."

"Surprised?" said Thomas. "Yes, I was surprised. I'll tell you something else. I was more than surprised. I was stupefied and amazed and began to have serious doubts about your sanity."

"Thomas!" She had to laugh. "Just because I didn't take your advice—"

"Hell, I wasn't so naive as to think you would, but I thought there was no harm in trying. I guessed that if you once saw him again you'd be right back where you started. You're a sensible girl, Karen—you don't have to convince me of that—and your judgment of men was always so damned impeccable that it was irritating, but even sensible girls have their blind spots, and Neville Bennett just happens to be yours. Okay, fair enough! It's your life and if he makes you happy, that's swell, but he didn't make you very happy the other time, did he, and I don't know why you should think he'll make you any happier now than the time before."

"Oh, stop that, Thomas—"

"Honey, I've met men like Neville before—you find them often enough in the acting profession, strange as that may seem to you. They're handsome and smart and charming and

they're all hell with the women, but you know something? You
know who they really love better than anyone else in all the
big wide world? No, *not* their mothers—not their wives—not
even their mistresses. They're in love with themselves. They
love their cute little selves better than anything else on this
earth, and—"

"Surely not as much as you love the sound of your own
voice, Thomas," said Neville blandly from the doorway.

Thomas swung round.

Oh God, thought Karen. The carving knife slipped from her
fingers and fell to the floor with a clatter.

"You'd better let me do that," said Neville, moving forward.
He picked up the carving knife, wiped it clean and turned to
the chicken on the draining board.

Thomas said idly: "How's the kid? May I see him?"

"Why, yes, of course!" Karen grasped at the diversion with
such relief that she was afraid afterwards she might have
sounded too pleased. "I'm surprised he hasn't ventured downstairs to inspect the new arrivals. Come up and say hello to
him."

They escaped upstairs.

"You *are* a fool, Thomas!" whispered Karen wretchedly.
"What on earth did you want to say all that for? And besides,
it's not true any more—you had no right—"

"Okay, okay, I'm sorry." Thomas had the grace to look con-
trite. "But how was I to know he'd come sneaking into the
kitchen after us? Look, after we've seen the kid let's go outside
for a stroll where no one will disturb us. I want to talk to you."

Snuff, evidently overcome with the excitement of being in a
new place and the strength of the Highland air, was fast
asleep.

"That explains why he didn't come down to see you," she
murmured to Thomas. "I think we'd better wait till tomorrow."

They returned cautiously to the kitchen. A lamp was still
burning and there was a plate of newly-carved chicken on the
draining board, but Neville had evidently returned to the
living-room. Thomas picked up a slice of chicken absent-
mindedly and moved to the back door.

"Let's go across the creek a little way."

"Burn," said Karen automatically, reaching for the coat which hung on the back of the door. "You're not in Minnesota now."

They went outside. Across the creek they took the track up the mountainside and after about five minutes found a flat rock where they could sit and survey the sweep of the moors and the lighted windows of the farmhouse below.

"I hope you haven't got mixed up with Melissa, Thomas," said Karen presently.

He was scandalized. "Melissa? Now, wait awhile—"

"Since you so kindly advised me about my private life I thought I'd return the compliment and advise you about yours," said Karen dryly. "And since you must have spent about forty-eight hours in Melissa's company, and bearing in mind that you must have stopped over somewhere last night—"

"Separate rooms," said Thomas.

"And the night before?"

"I had your room at her apartment. Hey, what *is* this?"

"And nothing happened?"

"And nothing happened," said Thomas virtuously.

"But I bet you tried!" She was teasing him now, a smile hovering at the corners of her mouth. "What a blow to your ego!"

"Well, of course I tried," said Thomas crossly. "Why not? But I might have guessed it was a waste of time. She was always cold, even when I first met her."

"She was warm enough to please Neville for over a year."

His mouth dropped open. He looked so comical in his surprise that she laughed out loud.

"You're kidding."

"No, it's true. He was just trying to end the affair discreetly when I arrived."

"Well, I'm damned . . ." He brooded on the information for a moment. Then: "But in that case what the hell's she doing here?"

"I was hoping you were going to tell me. I suppose she's just malicious and seized on the opportunity to make Neville feel embarrassed."

"Neville!" said Thomas. "Neville! Who cares about Neville? You're the one she's embarrassing!"

"If she really is acting out of malice, I just feel sorry for her making such a futile exhibition of herself."

"That's amazing," reflected Thomas. "To think that I've been traveling with her for two days and she never once mentioned her relationship with Neville. You'd have thought she'd have said something bitchy which would have given her away."

"Melissa's much too clever for that."

"But we talked a lot about Neville," said Thomas. "We both agreed—" He stopped.

"Well, go on," said Karen. "Don't stop. I know what you think about Neville, and I can guess what she must be feeling by this time. What did you agree?"

"Only that we thought you were—ill-advised to return to him," said Thomas with reluctance. "We talked of April—she asked me exactly what had happened . . ."

"Did she suggest that April was dead?"

He looked at her quickly in the darkness. "Did she suggest that to you?"

"She mentioned it was a possibility."

"Well, it is possible, I guess."

"Here in Scotland?"

"It would explain one or two puzzling things." He was hedging, defensive.

"Did she think it was an accident?"

"We—mentioned something about that—"

"You mean," said Karen, "that between you, you agreed that April's dead and Neville murdered her."

"For Christ's sake, Karen—"

"That's too much, Thomas!" She felt all the more angry because she recognized the panic trembling at the back of her mind. "It's slander and you know it, and how you dare, how you have the nerve to suggest such a thing when we have no proof that April's even dead—"

"But listen, Karen," interrupted Thomas. "Before you get really excited, just think for a moment. Go back step by step over what happened three years ago, and you'll see that there are one or two strange angles to the situation. Forget the possibility that she was murdered. Just concentrate on the possibility that she's dead."

"I don't want to," Karen said stubbornly, and in spite of herself she shivered. "I won't."

"Look," said Thomas patiently. "Nobody's saying Neville killed her. Say I killed her, if it'll make you feel any happier. Lord knows I felt like it often enough from the age of two onwards—you know we never got along together. I think in some ways—but not all, thank God—we were more alike than any of the rest of the family; we were certainly the two black sheep of the all-white batch, and because we were alike I always saw right through her. She might have fooled you, Karen, but she didn't fool me. She wasn't just a bitch and a phoney—she was a parasite exploiting you whenever she felt you had something to offer—"

"No," said Karen instinctively. "It wasn't like that."

"Unfortunately it was," said Thomas with unexpected firmness, "and half your troubles sprang from the fact that you refused to admit it. You can play the part of the ostrich much too well if you want to, Karen, but please don't play it now. Take a good long cool look at the possibility of April's death. To start with, if she's alive where is she? I've sounded the grapevine, even called up one or two of the producers she used to run around with. Nothing. They'd almost forgotten who she was. I haven't heard from her, you haven't heard from her, the family hasn't heard from her. So if she's alive what the hell's she doing? Okay, so she might have found herself some rich man and be living quietly in retirement—I concede that that's possible, but even if that's true I still think it's odd that she hasn't contacted any of her old friends to parade in front of them in mink and demonstrate her good fortune. You know how April loved to show off. Conversely if she was ill or starving you can be sure we'd have heard from her. She'd know Mother and Dad would always pay her medical bills and take her back with everything forgiven and forgotten.

"Secondly, if she's alive that means she must have left the farm that same morning that you found her with Neville. She was there when I rowed you across the lake at nine-thirty and yet Melissa tells me that by the time Leonie returned to the farm an hour and a half later after a visit to the lodge to see Marney, the farm was deserted. You were lost somewhere on

Plantation Q, Neville was looking for you and I had gone back
to the hotel at Kildoun to wait for your phone call to tell me
what had happened. (Incidentally, I still think I should have
insisted on landing with you and walking up to the cottage!
I know it was none of my business, but my God, I'd have told
the two of them where to go!) Anyway, during that hour and
a half April must have left the farm—if she ever left—and got
away. Now what puzzles me is why ever did she choose that
time to leave? She'd succeeded in her plans to drive a wedge
between you and Neville and she would shortly have Neville
to herself for as long as she wanted. Why walk out just when
she was on the brink of victory? It doesn't make sense."

"Neville had quarreled with her. He was full of remorse and
told her to go."

"So he says."

"Look, Thomas—"

"Okay, we'll take the situation from another angle. April
decides to leave—never mind why. Now as we both know, the
farm is not just one of those places where you can walk outside
on to a main highway, stand at a bus stop and get public
transport in a couple of minutes. It's a very hard place to
leave on the spur of the moment. You either have to walk over
to Plantation Q by the trail over the mountain—an uphill hike
which April couldn't possibly have attempted with high heels
and a couple of suitcases—and then get a lift from someone
at the lodge to the railroad station at Fort William, or else
you have to row across the lake and hang around outside
Kildoun until some driver in a passing car takes pity on you.
Now can you honestly imagine April teetering down to the
jetty with her suitcases, stepping into the boat without falling
in, and rowing—actually rowing—across the lake? It took
Neville a quarter of an hour to row across this evening, and
Neville's a man in good physical condition. April hated rowing always and couldn't even row for five minutes, let alone
for fifteen or twenty-five."

"If she were desperate—"

"Why on earth should she be desperate? As I've already
said, why should she even go away? If I were her and had
wanted to leave in a hurry I would have done one of two

things. Either I would have phoned the lodge and asked if there was a spare jeep and an off-duty forester who could come over the mountain, take me to Plantation Q and then give me another lift on to Fort William, or I would have called the hotel at Kildoun and asked if they could send over someone to pick me up in his boat and row me across the lake. People don't mind hiring out their boats now and then to make a bit of extra money—the boat I hired to row you across the lake that day belonged to a farmer. But April didn't do either of those two things. If she'd called the lodge we would have heard about it, and she didn't make use of a hired boat."

"Exactly! One of Neville's two row-boats was on the Kildoun side of the lake so that proves she must have rowed herself across no matter how unlikely that seems to us now."

"That doesn't prove anything," said Thomas at once. "That boat could have been towed across by himself in the second boat who then rowed himself back to the croft again. In other words the boat situation could have been rigged to make everyone think that April had gone away."

"Someone at Kildoun might have seen the boat towed across."

"So what? As far as they know the boat might have been towed across there for some visitor expected at the farm. Anyway, probably no one saw anything—Kildoun is such a tiny place and always seems so deserted. What a pity my hotel room didn't face the lake! If it had I would probably have seen exactly what happened, but all I did was sit by the bedside and wait for your call to come through. I didn't even dare leave the room for fear you'd try to get through to me when I wasn't there."

"And then finally I called you from the foresters' lodge and asked you to drive round to Plantation Q to collect me and take me away." The memory still hurt even now. Her heart ached for a moment before she pulled herself together. "But that was much later," she said abruptly. "It must have been nearly one o'clock when I called you."

"And meanwhile April had disappeared." He stared moodily out into the dusk. "I'm sorry, Karen, but I still think she's dead. I know you don't want to think that, but—"

"You mean someone killed her."

"Well—"

"Neville, for instance."

Thomas looked at her warily. "Or Leonie. She never liked April. Incidentally, why was Leonie at the farm then? I can't see why Neville arranged a rendezvous with April if he knew his sister was going to be there."

"There was no rendezvous. Leonie was on vacation there when Neville came up on business. As for April, Neville says she chased up there after him, and I—well, I believe him. April had already figured my marriage wasn't going so well and fancied the idea of stepping into my shoes. She wouldn't have waited for an invitation to spend a few days alone with Neville—she was quite capable of following him and issuing the invitation herself. She didn't realize till too late that Leonie was at the farm and Neville wasn't alone there after all."

"True." Thomas couldn't help chuckling to himself as he pictured the scene. "Imagine Leonie's face when April arrived!"

"Yes, I'll bet she was upset. I think that might have been why she set out for the lodge to see Marney the very next morning after they arrived. I expect she wanted to have a good grumble and it would have given her a convenient excuse to see him."

Thomas said idly: "Do you know if she really did see him that morning?"

"I've no idea. I should imagine so. Why?"

"Just wondering."

Karen stared out across the valley. The moon had risen and turned the dark waters of the lake to silver. Clouds floated past the shadowy mountain peaks to the north and wreathed the black moorland in eerie shades of light and darkness.

"Melissa's wondering too," she said with irony, and added with a flash of bitterness: "I'd like to know just what kind of game she's playing right now, first planting insinuations in my mind and then following me here."

"Could it be that she wants to scare you off Neville so that she could have him back? Perhaps she thought that if she could make it seem as though he killed your sister you would be horrified enough to retreat to America again."

"Even if I did, and I certainly don't intend to, he wouldn't go back to her."

"Yes, he would," said Thomas cynically. "If he found himself alone again and there she was ready, willing and able, the least he would do would be to give the situation a new try. I would. Any man would. It's common sense."

Karen opened her mouth to object to this, but then closed it again; she didn't feel inclined to argue with him on such an intricate subject. "Shall we go?" she asked after a pause. "It's getting chilly up here, and we've been talking a long time."

He agreed in silence and helped her to her feet. Presently he said: "You think it's going to work this time with Neville?"

"I know it is."

He was uncomfortable suddenly. She was so convinced, so certain.

"He's changed, Thomas. He seems less selfish, less concerned for himself. If it were possible I'd say he wanted the reconciliation even more than I did."

"I see."

"And I can tell you this, Thomas. If April was killed, and no matter what you or Melissa say I don't believe she was, then Neville wasn't the one who killed her. That I do know."

"Which Neville are you speaking of?" he couldn't help saying. "The new Neville, who's determined to make your marriage succeed, or the old one who was so determined to drive it on to the rocks?"

"He had no reason to kill April."

"Ever heard of a 'crime passionel'? Ever heard of blackmail? Ever heard of—"

"He didn't kill her, Thomas. I know it. Neville's not a murderer."

"We're all potential murderers," he said wryly. "Some just have more opportunity for realizing the potential than others, that's all."

She didn't answer and he knew he had upset her.

"I'm sorry," he said at once. "I don't mean to say all these things against Neville. If he can make you happy, then I'm

willing to be the best brother-in-law a man ever had. If I say
anything against Neville it's only because I'm worried silly
about you—I want you to be happy more than anything else
in the world, Karen, and I'd go to great lengths to see that you
were happy. You know that."

"I know," she said. "I know, Thomas."

She took his hand and they went down the steep hillside
together, not speaking but conscious that they understood
each other. At the back door once more, Karen turned to him
with a smile in which he glimpsed a flicker of relief.

"I'm so very glad you're here, Thomas," she said simply at
last, and something in her expression made him wonder just
how far she really did believe her husband to be uninvolved
in April's disappearance.

# FIVE

## I

The cottage was very quiet. In the living-room Neville was sitting alone by the fire, a novel in his hands, the radio murmuring a Beethoven quartet. He looked up as they came in.

"You were gone a hell of a long time," he said pleasantly, more to Thomas than to Karen. "Melissa decided not to wait for you and Marney volunteered to row her across the lake. Leonie's gone to bed, but I thought I might as well wait up for you as somebody will obviously have to ferry you across to join Melissa."

There was an inflection in the way he said the last two words which made Thomas look at him sharply.

"Who says I have to join Melissa? I'll stay overnight on the couch here."

"What a good idea," said Karen relieved before Neville could comment. "That'll save Neville a journey. Are you sure you wouldn't mind, Thomas?"

"I'd prefer it." He sat down on the couch without waiting for a further invitation and crossed his ankles leisurely.

"I'll go and get some blankets," said Karen. "It'll be cold when the fire burns out."

"One'll be enough." After she had left he went over to the phone. "Will Melissa be at the hotel by now, do you think?"

"Presumably," said Neville from the pages of his book. "They left at least half an hour ago."

"You know the hotel number?"

Neville did. Thomas began to make the call and within min-

utes was speaking to Melissa to tell her he was staying overnight. He had just replaced the receiver when Marney arrived
back from the lake and came through into the living-room to
join them.

"I must be getting back to the lodge, Neville," he said. "Has
Leonie gone to bed? Perhaps you'd thank her again for me
for the excellent dinner. Will you be coming over tomorrow?"

"Yes, I suppose so." Neville did not sound enthusiastic at
the prospect of resuming his work. "What time do you plan to
make a start? I was thinking of driving over at about nine."

"Fine, I'll tell Kelleher. Good night, Thomas."

"So long, Marney, I'll be seeing you."

"Good night, Neville."

"I'll come out and see you off." Neville put aside the book
with alacrity and moved out of the room to leave Thomas
alone by the flickering flames of the fire.

Thomas picked up the discarded book idly, read a page
and put it down again. He was just trying to find some light
music on the radio when Karen returned with some blankets
and Neville came back into the house after having seen
Marney leave in his jeep.

"I hope you'll be warm enough," Karen was saying as she
came into the room. "These are all I could find."

"That'll be fine."

From the distance they heard Neville's footsteps on the
stairs as he went up to his bedroom.

"I guess I'm not exactly welcome here," Thomas observed
wryly. "He'll find it hard to forgive me for the things he heard
me say earlier. I just hope he doesn't take it out on you."

"He'll keep it to himself." She kissed him briefly. "Don't
worry, Thomas. I hope you sleep well."

She left him looking guilty and apologetic and went upstairs to join Neville. On her way she glanced in at Snuff. He
was still fast asleep, small and peaceful, his thumb trailing at
the corner of his mouth, his long lashes shadowing his cheeks.

In the bedroom Neville was undressing; he looked up as she
came into the room and closed the door, but did not speak.

Presently she asked: "Did Melissa cause trouble?"

"No, Marney was there to keep the peace. She soon got

bored and was relieved when Marney offered to row her back to Kildoun."

"Well, that's something." She decided not to refer to Thomas. Moving across the room she began to wash at the basin, and when she had finished Neville was in bed, a cigarette between his fingers, his eyes watching her intently.

She began to feel uneasy. Perhaps it would be better to mention Thomas after all.

"Thomas and I—" she began but he interrupted her.

"There's no need for you to try to defend him or apologize for him," he said abruptly. "Let's just forget about him for the moment."

She knew she ought to feel relieved at his willingness to dismiss the subject, but she did not. She began to undress. When she came to the bed at last he crushed his cigarette into the ash tray and blew out the light.

"Karen . . ." He had turned to her, pulling her towards him as she slipped between the sheets, and she felt his hard strong body press against her own, his mouth seeking hers in the darkness.

She knew at once that she would have to pretend and so she poured her whole being into acting her part convincingly. If Neville in any way suspected her of being unresponsive he would immediately blame Thomas and accuse him of upsetting her, and whatever happened she was determined that that was something he would never suspect. Afterwards, spent by the effort of deception she lay motionless in Neville's arms, but it was only when he turned and whispered his love for her that she was sure the deception had been successful.

II

The next morning Snuff came pattering into the room soon after seven and woke them by clambering over their feet. He had just settled himself comfortably on Neville's back when the alarm clock shrilled into life and began to dance angrily across the bedside table.

Neville muttered something bad-tempered, but when the child promptly silenced the clock he opened his eyes and smiled at him without a trace of ill-humor. "Thanks, Snuff. How are you this morning?"

"All right." He slipped off the bed as Neville sat up. "Daddy, can we go for a walk after breakfast?"

"I wish we could, but this morning I have to go back to work. Maybe Aunt Karen would go with you instead."

"Would you, Aunt Karen?"

"Uh-huh. If it's not raining."

"It's not." He pattered over to the window and peered up at the sky. "The clouds are big and high up and moving quickly and the sun's almost shining." He danced over to the door. "I'm going to get dressed."

"Snuff!" called Karen, but he was already out of earshot.

Slipping out of bed she pulled on her robe and went after him to see if he needed any help but he appeared to be self-sufficient. He looked up astonished as she came in, as if he considered her intrusion a trespass on his privacy.

"What are you wearing today?" Karen said lightly. "Aren't you going to wear some jeans instead of those little short pants? Then your legs wouldn't get so scratched by the heather."

"They're trousers," said Snuff. "Not pants. And I don't have long ones. Nobody does until they're twelve." He remembered she was a foreigner and added kindly: "It's tradition."

"But I've seen other English boys your age wearing long trousers!"

"Common boys do."

"I beg your pardon?"

"It's common," repeated Snuff, raising his voice. "Common boys wear long trousers at any age. That's tradition too."

"Who said so?"

"Aunt Leonie."

Karen opened her mouth and shut it again. She was conscious not for the first time how difficult her position was in regard to the child. If she openly ridiculed Leonie's snobbishness, it would confuse Snuff and further antagonize Leonie herself if Snuff repeated the criticisms to her.

"Jeans are different from regular long trousers," she said at last. "They can be worn by anyone anywhere. That's tradition too."

"Well, I haven't got any," said Snuff crossly and struggled into a dirty red pullover.

She wanted to tell him to wear a clean one but knew instinctively that he would dislike the idea. Besides, she reflected philosophically, a clean sweater would only end up dirty at the end of the day; why not let him get the dirty sweater dirtier? Resigning herself to be patient she opened the door to go and then glanced back at him.

"It'll be fun to go for a walk together," she said. "I was wondering what to do with myself once your father had gone but now you've solved the problem for me. That was a good idea of yours."

He tried not to look flattered and didn't quite succeed. She was reminded with amusement of Neville.

"Where shall we go?" she asked him. "Shall we walk along to the end of the lake?"

"Okay," he said agreeably, using one of the expressions which his aunt would have detested. "If you like."

"Fine!" She smiled at him. "I'll be looking forward to it." And she stepped out on the landing, closed the door behind her and went downstairs to the kitchen.

Leonie was already dressed and stirring the porridge on the stove. Within a short time of her arrival she had made it clear by her actions that it was she who owned the cottage and she who was responsible for the food and the meals. She also, by means of subtle hints and allusions, had contrived to make Karen feel an interloper.

"I see Thomas stayed the night," she said as Karen entered the kitchen. "I went in to do the fire and found him sprawled on the sofa. It gave me quite a shock."

"It did? I'm sorry—we would have told you but you'd already gone to bed."

"I was wide awake actually," said Leonie. "I can never go to sleep while other people are still up and moving around." She

left the words "and making a noise" unsaid but the implication
hung in the air with unmistakable clarity.

"I'll set the table," said Karen, refusing to be drawn into
further apologies.

"Would you? Thank you so much. Of course I've no idea
what Thomas eats for breakfast."

"You needn't worry about Thomas," Karen said. "He'll be
asleep for hours yet."

"I hope not. I wanted to clean that room this morning before
I go into Fort William to do some shopping."

"In that case," said Karen with a serenity she was far from
feeling, "I'll wake him up and get him his breakfast myself.
Please don't worry about it."

She went into the dining-room, set the table briskly to conceal her annoyance and went into the living-room. Thomas
was sprawled on the sofa, blankets piled on him from the waist
downwards, his chest masked by a snow-white T-shirt.

"Thomas!" Karen shook him mildly. "Wake up."

"Go away, Leonie."

"That's not good enough, Thomas. You know very well it's
me. You'll have to get up because Leonie wants to clean the
room directly after breakfast."

"Grrr," said Thomas.

She left him, and moving back to the kitchen found Snuff
waiting as Leonie filled his bowl with porridge.

"You don't want porridge, do you, Karen?" The implication
was that Americans were not capable of appreciating such
food.

"Yes, please," said Karen. "Would you like me to cook
Neville's eggs and bacon?"

"No, I'll do it. You're on holiday. Besides, I'm used to cooking them."

"I did live with him for nearly two years, you know," said
Karen, helping herself to porridge while Snuff poured himself
a glass of milk. "I have had experience of cooking his breakfast."

"Well, of course, I didn't mean—"

"Is there toast and marmalade, Aunt?" said Snuff.

"Don't interrupt," said Leonie automatically, but she had already forgotten what she was going to say.

"I'll make you some toast when you've finished your porridge, Snuff," said Karen over her shoulder as she went into the dining-room. "Warm toast tastes nicer than traditional English cold burnt bread."

I must stop, she told herself as she put down her bowl of porridge on the table, I mustn't let her make me angry. To calm herself she went in to look at Thomas. He was, as she had suspected, still asleep.

"Thomas!" She shook him in exasperation. "Thomas!"

"Pas aujourd'hui, cherie," said Thomas distinctly and turned his back.

"You're impossible," retorted Karen, who spoke no French but knew enough to recognize the occasional phrase. "Impossible!" She returned to the dining-room next door, found Snuff already eating with gusto and sat down beside him. Perhaps she would feel less irritated if she had some coffee.

But the pot on the table contained tea.

"Leonie, is there enough water in the kettle for instant coffee?"

"What? Oh no, I'm so sorry, I forgot."

It was obviously going to be one of those mornings.

Presently Neville came down, wearing worn casual clothes and still contriving to look elegant. His presence eased the awkwardness in the atmosphere for a while, but he did not linger long over his breakfast and ten minutes later he was on his way outside to the jeep to begin his first day's work at the plantation.

"I won't be back for lunch, I'm afraid," he said as he kissed Karen goodbye. "Expect me back about six. Will you be all right here alone? Leonie says she's going shopping in Fort William."

"I'll have Snuff with me—and Thomas."

"Well, ring the lodge if anything crops up. There'll usually be someone there who knows which section of the plantation I'll be working in."

"Fine. But I'll be okay, you don't have to worry."

He smiled, kissed her again and was gone.

She went back to the dining-room to find Leonie clearing away the dishes and Snuff lingering over his last crust of toast and marmalade.

"Is Thomas up yet?" said Leonie, casually stacking two cups together.

"Lord, I'd forgotten him!" She went back into the living-room next door with a mingled feeling of irritation and guilt, and succeeded in waking him, but he was intent on returning to sleep as soon as possible. In the end he grudgingly transferred himself to her bedroom and promptly fell asleep again on the double bed, much to Karen's annoyance.

"Why's he so tired?" inquired Snuff who had been watching the scene with interest from the doorway.

"He's not especially tired, darling. It's just that he's an actor and actors get used to working at night and sleeping in the day. Shall we go out for our walk as soon as I'm dressed? Are you ready?"

"Yes."

"Sure you don't want an extra sweater?"

"No, thank you." He went away politely after she had said she wouldn't be long, and she closed the door after him and began to dress to the accompaniment of her brother's heavy breathing. She put on dark slacks, selected a thick sweater that clung warmly to her body and remembered a scarf for her hair. Her suede walking shoes were still caked with yesterday's mud, but she scraped off the worst of it with a spare nail-file and brushed the pieces out of the window into the flower bed below. When she left the room a minute later she found Snuff sitting on the stairs as he waited for her, and gazing soberly out into space.

"What were you thinking about?" she said lightly, but her words only served to make him shy and he shook his head and went downstairs ahead of her without replying.

Leonie was in the kitchen washing up. She had already declined Karen's offer of help and was now concentrating on her task with an air of efficient martyrdom.

"Snuff and I are just going for a walk," Karen said. "I don't know how long we'll be."

"Oh? I'll probably be on my way to Fort William by the time

you get back. I'll be home again later this afternoon, I expect. Snuff, you should put on another pullover—it's cold out and it might rain."

"Aunt Karen said I needn't," said Snuff with cunning and had skipped out of the back door in a flash before Leonie could open her mouth to disapprove.

"I asked him if he wanted another sweater," said Karen awkwardly, "but he said he didn't."

"Well, of course," said Leonie with a shrug. "He always does say that." She was very careful not to say: "I know him better than you do" but the implication was obvious. "I hope you have a pleasant walk."

"Thanks," said Karen shortly, and followed Snuff outside into the cool fresh air of the Highland morning. Snuff was already dancing on to the wooden bridge which crossed the stream. He turned to see how far she was behind him, and then danced on again so that he was once more at a distance from her.

"Hey, wait for me!" she protested with a laugh, but he ignored her, and she wondered with a sinking heart how long it would be before she ceased to be a stranger who had left him once and might leave him again, a stranger whom he was determined to keep at arm's length.

He took the path which led west along the shore of the lake, and she followed him at her own pace while he darted to and fro, skipping from side to side and jumping over mud pools. Once when he slowed down for a moment and she came within earshot of him, she heard him humming "Frère Jacques."

"Did you learn that at school, Snuff?"

He nodded, not looking at her, and then saw the tumbled-down ruins to their right by the shore. "What's that place?"

"It's just an old house which nobody has lived in for years. No, Snuff, don't go in there! The walls may not be safe—"

But he had gone and didn't hear her. She followed him with reluctance, remembering how the ruins had reminded her inexplicably of April, and when she reached the doorway, she saw that he was exploring the one large room with excitement.

"There's nothing there, Snuff. Let's go on." Already the

smells of damp and decay were making her shiver and she longed to turn back once more into the sunshine.

"Perhaps the people buried their treasure before they left," said Snuff, prodding the soft earth with his toe. "People often did that if they ran away from their homes. Wherever there's a Roman villa they find lots of coins buried in the ground. Monsieur le Professeur says so."

"This isn't a Roman villa, Snuff, just a shack where some poor farmers once tried to make a living. And they didn't run away leaving their money buried—they went away willingly because they had no money and wanted to try to find some elsewhere."

"Oh," said Snuff, not sounding in the least convinced, and went on prodding.

"Come on, let's walk on further. There are plenty of other things to see, and we might come to some better ruins later. This part of the country is full of them."

"Why?" said Snuff. "Why did everyone go away?"

They walked on back to the path while Karen began to explain what little she knew of Highland economics and social history, and presently they were some way from the ruined house and she was able to relax again.

They walked for another half hour and still did not reach the tip of the lake which had seemed deceptively close at hand. The path had become much muddier, and at length Karen decided to turn back. They were within sight of the ruins once more when Snuff asked if they could rest for a few minutes and Karen, agreeing, seated herself on a slab of rock and looked out across the lake to the hotel at Kildoun and the road running past it on the other side of the water.

Snuff began to wander off idly in the direction of the ruins and Karen, restraining her first impulse to call him back, pretended not to notice. After all, she reasoned, if he wanted to look for buried treasure, why should she spoil his fun? She settled herself into a more comfortable position on the rock and went on watching the changing hues of the lake, but when he had not returned after five minutes she got up and went over to the ruins to see what he was doing.

She found him on his hands and knees, scraping at the soft

damp earth in one corner of the house with a sharp piece of slate.

"Snuff, what are you doing?" Despite herself, her voice held an echo of uneasiness. It was dark in the ruins and again she felt conscious of her acute dislike of the place.

"I found some treasure," said Snuff complacently, and went on scraping.

"That's not possible, darling," she said sharply. "It's just some old stone embedded in the ground." Still she could not bring herself to step forward across the threshold. And then suddenly her spine was tingling and the panic began to crawl down the back of her neck.

"No, it's not a stone," said Snuff triumphantly. "It's a suitcase. Look! Can you see? Do you think they put jewels in it, or will it just be gold coins?"

There was a silence. Karen was rigid with the full force of appalling suspicions. Movement, even speech, was impossible.

"Here's the other clasp," said Snuff, still scraping patiently. "Now I can open it and see what's inside."

"No!" Her cry startled him so much that he jumped to his feet. Scarcely knowing what she was doing she moved across to him and saw the top of the old suitcase he had unearthed, the clasps rusty and clogged with mud.

"Snuff darling, can you go outside for a moment? Please— just for a moment."

He stared at her, recognizing her distress but puzzled about its cause. At last he said kindly: "Don't be frightened, it's probably only gold coins. You can look the other way, if you like, while I open it."

"Snuff, please—" But she was too late. He had already pulled back the clasps using all his strength to overcome the rust and mud, and while she watched, too horrified to stop him, he heaved open the lid.

A smell of rotting material floated up to meet them, the damp of mildew and decay.

"Well!" said Snuff in disgust. "Look at that! I thought there would at least be gold coins, but all that's there is lady's clothes! I wonder who they belong to."

## III

Afterwards Karen wondered why she had not felt dizzy with the shock, but all she was conscious of at the time was a feeling of dreadful clarity, as if she had faced an intricate puzzle for a long while only to have the mystery solved when she least expected it. As Snuff turned to her, his baffled annoyance showing clearly in his eyes, she felt herself move over to him and gently draw him to one side so that she could examine the open suitcase more closely.

A garment made out of a material which had once been green lay on top. Resolutely repressing her distaste for handling the mildewed cloth she picked it up and recognized the smart green sheath dress April had worn during her last visit to London. Beneath it were articles of underwear, the lace rotted away, the nylon discolored. A small woodlouse burrowed furtively out of sight as it was so unexpectedly exposed to the sight of day.

"Ugh!" said Snuff. "Creepy-crawly."

"I expect the suitcase is full of them—these clothes won't be any use to anyone now." She scarcely noticed what she said. April, she knew, had had two suitcases. Could the other one be buried here as well? She began to glance swiftly at the damp earth nearby.

"Let's go and tell someone about it," said Snuff. "Will Daddy be back from the plantation soon? Let's tell Daddy."

"No," said Karen abruptly, "we won't tell anyone just yet. Let's make it a secret between the two of us until I find out who the clothes belong to."

Snuff looked pleased at the idea of a secret and then chagrined that he could not boast of his buried treasure.

"Well, it wasn't much of a treasure anyway," he said aloud, consoling himself. "Just a lot of old clothes."

"Then it's a secret between the two of us for the time being," said Karen.

"Okay."

He wandered to the door of the hut and she followed him outside reluctantly, not sure what she should do but knowing only that she wanted a chance to be alone in the ruins for a while. Fortunately the problem was solved for her when Snuff danced back to the path and raced uphill to examine an outcrop of rock. The treasure had apparently lost interest for him.

"I'll follow you more slowly," she called after him. "When you get back to the house see if Uncle Thomas is awake."

That would give him something to do.

He waved to show that he had heard, and when he had disappeared among the rocks she went back again into the ruins. The chill of the place struck her anew as she re-entered it. She shook herself determinedly, and going back to the suitcase, she replaced the dress, drew down the lid and began to scrape back the earth to cover it again. When this was done she found a sharp stick outside and began to prod carefully in the area nearby. She found the second suitcase less than three minutes later. It was buried in another shallow grave, and without much difficulty she unearthed one corner, just to prove to herself that she was not mistaken.

After that she went outside, walked a little way from the ruins and sat down calmly on a rock to gaze out over the lake before her.

Suddenly she began to tremble. April's two suitcases were buried here near the house! And obviously it hadn't been April who had done the burying. April had almost certainly never left the house that morning. She was dead, and someone . . . someone had buried the suitcases to create the illusion that she had left safely, someone had towed the boat across the lake to hint at her escape route, someone had disposed of the body.

Her thoughts raced on with frightening speed. Why had the suitcases been buried and not thrown in the lake? Because they might have been discovered by fishermen fishing in the clear waters in high summer, or by sportsmen shooting wild duck in the rushes which fringed the lake below Kildoun. But no one was going to go digging in ruins long forgotten. No one except a child bent on finding buried treasure.

Buried. Buried in a grave.

Karen thought of her sister for one long icy moment of fear. If April was dead, where was the body? Perhaps the ruins . . . But no, that couldn't be. Putrefied flesh stank. A shallow grave wouldn't have been able to contain the smell.

She felt she was going to be sick. She got up hurriedly and stumbled back to the path, and presently the feeling of nausea passed, leaving her feeling weak and shaken. She did not know what to do. She was convinced now that April had been murdered, but when she tried to consider who had killed her and concealed both crime and victim with such hideous efficiency, her mind shied away from the possible suspects confronting her. Thomas, Leonie, Neville, Marney . . . She forced herself to consider each of them for a long moment. Thomas, she decided, could not be guilty. If he was, he wouldn't be so ready to proclaim that April was murdered (but wasn't he only doing so in an attempt to turn her against Neville?). "Oh nonsense!" she said aloud to herself with a conviction she was far from feeling. "Thomas isn't a murderer." Then there was Leonie. Karen hastily turned from Thomas to a consideration of her sister-in-law. Leonie had loathed April, but one hardly committed murder merely because of loathing (Or did one? People could murder each other for a nickel. Yes, but it wasn't that kind of murder . . . What kind of murder?). Well, thought Karen, never mind Leonie. The next suspect was—well, she wouldn't think of Neville just yet. The last suspect was Marney. Could Marney conceivably be a murderer? Marney with his gentleness, his courtesy, his old-fashioned charm . . . "But he had the brain to commit the crime," she told herself stubbornly. "Or rather, to cover up the crime. And whoever covered up the crime was no fool. Everything was remembered, even the last detail of leaving a boat on the Kildoun side of the lake to create the illusion that April had rowed herself across to escape."

Marney had been attracted to April; she could remember noticing three years ago in London how April had affected Marney when they had first met. Karen had thought little of it at the time because she was so used to seeing the effect which April had on men, but now she began to wonder. Supposing Marney had become involved with April. Supposing . . . But Neville had been the one involved with April, not Marney. Her thoughts balked again at the thought of Neville's possible guilt, but at last with a feeling of panic she let the possibility sink into her mind.

But no, Neville could not, would not have committed murder. Surely there would have been something to give him away, something which would have enabled her to detect his guilt! She would refuse to believe him guilty. She would not admit it. Nothing would make her admit it.

"But if I tell Thomas about the clothes," she said aloud to herself, "he'll at once believe Neville killed her."

The thought made her rigid with horror. Supposing Melissa should somehow discover about the clothes! It would give her just the lever she needed to strike back at Neville. Whatever happened neither Melissa nor anyone else must find out about the clothes.

But then what was she to do? Live the rest of her life with all her terrible suspicions? Conceal the fact that her sister had been murdered? Besides, it would be useless to expect Snuff to keep quiet forever about his startling find in the ruins. Sooner or later he would forget it was a secret or unwittingly give the game away, and all the details would come out.

She stopped, confusion bringing her to a halt. She did not know what to do, and yet knew that she must do something. And as she stood there, perfectly still, staring across the lake to the mountains beyond, she had the faintest glimmer of an idea.

If she could prove conclusively to herself who had killed April, then at least she would not have to live with her doubts and suspicions. After all, she thought uncertainly, in some ways Thomas had been right when he had said April had got what she deserved. All Karen was concerned to prove was whether or not Neville was guilty. If she managed to prove to herself that Leonie or Marney had killed April, then there was no need for her to resurrect the matter by going to the police. She would let sleeping dogs lie. As long as she knew that Neville was innocent she could come to terms with the situation without difficulty.

A coldness gripped her heart again, making breathing painful. She was revolted by the thought of proving any of the

four people guilty of murder, and frightened of what she might
discover, but the prospect of living in doubt, of forever wondering what had happened was more horrifying still. Moving
very slowly, the expression in her eyes remote and unseeing,
she reached the house and raised an unsteady hand to unlatch
the back door.

## IV

Upstairs Thomas was awake and telling a round-eyed Snuff
the story of his life. Karen came slowly into the room to ask if
he wanted coffee.

"And bacon and eggs," he said, "and toast, please."

"Porridge?"

"You're kidding." He turned again to Snuff. "Well, where was
I? Yes, when I was fourteen I went waterskiing . . ."

She left him to his reminiscences and went down to the
kitchen. Leonie had evidently left for Fort William, for there
was no sign of her. Presently Thomas came downstairs to eat
his breakfast while Karen and Snuff had a snack lunch, and
later Snuff wandered up the stream again on another of his
private expeditions, his sweater bright against the green-brown
of the mountainside and the purple of the heather.

The telephone rang just as Thomas was finishing his third
cup of coffee. He reached back and grabbed the receiver.

"Hello? Oh hi, Melissa . . ." He made a face at Karen. "Well,
I haven't made any plans—I've only just got up . . . Let me
call you back in ten minutes." He dropped the receiver hastily
back in its cradle.

"What did she want?"

"I don't know—I didn't stay long enough to ask." He gulped
down the rest of his coffee. "Why doesn't she go off to her
tweed mill?" He stood up, stretched and yawned. "I guess I'll
get dressed and maybe try a bit of fishing up the stream. Do
you want to come fishing with me?"

"If I can catch Snuff to tell him where to find us."

Snuff decided to join them and they set off together about half an hour later after Thomas had assembled Neville's fishing tackle and gear. The telephone shrilled angrily again just as they were leaving.

"Don't answer it," said Thomas. "I'll call her when we get back, but I don't want to talk to her now."

When they returned to the house some time later Leonie had arrived back from her shopping expedition and was putting away the provisions in the kitchen.

"I decided not to go to Fort William," she said, "so I stopped at the general store on the way there to buy the things we needed most. Melissa rang up, Thomas, and wanted you to phone back whenever you came in."

"Hell," said Thomas and went moodily into the dining-room to the telephone.

"Thomas," said Karen, following him, "I think I'm going to walk over to the plantation to the lodge and meet Neville when he stops work. Leonie's here now to look after Snuff so you don't have to worry about him. I'll be coming back with Neville in the jeep around six."

"I'll come with you," he said instantly, seizing the opportunity to avoid Melissa.

"No," said Karen firmly. "You call Melissa and find out what she wants. After all, she did give you a free ride up here, don't forget. You owe her something."

Thomas didn't seem to think so, but after a few minutes' wrangling he ungraciously picked up the receiver. Leaving him glaring after her, Karen went into the kitchen to tell Leonie where she was going and then paused to say goodbye to Snuff before going outside once more into the cool air of late afternoon.

Outside she crossed the stream by the wooden footbridge, and began the walk up the rough track which led uphill to the pass. The climb was steep. Several times she had to pause to get her breath, and as she turned to look back over the way she had come she was impressed afresh by the magnificence of the scenery, the lake ringed by hills, the hills hemmed in by mountains, the varying shades of the moors as the sun appeared and disappeared behind enormous banks of cloud.

It was lonely. There was not another living thing in sight. Swiftly she walked on uphill and at last reached the pass and stood between the twin shoulders of the mountain to gaze into the next valley, to the dark silent acres of Plantation Q.

It began to rain as she walked downhill, a light Highland drizzle, but before she could concern herself about getting wet it had stopped and the track had straightened out to follow the cut through the trees. The conifers were on all sides of her now, their dark boughs shoulder to shoulder, the ground beneath them a grave of pine needles. The silence was immense, unnerving. There seemed to be no birds singing or calling to one another, and there was no wind to sigh through the branches. Karen quickened her pace instinctively, and then at last the trees ended as abruptly as they had begun and she saw the mellow red brick of the lodge with the barn nearby which housed the fleet of foresters' jeeps.

The cook, an old Highland woman who had never been further south than Edinburgh, saw her through the window, gave her a toothless smile and told her that Neville was still out on the plantation.

Karen had guessed as much; on reaching the front of the house she went through the open front door into the hall and immediately met one of the young foresters who repeated the cook's information.

"Dr. West's here, though," he told her helpfully. "He's working in his office—second door on the right."

She felt reluctant to disturb Marney, but then realized with an even greater reluctance that here was an ideal opportunity to see him alone and encourage him to talk of the past. Summoning her determination she knocked softly on the door, opened it and went through into the room.

His smile seemed to be genuine enough. "Karen!" He rose to his feet. "Well, this is a surprise. I suppose you walked over? Do sit down."

He began to clear some files off one of the chairs.

"I don't want to interrupt you—"

"No, that's all right. I'm almost finished. Would you like some tea after your walk?"

"No, but if there's a glass of water . . ."

He brought it instantly from the kitchen and sat down again behind his desk as she drank it.

"I'd forgotten how long it takes to walk over," she said between sips, "and what an uphill climb it is to the pass."

"I hope you don't intend to walk back!"

"No!" she agreed ruefully. "I'll wait for Neville. Whereabouts on the plantation is he?"

"Somewhere out in section five. Would you like me to drive out there to find him?"

"Oh no—no, I mustn't interrupt him—"

"They're planting new seedlings out there . . ." He began to tell her about the trees with a curious zest, and described how an experiment in planting them in a certain area of the plantation had failed. "The ground was too rocky," he said. "I advised from the beginning that they would be better off in section five. Section five has a good sub-soil—it's further from the rocky slopes of the mountain, closer to the floor of the valley."

The image of planting the seedlings in soft earth reminded her of the suitcases buried in their shallow graves. She put down her glass of water, and fumbled for a cigarette.

"I'm sorry," said Marney suddenly. "I must stop talking shop. I'm sure you're not interested in all these details about the trees."

She inhaled from her cigarette, shook out the match slowly. "It's odd to be back here again at Plantation Q," she said, "and hearing you talk about the trees." She glanced around the room. "Of course last time I was here I couldn't have cared less what anyone was talking about."

There was a pause. Then: "No," said Marney awkwardly. "I suppose not."

She pretended to think that he did not remember the occasion of her last visit to Plantation Q. "I ended up here the day I found Neville and April at the house," she said baldly. "I rushed out stupidly without thinking and got lost on the plantation for hours before Neville found me within half a mile of the lodge and brought me here—I expect he told you about it afterwards."

"He mentioned it, yes." Marney's voice was strained.

"The funny thing is that I don't recall seeing you at all, but you were at the lodge then, weren't you? Or were you out on the plantation at the time?"

"Yes, I was out all morning working on my own about three miles from here. I became so absorbed in my work that I didn't even drive back to the lodge for lunch till nearly two. That was why I didn't see you or learn what had been going on until it was all over. Thomas fetched you from the lodge, didn't he? I think I got back soon after he had taken you away. Neville was in a frightful state and I gave him a whisky and tried to calm him down before driving him back to the house. We left Scotland that same afternoon, I remember—my work was completed by then and Neville decided to dash back to London after you. He never caught up with you, did he? You got on a plane to New York and that was that . . . I'm sorry, I'm digressing unnecessarily. Forgive me."

"No—no, that's all right. Leonie was there when Neville got back to the house with you presumably."

"Yes, Leonie was waiting for us, and—no, Snuff wasn't there, of course. I was forgetting."

"I'd left him in London with a cousin of his mother's. Was Neville surprised to find April had gone?"

"Yes, he immediately asked Leonie where she was and Leonie said she had assumed April was with him. After that they went upstairs to look for her and found her clothes and suitcases were gone—and so had one of the boats from the jetty. Leonie said she supposed April must have left just before she had arrived back at the house from the lodge at eleven that morning."

Marney looked guilty. "You know, I felt very badly about that afterwards. Leonie had telephoned me the night before from the house soon after April's arrival, and said she wanted to see me as soon as possible. Since it was late I suggested she come over to the lodge the following morning but . . . well, when I woke up the next morning I completely forgot I'd arranged to meet her at the lodge at ten. The trouble was that I had had a most absorbing talk with Kelleher at breakfast about my project and I was so anxious to get to work that the thought of Leonie simply didn't enter my head. I felt very embarrassed later when I returned to the lodge and found the note she had left me."

"She left you a note?"

"Yes, it was all about Neville's behavior in suggesting April came to the farm while Leonie was on holiday there. I know Neville swore there was no rendezvous, but not unnaturally Leonie found it hard to believe him. She was furious. I think she'd come to see me to seek moral support before she asked Neville to leave."

"Was that the first you knew of April being at the farm?"

"No, I knew April was there before I heard from Leonie that she too was at the farm. Before Leonie spoke to me on the phone that evening—the evening April arrived—I rang up the house to have a word with Neville and he told me then what had happened. He didn't say much, just that it was all awkward, that April was there, and he couldn't talk for more than a moment. He didn't mention Leonie at all." He made a grimace of distaste. "As soon as he told me April was there I wished he hadn't mentioned it. Naturally I thought they were alone at the farm together, and the knowledge made me feel shabby, as if I was somehow helping him to be unfaithful to you simply by knowing what he was doing. Even when I found out Leonie was there too I still felt guilty. To be very frank, Karen, I think Neville got out of that corner much more easily than he deserved. April might have given him a lot of trouble. I'm only surprised he didn't have more difficulty in getting rid of her."

"I think he had a huge row with her before he left the house to look for me—"

"All the more reason why she should want to make trouble for him afterwards." He stood up abruptly and walked over to the window, his hands thrust deep in the pockets of his worn corduroys. "Neville says he's never heard from her since."

"No." She decided to change the subject quickly in case he was on the brink of bringing up the possibility of April's death, accidental or otherwise. "Talking of Neville, Marney—"

"Yes, are you sure you wouldn't like me to drive you out to section five? He should still be there."

"Well, perhaps if it's not too much trouble—"

"No, I'd like some fresh air."

He put on an old tweed jacket, locked away his papers and took her outside. Rain was falling lightly again, but there was blue sky in the west and the shower was already half over. There was a jeep in the barn, and after Marney had helped Karen inside he sat down behind the wheel and started the engine. A moment later they were driving away from the lodge and swinging into a wide cut which led westward parallel to the mountain slopes.

After ten minutes of rough driving they reached another cut and beyond it lay a forest of little trees no more than two feet high. Bordering this plantation of embryos was a muddled section where trees had been felled and the ground ploughed up. Among the furrows the earth shone black as pitch in the clear afternoon light.

Neville and a group of men appeared to be bent over a fallen tree. Karen wondered what they were doing and marveled idly at the complexity of a subject which she would have thought so simple. She would not have imagined that trees could assume such importance that one small fallen conifer could hold the interest of six men. "What are they doing?" she asked Marney automatically.

"I don't know. Perhaps there's some malformation of the roots."

Neville had seen them and was waving his arm in greeting. Marney halted the jeep.

"Trouble, Neville?"

"No, just a minor puzzle. It seems there's granite nearer the surface here than we thought . . ." He went on talking, speaking competently in technicalities, but Karen didn't hear him. She heard nothing at all. Her whole mind was suddenly focused on the little fallen conifer and the hole in the ground where its roots had been. An idea filled her mind, chilling her spine and prickling her scalp. No wonder April's body had never been found. The murderer had never thrown it in the lake at all, never tried to bury it in the rough ground near the farm. April's body was somewhere on this side of the mountains, somewhere in the black earth of Plantation Q.

# SIX

## I

Reason and logic succeeded her panic less than a minute later, but Karen was still aware of feeling shaken. The idea that April's body lay buried somewhere on Plantation Q was a mere quirk of her mind, she decided, a sequel to the events of the morning when she had found the suitcases in their shallow graves. Now she was imagining possible graves everywhere without any substantiating evidence whatsoever. She was fast allowing her nerves to get the better of her; it was time she pulled herself together and ceased to give full rein to her imagination.

But her tenseness persisted. Marney was out in a jeep that morning, she found herself thinking; he was all alone in a remote section of the plantation; he could have driven over to the farm, killed April and driven the body back to the plantation for burial. Or perhaps Neville . . . no, Neville and April must have approached the house by hired boat from the lake the night before because when Karen had arrived the following morning there had been no sign of any jeep parked by the croft. But where had Neville been during the morning of April's disappearance? She only had his word that he had spent three hours looking for her; he could have walked to the lodge in three quarters of an hour, taken one of the fleet of jeeps, driven back, killed April and removed the body . . . For that matter Leonie could have done the same thing; it was a fact that she had walked over to the lodge that morning; she could have taken a jeep from the barn; by the time she had arrived

for her ten o'clock rendezvous with Marney everyone would
have been at work on the plantation and the lodge would have
been deserted save for the deaf old Highland cook in the
kitchens . . .

"Are you all right?" she heard Neville say suddenly. "You're
very quiet."

"Yes, I'm fine. Just a little tired." Karen resolutely tried to
close her mind against the past and concentrate on the present
before Neville became more suspicious and asked further
questions. They had left the lodge by this time after saying
goodbye to Marney and the foresters. Neville was coaxing his
jeep uphill on their way back to the farm in the next valley,
and as they reached the pass Karen made a great effort to become entirely absorbed in the scenery once more. But the effort was useless. Still she could think only of a hidden grave
somewhere beneath dark firs, the soft black earth concealed
by pine needles and protected by the regulations covering the
plantation.

"Neville."

His eyes continued to watch the rough track as he concentrated on the task of driving. "Yes?"

"How often are the trees cut down and the ground ploughed
up?"

He laughed. "Darling, forestry isn't quite so simple as that!
There's no clear-cut answer. Why?"

"I was just wondering. No special reason."

They began the descent into the valley. Far below them
lay the lake, its waters still and calm, the surrounding hills
mellow in the evening light. Suddenly without warning Neville
halted the jeep and switched off the engine.

"What's the matter, darling?" he said casually, turning to
face her. "I hope you're not worrying in case April fell into a
furrow on Plantation Q and obligingly buried herself afterwards."

His perception both frightened her and took her breath
away. "I thought we'd agreed to forget April?" she heard herself say automatically.

"I thought so too," he said, "but I can see you're thinking

about her all the time—wondering if there was anything in what Melissa said—"

"No, Neville!" Yet she was unnerved by his betrayal that he too had been thinking of April and worrying about Melissa's malice.

"Well, in case you were wondering about the plantation—"

"I wasn't."

"No? Well, why—"

"Neville, let's drive on and not discuss it any further. I'm tired, and I'm sure you are too, and I want to get home."

He did not answer, but glanced aside at the lake in the distance. His mouth was a hard line, his eyes sullen. Presently he said: "I wasn't wholly honest with you the other night when we first discussed April's disappearance. For a long time now I've been wondering if she was dead, but I didn't see how she could be. Suicide was out of the question, and if she had had an accident the body would have been found eventually, no matter where it was, and you would have been traced and notified. Eventually I considered the possibility of murder and put it aside as being too far-fetched, but when Melissa made her bloody insinuations I considered the possibility again. It still seemed unlikely, but after thinking very carefully I could see one could make out a case for saying it was unlikely that April had ever left this area. And if she had never left this area and her body had been deliberately hidden, that meant without a doubt that she had been murdered." He was fumbling for a cigarette. After a moment he found a packet and struck a match. Then: "Well, of course I considered the plantation," he said. "In some ways it presents a better place for a grave than the ground around the house which is stony and hard. The murderer would have wanted to dig a grave as quickly as possible, but to dig a grave near the house would have taken some time and a lot of effort."

Karen thought in a flash of the soft floor of the ruined house, but she remained silent, waiting for him to go on. "The plantation has a hard stony soil in some areas," he was saying, "but there are also areas where the earth is soft and pliable. If the murderer knew where to dig he could conceal the body quickly in a place no bull-dozer would ever disturb."

It suddenly seemed very cold. Karen shivered. "If the murderer knew where to dig . . ."

"Exactly." He shrugged with impatience. "But the proposition that April's buried in the plantation is untenable anyway because of the problem of transportation. No murderer would walk from the farm up the mountain to the pass and into the next valley with his victim's body under one arm and a spade under the other, and there was no jeep. I had only arrived at the house the night before—three hours before April—and I had come across the lake, not over the hills by jeep from Plantation Q."

"Then where's April buried?"

"I've no idea, but I know this. If we could find April's grave I think we'd have a good idea who killed her. But until we find the grave there's no concrete evidence that she's dead and not merely missing."

Karen shivered again. "Do you—is there anyone who—" But her voice refused to put the question into words.

"Is there anyone whom I suspect of murder? Well, frankly, no." He laughed shortly, without mirth. "As far as I can see we two are the only ones who had any motive for murdering her, and as I know as sure as hell that I didn't and as I can't quite visualize you killing a butterfly, let alone your own twin sister, that hypothesis doesn't seem very convincing to me."

The notion that she herself could be considered a suspect for the crime so appalled her that for a moment she could not reply. Then: "I guess the police might suspect me, if they knew about it," she said panic-stricken. "I could have pretended to be lost on the plantation. After shaking you off my trail I could have crept back to the house, killed her—"

"Rubbish," said Neville. "For one thing you didn't know I was going to rush out after you after wasting ten minutes quarreling with April. You didn't even know I was trying to find you until I finally discovered you half a mile from the lodge three hours later. I saw you enter the woods of the plantation when I reached the pass, but you never looked back. So if you decided to kill April, how did you know she'd be alone at the farm without me to protect her? Also, if you were going to kill her—how fantastic it sounds even to put such a theory into words!—you'd have killed her in a rage on discovering her with me. You would never have summoned up the will to kill her once your anger had cooled. Then again we come back to this problem of the corpse. If you killed April what did you do with her afterwards? I don't believe you'd be cold-blooded enough to work out all those details covering up the murder —you didn't hate April enough for that. I think if you'd killed her you'd have simply phoned the police and confessed."

She smiled in spite of herself. "In other words you think I'd be a bad murderer!"

"I don't think you'd have either the physical or emotional stamina to run backwards and forwards between the house and the plantation, kill April, dispose of the body, tow the spare boat across the lake, and run back to the plantation in time to be discovered by me half a mile from the lodge! The idea's absurd and I think the police would be the first to admit it."

She was vaguely aware of relief but such was her tension that it made little impression on her. After a moment she said unsteadily: "Neville, what did April say when you quarreled with her? Was it a very bad quarrel?"

His eyes were dark and withdrawn. He glanced at her, then glanced away. "It was unpleasant. I don't remember it clearly."

"Did she—"

"Oh yes, she stormed, raged, threatened, screamed—thank God we were alone and there was no one else within earshot! In a way the quarrel was my fault. I was so appalled that you should have come upon us like that, so shattered at the realization of what you must have been thinking. It was as if someone had slapped me across the face and woken me up in the most unpleasant way possible. I said a few curt words to April, telling her she'd better start to pack her things, and she immediately flared up—it all happened so quickly. Within seconds she was accusing me of all manner of things, and as I thought that was merely a case of the pot calling the kettle black, I was stung into replying . . . Then she started accusing you. When I saw how much she hated you, I—"

"She was always jealous. I tried to make it up to her so many times but she wouldn't let me."

"Yes, so she said. She laughed and said how she despised you."

"What did you say to that?"

"I hit her," said Neville.

She stared at him in disbelief. She saw his mouth twist in a wry smile.

"I have to admit I wasn't acting like a true English gentleman at that stage of the proceedings."

"But—"

"Of course, I shouldn't have hit her but I was so furious at the thought of what she had done, so furious with myself—the whole situation." He shrugged. "I hit her across the mouth, and she flew at me like a wildcat, clawing and screaming. I pushed her aside, and she overbalanced and fell to the floor. While she was picking herself up I walked out of the house and set off to try to find you."

"And—and you never saw her again."

He looked at her. His face, she noticed for the first time, was very white. "No," he said, "no, I swear to you, Karen, that I never saw her again. And when I last saw her she was alive."

II

The clouds had drifted inland to leave the mountains silhouetted against the clear summer sky, and the lake was a slim blue mirror on the floor of the valley. Even though it was after six by the time the jeep reached the farm the light had not yet turned golden, and Karen was reminded of how far north this land was and how short the nights were in consequence.

Neville halted the jeep, helped her to dismount and walked with her across the burn and past the rockery to the back door. In the kitchen a variety of pots simmered on the stove, but there was no one about. Karen went through into the hall and almost at once heard Snuff's clear treble say querulously:

"But it was a very disappointing treasure. Just a lot of lady's clothes."

My God, thought Karen, jerked to a standstill. She could feel the color drain from her face with the shock.

Neville bumped into her. "What's the matter?"

She could not answer.

"Neville?" called Leonie's voice from the living-room and the next moment she was confronting them in the hall. "Thank God you're back!" she exclaimed with relief. "Snuff has been telling us the most extraordinary stories . . ." Her voice trailed off as she darted a highly suspicious glance in Karen's direction.

The color flooded back to Karen's face as suddenly as it had left it. To her helplessness and fury she felt her cheeks burn scarlet. Neville wheeled round to face her. "What's this?"

"I—" Karen began faintly but Leonie interrupted her.

"Snuff says he discovered two suitcases full of women's clothes buried beneath the floor of the ruined house—"

"What!" Neville stared at her. Then: "Where is he?" He pushed past her. "Let me talk to him. He must be making it up."

"He says Karen told him to say nothing."

There was a short, electric silence. Karen found herself speechless, unable to meet either Neville's or Leonie's eyes. And then somewhere far away Melissa's voice, low and indolent, drawled: "But Snuff darling, why did Aunt Karen ask you to keep it a secret?"

Neville moved involuntarily. "What's Melissa doing here?"

"Don't ask me," said Leonie in a tone which indicated she couldn't possibly be held responsible. "Thomas brought her over here this afternoon."

Neville without a word went past her into the living-room, and Karen, not wanting to be left alone with Leonie, followed him automatically.

Snuff was sitting on the floor with his story-book, and on his face was a cross expression which seemed to suggest that he wished all adults would go away and leave him alone. In one of the armchairs sat Melissa, faultlessly elegant, noticeably undisturbed by Neville's arrival.

"What are you doing here?" said Neville abruptly, and her eyebrows raised themselves in disapproval of his tone of voice.

"Thomas took me for a row on the lake and then when it came on to rain I suggested we shelter at the cottage," she answered unruffled. "It was a heavy squall and the cottage was close at hand . . . I must say, darling, you're not exactly the perfect host this evening."

"Where's Thomas?"

"He's gone down to the ruined house," said Melissa, "to confirm Snuff's tales of buried treasure."

"Neville—" Leonie began.

"It wasn't treasure!" Snuff objected aggressively. "Just a lot of old clothes!"

"Snuff!" said Leonie sharply. "You sounded very rude—how dare you speak like that!"

"Aunt Karen didn't say it was rude," said Snuff nastily, and began to scramble to his feet to make his escape, his story-book tucked tightly under one arm.

"Never mind what Aunt Karen didn't say! Apologize to Aunt Melissa at once."

"She's not my aunt."

"Snuff—"

But he took no notice. Karen suddenly realized he was standing before her, looking up at her in fury. "I didn't mean to tell," he said aggrieved. "But I said something I didn't mean to say and they went on and on and on at me—"

"It's all right, Snuff. I understand."

"It's all right, Snuff," said Neville kindly, stooping to comfort him. "It doesn't matter. Nobody's cross with you." He glanced at Karen abruptly. "What on earth's this all about?"

All eyes were upon her. She struggled to pull herself together, to talk in a normal tone of voice. "I—I went for a walk with Snuff. He found—accidentally—in the ruined house—"

"Two suitcases of women's clothes," said Leonie crisply. "Buried under the floor."

"Why didn't you tell me about it?" Neville said at once to Karen. "Why did you say nothing?"

"I—I wanted to think—"

He turned and strode over to the front porch. "I'm going to join Thomas."

"So you said nothing," said Leonie disapprovingly to Karen as the front door slammed. "What a foolish thing to do."

Karen was stung to defend herself. "What do you suggest I should have done?" she flared. "Phoned the police?"

"Well, you might at least have told me. After all, I was here three years ago when—and you should have told Neville too, of course."

"I think she should have called the police," drawled Melissa from the hearth. "If they're April's clothes I think it proves pretty conclusively what happened to April."

Leonie was incensed. "Are you suggesting—"

"You ask your sister-in-law again why she didn't tell her husband about her little find! Ask her if she wasn't worried that she'd just become reconciled to a murderer!"

"How *dare* you!" Leonie's face was crimson. "How dare you insinuate such things about my brother!" She turned to Karen. "How can you stand there and let her say such things?"

"I—"

But Leonie had turned back to Melissa. "Please leave my house at once—this instant! I never invited you here anyway. Go on—get out! I never want to see you again."

"Dear me," said Melissa, "how dramatic." She began to draw on her beautiful leather gloves carefully, smoothing the material over each finger. "And who, pray, is going to row me across the lake? Or am I supposed to swim?"

"Row yourself over," said Leonie, and trembling with rage stalked out of the room to the kitchen. The door slammed after her with a force that shook the house.

Snuff was round-eyed. Karen stooped over him and took his hand in hers. "I think if you want to read in peace, darling, you'll have to read upstairs. Shall I come with you?"

"No, thank you," said Snuff, withdrawing his hand with dignity, and walked away without looking back.

Something seemed to twist beneath Karen's heart as she watched him go. She longed to be able to reach him, but knew that the barriers he had raised to reject the adult world were at that moment insuperable.

"My dear," said Melissa, smoothing her hands over her hips and glancing at herself in the mirror. "*What* a scene."

Karen did not answer her. She did not trust herself to speak.

Her feet carried her across the hall again and she found herself opening the front door and stepping out into the cool air of early evening. After taking a deep breath to steady herself, she set off towards the ruined house beyond the stream and less than three minutes later had reached the crumbling walls.

Neville and Thomas were stooped over the two suitcases which lay excavated amidst the upheaval of dark earth, but as they heard her approach they straightened their backs and turned to look at her.

"Karen," said Thomas soberly, wiping the sweat off his forehead with the back of his hand, "you should have told us."

"I—I know . . ." She leant against the doorway suddenly in exhaustion and closed her eyes. As if from a long way away she heard herself say: "I was too shocked—too dazed—I just wanted to think." And then all at once Neville's arms were around her and holding her close to him, and Neville's voice was saying softly: "I understand."

She opened her eyes gratefully and saw his face inches from her own. There was compassion in his eyes but also something else, a hint of wariness, or reserve, of speculation.

"Maybe we ought to dig up this whole floor, Neville," Thomas was saying. "Do you reckon anything else could be buried here besides the suitcases?"

"I doubt it. We can try digging, I suppose, but I'd be surprised if we found anything. The suitcases take up most of the soft ground here—you can see that over there by the wall the granite is showing beneath the weeds. If you were to take a sharp stick and poke around I think you'd strike rock close to the surface except in this section where the suitcases were buried."

"Where can I find a sharp stick?"

"I believe there are stakes for sweet peas and runner beans in Leonie's gardening shed by the house, if you want to get one. I'm going to take Karen back to the house."

"Thomas," said Karen, "I wish you'd row Melissa back to Kildoun. Leonie has just ordered her out of the house but she won't go for lack of transport."

Thomas made a rude comment about what Melissa could do with herself and began stabbing the earth savagely with the sharp edge of the spade.

"You've got the hell of a nerve to say that," said Neville annoyed. "If it hadn't been for you she wouldn't be here now."

"Please!" said Karen in despair. "Don't you two quarrel as well! That would be more than I could bear!"

"I think we ought to have some sort of conference to decide what should be done," said Neville. "Perhaps we'd better not get rid of Melissa until we've agreed on some course of action. Why don't you come back with us now, Thomas? I doubt if you'll find anything else here, but if you're not satisfied you can come back and search again later."

"Thanks," said Thomas curtly. "I will." He left the spade leaning against the wall and followed them outside with reluctance.

They returned to the house in silence. Karen was conscious of a sense of approaching disaster. Now what would happen? Would someone call the police? But there was still no body, no proof of murder. She shuddered violently, the wave of revulsion shaking her through and through, and glanced at Neville, but he was staring straight ahead, his face expressionless, his hands tight fists in the pockets of his trousers. She wondered what he was thinking.

They reached the house.

"Leonie?" called Neville abruptly as he entered the hall.

There were footsteps in the kitchen; the door opened. "Ah there you are, Thomas," said Leonie, looking past her brother and glimpsing Thomas on the porch. "Could you kindly row your friend back to Kildoun as soon as possible? This is my house and I'm becoming a little tired of uninvited guests."

"Before Melissa goes," said Neville abruptly, "we have to decide what should be done about Snuff's 'treasure.' Could you come into the living-room a moment?"

Leonie looked as if the last thing she wanted to do was to breathe the same air that Melissa breathed, but she gave in with bad grace and followed them through the small dining-room into the living-room beyond. Melissa had mixed herself a drink and was standing by the window; from the radio came the sound of an interview, a discussion of the approaching Edinburgh Festival. Neville turned the switch; the radio died and silence fell upon the room.

"It seems the suitcases are April's without a doubt," he said to Melissa. "Both Thomas and I were fully agreed on that."

"But of course!" said Melissa ironically. "Did you really expect them to be anyone else's? I've said all along that she was murdered, and this merely confirms my suspicions."

"Seeing you're so smart, honey," said Thomas, "maybe you can tell us where the body's buried? It might save us a lot of waltzing around if you could exercise your clairvoyant talents in that direction."

Melissa seemed impervious to sarcasm. She shrugged her shoulders. "How should I know? I wasn't even here three years ago. Why not ask someone who was?"

"Neville," said Leonie. "The ruined house—"

"No, I'm fairly certain there's nothing else there except the suitcases although Thomas is going to have another look later."

"Then where—" Leonie broke off, the question unphrased.

"I don't know," said Neville. "I don't know where the body can be."

"How about Plantation Q, darling?" said Melissa. "That would be a good burial ground, wouldn't it? Very convenient for anyone who knew their way around there well."

Leonie and Karen began to speak together. In the pause while they each broke off and waited for the other to speak, Neville said: "Whether she's buried on the plantation or not, there's a chance that the body may never be found. The question at the moment is not where the body is but what we should do—if anything—about the discovery of the suitcases."

Leonie said rapidly: "I suppose there's no chance of it being some sort of accident? There's no possibility—"

"None, as I see it," said Neville flatly. "Someone deliberately created the impression that April had packed her bags, left the farm and rowed over the lake—the impression that April had left alive. Why should April herself bury her suitcases and leave without her belongings?"

There was an awkward silence which began to lengthen

unbearably. Karen felt her heart bumping fast against her ribs, her nails digging into the palms of her hands.

"Well," said Melissa, "to be quite frank, I think the police should be informed. It's obvious that there's been some sort of foul play."

"But nothing can be proved," said Neville. "Even if the body is found they'll probably still be unable to prove anything. All it will mean is that the five of us who had access to the house at the time, and who therefore come under suspicion, will be questioned and cross-questioned by the police and caused endless unpleasantness."

"Well, why shouldn't you be?" said Melissa coolly. "It's obvious that one of you is a murderer."

"But what of the four who are innocent?" demanded Thomas. "Besides, personally I think that whoever killed April did more than one person a good turn."

Leonie opened her mouth to protest automatically against this condonation of murder, but only succeeded in looking as if she agreed with what he had said. Then: "How can you be sure, Neville, that one of us five . . . I don't understand. Perhaps one of the foresters went berserk—perhaps one of them came over to see her, attacked her for some reason—"

"I doubt if anyone who went berserk like that could have covered up the crime so efficiently afterwards, and anyway no one at Plantation Q except Marney knew April was here. I didn't advertise her presence to all and sundry. Also, how could anyone not familiar with the farm or this side of the mountain have known where to find April's clothes and where to bury the suitcases quickly in soft ground? It's out of the question."

"Marney should know about all this," said Leonie suddenly. "Let me ring him up and ask him to come over."

"No, wait," said Neville. "Let's first decide what we're going to do. Normally I would favor going to the police, but at this stage I can't see what such a move would achieve apart from engulfing us all in notoriety in the press and putting each one of us through a hell of inquisition—to no avail."

"What fine advice," said Melissa, "from such an upstanding pillar of society and a senior member of the civil service."

"Melissa dear," said Thomas, "if you weren't a woman I'd
tell you in no uncertain terms to shut your beautiful god-
damned mouth. What's this got to do with you anyway? You're
not even involved! Why don't you stop posing as the lady with
the scales of justice and get the hell out of our lives? I don't
often agree with Neville, God knows, but this time I'm with
him one hundred percent. There's no point in going to the
police. It's possible I might feel a little differently if April were
worth avenging, but I'm her brother and I'm prepared to let
things be. We can achieve nothing by going to the police except a lot of grief for ourselves. Besides, it's all very well,
Neville, for you to doubt whether the police could ever make
an arrest, but supposing they did and arrested the wrong
person."

"This is England," said Leonie. "Our police don't make mis-
takes like that."

"I bet they do," said Thomas. "They're only human, aren't
they? Now supposing the police arrested Karen. She must be
suspect number one as far as motive goes, but not even her
worst enemy (you perhaps, Melissa dear?) could ever believe
her guilty of murder."

"Just a moment, Thomas," interposed Neville. "Let's not start
speculating about guilt and motive. Let's just concentrate on
whether we're going to tell the police about the clothes. I personally am against it. So are you, Thomas. Karen darling—"

"I'm against it too," Karen heard herself say, and thought
instinctively of the police questioning Neville, suspecting him,
putting him under arrest . . .

"So am I," said Leonie at once with a fervor that Karen
found surprising. She must have realized the extent of her
brother's danger. "There's nothing to be gained from going
to the police now. She was a most unpleasant girl—although
I suppose I shouldn't say that—and she's dead and that's all
there is to it. It would be senseless to resurrect it all now."

"Well, well, well," said Melissa. "What a united front all of
a sudden!"

Nobody spoke. Then: "I still think Marney should know
about this," said Leonie stubbornly. "Let me phone him,
Neville."

"If we're not going to the police I see no point in worrying him with it."

"But I think he has a right to know," Leonie persisted. "He was, after all, involved—he was here three years ago, and even though he was staying at the lodge, he knew his way around the farm and this side of the valley. He's one of the five whom the police would suspect."

"But we're not going to the police."

"May I," said Melissa, "just ask one question? What makes you so sure that the child won't talk? He's given the game away once—how can you be so certain he won't do it again?"

"He doesn't know the significance the clothes have," said Neville. "As far as he's concerned the buried treasure turned out to be a big disappointment. He'll soon forget about it."

"You're crazy," said Melissa frankly. "All of you—you're quite mad. The whole thing's bound to come out and you'll all be charged—not with murder, perhaps, but with conspiracy to conceal a murder—"

"I hope," said Thomas, "that you're not proposing to interfere in any way, Melissa."

"Well, if you think I'm going to sit back and implicate myself in all this, you couldn't be more wrong! I for one don't intend to be charged with conspiracy!" She ground her cigarette to ashes and stood up. "If someone hasn't informed the police before noon tomorrow, I most certainly shall."

There was a silence. She looked up suddenly, as if she found the silence surprising and saw everyone's eyes watching her.

"Melissa," said Thomas politely, "this is none of your—business."

"It most certainly is if you involve me in your conspiracy!" Melissa retorted. She moved to the door. "Well, I'm going. Perhaps someone could row me across to Kildoun."

There was another pause. Then:

"I will," said Neville.

"Thank you," said Melissa very pointedly, "but no. I'm sure someone else would do just as well. Perhaps you would, Thomas."

"Not on your sweet-natured little life! Row yourself."

The silence was so intense that it became almost audible.

"I'll row you across," said Leonie at last. "I'm used to the journey." Her tone of voice implied that she had reached the stage where she would welcome any opportunity to take Melissa as far away as possible. "But first I'm going to phone Marney and tell him what's happened."

"No, don't tell him a word on the phone," Neville ordered abruptly. "The local telephone operator might overhear something. Just ask Marney to drive over for dinner."

"Dinner! My God, I'd forgotten it! Everything will be terribly overdone." She hurried off anxiously towards the kitchen.

"I wish you'd let me row you over, Melissa," said Neville irritated. "Leonie's got more than enough to do here at the moment. What do you expect me to do—push you in the lake in broad daylight?"

"It's clouding over and getting very dark, as a matter of fact."

"Oh, for God's sake!"

"I'll wait till Leonie's ready, thank you."

"Thomas—" began Neville.

"No," said Thomas. "Absolutely not. *You* might not be tempted to push her into the lake but I most certainly would."

"Thomas!" Karen protested. "Don't, don't make such a joke just now . . ."

Neville was beside her in an instant. "Darling, why don't you lie down upstairs for a few minutes? You look exhausted and I'm not surprised. I'll bring your supper up to you in bed."

"I'm not hungry." She turned aside, conscious of a longing to escape. "But I think I will lie down."

Neville kissed her, and she made her way upstairs as quickly as possible. To her amazement she noticed that her legs were weak and her hands were trembling. When she reached her room she lay down on the bed for several moments, her eyes closed, her mind numb, and then directly below her in the dining-room she heard Leonie ask the operator for the number of the lodge at Plantation Q.

The telephone was by the window in the dining-room, and the window, like the window in the bedroom, was obviously wide open. Karen heard Leonie's voice travel clearly towards her on the still evening air.

"Dr. West, please . . . Marney? Could you come over to dinner? Something quite awful's happened, and—would you? Thank God . . . Yes, come as soon as you can."

There was a faint noise as the receiver was replaced. Presently Neville said from somewhere at hand: "Is he coming?"

"Yes, he's coming straight away. Now, let me get rid of that dreadful woman."

There were footsteps, the murmur of distant voices, and then at last silence. Karen struggled to keep awake and think clearly about the situation confronting them all, but her nervous exhaustion coupled with the physical exercise of the walk to the lodge earlier made sleep impossible to combat. Almost without realizing it she had slipped into unconsciousness, and when she next opened her eyes she heard the roar of the jeep as Marney arrived at last from Plantation Q.

## III

She rose, changed into a dress, adjusted her hair. When she was ready she went next door to Snuff's room to suggest it was time he went to bed, but Leonie had evidently been there before her for Snuff himself was sitting up in bed in his pajamas with his favorite well-worn story-book open before him. He seemed flattered that she had called in to say goodnight, and she stayed with him for a few minutes to read aloud to him from the book. Finally when she could put off the moment no longer she went downstairs and through the dining-room to the living-room where Neville was handing Marney a double whisky and soda. Thomas was propping up the window frame, an alert expression in his eyes, but there was no sign of Leonie; evidently she had not yet returned from rowing Melissa across to Kildoun. Karen glanced out of the window to see if she could see the boat, but outside heavy clouds had brought an early twilight and inside the light from the lamps made the windowpane a mirror reflecting the interior of the room.

Everyone turned to look at her.

"Good evening, Karen," said Marney, rising to his feet in an automatic gesture of courtesy. He looked tired, she noticed, and there was a strained set to his mouth. "Neville's just told me what's been happening here today."

She did not know what to say. She heard herself murmur awkwardly: "We thought you should know."

There was a pause. Then: "Well, there you have it," said Thomas abruptly. "Either we go to the police before noon tomorrow or else Melissa does the job for us. It's as simple as that."

Marney sat down again, sipped his drink and clasped the glass tightly in his long bony fingers. "Then it looks as if one way or the other the police will be informed, doesn't it?"

The comment drew no response.

"It's a pity someone can't persuade Melissa . . ." Marney let the sentence trail off into vagueness.

"Her mind's made up," said Neville flatly. "Besides, she's enjoying her position of power over me. There's nothing more I could say which would dissuade her."

Marney turned to Thomas. "Since you arrived with her, I assume you've both been seeing a lot of each other. Isn't it possible that you would be able to persuade her—"

"She's not my mistress, if that's what you mean," said Thomas righteously at once.

"That wasn't what I meant," said Marney without inflection. "It just occurred to me that if you were at all friendly with her—"

"I'm not."

Marney shrugged. "Well, there's certainly nothing I can do," he said at last. "There's no reason on earth why she should listen to me."

The front door opened. The next moment Leonie was moving into the room.

"Marney, thank God you're here—"

Karen was surprised how distraught Leonie looked. Her face was haggard, her hair straggling, her movements staccato with her nervousness.

"Has Neville told you? Neville, what have you said? Did you tell him—"

"Yes, yes," said Neville, poorly concealing his irritation at this display of panic. "We've just been talking about it. Sit down, Leonie, for God's sake, and relax and let me get you a drink. It won't solve anything if you get worked up over all this."

"Have my chair," said Marney at once, and insisted in installing her in it while she smiled up at him gratefully.

"So kind . . . thank you . . . perhaps we really ought to eat dinner straight away—if we wait much longer it'll be ruined—"

"Never mind about the dinner for the moment," said Neville dryly. "That's the least of our worries. The question is what are we going to do about Melissa?"

"A curiously sinister word-choice, Neville," Marney was smiling slightly. "What on earth can we 'do' with Melissa? Come, let's be realistic about this. There's nothing we can do. We can't persuade her to change her mind, and obviously if we attempt to force her hand in any way it will only underline our own guilty feelings."

"But Marney," said Leonie white-lipped. "Marney—"

"Look Marney," said Thomas. "You may not be directly involved in this, but we are—"

"Actually that's incorrect, Thomas. I'm every bit as involved as you are. I know the farm and this side of the mountain almost as well as I know Plantation Q, and I knew April was staying here three years ago. If the police investigate this I shall come under suspicion, just as you will."

"Well, then—"

"Listen," said Marney, leaning forward in his chair, "if we try to bargain with Melissa we make it look as if we have something to hide—as if one of us really did kill April three years ago." He paused. "One of us, you understand? You, Neville—or Karen—or Thomas—or you, Leonie—or myself. Now, let me ask you all this: are we sure that one of us is guilty? How can we be?"

"You're surely not expecting a confession, Marney," said Thomas ironically.

"No," said Marney, "I'm not. Because I don't believe any one of us is guilty of murder. How do we know April was murdered? We don't. There's no body. All we have is pure conjecture. Supposing she had an accident, for example—supposing she was accidentally killed in such a way that to any outsider it might seem that she had been murdered? That would account for the fact that someone very much concerned buried the clothes and created an impression that she had left. Or else supposing, again, that she had an accident, and someone seized on the opportunity to spare another person all the distress of an inquest and inquiry by deliberately creating the impression that April was still alive while he himself removed all trace of her from the scene of the accident? Or supposing April herself packed her bags, took them to the jetty and then slipped, hit her head and drowned in a few feet of water nearby? Whoever buried the suitcases wouldn't even have had to go into the house to pack her clothes. You see how insubstantial all your theory of murder is? There's no evidence of murder, none at all. Certainly the police could never prove a murder charge against any one of us—they would suspect, yes, but suspicion and proof are two very different things. Even if they find the body, and it's just possible, I suppose, that they might, they'd still have no proof of who killed her. If she was killed at all. I don't think we have anything to fear from the police. If Melissa didn't intend to go to them with the whole story, I'd let the matter rest, but since she's made up her mind to tell them about the clothes I think we should be first to contact them. We should show them that we've nothing to hide."

"But Marney," said Leonie, "the investigations, the publicity, the police searching for the body—"

"If they find the body and find April's skull smashed in," said Thomas, "they won't think it's an accident, Marney."

"How do you know April's skull's smashed in?"

"The point is," said Thomas, "how do you know it isn't? Personally if I were a policeman, I'd be a lot more inclined to believe the murder theory than the accident theory, and I'd guess that it'd be a hell of a lot easier to prove murder than accident."

"I don't think the police would ever be able to prove anything."

"I think they could," said Neville unexpectedly. "They could establish motive and opportunity in some cases."

"That's still not proof, Neville."

"Hell," said Thomas. "Do your police expect every case to have the proof neatly displayed on a silver platter? I'll bet they don't! I'll bet they're as eager to make two and two make four as any other police force, and just as eager to accept circumstantial evidence."

"I think we're losing track of the argument," said Marney. "The point is that Melissa's going to the police. If we contact them before she does we create a good impression. If we leave her to tell the story we all look guilty. The police are going to ask us all why we didn't contact them as soon as we discovered the suitcases, why we haven't in fact contacted them at all. Can't you see how it's going to look to them?"

"I suppose," Karen said slowly, "we couldn't destroy the clothes—and the suitcases?"

Everyone stared at her.

"I mean, if we took them away and the police came and found nothing . . . We could easily make Melissa out to have been motivated by jealousy into making a false accusation—"

"That's a marvelous idea!" cried Leonie, flushing in her relief and enthusiasm. "Why didn't we think of that before?"

"Of course!" said Thomas, snapping his fingers. "You're a smart girl, Karen. That'll take care of Melissa and make her look a fool, and it'll save us all the public resurrection of the past."

"We could burn the clothes," Neville mused, "and scatter the remains in the lake."

Leonie sprang to her feet. "Let's do it now."

"No!" said Marney so strongly that she jumped. He set down his glass. "I'm afraid I can't possibly agree to that—I'm surprised you agree to it, Neville. It may make Melissa look a fool, but the police are going to say 'no smoke without a fire' and make inquiries just the same. Besides, you're all entirely forgetting Snuff. If the police question him he'll tell them all about the clothes—how can he do otherwise? How can we ask a child of seven to lie to the police for reasons beyond his comprehension?"

Oh God, thought Karen stricken. She had forgotten. So

deep was her confusion and anxiety that she had even forgotten that it was Snuff who had discovered the clothes.

"I suppose that argument's unanswerable," said Neville with reluctance, and even Thomas and Leonie had no defence to make.

There was a heavy silence.

"Let's have dinner," said Neville abruptly. "Maybe my brain will function better after I've had something to eat."

Dinner was a sombre meal. Afterwards over coffee they tried to discuss the situation again, but the arguments became circular and it became evident that no decision was likely to be reached. Marney maintained that they should go to the police at once, but no one was prepared to accept this as a tolerable solution to Melissa's ultimatum. In the end Thomas stood up and moved to the door.

"Look," he said, "let me row myself back to Kildoun and spend the night in my room there. I'll have a talk with Melissa and exert a little charm and see if I can't persuade her to change her mind. Would you agree to wait till tomorrow morning, Marney?"

Marney shrugged. "The longer we leave it the worse it'll look to the police, but if everyone agrees to wait till tomorrow morning then I suppose I'm prepared to wait too."

"I'll call you first thing tomorrow, Neville," Thomas said, "and let you know if I had any success."

After he had gone they all remained in the living-room and discussed the situation further. Leonie was very over-wrought still, Karen noticed, and was constantly getting up and moving restlessly over to the window and then back to the chair again. Marney was drinking steadily, the glass of whisky never leaving his hand except to be refilled. Neville was chain-smoking, and so was she, cigarette for cigarette, almost inhalation for inhalation, her nerves seemed unable to get enough of the soothing benefits of the drug.

Suddenly the phone rang. Neville leapt to his feet and picked up the receiver. "Hello? Yes, Thomas. What—you didn't? . . . Why? . . . I see . . . yes, all right, I'll tell them . . . Thanks." He replaced the receiver and slowly turned to face them.

"What's happened?" said Leonie tautly.

"Melissa wouldn't answer when he knocked on her door. She wouldn't even answer when he rang through to her room on the telephone. I'm afraid it seems she's quite determined not to reach a compromise."

# SEVEN

## I

When Neville had finished speaking there was a silence. At last Karen heard herself say slowly: "What are we going to do now?"

"Nothing." Neville began to mix himself another drink. "Thomas said he'd try to talk to Melissa in the morning and that he'd phone back again after breakfast."

"So we wait until tomorrow?"

"I don't see what else we can do."

There was another uneasy silence. Then: "That stupid interfering woman!" Leonie burst out, and Karen saw with a shock that her mouth was trembling and her eyes were bright with tears. "Why does she want to create trouble for us all? Why did she even have to come here?"

Marney stood up as if he suddenly wanted to escape. "I think I must be going back to the lodge, Neville. It's getting late, and it doesn't seem as if there's anything more we can do at the moment. Thank you for the dinner, Leonie."

Leonie made an effort to compose herself. "I'll come and see you off."

"No—no, please don't trouble—"

"Don't forget your coat. It's hanging up on the back door." She went out of the room to get it for him, and he wandered out after her, his head bowed, his shoulders hunched as if to ward off the memory of Melissa's ultimatum. "Goodnight, Karen. I'll see you tomorrow, Neville."

"All right, Marney. Goodnight."

He left. A minute later they heard the roar of his jeep as the engine flared into life, and then the noise receded as the jeep crawled away up the mountain track.

"I think—" Karen began, but was interrupted as Leonie called out from the kitchen: "Oh, he's left some papers behind! They must have fallen out of his coat pocket in the dark and he didn't notice."

"Never mind," said Neville. "I'll take them over to the lodge with me tomorrow."

"All right. Well, no, perhaps I'll go after him now. If I take your jeep he'll see the headlights behind him and wait for me to catch him up so I won't have to drive all the way over to the lodge. Anyway I want to get away from the farm for a little while. I feel one of my headaches coming on and I'm sure I'll never be able to sleep if I try to go to bed now. Do you have the keys to the jeep, Neville?"

"They're in the ignition."

"I feel the opposite to Leonie," said Karen to Neville as the back door closed and they were alone together. "I'm exhausted and all I want to do is to fall into bed and sleep for twelve hours." She did not add that she wanted to escape from further discussion of Melissa. "What are you going to do now, darling?"

"I may join you soon." He was by the window, his hands in his pockets, and he did not turn to face her as he spoke. "I think I'll go for a short walk. I feel very restless and the exercise will probably calm me down."

"I'll see you later, then," said Karen and went upstairs without further delay. When she reached the room she closed the door and then moved over to the window to stare outside for a long moment. All trace of that gloomy clouded twilight had now faded into suffocating darkness; night had come, and suddenly dawn seemed intolerably distant, as if it lay at the far end of an interminable corridor of time.

Karen undressed slowly and spent a long time preparing herself for bed. It was as if she had changed her mind and were putting off the moment of inactivity as long as possible, clinging to any mundane movement which would help take her mind off the situation. Everywhere was very quiet. She wondered vaguely if Leonie had managed to catch up with Marney before he reached the pass.

At length the time came when there was nothing else to do but pull back the covers and slip between the sheets. She turned down the lamp, but presently the darkness seemed too overpowering so she slipped out of bed and drew back the curtains.

To her surprise she found the heavy clouds had broken and were drifting stormily across the face of a ragged moon. The scene had the eerie silver-black quality of an unreal landscape delineated in some strange medium. Karen shivered, turned aside, but could not bring herself to go back to bed. Presently she went downstairs. There was no one there, but the lamp was still burning in the living-room and the ashes still flickered in the grate from the evening fire. Karen had a sudden absurd wave of revulsion against being alone in the house. Shaking herself resolutely she walked to the decanter, mixed herself a stiff scotch and soda, and with the glass in her hands sat down on the couch and gazed at the red embers in the grate. But the blankness of the dark windows forced themselves to her attention; seconds later she was standing up to draw the curtains.

It was very quiet.

Of course she was not alone in the house. Snuff was there too, upstairs, fast asleep. Lucky Snuff, able to dismiss the suitcases as mere disappointing buried treasure.

She began to move restlessly about the room, but presently even the shuffle of her slippers sounded so loud that she stopped to listen. The silence closed in on her at once, stifling walls of soundlessness. She began to walk up and down again.

It was foolish to be nervous, she told herself, foolish and neurotic. If the farm were by the road on the other side of the lake she would have had an excuse to be nervous of the loneliness, but here the very isolation made it perfectly safe. There was no chance of a visit from some stray hitchhiker, not even the threat of a passing car.

She opened the door, moved through the dining-room and paused by the front door. It was unlocked. Neville always left it unlocked while they were staying at the house. There was no reason to lock it because there was no possibility of intrusion. It was so safe, so isolated.

Karen stared at the door. Supposing it were to open now. She pictured it swinging silently inwards on its hinges, motivated by some hidden force outside, and there on the threshold was April, her body rotted from three years in the black soft earth, her eyes bright and insanely alive.

Karen leant back against the wall and closed her eyes. She must not, would not give way to hysteria. She forced herself to look at the closed door calmly, and as she looked, willing herself to remain calm and self-possessed, she saw the door handle begin to turn slowly as if it had a life of its own.

"Neville!" The cry was a reflex born of panic, and then suddenly he was there beside her and closing the door behind him as he entered the hall.

"What's the matter, darling? You look white as a ghost! I'm sorry I was so long—I went further up the stream than I intended. Couldn't you sleep?"

"No, I guess I was more restless than I thought I was. Wasn't there any sign of Leonie returning?"

"None, but I doubt if she managed to catch Marney this side of the pass. Besides, she might have driven all the way to the lodge to have a private conference with him—that would be typical! I hope Marney doesn't have too much difficulty in getting rid of her if she turns up at the lodge." He moved towards the living-room. "I'm going to have one final drink and then I'll join you upstairs. I shan't be long."

She went back to their bedroom, her knees weak, her body trembling, and this time the effects of shock combined with the whisky so that she was glad to lie still and close her eyes.

She never even heard Neville come to bed.

When she awoke it was dark and someone was moving about the room.

"Neville?" she said nervously, still not fully awake.

"Yes, I can't sleep. I'm going downstairs for a while. Don't you worry—just go back to sleep and relax."

His voice was reassuring; unconsciousness was close at hand and presently she was slipping back into sleep again, her mind disturbed by brief flickers of dreams which made no sense and which memory would not retain. She was aware of tossing and turning but when she next opened her eyes it was dawn and the room was filled with a pale unearthly light.

Something was wrong. She twisted round in bed instinctively and then she recognized the source of her uneasiness. She was alone; Neville had never returned.


## II


She went downstairs, but there was no sign of him. Still wearing only her nightdress and peignoir, she opened the back door and walked a few yards up the hillside behind the house so that she had an uninterrupted view of the surrounding country, but as far as the eye could see there was no hint of life. Neville's jeep was parked near the stream to indicate that Leonie had returned safely during the night, and the jeep seemed as small as a toy against the vastness of the mountains and the moors. The dawn was breathtaking in its translucent colors, but the air was cold; Karen shivered, drew her peignoir closer around her and returned to the house, but even after pausing in the kitchen, the warmest room in the house, she was still shivering. At length she was about to return to her room when she heard the noise of a door opening somewhere above her and the next moment Leonie, wearing a long drab dressing-gown, was coming quietly downstairs.

Leonie saw her and gave a start of surprise. "I thought I heard someone moving about! What's the matter? Couldn't you sleep?"

"Neville seems to have disappeared," Karen heard herself say, aware that Leonie was no longer a source of irritation but a welcome presence in the isolated silence. "I woke up in the middle of the night and found him about to go out for a walk as he couldn't sleep, but when I woke up again just now he still wasn't back."

"Did you notice the time when Neville left?"

"No—no, I didn't."

"It might only have been a short time ago—dawn has only just come and half an hour ago it was still dark." She crossed to the gas stove, reached for the kettle and filled it with water. "I couldn't sleep either. I'm going to have a cup of tea, but I suppose you'd rather have coffee."

"Please." They waited in silence while the water was heated, and presently they were sitting down together at the kitchen table with the steaming cups and Karen was watching the lake change color as the sun rose higher in the sky.

"I wish Neville would come back," she couldn't help saying. "I wonder where he can be."

"Perhaps he's gone over to the hotel to try to talk to Melissa," Leonie said unexpectedly. "I know Neville felt very strongly how important it was for Melissa to see reason about going to the police."

"But if Melissa won't change her mind, what could Neville do? We're all powerless."

"If anyone can persuade her," said Leonie firmly, "Neville will. He knows how important it is for all our sakes."

Karen was aware of irritation. "All?" she said. "But you won't be much affected if Melissa goes to the police! You were at the lodge when April disappeared—you weren't even here! You don't have to worry."

"Well, of course," said Leonie, bridling at Karen's tone of voice, "I don't worry on *my own* account. I'm worried about Neville—and you, naturally. And Marney."

Karen opened her mouth to say that Marney had been working on the plantation all morning on the day of April's disappearance, but then shut it again instinctively. Instead she said: "Yes, I guess the situation is awkward for Marney."

Leonie shot her a suspicious glance and took a sip of tea thoughtfully.

Karen changed her tactics. "Marney didn't see April that morning, did he?" she demanded, deciding on a direct approach. "He didn't come to the farm?"

There was a silence. "Well, actually," said Leonie after a long pause, "yes, he did."

"But I thought—" said Karen and stopped.

There was another long silence.

"Well, after all," said Leonie practically, "I might just as well tell you—we're all in the same boat. I'd already decided to tell Neville as soon as I had the opportunity, so I suppose it won't do any harm to tell you. Anyway perhaps you really should know the exact situation—especially now that we're all in such a dangerous position."

She absent-mindedly helped herself to more tea. The dark water swirled in the cup and a monstrous tea-leaf, swollen and bloated, floated to the surface and stayed there. Karen watched it drift around and around in circles as Leonie stirred the tea twice with her spoon.

"I left the farm at nine that morning," Leonie said at last. "The morning April disappeared, I mean. I got up early and had breakfast on my own. Neither April nor Neville were up, much to my relief, and I didn't see them before I left. I had arranged by phone the night before to meet Marney at the lodge at ten o'clock that day because I wanted his advice on how I should handle the situation—I was really so angry with Neville that I hardly trusted myself to speak to him at all, and I thought Marney could help me, tell me what to do."

The whirling eddies died in the tea-cup. She scooped out the monstrous tea-leaf with her spoon and laid it neatly in the saucer.

"After all," she was saying, "the farm *was* mine! Wouldn't you have felt angry if you'd been in my shoes? I know Neville insisted that April had chased after him without his consent, but . . . well, he wasn't exactly displeased to see her, you know! In my opinion he should have told her to stay at the hotel when she rang up from Kildoun to ask him to row across the lake to fetch her—but no! Such a thought obviously didn't enter his head. He brought her across to the farm as if they expected *me* to go to the hotel and leave them alone together! Really it was shameful how little consideration they had for my feelings! The whole episode was so degrading, so sordid." She shuddered suddenly at the memory. "So I decided to go over and see Marney. It took me about fifty minutes to walk over to the lodge, so by the time I arrived it was about ten minutes to ten. I was a bit early so I wasn't surprised when Marney wasn't there to meet me. I waited for a while in his office, and then one of the foresters came in and told me that Marney had gone out to the furthest boundary of the plantation to complete a project and wouldn't be back till lunch-time. He had forgotten all about my appointment with him—Marney's so absent-minded sometimes. Anyway I left him a note telling him what had happened and saying I wanted to see him, and then I walked back over the mountain to the farm.

"It was about eleven by the time I arrived, and the first thing I saw was the jeep parked by the stream. I was puzzled because Neville—and later April—had arrived by boat the night before, but I supposed that Neville had followed me over to the plantation, taken a jeep from the barn and driven back here while I had been in the lodge waiting for Marney. So I walked past it over the footbridge and slipped in the back door.

"I heard them almost at once. They were in the living-room. I went through the kitchen, across the hall and into the dining-room. The living-room door was ajar and I—well, I listened. I was too stupefied to do anything else, because it wasn't Neville with April at all. It was Marney. Marney had driven over to see April when everyone else thought he was out at work on the plantation. There was no sign of Neville, of course, although I didn't find out till later that he was searching for you on Plantation Q. I didn't even know of your arrival then because I had left the farm before Thomas had rowed you across the lake from the hotel at Kildoun.

"All I knew was that Marney and April were talking together in the living-room just a few feet away from me, and as I listened to the conversation I realized—" She stopped. An ugly red stain spread upwards from her neck. She was staring down into her tea, her elbows on the table, her hands clasped tightly together. At last she managed to add: "I realized they knew each other very well, much better than I'd ever imagined."

Karen was aware of shock. It took her a moment to speak. "You don't mean—you can't mean that April and Marney—"

Leonie said nothing.

"They couldn't have been having an affair! I don't believe it!"

"No," said Leonie, still not looking at her, "they weren't. But that was apparently what Marney wanted."

"My God . . ." Karen was too amazed to say more. She had been aware that Marney had admired April, but not that he had been infatuated with her.

"April seemed to find the idea quite amusing," said Leonie.

April would. Karen had a shaft of understanding. Marney wouldn't have been the first ascetic, self-contained man who had suddenly and for no obvious reason become blindly infatuated with a woman as unsuitable as April. No wonder April had been amused! Another man to her credit—another notch on the tally-stick, but this time the man would have had no attraction for her whatever.

"I didn't stay after that," said Leonie in a muffled voice. "I was too shocked. I ran outside again, over the footbridge and along the lakeside past the ruined house. I walked and walked. I walked to the very tip of the lake, and after that I walked back again. I felt more composed by that time, more in control of myself, and physically I was too exhausted by all the exercise I had taken that morning even to summon the strength to make a disastrous scene. But I needn't have worried about making a scene. When I got back to the house at last, they had both gone and the place was deserted. After a while I began to wonder where Neville was so I telephoned the lodge and spoke to him there. He told me what had happened, said you had left with Thomas and he didn't know what to do. Then he said Marney had just come in from the plantation for lunch and he wanted to talk the situation over with him. In the end they both arrived at the house shortly afterwards, and it wasn't until then that we discovered April had packed, rowed herself across the lake and departed—or so we thought at the time. We were all so relieved. Later that day Neville and Marney left Scotland together, but I stayed on alone for another week to complete my holiday before rejoining Neville in London. I didn't know what to say to Marney about the scene I had overheard, so in the end I said nothing and never revealed that I knew he hadn't spent the whole morning at the plantation. I half-wondered if he would guess I'd seen him when he heard I'd been back at the farm by eleven, but Marney's so vague about time and while he was with April I'm sure he didn't stop to look at his watch. After leaving the house he must have driven straight to the section where he was supposed to be working; since he didn't go all the way back to the lodge he wouldn't have wondered later why he hadn't met me while I was walking back again over the mountain. He would simply have assumed later that he must have just missed seeing me before he turned off the main track to drive out to the remote section of the plantation where his work lay, and I thought it best not to let him know I had already reached the house before he left. I was right, wasn't I? It wouldn't have helped if I'd told him what I knew."

"Did you tell him when you saw him last night?"

"No, I didn't see him last night. I dropped the papers at the lodge and didn't stop to talk to him. Besides, I think he had gone straight up to bed."

"And you never told Neville?"

"Neville? Of course not! This was strictly between Marney and myself. Why should I have told Neville?"

"But if Marney was the last person to see April alive—"

"At the time we didn't think she was dead. We thought she had simply gone away."

"But now—"

"Oh, *now*," said Leonie impatiently. "Yes, I told you I was going to tell Neville about it as soon as I had the opportunity, but of course it still doesn't prove Marney had anything to do with April's death. Anyone could have gone to the house and killed her when Marney left in his jeep. I'm quite convinced that Marney left in his jeep. I'm quite convinced that Marney didn't kill her and that he's completely innocent of any crime."

Karen was silent. All she could think of was that April had been seen and heard by two people after Neville had left her. Neville couldn't have killed her. Neville wasn't guilty.

"Don't you agree?" Leonie was persisting. "Someone could have killed her after Marney left. Don't you agree?"

"Yes," said Karen, anxious not to upset Leonie by disagreeing. "I guess so."

"Marney's innocent," repeated Leonie, her voice high and strained in that still room, and Karen suddenly began to wonder if Leonie was protesting Marney's innocence so loudly because she had seen him commit murder and wanted desperately to protect him.

## III

The coffee tasted hot and bitter. Karen put down her cup after one sip, and stood up slowly. "Maybe I'll just slip outside again," she heard herself say, "to see if there's still no sign of Neville."

Leonie turned her head sharply. "But you do see, don't you, how important it is that Melissa shouldn't interfere in such a dangerous situation? You see how important it is that the police shouldn't be told?"

"Certainly I do, and I appreciate you telling me all this—it gives me a much clearer understanding of the situation." She escaped quickly, closing the back door behind her and taking deep lungfuls of the cool Highland air as she moved up the hillside again to the same vantage point.

There was still no sign of Neville. She wondered desperately where he could be and what had happened to him, and then decided that before she considered the problem further she should put on some thicker clothes to combat the chill of the northern morning. Ten minutes later, wearing warm slacks, a sweater and walking shoes she slipped out of the back door again and walked back to her vantage point to think clearly.

Perhaps Neville had walked over to Plantation Q to discuss the situation further with Marney. Yet would Neville have bothered to walk? Surely he would have taken his jeep and driven over to the lodge. Karen glanced back at the jeep parked near the stream and decided that in all probability Neville had not gone to Plantation Q. Yet despite Leonie's suggestion, Karen doubted if Neville would have gone to see Melissa at dawn when the hotel doors would be locked and Melissa would certainly be asleep. So where could Neville be?

She paced about restlessly, aware of her extreme tension

and the gnawing ache of anxiety. Perhaps after all Neville had walked over the mountain—he himself had said earlier that he felt exercise would calm him down, so perhaps on this one occasion he had walked instead of using the jeep.

He must have walked. He would be at the lodge and talking to Marney.

"I'll walk over myself," she decided suddenly, and at once felt better for reaching a decision. She felt herself unable to endure waiting any longer, and she had an immense desire to escape from Leonie and talk to Neville of the new suspicions which had insinuated their way into her mind and now refused to be put aside.

"I must find Neville," she thought, "I have to find Neville. I must talk to him."

She walked back to the farm, crossed the stream and went on past the parked jeep up the mountain track. Once or twice she glanced back at the farm, but Leonie evidently had not seen her, or if she had she was making no attempt at pursuit. Karen relaxed a little and began to walk at a more even pace so that the steep gradient would not exhaust her too soon, but presently her breathlessness drew her to a halt and she stood for a moment and looked back once more at the house now far below her on the floor of the valley.

The golden pallor of dawn had faded into the clear brightness of daylight; the sky was already streaked with clouds and across the valley to the west the mountains were partially obscured by mist. The moors were a curious shade of purple-brown, shifting and varying in hue as the clouds began to drift across the sun. Below, the lake was a long slender strip of immobility, sometimes blue as azure, sometimes dark as flint in the changing light. As far as the eye could see was nothing but magnificent yet oppressive isolation.

Karen reached the top of the pass and paused to get her breath, but in less than a minute she was moving on again. She was beginning to feel more urgently than ever that she must talk to Neville, warn him about Marney. What would Neville do? What would he say to Marney? There was so little time; Melissa would be going to the police at noon.

She was almost running now. The path was winding downhill, and directly ahead of her were the dark silent trees of the plantation, a direct contrast to the bare sweep of the surrounding moors. In a quarter of an hour—ten minutes—she could be at the lodge talking to Neville.

She stumbled on down the track, her eyes watching the ground to avoid the danger of tripping over a loose rock or stone. Soon she had reached the edge of the plantation and she slackened her pace again and glanced around her nervously. She had always hated the twilight of the woods, the unnatural stillness that prevailed there.

She saw the tire-tracks straight away. They bit into the wet earth and curved away around the perimeter of the plantation. They looked fresh and clear and clean-cut in the morning light, a trail blazed in darkness and now coming into its own as the sun rose steadily in the east.

Karen felt her heart bumping rapidly. She stopped, pushed the hair back from her forehead, and stared through the trees. Perhaps Neville—no, Neville wouldn't be working at this hour. Perhaps one of the foresters had just driven up from the lodge. Perhaps he would know if Neville was there talking to Marney.

She moved forward away from the path and followed the tire-marks skirting the edge of the woods. There was no sign of a jeep although Karen expected to see one with every step she took. She walked on, her feet making no noise on the soft pine needles, her breath sounding hard and uneven in her throat, and suddenly it seemed to her in a flash of fantasy that all the trees were watching, waiting in anticipation as she drew nearer the end of the trail. Her scalp began to tingle, but she did not stop. Her feet carried her across the pine needles until abruptly the trail ended in a muddy swirl where the jeep had been turned around and driven back to the main track.

There seemed to be no one about.

She was aware of an immense fear. She cast a quick glance around her but there was nothing except the pines on one side of her and the open moors of the mountainside on the other. And then suddenly she saw the grave.

Her legs carried her forward against her will; it was as if she were drawn forward by compulsion.

There was a rectangular patch of freshly-dug black earth. A few pine needles had been scattered over it but there was no mistaking its sinister measurements. Karen picked up a stick, sank it into the soft earth and struck flesh.

After that she was hardly sure what happened. Hands which did not seem to belong to her scraped at the earth and revealed a wrist, a slim elegant wrist still looking repulsively human, and on the wrist beyond the costume ring Melissa always wore were Melissa's meticulously manicured fingernails, shining, polished, and horribly alive.

But Melissa was without doubt very dead.

Karen was dimly surprised that she did not feel dizzy, but when she stood up there was no roaring in her ears, no weakness in her legs. All she was aware of was the absolute stillness and the silent watching twilight of the woods.

She stared down again at the grave. She looked and went on looking in mesmerized disbelief, but at last she raised her eyes slowly to the dark silent shadows of the trees beyond the grave and it was then that she saw him, standing there.

# EIGHT

## I

Her hand went to her mouth. She took a pace backwards.

"Karen!" His eyes were wide and blank. "My God, what are you doing here?"

She tried to move, but could not. She tried to speak but the words would not come. And then he began to walk towards her and the fear rose in her throat and forced her to cry out loud.

"No, Marney—"

He did not stop. He came on towards her without hesitation, his footsteps soundless on the pine needles, and suddenly, mercifully, the power to move returned to her and she was running blindly downhill through the dark trees, the harsh sobs jolting her body. He was running after her. She could hear him behind her but such was her terror that she did not even look back. How far was it down to the lodge? How long could she keep running like this? Supposing she should get lost. And she thought of that other time three years ago when she had rushed out of the house to escape from April and Neville and had lost herself hopelessly among the acres of trees.

The questions stabbed through her thoughts and seemed to cast jagged patterns across her consciousness. She had reached the track again now after cutting a diagonal path through the woods, and as her feet slid painfully against the rough stones she looked back for the first time and saw Marney swerving deeper into the woods.

Perhaps he was heading to cut her off. He knew the plantation so much better than she did. Still sobbing with her
exhaustion and panic she ran into the woods on the other side
of the track and began to run downhill among the trees again.
As long as she kept moving downhill she knew she would
eventually reach the level of the lodge. And once she reached
the lodge she would be safe.

A minute later a crippling stitch made her stop and bend
over double. She was fighting for breath. Perhaps she would
never get to the lodge. Perhaps Marney would catch up with
her in a matter of seconds. She twisted round, but he was nowhere in sight. Had he lost her? Or was he hiding, watching
her? Her thoughts spun dizzily, but even before she could
attempt to answer her own questions, the pain in her side
eased and she was running again.

The trees thinned; she came upon a wide cut through the
woods, and as she crossed it she saw him watching her far over
to the left. He would have known she had to cross the cut to
reach the lodge, and as she stumbled across the open track to
the trees on the other side she was aware with horror that he
was now probably between her and the lodge itself. She had
struck a course out to the west of the mountain track, and
wherever Marney placed himself between her and the track he
would succeed in cutting her off.

In panic she began to make a still wider detour, moving
even further out to the west. She must come round in a circle
and approach the lodge from the front. There was no other
way. If only she didn't get lost she might still reach safety.

The trees closed in on her again and met above her head
to obscure the early morning sunlight. Karen began to feel as
if she were suffocating in some terrible grave. She had stopped
running now on account of exhaustion and was half-walking,
half-stumbling down the hillside slopes. And then at last she
realized that the ground was no longer tilted beneath her feet,
and that she was on a different terrain. The lodge would be
to her left now. Cautiously, her eyes straining to pierce the
gloom and detect any possible sign of a pursuer, she began
to move to the left.

Ten minutes later she stumbled on the drive which linked

the lodge to the main road, and keeping among the trees for protection she changed course again and pressed northwards up to the lodge.

Suddenly she saw the barn ahead of her where the fleet of jeeps was kept. The house lay beyond, its walls mellow and tranquil in the morning light. Karen was ready to collapse with sheer relief. The tears of reaction were just pricking her eyelids when a car roared from the drive behind her and the next moment a white Fiat 600 flashed past and swung off the road to cruise to a halt on one side of the barn.

Karen had shrunk back instinctively into the trees as the car had passed her, but now she ran forward, summoning up new reserves of strength which she did not know she possessed. Rushing round the corner of the barn, she bumped straight into the man who was emerging from the driver's seat.

"Neville!" She was almost hysterical with relief. "Oh Neville, Neville, Neville—"

He was just in time to catch her as she fainted.

## II

When she next opened her eyes she found she was lying on the sofa in Neville's study at the lodge. Neville was sitting beside her holding one of her hands, and beyond him was Thomas, his face white, his eyes bright with anxiety.

"Thomas?" She groped dimly for some memory of what had happened and then remembered that Thomas had been in the passenger seat as Neville had emerged from the little Fiat. "What happened?" she said confused. "I don't understand. Why are you both here?"

They glanced at each other quickly. "We came to look for Marney," said Thomas. "But while you were unconscious just now Neville checked his room and he wasn't there."

"I rowed myself over to Kildoun as soon as dawn came," explained Neville. "The more I thought about it the less I understood why Melissa had failed to answer when Thomas knocked on her door and rang her room last night. Before I left I telephoned the manager MacPherson and he very nobly rose to the occasion, got out of bed and let me into the hotel when I arrived. We then discovered Melissa wasn't in her room, although all her clothes were still there and her car was still parked in the yard. Then Thomas—"

"I woke up next door and wanted to know what was going on." Thomas shifted warily from one foot to the other. "Neville and I had a conference and decided to drive round by road in Melissa's car to the lodge to see if Marney knew anything about the mystery. Karen honey, I hate to rush you but can you tell us now what you were doing here? Do you feel strong enough yet to tell us what's happening?"

"I didn't know where Neville was . . ." She still felt muddled. "I thought you must have walked over to the lodge for some reason, Neville, so I—"

"Didn't you see that both boats were missing from the jetty? Thomas took one last night and I took the other this morning."

"No, I—how stupid of me! I never thought to check the jetty or the boathouse. I simply thought you couldn't have gone across to see Melissa while it was still so early."

"Did you have some urgent reason for wanting to see me?"

"Yes, I—oh God, yes, I did . . ." She began to talk. She heard her voice, a low even monotone recounting her conversation with Leonie, her conviction that Leonie suspected Marney of murder, her journey over the mountain, the grave, the confrontation with Marney, the chase . . . Suddenly she broke off and shuddered as the shock of memory began to exist in comprehensible terms.

"Get her some more brandy, Thomas. There's another bottle in that cupboard over there. Well, it all seems plain enough, doesn't it? Marney must have killed April three years ago and he must have killed Melissa last night. I've no doubt we'll find April's grave close to Melissa's in that same section of the plantation."

"I should think so. The situation was probably aggravated by the fact that she was involved with me."

"Yeah, that makes sense. That gives him a motive, and that's what floored us when we were trying to figure out the situation just now at the hotel. Do you think Leonie saw him kill her?"

"No, I don't. If she had seen him kill her, I'm sure she would have said something, if not to me then to Marney himself. Good God, she could even have forced him to marry her if she'd witnessed him commit murder! At least she would have promised him her loyalty and sworn herself to eternal secrecy. She wouldn't have been able to keep the information to herself for three years."

"Then you think—"

"I think she was telling Karen the truth. She overheard part of the quarrel, then dashed out to recover from the shock and waited until she was exhausted. By the time she returned to the house Marney had killed April and driven the body off in his jeep for burial on the edge of the plantation."

"But would he have had time to pack the suitcases and tow the spare boat across the lake?"

"Plenty of time. If Leonie walked to the tip of the lake she would have been gone for well over an hour. He was alone at the house—and what's more as far as he knew he was certain to be alone there; he didn't know, remember, that you and Karen had arrived and had stayed the night at Kildoun. He only knew I was staying at the house with April and Leonie, and since Leonie was by that time at the lodge waiting for him (or so he thought) and since he naturally assumed I was at the plantation beginning my business by the time he arrived at the house to see April, he couldn't have foreseen any interruption. It all fits in."

The brandy was beginning to make Karen feel better. She had stopped shivering and her brain was becoming clearer. She drank the last drop determinedly and set the empty glass down on the table with a steady hand. "But Neville," she said evenly, "how could Marney have killed Melissa? I don't understand."

"Easy," said Neville at once. "As soon as he got back to the lodge last night he must have taken Kelleher's Rolls and driven round by road to the hotel at Kildoun. Unless—Karen, did Leonie say she saw Marney last night when she drove after him with those papers?"

"No, she didn't see him. She said she thought he had probably gone to bed and she simply left the papers at the lodge."

"There you are, then! Marney left immediately, arrived at Kildoun and sought Melissa out to discuss the situation. When she refused to change her mind about going to the police he killed her, drove her back to the lodge and finally took the body up to the top of the plantation for burial."

"You mean he killed her at the hotel?" Karen said doubtfully.

"No, I expect he suggested a drive in his car to talk the situation over."

"But how did he get in touch with her when he reached the hotel? She refused to speak to Thomas."

"Maybe he simply knocked on her door and told her who he was. Melissa would have been intrigued to know what he wanted. She probably hadn't foreseen an interview with Marney."

"But how did he know which room she had?"

"Couldn't he simply have asked? He's known at the hotel and they wouldn't have seen anything odd about him wanting a word with one of the English guests who happened to be known to him."

"What do we do now?" said Thomas abruptly before Karen could say anything else. "Shall we call the police?"

"I'd like to see Marney first. Damn it, where is he? If he was running after Karen he should have been here ten minutes ago! Perhaps he realized he couldn't catch Karen and decided to go over to the house to see me and try to explain away what had happened. After all, he doesn't know I'm here. He thinks I'm asleep in bed. Perhaps we'd better drive back over the mountain to the house."

"Then he's sure to come back here and we'll miss him," said Thomas sardonically.

"All right," said Neville, making up his mind. "You stay here at the lodge, Thomas, in case he comes back, and I'll take Karen over to the farm with me. I'm not letting her out of my sight after her adventures this morning."

"What do I say to Marney if he turns up here?"

"Tell him to drive over to the house to see me. Say I know

everything but I'd like a word with him before I actually telephone the police."

"Okay then." Thomas looked uneasy for a moment, but soon
managed to suppress any trace of nervousness. "Is that all
right with you, Karen? How are you feeling now?"

"I'm better, Thomas, don't worry about me." She stood up
and was surprised to find herself light-headed after drinking
brandy on an empty stomach. "I don't mind going back with
Neville."

"I'd better take another jeep," murmured Neville, rising to
his feet. "Kelleher will be cross since I've already got one at
the house, but I can't help that. Are you ready to leave now,
darling, or do you want to wait a few minutes longer?"

Karen said she was ready. She now felt so tense again that
she longed for some kind of action. The more she waited the
more nervous she became.

Neville brought one of the jeeps up to the door and helped
her up into the passenger seat.

"I'll see you later, Thomas."

"Okay, Neville. Good luck. Take care, Karen."

"You too, Thomas. 'Bye."

The jeep was rattling off across the yard towards the main
cut into the woods, and Thomas stood on the doorstep looking
after them, a small lost figure shading his eyes against the
sunlight.

There was no sign of Marney. At the perimeter of the
plantation, Neville halted the jeep to examine the trail of tire-
marks for himself and to look at the grave. He came back three
minutes later, his mouth grim and set, his hands clenched deep
in his pockets.

"No sign of him," was all he said. "The place was deserted."

They did not speak again until they reached the farm,
parked the jeep and crossed the bridge over the burn to the
back door.

"I think he's here," muttered Neville. "I can hear Leonie
talking to someone in the kitchen."

Karen felt the breath catch in her throat. Her nails dug into
the palms of her hands.

Neville opened the back door.

The voices stopped. Then:

"So there you are, Neville," said Marney in a strange hard voice. "I'm glad you've come back because I was just about to telephone the police and I wanted a word with you before I spoke to them. You bloody fool! You might have got away with April's murder, but what on earth made you think you could get away with Melissa's? Why the devil did you have to lose your head and kill her?"

## III

There was a long amazed silence. Neville had stopped abruptly and was for once at a loss for words. Leonie, looking drawn and haggard, had her back to the sink and Marney was standing by the stove. To Karen, on the threshold of the room, the scene seemed like a tableau hovering on the brink of some appalling animation.

"You did kill her, didn't you," said Marney, still speaking in his strange hard voice. His hands were clenched in tension, his scanty hair was windblown and untidy, his clothes muddy and creased. As he spoke he kept pausing to lick his lips. "You weren't out on the plantation for three hours searching for Karen the day April was killed. You walked to the lodge to get a jeep and then you drove back to the house after I had left and Leonie was far away at the tip of the lake. You found April alone and after you had killed her you drove her body up to the plantation and buried it near the place where you buried Melissa last night. If Karen hadn't interrupted me this morning I'm certain I would have found April's grave just a few yards from Melissa's. I got up early because I couldn't sleep and decided to walk over to the house to have breakfast with all of you—but then I saw the tire-marks running off the track and around the edge of the trees, and since I couldn't understand why anyone should have been in that section of the plantation I went to see what had been going on. Then Karen came. I tried to catch her to ask her how much she knew but when I lost her I decided to continue my journey to the house to have it out with you once and for all. How did you kill Melissa? I suppose you rowed across the lake last night and suggested you go for a drive in her car while you discussed the situation. Then you must have killed her, taken her to the lodge and driven the body by jeep up to that section of the plantation. Am I right? After that you simply drove back to the lodge and returned Melissa's car to the hotel before rowing across the lake to the house again. That's what happened, isn't it? Wasn't that what you did?"

Neville found his voice at last. "You know damned well I did no such thing," he said. He seemed mesmerized by Marney's transformation into an angry counsel for the prosecution. "You know bloody well you killed them both."

Leonie shook her head violently: "Don't—don't, Neville—"

Neville swung round to face her. "Leonie, it's too late for lies now. It's impossible to cover up for one another or pretend we can all overlook murder to save ourselves unpleasantness with the police. Melissa's dead—killed—buried up on the plantation with April—"

"So you admit it," said Marney. "You admit April's buried up on the plantation with Melissa." He moved towards the door leading into the hall. "I'm going to phone the police, tell them everything and suggest they look around for April's grave while they exhume Melissa."

Neville suddenly seemed to realize that Marney was in earnest. "You're going to tell the police that because you know damned well they'll find April there!" he shouted. "Your only hope of getting out of this unscathed is to try to blame everything on me!"

"Shout as much as you like," said Marney. "You won't convince me you're not guilty. Who else could have killed those two women? Leonie could never have buried April on the plantation because she could never have transported the body there from the house—she had no jeep. Karen couldn't conceivably have killed Melissa since she was at the house all last night. Thomas might have killed them both but he would never have buried the bodies in that particular place. He doesn't know the plantation well enough and he had no access to the jeeps anyway. So it's you or I, Neville, and since I know perfectly well that I could never—never, you understand—deprive another human being of life, that leaves you." He turned abruptly on his heel. "I'm going to call the police."

Karen heard herself call dizzily: "No, wait, Marney, wait—" But she was interrupted.

"But Marney," said Leonie in a loud harsh voice, "April's not buried on the plantation."

"Leonie my dear, I know you want to protect your brother, but I really feel that the time has come to tell the truth—"

"But I am telling the truth," said Leonie. Her eyes were dark and huge in their sockets; her mouth was working grotesquely. "I killed April and last night I killed Melissa. Don't you understand what I'm saying? I killed them. I killed them both."

## IV

They stared at her in silent disbelief, and as they stared she began to wring her hands, squeezing her long fingers until the bones cracked. "I killed April after you left, Marney. I waited till you had driven away in your jeep and then I slipped back into the house and killed her. I didn't mean to but I had had such a shock in discovering you were in love with her that I couldn't have been quite sane. I shook her so hard that she fell and stunned herself, and then when she was unconscious I gripped her throat until she didn't breathe any more."

"Leonie—" Neville, appalled, tried to argue with her, but she refused to listen to him.

"No, it's true, Neville, it's true! And I killed Melissa last night. I took her down to the water's edge to row her across the lake to the hotel and it was so dark, so gloomy with all those clouds hiding the mountains that I couldn't help thinking that no one would see me if . . . I didn't really stop to think, you see. I pretended I had to go into the boathouse and when she came after me I killed her, just as I had killed April. After that I carried her up to Neville's jeep. She was surpris-

ingly light—or perhaps I was just so strong . . . When Marney
left that evening I pretended to go after him—I'd already
removed the papers to give me an excuse—but all I did was
drive Neville's jeep with Melissa's body in it up to the plantation and dig that grave. Afterwards I went on to the lodge,
dropped the papers through the letter-box, and drove home.
I had to bury her on the plantation because the ground is so
rocky and hard all around the house—it's impossible to dig a
grave here without a lot of effort and trouble and I wanted so
much to get rid of the body, bury it, forget about it—" She
stopped. Harsh sobs shook her from head to toe; her face
crumpled as she pressed her fingers against her eyes to try to
obliterate the tears.

There was a deep horrified silence.

At last Neville said slowly: "I don't believe you, Leonie.
You're making it up to protect us both."

She shook her head dumbly, her sobs muffled.

The silence fell again. And then into that silence Karen
heard herself say calmly: "If you killed April, Leonie, you'll
know where her grave is. Where is she buried?"

For a moment she thought Leonie wasn't going to answer.
Then: "I shall tell the police," Leonie managed to say unevenly, "but I shan't tell any of you. I shall tell the police to
prove to them that I killed her."

"They might still think you were covering up for one of us."

"No," said Leonie with a strange incisiveness. "I was the
only person who could have buried April in this particular
place. I shall explain to the police and they'll understand
why."

"Then tell us."

She shook her head stubbornly. "No."

Neville's glance met Marney's. They looked at one another
for a long moment. Then:

"In that case I suppose I'd better call the police, hadn't I,"
said Marney bleakly, and moved with bowed head out into
the hall.

# V

The police arrived from Fort William towards the end of the morning. Leonie had retired to her room as soon as Marney had made the telephone call, and on Neville's advice. Karen had also gone upstairs to rest for a while. When he and Marney were alone together Neville had telephoned the lodge, spoken to Kelleher to say he and Marney would be at the house until further notice, and had then had a word with Thomas. By the time Thomas himself arrived at the house, three quarters of an hour later after walking over the pass from the plantation, Snuff was up and Karen had returned downstairs to cook breakfast.

But except for the child no one was hungry.

The morning seemed interminable. At last Karen, her head aching with the tension, went to lie down again, and when she awoke later from a brief sleep it was almost noon and the police were downstairs in the living-room. She was just wondering whether she should join them when she heard Neville go into Leonie's room next door to summon her.

"Leonie . . ." She could hear his voice faintly through the wall, but then there was a long silence. After a minute or two of further silence she heard him leave the room and run quickly downstairs.

She got up, spurred on by an unreasoning sense of dread. She was just slipping on her robe when there were footsteps on the stairs again, and the next moment Neville came into the room.

He was very white.

"Neville—"

"I'm afraid Leonie's taken too many sleeping pills," he said unsteadily. "We've phoned for a doctor and one of the policemen is just trying artificial respiration."

"My God." Her mind was spinning dizzily, and as she sat

down again on the edge of the bed she did not at first hear
his next words.

"Karen—did you hear me?" He was leaning over her, his
face taut and strained. "She left a confession, Karen, a written
confession for the police. She told them where to find April's
grave."

She stared up at him blankly. "Where is it? Where did she
say it was?"

"Beneath the rock garden," said Neville. "The rock garden
she was beginning when I brought April to the farm three
years ago."

## VI

Leonie's note was more stark than Karen had expected. She
had simply written:

To Whom It May Concern:
    In the presence of my brother Neville Bennett, his wife
Karen, and Dr. Marney West, I explained how I killed
April Conway and Melissa Fleming. They also know why
I killed each woman, and know that Melissa's grave is on
the boundary of the plantation nearest to the house.
April's grave is beneath the rock garden. No one else
knows that except me, because no one else could have
buried her there. I was beginning the rock garden when
I arrived at the house for my holiday that year—I already
had a pile of stones and small rocks assembled and I intended to spend my holiday arranging them and planting
flowers. When I killed April my first thought was to hide
the body before Neville came back to the house, so I took
the body outside and piled the rocks and stones over it
until it was completely hidden. Once that was done I
packed her suitcases and took them to the only soft
ground I knew, the floor of the ruined house. It wasn't
until both suitcases were buried that I realized I wouldn't

be able to bury the body there as I'd hoped—the rest of the floor was granite and there was no more room. I then towed the spare boat across the lake to make it look as if she had rowed herself across, but I didn't dare set about digging a grave for the body because I knew it would take a long time and I was frightened of being discovered before I had finished. I decided to leave the body where it was until I knew I would be alone for some hours. In the end, however, the opportunity to dig the grave arrived sooner than I had expected—Neville left Scotland that same day to follow Karen and Thomas back to London, and Marney, his business completed, went with him. Those are details that can be verified, and they're important because they prove that neither Neville nor Marney had the chance to dig a proper grave for the body. I did. I stayed on at the house and managed after much labor and effort to do what had to be done. The ground was very hard and stony and I nearly despaired of ever being able to go deep enough. This also can be verified when the body is exhumed, and it will prove that whoever dug the grave spent several hours digging it. Finally when I had finished I piled the rocks and stones up over the grave and spent a long time working on the rock garden so that no one would ever suspect what lay beneath it.

I have no more to add except that both women were despicable creatures and if it were not for the fact that to kill is evil and unchristian I would never regret that I had caused their deaths.

Please conclude any public investigation as quietly as possible for the sake of my nephew, who is as yet too young to understand why I should feel my life is finished and why I should thus seek to end it of my own accord.

## VII

"I feel numb," said Karen slowly to Neville. "Numb and upset and very, very tired. I feel as if I'm incapable of making any decisions about what to do next."

He smiled. Strain and shock had made him look suddenly older and less debonair, but despite his careworn looks his smile still held a trace of his old self. "You needn't worry," he told her wryly, "because I've already made your decisions for you." He put his arms around her and stooped to give her a kiss. "After all this is over, I shall take you on a cruise—perhaps a Hellenic cruise to Greece. I know you always wanted to go there, and cruises are the ideal way to travel—we'll both get plenty of opportunity to rest and push Scotland to the back of our minds. Snuff can come with us—if you don't mind him coming—"

"Of course he must come! How could we go without him?"

He smiled at her again. "Then it's settled! We'll have a long holiday and then when we get back to London after the cruise I might consider leaving the British Isles for a while—I'll certainly sell the farm. I couldn't return here for a holiday again. As far as my work's concerned, I've had an excellent offer recently from some forestry people in Canada, a two-year assignment—" He saw Karen stiffen. She was by the window, looking out towards the burn. "What's the matter?"

She shook her head. "Nothing, just the police. They're starting their investigations of the rock garden."

## VIII

They were already investigating at Plantation Q. The police inspector in charge believed in being thorough and taking nothing on trust, not even a convenient suicide note, and so even as Leonie's rock garden was carefully dismantled, the area around Melissa's grave was being subjected to close scrutiny. The police worked methodically and patiently, and then just as they were debating whether to explore deeper in the woods, a jeep arrived from the house with word that the body of a young woman had been uncovered beneath the rock garden which Leonie had tended for so long with such loving care.

# CALL IN THE NIGHT

# ONE

It was in the afternoon when the phone call came from Europe, one of those long shimmering afternoons of high summer when the distant reaches of the avenue dissolved into a haze and the heat was locked into the streets by the tall buildings. As soon as I had crawled home from an ill-advised window shopping spree along Fifth Avenue I went to the air conditioner, pressed the switch and stood for a few moments before the fan as I stared out of the window. Eighteen floors below me pedestrians toiled along the pavement and traffic broiled at the intersections; twenty blocks away to the northwest a helicopter prowled through the sky and tip-toed to a landing on the summit of the Pan Am Building. I was reminded of a fastidious fly examining a piece of angel cake.

I turned, moved away from the window and opened the door of the closet which the owners of the apartment hopefully described as a kitchen. There was a bottle of Bitter Lemon in the icebox; underneath the sink was the small bottle of gin which I always kept in readiness against the possibility of unexpected guests, although why I bothered to keep such a thing I don't know since none of my girlfriends had a penchant for alcohol and I had hardly reached the stage of being a secret drinker. However, I had fallen into the habit of keeping an unopened bottle of gin in the apartment ever since the time several months ago when I had been in the embarrassing position of being unable to offer a date anything stronger than ginger ale, and habits, unlike male escorts, are easy to acquire and hard to shake off. Now, because I was so exhausted and felt totally limp with the heat, I seized the gin bottle and poured a minute measure into the glass to join the ice and the Bitter Lemon. I smiled, feeling pleasantly wicked to be drinking alone, and thought how shocked my parents would have been if they could have seen me. Both had been total abstainers, pillars of a very proper little New England community in New Hampshire; my father had even refused to grow apples on the small farm where we had lived because he disapproved so strongly of cider.

I sighed, half in irritation, half in regret at my memories. That chapter of my life was closed now, and although I missed my parents and occasionally suffered vague pangs of nostalgia for the New Hampshire countryside, I was in fact thankful to be free of that strict New England upbringing. Even now I sometimes wondered if I were completely free of it. After twenty-eight years in the world and three years in New York City I was still smitten with guilt if I bought clothes which were frivolous rather than useful, and worried myself silly if I didn't have a healthy balance at the bank.

"So *sensible,* darling!" Gina always used to say. "If *only* I could be more like you!"

But she wasn't. Gina was utterly different, so different that I had no idea how we had managed to maintain close contact with one another after our parents' deaths. She was five years younger than I, and so had had five years less of exposure to the New England influences. For a time while she had worked in New York I had conscientiously tried to keep an eye on her, but after a while I gave up. It was much too exhausting, and anyway I had no wish to quarrel with her by criticizing her shortcomings. So we went our separate ways, and later I had my somewhat dubious reward when she went to Hollywood and scribbled reams of rushed letters to me concerning her work and her excessively complicated love life. Evidently my tolerant resignation, which my parents would undoubtedly have judged to be cowardice to tackle a moral issue, had encouraged Gina to cast me for the rôle of confidante. The mail from California came with great regularity. At first she had tried to phone collect, but I didn't take kindly to that.

"Three minutes only," I told her. "I'm sorry but I'm rather

broke at the moment and can't afford any more. I don't want to have to eat yogurt for dinner as well as for lunch."

"But darling, how *can* you be poor!" She sounded so upset at the thought of it that I began to feel touched by her concern. "I mean, you must make such an awful lot of money teaching those terrible children—"

"Not as much as you make in a thirty-second soap commercial," I said with truth, and then felt guilty lest she should think I was being mean, so I encouraged her to talk for ten minutes and postponed buying the *Antony and Cleopatra* album until another time.

However, she took the hint, and after that the letters started to arrive. I began to feel that perhaps I had missed my vocation in life and that I should have been running an advice column for females in distress. "I hardly know what to say," I wrote despairingly in an early letter back to her. "I don't think you'll find my comments any use to you at all. I can't imagine why you should think that just because I'm five years older than you I have a total, all-enveloping knowledge of human relationships and problems."

"But you're so sane!" cried Gina's pen, weeping purple ink on to pink paper in reply. "So sensible! If you only knew how comforting it is in this mad crazy mixed-up beastly city to have *someone somewhere* who can talk sense and behave normally. . . ."

In fact I think I had become a parent-substitute for her, a symbol, however inaccurate, of the orderly world she could remember from her childhood, and that although nothing would have induced her to return to the discipline of a New England existence, it comforted her to think that it was always there if ever she needed it.

After a few months of this peculiar correspondence, I found I was becoming much fonder of her than I had been when we had both lived in New York; distance lends enchantment. When she came through New York en route to a modeling career in Paris we had a very enjoyable week together, but I could not pretend to myself that I wasn't slightly relieved when the time came for us to part again. I felt like a quiet, placid house in a quiet, tree-lined road of some quiet small town which has suddenly been hit by a tornado, lifted off the ground, spun round three times in mid-air and then dropped back into place with an earth-jarring jolt.

Gina had been six months in Paris on that afternoon in early July when I returned from my window shopping stroll along Fifth Avenue. I had had lunch with an old college friend, and had left my apartment building before the arrival of the mail, which was never delivered before noon on Saturdays. When I returned exhausted at four o'clock I almost forgot to check the mailbox but fortunately I remembered, and there, waiting for me, was the familiar airmail envelope and the familiar dizzy purple-inked handwriting beneath the familiar French stamps. After I had mixed myself my illicit Bitter Lemon, I subsided on to the couch, shook off my shoes and put my feet up. Then with my glass in one hand and Gina's letter in the other I settled down to assume my well-worn rôle of guide, philosopher and friend.

It started in the usual way. According to Gina, this was "just a little note." Sighing with resignation I began to count the pages of whirling purple loops and curls, and then curiosity got the better of me and I went back to the beginning again.

". . . this is just a little note, darling, honestly, as I'm so rushed I'm nearly going out of my mind and I'm supposed to be in three different places at once right now and oh! life's so complicated just trying to fit everything in, and sometimes I wish I was like you, darling, honestly, with your nice steady job and your regular salary and your dear little apartment the size of a dime and your view of midtown Manhattan, and sometimes I really do wish I was back in New York with the luncheonettes and the pizza shops and the bars and the heat that bounces up from the sidewalk to meet you, because although Paris is so glamorous and so exciting and so *soigné*, it does nothing but rain and one does get just a *little* tired of all those dashing French males pinching one's bottom on the Metro. Talking of males, I've just discovered the most enthralling specimen you could ever imagine, and—just for a change —he has absolutely nothing to do with the world of fashion or photography, and he's not even French either, and let's face it, darling, I'm just about due for a change of nationality

romance-wise after six months of warding off/egging on
would-be Latin lovers. This latest gem is British, but not
the bowler-hatted variety or even the Carnaby Street variety
either (yes, believe it or not, there *are* other kinds!). His name
is Garth Cooper. He seems to be unmarried, but I can't think
how he's managed to escape for so long because he's about
thirty-five and there's nothing wrong with him, quite the reverse in fact, as I've been discovering recently when we've
been out on the town together. In fact that reminds me, we
went out together last night and GUESS who we saw! Just
guess! You never will, never in a million years—Warren
Mayne! And if you'll believe it, he came right up and kissed
me as if he was still my fiancé. Some people have an awful
nerve, don't they? I was embarrassed to pieces and didn't even
dare look at Garth but afterwards he seemed amused and said
it looked as if Warren had come to work in Paris so that he
could get in touch with me again. Of course I denied it, but I
*did* wonder. Oh, it's just too much of Warren if he has followed me to Paris! It'll make life so horribly complicated and
I just can't bear it, it's complicated enough already, and sometimes I can't help wishing you were here to sort it out for me
—incidentally hasn't school finished for the summer yet? What
are you doing about a vacation? Rake those surplus dollars
out of your bulging bank account and buy yourself a round
trip excursion flight to Paris! Must rush, darling, no more now,
love and take care and all the rest, GINA."

I sighed again, sipped my gin and reflected what a mysterious thing sex appeal is. Gina and I look rather alike—or at
least we used to before Gina took to false eyelashes and the
hollow-cheeked look—but she obviously has a certain mysterious quality which I lack. I really can't believe the mystery
rests on false eyelashes alone so I suppose some extraordinary
fusion of the hereditary quirks of our very ordinary parents
must be responsible. Whatever it is, it never seems very fair.
But then unless one is a complete ingenue one hardly expects
life to be fair; I had long ago resigned myself to that basic
truth so I was always cross when I caught myself behaving
like an ingenue again and envying Gina her good luck.

As if, I thought disgusted with myself, I even wanted to be

a model. She was welcome to it all, Paris, men and mink coats!
I was perfectly happy with my Shakespeare records and my
friends and the Metropolitan Museum on Sundays; I had a job
I liked, an apartment of my own, and perhaps, if I were careful
with my saving and my raise came through shortly, a shining
little red Volkswagen. . . .

After day-dreaming for several minutes of stepping casually
into my very own car as the doorman held open the door for
me with an admiring smile, I roused myself, found pen and
paper and sat down again to consider a reply. I always found
Gina's letters easier to answer if I made the effort to write when
her initial impression was still clear in my mind. To write a
guide-philosopher-friend letter in cold blood after an interval
of several days was much too turgid a task to face.

"My dear Gina," I began, scratching away nimbly at the paper. "How you do ramble on, although I'm sure I'm just as bad
myself sometimes. Here are my comments in chronological order: 1) You know darn well you'd rather be in Paris in the rain
than in a ninety-degrees-ninety-percent-humidity New York,
so don't ask me for sympathy on *that* issue. 2) If the Metro is
such a danger spot for the more vulnerable parts of your anat-
omy, catch a bus and sit down at once. 3) I don't trust this
thirty-five-year-old Englishman. Why should he be (apparently) floating around Paris with money to burn? Also, what
do you mean when you say he 'seems' to be unmarried. That
sounds as if you really think he might be married. If he is, say
a tender goodbye now, and then maybe I won't have to offer
you my shoulder to cry on long distance in six months' time,
when he suddenly strikes a noble pose and decides to go back
to his wife. 4) Bad luck about meeting Warren again. However, if you don't want to see him in the future, there's one
quite simple remedy. Tell him so. 5) I'd love to come to Paris
and see you but am just about to get my little red car which I
told you about when you were here last winter. Maybe next
year? I'm not having a very ambitious vacation this year, just
a week in Boston with Sue and her husband and a week in
Martha's Vineyard at Nancy's cottage there . . ."

I paused to reread what I had written before continuing
my own news, and swallowed the last of my drink. I was just

picking up my pen again to resume the letter when the phone rang.

Reaching backwards I grabbed the receiver and knocked over my empty glass. "Yes?" I said confused, picking up my glass and retrieving my writing-pad which had slid off my knees to the floor. "Hello?"

"Miss Claire Sullivan, please."

"Speaking," I said dimly, puzzled by the unfamiliar man's voice and the hum of the long distance wire.

"Miss Sullivan, this is London, England. Will you accept a call, please, from a Miss Gina Sullivan who wishes to reverse the charges?"

I was so surprised that I even forgot to be annoyed at Gina's further attempt to call collect. "London?" I said in amazement. "London, England?"

"Yes, madam. Shall I—" He paused politely.

There was no mistaking the British courtesy. Or the British accent.

"Yes," I said rapidly. "Yes, I'll take the call. Thank you."

"Go ahead, please, caller."

"Gina?" I said at once incredulously. "Gina, what are you doing in—"

But she was already talking, not listening to me, her voice high-pitched and breaking with panic, her breath coming in sobs and gasps, and as I listened her terror communicated itself to me until I too was rigid with her fear.

"Oh Claire, Claire, please come," she was sobbing. "Please come, Claire. Oh Claire, I'm in such dreadful terrible trouble I don't know what to do—Claire, you just have to come, please, please—I don't know what to do—"

"Gina listen! Where are you, for God's sake? What's happened? What—Gina, are you there? Gina—"

But there was nothing there any more, just that long empty silence, and then across a distance of four thousand miles I heard the soft stealthy click of the receiver being replaced.

# TWO

The buzz of the disconnected wire produced a reaction from me of stupefied disbelief. I stared at the silent phone and listened to the dull *purr* as if I were completely paralyzed, and then at last I pulled myself together, called the operator, and asked for the international circuits.

"I was speaking to London—I was cut off—" I couldn't think clearly; I heard myself stumble over the questions the operator asked. "No—no, I don't know the number in London . . . yes, if you could please trace the call for me . . ."

I hung up, waited, mixed myself another gin. At last, just as I thought I could bear waiting no longer, the phone rang again.

"The call came from 16, Hereford Mansions, London W.8.," said the operator sedately. "Number: Kensington 21272. The number is listed under the name of a Mr. Eric Jantzen, that's J-A-N-T-Z-E-N. Shall I try the number for you?"

"Please." My pencil whispered across the paper, recording the information she had given me.

"Whom are you calling, please?"

"Gina Sullivan." I spelled it.

"One moment, please."

I waited, listening. Presently I heard the dialing, followed by the sound of the bell ringing far away.

"Trying to connect you," said the operator.

"Thank you."

It went on ringing.

"Still trying to connect you," said the operator.

"Thank you."

A long pause.

"I'm sorry," said the operator. "There's no reply. Can I try the number again for you later?"

I couldn't think what to say. At last I said: "No, thank you, but could you check the address of the call again? My sister has never mentioned anyone called Eric Jantzen and I want to be quite sure there was no mistake."

"Call you back," said the operator, impersonal as an automaton, and hung up.

I replaced the receiver and sat staring into my glass. Supposing I kept trying the number and still got no reply? What was I to do? I'll wait till midnight, I thought and then if I haven't managed to contact Gina or if she hasn't called back. . . . My scalp prickled. What was I to do then? It would be no good calling the police of the local precinct about something which had happened in London. And if I called the police in London, spoke to Scotland Yard . . . I tried to imagine the conversation.

"My sister called me from London just now," I would say. "She sounded very frightened and hysterical. Then we were cut off and the receiver was replaced and now I can't re-establish contact with her. Could you check the address of this apartment belonging to Eric Jantzen and see if she's all right?"

Did one ask Scotland Yard to give reassurance about one's relatives? I mentally tried a more dramatic approach. "I'm afraid something dreadful has happened to my sister—we were cut off in the middle of our conversation and it sounded as if someone had silenced her. . . ."

But that wasn't true. Gina hadn't mentioned that she was in danger, only 'in trouble.' If she had been interrupted by someone who had silenced her and replaced the receiver, she had given no indication of it. There had been no scream, no gasp of horror, only the hysteria and sheer panic which I, perhaps mistakenly, had interpreted as a hysteria born of fear. I rephrased my approach to Scotland Yard and imagined the subsequent conversation.

"I've had a very disturbing phone call from the apartment of a Mr. Eric Jantzen," I would say. "My sister was hysterical and sounded immensely frightened—I think it's vital that the call should be investigated—"

And Scotland Yard would interrupt: "What was your sister doing in London? How well did she know this Eric Jantzen?"

"I don't know, but she was friends with an Englishman called Garth Cooper."

"You say your sister's a model by profession?" Scotland Yard would say instantly. "Young—smart—presumably attractive to men?"

"Yes, but—"

"Isn't it likely that she was hysterical as the result of a crisis which was possibly brought on by her relationship with either or both of these two men?"

"Well, yes, but—"

"Did she actually say she was afraid? Or in danger?"

"No, but—"

"What were her exact words?"

I winced. I didn't have to imagine Scotland Yard's comment on that particular phrase. I was just wondering if I should call them anyway, when the phone rang again. It was the operator confirming Jantzen's name and address. I told her I had changed my mind, and asked her to try the number again for me in an hour's time. After I had replaced the receiver, I had a brain-wave, and going over to the bureau on the other side of the room I got my writing case and found the phone number of Gina's apartment in Paris. Gina shared the apartment with another American girl, whom I had never met, called Candy-Anna; I particularly remembered the eccentric hybrid of a first name, although I had long since forgotten the second. Presently I was talking to the international information department again, and placing yet another call to Europe.

This time I was more successful. A voice as languid as melting maple syrup answered the ringing phone and breathed a tingling hello into the mouthpiece.

"Go ahead, caller," the operator said.

"Candy-Anna?"

"Ye-es," said the voice, sagging a little with the realization that I wasn't an escort calling for a date. "Who's this?"

"Gina's sister Claire in New York. I—"

"Well, *hi!* I've heard *so* much about you! Gina was saying only yesterday—"

"Yes, I'm trying to find her." My interruption was hardly very adroit but she appeared not to notice my abruptness. "Do you know whereabouts in London she is, please?"

"Why, how clever of you to know she's in London! She only decided yesterday to—"

"Do you know where she's staying there?"

"Well, no—no, not really . . . She traveled over with a friend of hers, a wonderful, wonderful man who you'd just love to meet—"

"Garth Cooper?"

"Why, you *know* him! Isn't he the most—"

"No, I haven't met him. Do you know where he lives in London?"

"Gee, no—is it important? Gina'll be back on Monday—she was only going for the weekend and she said—"

"Did she ever mention the name Eric Jantzen to you?"

"Eric who? Honey, I just don't remember! If you knew how many wonderful men Gina has absolutely panting on our doorstep—" Sour grapes tinged the maple syrup sweetness briefly and was gone. "I'm sorry I just can't remember—honestly. I don't *think* she ever mentioned an Eric, but it's just possible I might have forgotten. I forget terribly easily. My memory's just the most hopeless thing you could ever imagine . . . Say, how's New York? What time is it there? Tell me all about it!"

Not at three dollars a minute, I thought with wry amusement, but I said politely that it was afternoon in New York and the weather was fine and I was so grateful for her help and hoped to meet her one day. Having escaped from the conversation as gracefully as possible I got up and moved restlessly over to the window.

I simply did not know what to do. I glanced at my watch. It was five-thirty, ten-thirty in England. In half an hour the operator would try the Jantzen number again. I at least had till six o'clock to decide what to do if I were unable to make contact with Gina.

I tried to consider the situation quite dispassionately. What did I really think had happened? If I were honest I had to admit I believed Gina had got into some sort of emotional tangle with Garth Cooper and Eric Jantzen. I knew from past experience that Gina had an enormous talent for tying her love life up into the most preposterous knots. She had probably gone to London with Cooper and then discovered from Eric Jantzen, whoever he was, that Cooper was married after all. In her shock she had characteristically dramatized the situation by believing her heart to be utterly broken for all time, and carried away by a sense of tragedy had made the phone call to tell me what trouble she was in.

Then why had she hung up in the middle of the conversation?

I worried over the question until the phone rang again at six o'clock.

"There's still no reply from the London number," said the operator. "Shall I call again at seven?"

I made a spur of the moment decision. "No," I said. "Could you please place a call for me to Scotland Yard?"

I suspected that by this time even the automaton of an operator was beginning to doubt my sanity.

"Scotland Yard, London?"

"Yes," I said. "The police."

"Person to person?"

"No, no—anyone will do. I want to report something."

"Call you back," said the operator in the kind of voice one uses to the mentally disturbed, and left me listening once more to the dull buzz of a severed connection.

I began to rehearse my story again and tried to suppress a feeling of mounting nervousness and panic. When I was finally called upon to tell my story some minutes later I found myself, much to my fury, stammering over my carefully rehearsed words while my face burned with my embarrassment.

Fortunately the policeman at the other end of the wire, Detective-Inspector Fowles, listened and commented courteously enough and asked the right questions to straighten out my confused story. When I asked in desperation at last if the police would be able to help, he was reassuringly placid.

"Yes, we'll send someone round to make an inquiry at the Jantzen flat," he said. "Don't you worry, we'll look into it straight away. If there's been any funny business going on we'll sort it out and find out what's happening to your sister."

"Can you let me know any news as soon as possible? I realize these phone calls must be very expensive, but I'd really appreciate it if—"

"Yes, of course, Miss Sullivan. Now I have a note of your number here, don't I? I'll give you a ring myself as soon as the report comes through and I have some news for you."

I thanked him gratefully, replaced the receiver and then leaned back on the couch and closed my eyes. I felt exhausted. After a while I went to the kitchen and half heartedly tried to cook myself some supper, but I found I could eat nothing.

I walked restlessly about the room, stood by the window, stared out at the Pan Am Building and the other giant buildings. Another helicopter landed and departed. Seven o'clock came. Lights were pinpricking the dusk; night-time New York was coming alive, and far below me on the Avenue I could see the red tail lights of the cars as they cruised *en masse* to the midtown restaurants and the glitter of Broadway. Soon it was eight o'clock. Then nine. Twice I nearly picked up the phone in an agony of impatience, but managed to restrain myself; the man at Scotland Yard would call back. It was senseless calling him again when he might not yet have the news I wanted. I was just making myself another cup of coffee shortly before eleven-thirty when the ring of the phone made me spill boiling water over the floor.

"Hello?" I said nervously into the receiver. "Claire Sullivan speaking."

It was Scotland Yard, Detective-Inspector Fowles again. My knees were unsteady suddenly; I had to sit down.

"Miss Sullivan, I'm afraid we have no real news of your sister but all seems to be quite in order so perhaps no news is good news. Mr. Jantzen had invited her to have a drink with him, but he was delayed and couldn't keep the engagement—he tried to contact her to cancel the evening but couldn't get in touch with her. He was completely unaware that your sister had ever been in the flat."

"But—" I was confused. "How did she get in if he wasn't there?"

"He suggested that she might have come with a friend of hers, a Mr. Cooper. Apparently this Mr. Cooper has a key to the Jantzen flat."

Somewhere far away at the back of my mind I was conscious of a slight unreasoning stab of fear.

"Did you check with Mr. Cooper?" I said uneasily.

"We haven't been able to contact him so far, but I shouldn't worry too much, if I were you, Miss Sullivan. Apparently your sister came over from Paris with this Mr. Cooper—"

"Yes," I said. "I know."

"I expect they've gone out on the town tonight—your sister's probably having the time of her life, and enjoying every minute of her visit!" He sounded comforting, reassuring; I could tell that he himself was convinced nothing was wrong. "Look, I'll tell you what I think happened—she and Cooper went to his friend's flat for a drink and had a tiff about something. Maybe he pretended to walk out. Well, you know these young girls—and your sister probably enjoyed a spot of drama now and again. She put through her call to you to weep on your shoulder—and then lo and behold he turns up again all ready to apologize and they go off together quite happily as if nothing had ever happened. You mark my words, you'll have a call from her tomorrow saying she's sorry she gave you such a fright."

All I could say was: "Supposing she doesn't call?"

"Well, if she doesn't . . ." He paused to consider this remote possibility. "Give it till Monday and then check up to see if she got back to Paris safely. If she didn't and if there's still no word from her, then get in touch with me again."

"All right," I said slowly. "All right, I will. And thank you very much for all the trouble you've taken."

"Not at all, Miss Sullivan. Don't mention it."

We said goodbye, he very cordial and friendly, I stilted with anxiety and uneasiness.

Presently I sat down on the couch and remained there for a long while, but the more I told myself that it was foolish to go on worrying, the more worried I became. The thought of waiting another forty-eight hours until Monday without doing anything except wile away the time was not a pleasant thought.

At last, in an agony of indecision and nervousness I got up, went over to my purse and had a look at the balance in my checkbook. After a little simple arithmetic with the balance in my savings account I sat thinking for a long while. I was remembering the car again, my little red Volkswagen waiting patiently for me to save up the money to buy it. I thought of the trips I had planned, the luxury of excursions out of town to the beach in summer without the tedium of the long subway ride, the six-week expedition to the West I had visualized during next year's summer vacation.

I thought for a long time.

"Well," I said aloud to myself at last, "perhaps it would all have been rather extravagant. And everyone says that keeping a car in Manhattan is more of a liability than an asset. I can wait a little longer for that sort of extravagance. And I always did want to go to Europe."

Having reached my decision I felt much better. I went to bed, snatched a few hours' sleep, and as soon as I awoke next morning I dialed Pan Am to inquire how soon they could offer me a seat on a flight from New York to London.

Fate then took a hand in the proceedings; I discovered that because it was the height of the summer tourist season at that time, all the planes were fully booked on the flights to London. I put my name down on several lists, and then, nearly beside myself with frustration, I paused to consider the situation. It was now Sunday morning. Even if I got a flight that same day I would hardly be able to reach London before Gina left England to return to France—assuming, of course, that Gina was safe and well. That being the case it would be more sensible for me to try to obtain a flight not to London, but to Paris. I went back to the phone again and eventually, by a stroke of luck, found there was a cancellation on a TWA flight to Paris on Monday. Having made my reservation and committed myself positively to my decision to go to Europe I was at last able to relax a little, but there was too much to do to enable me to relax for long. I set out for Forty-second Street to exchange a check for a ticket to Paris, and as I walked I found myself again thinking of Gina, her suave Englishman Garth Cooper, Candy

Anna saying in her carefully preserved southern drawl: "Such a wonderful, wonderful man. . . ."

I began to be nervous once more. I could hardly reach the airlines' building at Forty-second Street quickly enough.

Half an hour later with my ticket safely in my purse I returned home and tried to prepare for my journey in an organized manner, but I found I was still too distraught to conform to any careful routine. I checked my passport and smallpox vaccination certificate; eternally optimistic, I had always kept both valid. The dreary task of packing lay before me. Finally when my suitcases were closed I called a couple of friends to tell them that I had decided to take a surprise trip to Europe. Both friends were suitably amazed. I began to wonder vaguely if I were indeed demented, but pushed the thought out of my mind as I sent a cable to Gina's apartment in Paris to announce my arrival.

Perhaps, I thought, determined to be optimistic and believe that all was well, perhaps Gina would be at the airport to meet me.

But somehow at the back of my mind I remained uneasily convinced that no one would be there when my plane touched down at Orly. I started to worry again, worrying all through Sunday night, and then at last it was Monday and I was rushing to my bank at nine to buy travelers' checks before taking a cab out to Kennedy to catch the morning flight. Fortunately all went well; there were no delays, no last minute disasters, and within forty-eight hours of Gina's phone call from London I was on my way to Europe to find her.

The flight seemed endless. For hour after hour the plane seemed suspended in a blue vacuum, and at last the time difference between Europe and America manifested itself in a spectacular sunset and an early twilight. By the time we reached Paris it was night, although my watch told me that in New York it was still late afternoon. I thought of the long avenues dissolving into a heat-haze, the stifling sidewalks, the drone of a million air conditioners, and suddenly that was far away on the other side of the world and the plane was beginning its long downward path to the runway and French soil.

I roused myself from the torpor of the long flight, put away my book, forgot to feel nervous. Below me I could see lights, European lights, pinpricking the darkness of the summer night, and my excitement was such that for a moment I forgot Gina altogether. The plane sank lower and lower; the lights stretched as far as I could see. Presently I saw the lights of the airport, and as the plane sank still lower to meet them I remembered to fasten my safety belt. Within a quarter of an hour the plane had landed and I was stepping out into a new and different land.

My excitement rose in a crescendo and then ebbed. I felt alone, foreign, shy. I did have a slight knowledge of French so I was not completely at a loss but the rapid cross-fire of conversation around me was far removed from the simple phrases I had learned at school. Feeling very lost and helpless I filtered through Customs and Immigration and was directed by dual-language signs to the place where I could get a bus to the terminal. I hung back, hoping in spite of myself that there would be some sign of Gina, but there was no face I knew; I remained a stranger among strangers and the airport continued to seem cold and impersonal.

After a delay I managed to cash a traveler's check, and was able to pay my fare and board the bus. My second stage of the journey began; the bus roared through the Parisian suburbs, over cobbled streets, past outdoor cafés and shabby houses. And then suddenly the shabbiness was gone and there were wide boulevards, illuminated vistas, floodlit buildings, incredibly familiar landmarks. We seemed to drive through the middle of the city, and soon my excitement was such that I forgot I was alone and thought only that this was Paris and I, Claire Sullivan, was seeing it all with my own eyes.

I reached the terminal, found my luggage again, hailed a waiting cab.

"*Numéro vingt-deux, Rue St. Thomasine, s'il vous plaît.*"

The driver nodded, assuming an expression of what I supposed was typical Parisian *ennui*. We shot off like a bullet from a gun, bounced over cobbles, screeched to a halt at an intersection. Finally as we cannoned forward again I became adjusted to this spastic form of transport and instead began to feel nervous in case my cable had failed to reach Gina's apartment.

But it had arrived safely. After I had paid the driver and left the cab I found my way into the apartment building with my luggage and shut myself in a small but modern elevator. Gina lived on the third floor. On emerging into the passage I couldn't find a light and had to strike a match, but at last I was outside the right door and reading Gina's name above Candy-Anna's on the name slot.

I was conscious of immense weariness mingled with relief. I rang the bell, waited, and presently the door opened and I was facing a slim willowy girl with honey-blonde hair and limpid blue eyes.

"Well, hel*lo* there!" said Candy-Anna, effortlessly hospitable. "Welcome to Europe! It's just wonderful to see you but I hope you're not going to be terribly disappointed. Gina must have decided to prolong that weekend in London—she didn't come back last night after all and I just haven't the remotest idea where she is. . . ."

# THREE

"Who is this man Garth Cooper?" I said. "Have you met him?"

Half an hour had passed since my arrival, and we were sitting drinking Swiss coffee in the large dishevelled living room. Candy-Anna had been pardonably curious about the suddenness of my trip to Europe and my concern for Gina, but I am not naturally inclined to confide in complete strangers so I had edited and omitted large sections of the story.

"Gina's been pressing me to come to Europe for a vacation, so I decided I would," I had said. "I had a phone call from London on Saturday night in which she sounded very odd, to say the least, but when I called her back I couldn't get in touch with her. That was when I called you to try and find out why she was in London and who she went with."

"Well, she went with Garth," Candy-Anna had answered. "But it wasn't just a wild lost weekend together—my, but you mustn't think that!" Her limpid eyes assumed a carefully cultivated expression of innocence. "Garth was going back to London after being in Paris on business and Gina decided to go too, just for the weekend and to see a bit of England. But I guess the weekend must have been a real blast and she decided to stay on. Why was her phone call to you so odd? You don't think anything's happened to her, do you?"

"She just didn't seem like herself." I had finished my cup of coffee, and then asked my question about Garth Cooper. "I believe you said on the phone that you'd met him," I added, remembering. "What kind of man is he, do you think?"

But I might have known Candy-Anna would be quite incapable of giving a straight answer to such a question.

"Garth? Why, he's just a wonderful, wonderful person! We both absolutely love him to pieces—"

"Yes," I said, trying not to sound impatient, "but what does he do? Why was he in Paris? Does he live in London?"

"My, I've no idea! I guess he must. But I think he has a small place in Paris too—I remember him saying he was always traveling back and forth between the two places . . . So glamorous!" She sighed. "Imagine living and working in London *and* Paris—"

"Yes," I said again, digging my nails into the palms of my hands. "But what does he *do?*"

Candy-Anna frowned for a moment, probably from the effort of mobilizing unused machinery for thought. "Well, gee," she said at last, vaguely surprised, "isn't that the strangest thing? I've just no idea at all."

"Did he seem rich?"

"Oh *yes!* He took cabs everywhere and never used the metro. And he and Gina went to simply wonderful places to eat and did marvellously glamorous things like going to the opera and the theatre. It was lovely for Gina! I was so happy for her."

I had my doubts about that, but kept them to myself. "How long has Gina known him?"

"Oh . . . about six weeks, I guess. But he hasn't been in Paris for the whole of that time. He was here all last week and they saw each other nearly every night. Then on Friday night they took off for London together."

"I suppose you don't know when he himself is scheduled to come back to Paris?"

"Gee, no! I've no idea. It could be that he'll stay in London for a while now. I just don't know."

I wondered what to do. It was beginning to look as if I should take a plane to London as quickly as possible, find this man Cooper and ask him point blank what had happened to Gina. But then . . . I sighed. I was no doubt being melodramatic and foolish. In all probability Gina was hopelessly in-

volved with him by this time and had no intention of returning
to Paris while her romance was flourishing so successfully in
London. She wouldn't thank me for interfering. I began to
feel as if I had made a complete fool of myself. Against
Scotland Yard's advice I had taken a melodramatic view of
the phone call and now I was taking an equally melodramatic
and misguided approach to Gina's continuing absence from
home. I was just telling myself bitterly that it would have been
more sensible to have remained in New York instead of rushing across the Atlantic Ocean like a lunatic, when the phone
rang.

We both jumped.

"It's Gina," I said at once. "It must be. She's back."

Candy-Anna grabbed the receiver. "Hello?"

I leaned forward on the edge of the couch, my limbs aching,
and saw her eyes widen with surprise. "Why, Warren! How
are you? What? No, she's not here right now—she's not back
yet. Yes, that's right. . . . No, I haven't heard from her—"

I interrupted sharply. "Is that Warren Mayne, Gina's ex-
fiancé?" I was remembering Gina's letter which had reached
my apartment shortly before the phone call.

"Just a moment, honey," she said into the receiver, and then
to me: "Yes, it is—do you know him?"

"Can I speak to him, please?"

"Sure." She was surprised. She turned her attention back to
the receiver. "Honey, just guess who's here wanting a word
with you! Someone out of your past!" And having fulfilled
her obligation to be mysterious and tantalizing she handed
the phone over to me with a dazzling smile and reached out
for another cigarette.

"Warren?" I said quickly. "This is Claire Sullivan, Gina's—"

"Claire!" He was amazed. And suddenly I could see him,
very young and clean cut, his fair hair too short, his serious
face pleasantly ugly, his brown eyes shining with affection
like those of a well-trained spaniel. Gina had led him a terrible
dance the previous year in New York; I had spent most of
our meetings feeling sorry for him.

"Yes!" I said, smiling in spite of my anxiety. "Yes, it really is me! How are you, Warren? I had heard from Gina that you were in Paris now."

"She mentioned me?" He was touchingly gratified. "Yes, I'm working for an American company with offices here. It's—" He stopped, as if halted by the realization that I should be in Manhattan and not in Europe at all. "Well, I'll be darned!" he exclaimed. "Gina didn't mention you were vacationing here! I didn't know you were in Paris!"

"Neither does Gina. It's all an involved story and I seem to have got into a muddle, to say the least. I'm told Gina's in London with someone called Garth Cooper."

Candy-Anna clapped her hand over her mouth and shook her head frantically, but she was too late. There was a sharp gasp from the other end of the wire, and as I blushed scarlet in my confusion Warren shouted: "What! Cooper? Gina went to London with Garth Cooper? Why, she told me—"

I inwardly cursed myself for not having the presence of mind to foresee the situation. "They weren't together," I said helplessly, making things worse. "They just took the same plane."

"Well, where is she now, for Pete's sake? Why isn't she back? My God, if I'd known that Cooper was going to London with her—"

"Warren, you must excuse me, but I don't really understand any of this myself. I've only just arrived and I'm not at all sure what's been happening as far as Gina's concerned. Could we meet tomorrow and talk about all this? I'm a little confused."

"Well, I'm not." He was obviously still beside himself with rage. "It's all as clear as daylight to me. That damned Englishman flashed his money around and invited her to come with him on a guided tour of London! My God, if I ever see him again—"

"Perhaps if we could talk about it tomorrow, Warren, I—"

"Breakfast? Lunch?" he asked quickly.

"How about lunch?" I suggested, hoping I'd hear from Gina before then.

"Fine. I'll stop by at your place at noon," he said furiously and slammed down the receiver.

"Oh dear," I said ineffectually. "Why on earth did I have to be so stupid? Now I've made the situation worse for Gina than it was already."

Candy-Anna was reassuring. "Gina doesn't care about Warren anyway. She'd be glad for the excuse to get rid of him forever." Her eyes held a hint of speculation. I guessed she would be glad too, but for different reasons.

"I must go to bed," I said exhausted. "I feel worn out. I apologize for descending on you like this, Candy-Anna, and putting you to such inconvenience . . ."

I was assured that I was very welcome and that there was no need to apologize.

In the end I slept in Gina's bed with Gina's familiar belongings strewn around me. Candy-Anna breathed peacefully across the room, but I slept lightly, half-expecting the phone to ring again with news, good or bad, from London. But there was no news and no phone call and when I opened my eyes at last it was eight o'clock and the sun was streaming through the slanting slats of the Venetian blinds.

Warren arrived punctually at noon. Candy-Anna had left earlier for a business appointment ("Modeling engines, honey —would you believe? I have to pose with a truck and a baby elephant.") and I was on my own when the bell rang. I went across to the door to open it.

Warren looked exactly the same as when I had last seen him. He was, I suppose, nearer my age than Gina's but I always thought of him as being at least five years my junior. When Gina had come to New York after our parents' deaths she had studied art for a while in Manhattan and had met Warren while they were both going through the long-haired Greenwich Village stage. Unfortunately for Warren, Gina had outgrown the phase more quickly than he had, and after finding success as a model in New York she had moved away, first to Hollywood and then to Paris, and there had been copious stormy scenes with the diamond engagement ring being pushed back and forth and finally discarded altogether. I could not help feeling Warren had been unlucky, since he was in his own way extremely eligible and plenty of girls would have been very anxious to catch him. He came from a good family; his father was in the diplomatic service in Washington. He was not particularly cultured or intellectual, but then neither was Gina; I thought it would have been a good match, but Gina had thought otherwise, and had gone off to fresh fields and new pastures in pursuit of what she had considered to be a more glamorous existence.

"It's good to see you again," he said, offering me his hand and smiling his bright naive smile. "I'm sorry I was so rude on the phone last night, but I was upset."

"It was nice of you to come around," I said politely, "I was hoping that perhaps you'd be able to tell me what's been going on."

"I was hoping you were going to tell *me*," said Warren. He glanced at his watch. "Look, there's a small restaurant just down the road—why don't we go out and get something to eat there? I'll bet there's nothing in the ice-box here except yogurt. Models never eat anything."

I had naturally assumed that we would go out to lunch, so his bland assumption that I might have been prepared to cook him a meal rather took me aback. I said hastily that I would be very interested in trying a French restaurant, and together we left the apartment and went into the cool fresh air of the street outside.

I caught my breath. Looking down the road I could see the Seine and beyond that, further up the river, the shining splendor of the Eiffel Tower. The sky was blue, the sun warm, but there was little humidity. New York seemed a million light years away.

"How wonderful it is to be in Paris!" I exclaimed spontaneously. "I can't think why I never made the effort to come before."

Warren smiled condescendingly. "It does seem exciting at first, doesn't it?" he said in the indulgent tone of a father talking to a child. "I felt the same too, when I arrived."

I could have murdered him.

However, my irritation ebbed when we reached the little restaurant and sat outside on the pavement under a striped umbrella. We ordered steaks and wine and then relaxed in our chairs to wait.

"They'll take hours," said Warren. "French service is the slowest in the world."

"That doesn't matter," I said firmly, putting him in his place, and to change the subject I began: "Now about Gina—"

"Exactly," said Warren with alacrity. "Look, what's going on? How did you know she was in London with Cooper? What did she tell you? Did she say she'd be back in Paris to meet you? Why isn't she here? Where is she?"

I began the weary task of explanations. I told him everything, partly because I knew him well, partly because he was obviously as worried about Gina as I was, and partly because I felt I had to discuss the situation with someone. He listened intelligently enough to begin with, but after a while I sensed he was rapidly becoming too jealous to concentrate on what I was saying.

"So there it is," I concluded at last, ignoring the sulky droop of his mouth and the introspective look in his eyes. "I don't know where she is or what's happened to her, and I'm worried —perhaps unreasonably." I hesitated and then asked the question I had put to Candy-Anna the previous evening: "What kind of person is this man Garth Cooper?"

The waiter arrived with our order and interrupted us, but I did not have to repeat my question. As soon as the waiter had left us Warren said angrily: "Well, he's English to start with. I never trust the English. The biggest fallacy in the world is to think they're just like us because they speak the same language—they're not like us at all."

I made an effort to avoid an argument on the subject of racial prejudice. "You mean you don't trust Cooper?"

"I never trust the English," said Warren obstinately. "You can never tell what they're thinking. They're always so polite, so cool and so damned charming, and then suddenly you find they're all set to stab you in the back. Cooper tried to give me the impression that he wasn't really interested in Gina at all and that he wished me well—and then what happens? I find he's taken her off to London for the weekend! Well, if that isn't two-faced double-dealing, damn it, I don't know what is—"

"But as far as I can gather they were merely traveling together—"

"Look," said Warren. "You don't seriously think they're going to shake hands at the London airport and go their separate ways, do you? Why do you think she went to London?"

"It's an interesting city," I said annoyed by his eagerness to read guilt in what might well have been an innocent situation. "Why shouldn't she have wanted to see it with or without Garth Cooper?"

"Because Gina's all tied up emotionally with this damned man Cooper. He's a rich, successful businessman of about thirty-five. He's sophisticated—he knows his way around Paris and I'll bet he knows his way around London too. He's the sort of man women drool over as soon as he enters a room, while men ask each other what the hell he has that they don't have. Gina, as usual, has gone into the whole business with her eyes tight shut—she never even stopped to ask herself if he was married or what kind of a background he had—"

"You mean he's the playboy type?"

"I mean he's a womanizer. He knows I came to France to be with Gina and yet that didn't stop him from taking her out on the town and spending all that money—"

I was becoming a little tired of Mr. Cooper's money. "But Warren," I said reasonably, "Gina chose to go out with him, didn't she? And you're not her fiancé any more, if you'll forgive my saying so. If she chose to go out with him it's bad luck for you, but in Cooper's eyes she doesn't belong to you any more than she belongs to him."

"She's infatuated with him," said Warren obstinately. "It's me she really loves."

I was silent. It was impossible for me to say that this was highly unlikely.

"If I can only get her away from Cooper—if I could only persuade her to notice me again . . ." He refilled his glass of wine; he was drinking much too quickly, ". . . she'd come back to me," he said. "I know it. That's why I'm here. I got my father to pull some strings and fix me this job for a year. It's not well paid but at least I'm in Paris near Gina—if only

Cooper would stay in England and leave me alone with her, I know, I just know, that everything would work out all right."

I almost said: "If it wasn't Cooper it would be some other man," but I checked myself. I had learned long ago that it's no good arguing with someone in love. "What *is* Garth Cooper's business?" I said after a moment. "Do you know what he does?"

"Sure. He deals in china and glass, some of it antique, some of it modern, but all of it valuable. He's involved with the importing and exporting of special lines of china and glass between England and France."

"His main office is in London, I suppose?"

"Yes, but he has a small base here in Paris. He told me it's an office-cum-apartment, where he stays as well as works when he's here. It's not a big firm—he's his own boss."

"Does he have any partners?"

He looked at me in surprise. "But I thought you knew? You mentioned the name when you told me where Gina's call came from. You mean to say you didn't realize all along who Cooper's partner is?"

"Not Eric Jantzen!"

"No," said Warren, "his wife. Cooper's partner is Eric Jantzen's wife Lilian."

It transpired that Warren had never met either of the Jantzens and that his knowledge of their existence was derived solely from his meeting with Cooper and Gina during the previous week.

"I arrived in Paris a month ago," he said. "It took me some time to trace Gina, and then just as I had managed to discover her address I met her by chance in one of the restaurants on the Champs Elysées. That was last Tuesday. She was with Cooper but I went up to her just the same—Cooper was very pleasant, or seemed to be, and asked me to join them for a drink, so I accepted and sat talking with them both for about twenty minutes. Or at least Gina didn't talk much; it was Cooper who carried the conversation—he went all out to give the impression that his relationship with Gina was a very casual one, but I'm not a fool and I wasn't taken in by what he said. And when I called up Gina later—" He winced. "We had several rows over the phone. I soon realized that Cooper had misled me, and that in fact she was heavily involved with him. On Thursday I asked her if I could see her over the weekend and she said she was going to Brittany sightseeing with Candy-Anna. So I call Monday night to ask her how she made out and you tell me she went to London with Cooper."

I was silent, thinking of Gina, wondering for the hundredth time what I should do. We had finished our meal and were drinking the last of the wine.

"Maybe I should go to London," I said uncertainly. "I'm so worried about her."

"Because of the phone call?"

"Yes—yes, I suppose mainly because of the phone call. If I thought she was merely busy carrying on with Cooper I would be reluctant to interfere, but I just can't believe that phone call has a completely innocuous explanation. I keep thinking about it."

"If you go to London," said Warren, "I'll come with you. If Gina's in any sort of trouble I want to be there helping her get out of it."

"Mmmm . . ." I was hesitant, not anxious to have him constantly at my elbow but willing to admit it would be pleasant not to face another foreign country alone. "Let me think it over. Can I call you later on this afternoon?"

"Sure." He found a pen and a scrap of paper and wrote down both his office and his apartment numbers. "I'll be home from work at six," he added, and then, glancing at his watch: "Talking of work I guess I'd better get back to the office. I've taken a long lunch hour."

Since he did not offer to pay for me we split the bill and then shook hands again as we parted in a stilted expression of comradeship. "Phone me as soon as you've made up your mind about London!" he called after me, as I made my escape. "I'll be all set to go, if necessary."

I seemed to be totally incapable of making up my mind on anything by that time. I could not decide whether I should go to London, and if I did go, whether I should go with Warren.

I was afraid that after a few hours I would find him excessively annoying, but there are times when any companion is better than none at all, and this might easily be one of those occasions. On reaching the apartment again, I absent-mindedly made myself some coffee and sat down on the window seat to gaze out on the Parisian afternoon.

After some concentrated thought I came to the conclusion that the situation was less complex than anxiety made it appear. I would simply go to London. If I found Cooper I would look like a fool, but that was the worst that could happen; at least I would be on hand to help her. But if I stayed in Paris. . . . I shrugged. In that case I might as well have stayed in New York. The best thing I could do was to go to London, and if Warren was willing to help I should accept his offer. I might need all the help I could get. If he got on my nerves too badly I could always manage to escape from him.

I smiled wryly. Poor Warren! I really rather liked him. I finished my coffee and went to my handbag to find the paper with Warren's phone number on it. I was just looking at it a moment later when I had an idea.

Two minutes' searching around the living room produced the telephone directory, and sitting down on the floor, I opened it to the C section and began to turn the pages to Cooper. If he had an office in Paris which also served as a *pied-à-terre* for himself, it was possible it was listed under his name as well as under the name of the company.

It was. I saw the entry COOPER, GARTH, and the address in the Rue Piedmont, and on an impulse I reached for the phone and began to dial. It was logical to assume there would be a secretary there, or at least an answering service, and I could find out from them how long he was expected to be away from Paris and perhaps also the address of his office in London.

The number started to ring. I was just wondering in panic if the secretary or the answering service would speak English, when someone picked up the receiver.

A male voice said casually: "*Âllo?*"

I fumbled for the remnants of my school girl French

vocabulary, but my mind, as so often happens in such a situation, went blank. "*Monsieur Cooper, s'il vous plaît,*" I said haltingly, and then added with an American accent which even I could hear: "*Est-il là?*"

There was a slight pause. Then:

"Yes, he's here," said the stranger in the perfect accentless English which only the British can produce. "You're speaking to him. May I ask who this is, please?"

# FOUR

I was so transfixed with embarrassment and surprise that I was dumbfounded. My fingers clasped the telephone receiver with a tight, hot, painful grip. My mind was blank, my tongue utterly paralyzed.

"Hello?" said Garth Cooper sharply. "Hello? Are you still there?"

I said very slowly: "Yes, I'm sorry. I wasn't aware that you were in Paris, Mr. Cooper. Please excuse me if I sound surprised." And remembering that he did not know who I was I added: "This is Gina's sister, Claire Sullivan."

Now it was his turn to be silent in astonishment. I tried to picture him, imagine his expression, but I could not.

"I've just arrived from New York for a vacation," I said, "but Gina doesn't seem to be here. I—I suppose you don't know where she is, by any chance?"

There was another slight pause. Then:

"She didn't know you were coming, did she?" he said unexpectedly. "She didn't mention it."

"No, it was a spur of the moment decision." I felt weak suddenly, dangerously close to tears. All my reassuring thoughts about Gina had sprung from the supposition that she was with Garth Cooper. To find out that he was back in Paris while she apparently was still in London was somehow horribly unnerving. "Mr. Cooper, if you know where she is—" I broke off, not knowing which words to choose.

"I last saw her in London," he said. "We flew over together last Friday evening, and on Saturday I introduced her to someone she wanted to meet, someone with show business connections. You know, no doubt, that she was hoping to break into films."

"Then you last saw her—"

"—on Saturday for lunch. I've been in Paris since Sunday night, but I'm returning to London again tomorrow morning. Perhaps I could make a few inquiries for you."

I did not know what to say. I was still so appalled by the realization that my worst fears had been proved valid that all I was conscious of was complete confusion.

"Perhaps we ought to discuss this in detail," said Garth Cooper after a moment. "Are you doing anything this evening?"

"No," I said numbly.

"Would you care to have dinner with me?"

"Well . . . if you're not too busy . . ."

"Not in the least," he said briskly. "Are you staying at Gina's flat?"

"Yes."

"Would it be convenient if I called for you at eight-thirty?"

"Yes . . . yes, it would. Thank you, Mr. Cooper."

"Not at all, Miss Sullivan," he said, very smooth, scrupulously courteous. "I look forward to meeting you."

And the line clicked with an air of finality as he replaced the receiver.

I had time on my hands, but did not know how to spend it. I should have passed the afternoon sight-seeing, visiting the Louvre perhaps, or Notre Dame, or Sacré-Coeur perched on the heights above Montmartre, but I had no heart for playing the rôle of tourist. I was too worried. For a while I considered canceling the date with Garth Cooper and going at once to London, but when I called the airlines I found that there were no seats available on the night flights across the Channel. On an impulse I made a reservation on the Air France morning flight, and then dithered for a while about whether or not I should contact my friend at Scotland Yard again. In the end I did put through a call to Detective-Inspector Fowles, more to ease my mind than in any hope that the action would have startling results. But I was out of luck; he was away from the office. I left my name and phone number and wondered if I should have spoken to anyone else, but then decided that if I were to be in London tomorrow anyway I might as well spare myself making explanations to a stranger on the phone. Having settled that issue, I began to wonder if I might have been too ready to believe Garth Cooper when I had spoken to him earlier. It was not improbable that he had lied to me, and that he was after all connected with Gina's disappearance. I told myself I must guard against being too credulous when I met him that evening.

At length, unable to endure the confining walls of the apartment any longer, I went out and walked down to the river, but it began to rain and I was obliged to turn back again to the Rue St. Thomasine. Time passed; Candy-Anna returned from work and rushed out again at six-thirty on a date. Left alone once more I had a bath, changed slowly and by a quarter past eight was sitting on the window-seat and nervously watching the street below.

I began to wonder what he would look like. What, in general, did Englishmen look like? One had a stereotyped impression of Spaniards, Italians and Frenchmen being dark, slim and excitable, of Swedes, Danes and Norwegians being tall, blond and bland. Germans were fair and jolly with overweight tendencies, Slavs fair and sad with a fondness for melodrama. But the English? Would he be dark or fair? Fat or thin? Withdrawn or volatile? Perhaps, I thought, resorting to a familiar image, he would be like a typical New Englander, a reminder of the countryside where I had been born and brought up. Logic rather than instinct told me this was unlikely. This man would be European, not American. He would think, act and speak like a European.

I was too inexperienced then to know that the English no more consider themselves part of Europe than they consider themselves part of America.

Below me in the street a taxi pulled up and my heart thudded in anticipation, but two very obvious Frenchmen got out and my nervousness receded. I glanced up and down the street. There was a woman, two children . . . and behind her a small man with middle European features. In the other direction walking up from the river were two more men, not together, of uncertain nationality. I was just wondering if either of these could be Garth Cooper when he came along.

To this day I have no idea why I should have been so positive of his identity as soon as I saw him, for he did not obviously stand out as a foreigner on French soil, but there was certainly no doubt in my mind. Perhaps the clue to his nationality was in his casual easy walk; Frenchmen are almost always either in a hurry or else idly stationary. His clothes were casual too, but not casual in the sense of being informal. On the contrary his suit was perfectly cut and his whole appearance immaculate, but he wore his clothes with an air of carelessness as if he knew he did not need to take trouble in order to look presentable. He had no hat, no umbrella and appeared to be unaware of the slight drizzle. Here was someone who expected it to rain a little during the course of each day and would have been surprised if it hadn't. His hands were in his pockets; as I watched, his right hand went to his head absent-mindedly to smooth his hair, and then with a quick glance up and down the street he crossed over to the pavement beneath my window and disappeared into the building.

I experienced a stab of nervousness followed by a wave of panic. I'm never very good at first meetings. With an abrupt, awkward series of movements I stood up, smoothed my dress over my hips, fidgeted with my collar and glanced in the mirror to check my appearance. I was just wishing I were four thousand miles away when the bell rang.

Moving very slowly I crossed the room and opened the door.

He smiled, polite, charming, unconcerned. "Miss Sullivan?"

"Mr. Cooper?" I said too efficiently, and opened the door a little wider. "Please come in."

"Thank you." He moved indolently across the threshold. His hair, which had looked dark at a distance, was in fact a light brown; I noticed again the trick he had of smoothing it with his hand as if he expected it to be perpetually untidy. He was tall, but not strikingly so, and without being solidly built he still managed to give an impression of durability. One felt he would wear well under adverse circumstances. He had a straight nose, a humorous mouth and wide set, unreadable light eyes.

"Can I offer you a drink?" I said uneasily.

"No, thanks," he said. "They have the most terrible bottle of whisky locked away in the bedroom somewhere, but since they always produce it with such enormous pride I haven't the heart to tell them it's undrinkable. Let's go straight out and have dinner. Incidentally, I must apologize for suggesting half past eight instead of half past seven. I forgot that Americans always eat early."

"When in Rome," I murmured, unable to think of anything else to say.

"Do as the Romans do?" he said. "Or do as your sister does and treat it like a little old-fashioned corner of Manhattan?"

I was unsure whether he was amused or not. "That's only a defense," I said. "One feels so foreign here."

"Depressing, isn't it?" he agreed, taking me aback. "The French look down their noses at anyone not born in France, but don't let it upset you. There's one race they hate even more than the Americans, and that's the British. They haven't yet got over Waterloo." He strolled over to the door again and held it open for me with a smile. "It'll be pleasant to dine out with a fellow-foreigner, for a change."

Since he had spent most of the previous week dining out with Gina I could not see why he should consider the prospect of dining with me a change but I made no attempt to argue with him. I opened my pocketbook, checked to see if I had my keys and glanced round the apartment automatically to see that all was in order. He waited by the doorway. The light from the corridor beyond seemed to slant oddly across his face, and as I passed him I looked up for no reason and found he was watching me with a closed, impassive expression which betrayed nothing.

I moved on, my face tingling, and felt his presence behind me as we moved down the corridor to the elevator. There was a curious, awkward silence. I was just racking my brains to think of some way of breaking it when he said lightly: "So this is what Gina would look like if she wasn't underweight and over-made-up!"

He meant it, I knew, to be a compliment, but I thought the remark disloyal and unfair to Gina.

"Gina's very attractive," I said glibly, not thinking.

"I didn't say she wasn't," he said in reply, and opened the doors of the elevator as it reached our level of the shaft.

I really couldn't let the topic lapse on that dubious note so I said as we stepped into the elevator and he closed the doors after us: "I only wish I were as slim and as clever with my appearance as Gina is."

He pressed the button to the ground floor and the cage began to sink downwards. "Well, I shouldn't worry about it too much if I were you," he said. "You really don't need to."

I had taken him too seriously. My face began to tingle again and I turned aside to hide my embarrassment. Fortunately before any further conversation was necessary we reached the lobby and went outside into the wet street. He hailed a cab, and as I scrambled into the car I heard him say in perfect French to the driver: "*Le Cicéro, S'il vous plaît.*"

"Have you been to Paris before?" he asked neutrally, as the cab shot off over the cobbles.

"No," I said. "This is my first visit to Europe." A thought occurred to me. "Have you been to America?"

"I've been to New York," he said, "but I'm told that that's no more America than London is England."

"Did you like it?"

"Well, yes," he said frankly. "As a matter of fact, I did. One is supposed to shudder, I know, and say it was terrible, but I rather enjoyed it. I took a fancy to the Pan Am Building."

"That's near where I live!" I told him how I could see the building from the window of my apartment.

"You have one of those large modern apartments with every imaginable convenience?" he hazarded.

"Well, it's not considered modern," I said, "since it's at least ten years old, but I suppose it might seem large to anyone who had previously lived in a cell. And the conveniences, though numerous, are imaginary, not imaginable. But it has a good view and it suits me and it's home, so I shouldn't complain."

He laughed. "It sounds like my apartment here in Paris!"

"But you have a bigger one in London?"

"Slightly bigger. But I don't like living in flats. My favorite place is a cottage I own in the country, in a village called Holmbury St. Mary in Surrey."

"You mean English villages really do have names like Holmbury St. Mary!"

He was amused. "That's a very modest example of a typical English village name! They come in much more exotic forms than that. My favorite name belongs to a village in the West Country called—if you can believe it—Compton Pauncefoot . . . hey, this driver's taking a very direct but unscenic route! We can do better than this." He leaned forward and began to speak in French. I caught the names *"Champs Elysées"* and *"Place de la Concorde"* and *"La Madeleine"*. The driver nodded wisely and turned the car into a sidestreet. "Since this is your first night out in Paris," said Garth Cooper, "you should be allowed at least a passing glance at a few landmarks."

And as he spoke the car swung into the Avenue Victor Hugo, and at the end of the wide boulevard I could see the floodlit splendor of L'Étoile and the Arc de Triomphe. Traffic roared past us, roared around us, roared behind us. Everyone seemed to be driving with a most reckless audacity. "Is traffic in Paris always like this?" I said doubtfully, remembering the stately pace of the New York avenues with the countless intervals of traffic lights and intersections.

"Always," came the wry reply.

We reached the Arc de Triomphe, circled it and hurtled into the Champs Elysées. There were lights among the trees, crowds strolling on the sidewalks and far away, at the end of the seemingly endless boulevard, more lights, a glimpse of greater brilliance to come.

I sighed.

"It's nice, isn't it?" said the man beside me. "I never get tired of it."

"Nice!" I said reproachfully, my eyes drinking in everything I could see and still thirsting for more. "What an understatement!"

"Where I come from everything is an understatement," he said. "It's good to hear someone who's not afraid to sound enthusiastic."

We traversed a smaller version of L'Etoile and went on down the Champs Elysées. There were buildings on either side of us now, enormous restaurant-cafés with tables on the pavement, hordes of people.

"Paris comes alive at night. When we come back this way later on there'll still be crowds everywhere."

"Is London like this too?"

"No, Londoners enjoy themselves secretively indoors in private clubs. Or else they cram themselves into a smoky little pub and see how much beer they can drink before closing time."

"*Are* the English really so odd?"

"We have to do something to preserve the illusion that we're different from any other race."

We reached the enormous width and breadth of the Place de la Concorde; with a dexterity born of sublime confidence our taxi skipped nimbly in and out of other cars which were weaving diagonal and horizontal lines in front of us. We turned north to La Madeleine, then east along the Rue St. Honoré and into the Rue de Rivoli which led past the Louvre.

"I'd like to go there and look around," I said wistfully, remembering that I was due to leave the following morning for London, and thought: I'll come back. As soon as I find out what's happened to Gina I'll come back here.

"You're interested in art, then?"

"In an amateur sort of way."

"Music?"

"Again—in an amateur sort of way."

"That means you must be highly professional at something!"

I laughed. "I teach English literature—I suppose you could say I was professional at that!"

"How interesting. Incidentally, what do the Americans really think of Shakespeare?"

"I suppose most of them are aware that he was born at Stratford-on-Avon, not Stratford, Connecticut."

"You surprise me. During August at Stratford-on-Avon one can almost imagine one is in Stratford, Connecticut. There's such a predominance of American accents in the High Street that I naturally assumed he was somewhat of a national figure in America."

I smiled. "The people who can afford to vacation in Stratford-on-Avon are usually people who have received a reasonable education."

"Do you like Shakespeare?"

"Yes—very much."

I thought he would make some comment at this point to reveal his own tastes, but he did not. Instead he leaned forward to say something else to the driver, and as he moved the glare from a street lamp momentarily threw a harsh light across his face and emphasized the fine line of his nose and jaw.

Somewhere far away, in the furthest recesses of my body, my heart skipped a beat and then went on as if nothing had happened.

He turned to face me again with his casual charming smile. "We're almost there. I hope you didn't mind the slight detour before dinner."

"On the contrary, I enjoyed it very much," I said. My mouth felt dry. My hands were clenched in tension and I consciously had to relax each finger. "Thank you." A mute voice was saying in my dulled brain: *not that. Please not that.*

Ever since I was old enough to distinguish between boys and girls, I seemed to have an unhappy knack of falling for men who were not only totally unsuitable but also totally uninterested in me. For a long time now I thought I had outgrown it, but now I began to wonder. It seemed as if my weakness had merely been in abeyance and was now showing unmistakable signs of awaking and returning to disrupt my life.

My hands clenched themselves again. I stared unseeingly out of the window as the car drew to a halt.

Outside the taxi I found myself in a narrow street leading off a wide boulevard, and presently we were making our way into a very plush, very intimate little restaurant where waiters fluttered like black and white moths and an imposing maître d'hôtel cruised across the thick carpet to greet us.

"Bonsoir, Monsieur Cooper, bonsoir, mademoiselle . . ." He

bowed gracefully, flourished an elegant hand, summoned a minion to escort us to a secluded alcove. I forgot my fears of a moment ago; feeling immensely important and supremely élite I allowed the waiter to pull out my chair and help to seat me as carefully as if my solid frame were as delicate as the most fragile china. A menu was put into my hands; I stared dizzily at all the French names and did not know where to begin.

"Do you want to try some French snails to start with?"

"I—don't quite feel brave enough for that," I said, overcome with cowardice. "After all, this is only my first evening in Paris. Is there something still French but not quite so exotic?"

"Vichyssoise?"

"Yes, that would be lovely."

We considered the menu for several minutes and made our decisions. A waiter took our order; Garth selected a wine. Finally when there was nothing more to do except to wait for our meal to be served, we sat back in our chairs and relaxed. Or at least, he did. I was too tense, too anxious to introduce the subject of Gina yet, not knowing how to begin, and in the end it was he who spoke first.

"I hope I'm not being too dense about this," he said casually, "but I'm still not really clear as to why you decided to come here on the spur of the moment without telling Gina. You don't strike me as being a scatterbrained little girl like Candy-Anna, so I find your actions all the more striking because they're so obviously out of character. Why did you decide to come?"

I hesitated for a moment, toyed with my snow-white napkin and smoothed it over my lap very carefully before I answered: "Your partner said nothing to you?"

"My partner?" he said astonished. "Lilian Jantzen? What does she have to do with your decision to come to Paris?"

"Gina called me from the Jantzens' apartment on Saturday to urge me to come over." I decided against telling him the truth. "She sounded so carried away with Europe—so insistent that she was having such an extraordinary time—that my imagination was fired and I made this ridiculous spur of the moment decision. I knew Gina was planning to return to Paris by Monday so I thought I would surprise her by arriving Monday night—however, I did send a cable forewarning her so that my arrival wouldn't be too much of a shock. But when I got here I found she wasn't back from England and Candy-Anna had no idea where she was. That's why I called you this afternoon—I figured that as you'd been in London with her you might have some idea how I could get in touch with her."

"I'm afraid I know little more than you do." His eyes, steady, quizzical, interested, met mine. It was quite impossible to read his thoughts or guess if he were as honest as he seemed to be. "As I said to you on the phone this afternoon," he went on, "Gina was very eager to break into films—just as many successful young models are, I suppose. It so happens that my partner's husband, Eric Jantzen, who is an artist of some standing in London, has show business friends, and I thought there was a possibility that he might be able to provide Gina with some valuable contacts. I'd discussed the matter with him previously and he'd said that he'd be happy to meet her, so when we were both in London last Saturday I managed to introduce them to one another. I believe he invited her to his home for a drink that evening, so that would explain her presence in the Jantzen flat, even if it doesn't explain anything else. I can't see why on earth she put through a call to America from the flat of a more or less complete stranger. That simply doesn't make sense at all. What did she say?"

The arrival of the Vichyssoise gave me time to consider my reply. "She had been trying to persuade me for some time to take my vacation in Europe," I said carefully, after the waiter had retreated. "I think her call was more of an impulsive, reckless gesture than anything else. A sort of gay, with-it, 'fun' gesture, if you can imagine what I mean. I know that sounds peculiar, but you knew Gina a little, didn't you?" I sipped my Vichyssoise, thankful of the opportunity to avoid looking at him as I spoke. "Gina is the sort of person who's quite capable of calling New York collect from the apartment of a stranger in London just to say 'why on earth don't you come over and join me?' It's just the sort of thing she would do."

He smiled. For some reason his smile made me feel uneasy, although I had no idea why it should. It was a friendly smile, frank, open and natural. There was nothing sinister about it at all, yet the sense of uneasiness persisted. "I don't actually know Gina very well, you know," he said after a moment. "In fact, although I met her about six weeks previously, I saw little of her until I returned to Paris from London about two weeks ago. Even then I only took her out a couple of times. She was having trouble with a difficult ex-fiancé."

"Yes," I said. "She wrote and told me that she had met Warren again in Paris."

"You know him? I thought he was a nice young chap, if a little stupid. If he had had an ounce of common sense he would have realized that the last way to win Gina back was to chase after her like an infuriated terrier who enjoys a good bark. He met Gina by chance when I was with her, and although he joined us for a drink and the meeting began pleasantly enough, there was a rather unnecessary scene before he could be persuaded to retreat."

"It must have been embarrassing for you."

"Well, actually I was sorry for both of them—sorry for him because he was carefully destroying the impression he was trying to create in Gina's eyes, and sorry for Gina because I'm sorry for anyone with a difficult ex-fiancé. She was much more embarrassed than I was. I was really hardly involved—I didn't know her well enough for the scene to make any emotional impact on me."

I said lightly: "Candy-Anna spoke of you as if you were the big romance of Gina's life!"

"Candy-Anna reads too many romantic magazines." He spoke lightly too. His eyes were clear and unconcerned. "There had hardly been time for such melodrama."

Now I was certain that he was deviating a little from the truth. "She probably read some tremendous meaning into the fact that you and Gina traveled to London together," I said placidly. "She's just the sort of person who would fasten on something like that and exaggerate it out of all proportion."

He sipped his Vichyssoise, effortlessly matching my attempt to appear nonchalant and unconcerned. "Probably."

I blushed, not knowing why, only feeling obscurely that his terse comment had been a rebuff. I made a great business of

dabbing my mouth with my napkin and cast around in my
mind feverishly for some way of changing the subject.

"Didn't the Jantzens mention to you that Gina had made
the phone call from their apartment?" I said at last, remembering that my friend at Scotland Yard had contacted the Jantzens
during his routine inquiry into the situation. "Didn't they
mention it at all?"

"I haven't seen either of the Jantzens since early on Saturday," he said. "We all had lunch together with Gina. After
that I was tied up for the remainder of the weekend on personal matters and then on Sunday night I returned to Paris."

"But haven't you spoken to them—to your partner—on the
phone since then?"

"Yes," he said, "I spoke to Lilian this morning, but we never
discuss by phone anything which isn't strictly business. Too
expensive." He smiled. "We Europeans don't possess your
American passion for the long distance call!"

"I hardly regard it as one of my ruling passions," I said
dryly, remembering ruinous little bills arriving in the telephone company's discreet buff envelopes.

"Ah yes," he said, "I was forgetting. You have other, much
more interesting ruling passions. How did you first become
interested in Shakespeare?"

He was, I discovered during the course of the evening,
extremely clever at manipulating the conversation into the
precise channels which interested him. Throughout our long,
elaborate and delicious meal I found myself talking far more
than I normally did with a stranger; the wine was heady,
powerful; my tongue seemed encouraged to give voice to a
surprising amount of detail. I spoke of New England and New
York, of a new life and a new world, of my parents, my work
and my interests. We talked of the theatre, films, the written
word, the spoken word, and I found myself to my amazement
giving bold, outspoken opinions in situations where reticence
would normally have made me retreat or waver. Finally as
we sat facing each other over the black coffee and Grand
Marnier, I realized that he now knew a great deal about me
whereas I still knew absolutely nothing about him.

"Which college did you go to?" I said, knowing that the

English educational system was very different from the American but assuming he would have received some form of advanced education. "University, I mean, not college."

"I didn't go to a university," he said unperturbed. "My father went bankrupt so I was put out to work at an early age, like David Copperfield."

"Oh," I said, not knowing quite what to say. "But you graduated from high school—you obtained the usual diplomas?"

"By a fortunate chance I did, since my father thoughtfully staved off bankruptcy till I was seventeen, but it wouldn't have mattered if I'd been forced to leave school earlier. It was one of those schools where merely to attend it is supposed to open all doors later on, regardless of academic merit. I say 'supposed to' because things are changing and now one is expected to learn something while attending school—a revolutionary idea, if ever there was one! My father would have been shocked."

"Is he dead?"

"Yes—perhaps fortunately for him. The world where he belonged died with the second world war. Afterwards in the late forties and early fifties there were too many changes for him." He spoke simply, with pity but without regret. "My mother died soon afterwards. I have a sister in New Zealand and three spinster aunts in Norfolk, but apart from them I'm as devoid of relations as you are. . . . I've never made up my mind whether that's a situation which calls for relief or regret. I suppose one is less restricted without relations, but—"

"—More lonely," I said. I was wondering how he had managed to make his money since he had clearly inherited nothing from his father. "When did you meet your partner? Have you known her a long time?"

"Yes, I met Lilian ten years ago when I was working in the china and glass department of a London store. I was a salesman and she was one of my best customers. One day, about six months after we first met, she asked me if I would like to try selling for her instead of for the department store. She was interested in the possibility of importing French china and glass and selling it in London—she knew people in the business, she'd worked in it herself, she thought she could create a market in certain glass which hadn't been imported since before the war. . . . Well, to cut a long story short, she had the money and the flair and she knew what she was doing. All I did was to sell a saleable product. Before we knew where we were, we found ourselves joint partners in a small but flourishing export-import business between England and France."

"I see." I could not quite believe he had ever been a mere salesman. He was so totally removed from my conventional picture of what a salesman should be like. "But do you—did you enjoy selling?"

"I enjoyed dealing with china and glass. Especially glass. Glass can be so beautiful, so exquisite. I always thought of selling as being nothing more than telling people who could afford to buy that they couldn't possibly spend their money in a more aesthetically pleasing manner. Do you know anything about glass?"

"Nothing at all."

He began to talk about it, interrupting himself only to order more coffee and liqueurs. Time, meaningless and unimportant, floated hazily away.

"Of course Lilian knows more than I do," he said at last after speaking with the authority and enthusiasm of an expert for some time. "She's taught me all I know." The phrase somehow struck a discordant note; he made an amused, impatient gesture with his hand as if to brush any possible *double-entendre* aside, and added frankly: "She's a remarkable woman."

"Yes," I said. "She must be. But what about her husband? Doesn't he have any part in the business at all?"

"Good God, no—Lilian wouldn't have that! Anyway, Eric's an artist, with a career of his own—the last thing he would want is to be involved in an office routine."

"I see."

"Of course, it was somewhat tricky when Lilian and I began our venture together. Eric was a little suspicious, I think, but he had no need at all to worry. I'm not interested, from the romantic point of view, in a woman ten years older than myself, and Lilian simply isn't interested in the romantic point of view. She's in love with her china and her glass."

I wondered why he felt it necessary to point this out to me; it was as if he were being automatically defensive on a subject which had caused him great difficulty in the past. I said impulsively, my mind veering back to Gina: "Do you think either of the Jantzens would know where Gina is? I'm really very worried about her."

He looked surprised. "Really? Why's that? I should think she enjoyed London so much over the weekend that she decided to stay on for a few days. After all she's a free lance model and can do as she pleases. And if Eric offered to introduce her to some show business contacts it's obvious she would stay on until she met them."

I nodded. Since I had misled him about Gina's hysterical phone call to me, I could not expect him to understand my anxiety.

"Have you contacted the agency she works for? Maybe they've heard from her."

"Candy-Anna spoke to them today but they've heard nothing. In fact, they were very annoyed because she hadn't reported for work today. They had a special job lined up for her."

"Hm." He was silent. "I'll ask the Jantzens tomorrow if they know what's happened to her."

I nearly told him that I had resolved to go to London myself, but then held back at the last moment. It would be foolish to trust him too much. I had only his word that he had not seen Gina since Saturday afternoon, and I had already had the suspicion that he was minimizing the importance of his association with her. I felt depressed suddenly, tired; the glow of the wine had dulled and the sparkle of the evening seemed to have effervesced into nothingness. And then all at once his hand slid across the table to cover my own in a gesture I would never have expected from him, and his voice, concerned yet still casual, said quietly: "You really shouldn't worry, you know. I'm sure she's quite all right." I felt the tears blur my eyes and the sudden tightness hurt my throat because I knew that he was trying to be kind.

"Some more coffee?"

"No," I said, making an effort and overcoming my distress. "No, thank you. I feel completely satiated! It was the most wonderful meal and I enjoyed it very much."

"Would you like to go on somewhere else for a few more drinks?"

"No—no, really, I couldn't, thank you very much." The depression about Gina was enveloping me again and I had a sudden absurd fear of bursting into tears in front of him and telling him more than I should about my predicament.

He glanced at his watch. "Well, the night's still young," he said lightly. "It's not even midnight yet. Would you like to drive into Montmartre and go up to Sacré-Coeur to see the city lights? Or would you like to stroll down the Champs Elysées for a little way? Or are you too tired and want to go back to the apartment?"

I nearly said: "Yes, perhaps if you'll excuse me . . ." but I did not. I looked up into his face and suddenly I forgot about my depression and my dread of losing my self-control. It didn't matter any more. Nothing mattered except that I was with him and that we were in Paris. I wanted to remember the evening as long as I lived and not mar a future memory by ending the evening too abruptly.

I said spontaneously: "Oh, I'd love to sit in one of those open sidewalk cafés on the Champs Elysées and watch the world go by!" and he laughed and said: "Why not? That's a splendid suggestion!" He paid the bill, leaving the notes carelessly on the check and not pausing to wait for change, and we left amidst the bows of the waiters and the good wishes of the Maître d'Hôtel. Outside it was warm and the night sky glowed in a reflection of a million lights and the cobbles of the street nibbled at my high-heeled shoes.

The next three hours are hazy in my memory, not because I was too tired to remember them but because they passed so quickly that afterwards my memory was only able to recall assorted moments. I can remember the smoke of Garth's cigarette curling upwards into the night air as we sat in the café on the Champs Elysées, the flame of the match reflected in his light eyes, the shadows his hands cast on the table. I can remember hearing the roar of the traffic yards away across the wide sidewalk, the murmur of the strolling passers-by, the incessant intensity of a strange language being spoken on all sides of me, but when I try to remember now I cannot hear our own voices or recall what we said. Later we took a cab to a place in Montmartre, danced a little, drank a little more, but I have no memory of being tired or even a clear recollection of the places we visited, until finally in the early hours of the morning we were on the steps of Sacré-Coeur and all Paris lay spread out before us beneath a summer moon.

"Oh!" I said, and the meaningless syllable expressed all that I felt at that moment, joy that the evening had exceeded my expectations, sadness that it was over and would almost certainly never be repeated, guilt that I could have forgotten Gina so completely when she had dominated my mind for so long. And as I sighed and went on gazing out over the city, he said casually from close at hand:

"How long do you intend to stay in Paris?"

The magic was broken. I didn't know whether he was asking the question because he wanted to see me again or because he wanted to know what I planned to do next to find Gina. I moved a little, turning slightly away from him. "I don't know," I said. "My plans are uncertain."

After a moment he said: "What's the matter?"

"Nothing!" I was startled. "Why?"

"I thought perhaps something had disturbed you."

"No. I was only wishing that there could be more evenings as enjoyable as this one."

"I see no reason why there shouldn't be."

I did not answer.

"Unfortunately I can't cancel this trip to London tomorrow, or I'd most certainly do so. I'll be in London at least five days, possibly a week. If you were planning to go to England—"

"I have no plans at the moment," I said too abruptly, and moved back towards the white ghostly walls of Sacré-Coeur. "I'll have to think about that in the morning."

"Couldn't you think about it a little now?" I could hear his quiet footsteps behind me. "I'd like to see you again, and it seems pointless that we should have to spend the next week in different cities."

"Well," I said, trying to speak lightly and only succeeding in sounding hard and unnatural, "no doubt we'll both survive somehow."

I thought he would make some quick clever reply, but he was silent. Surprised by this unexpected reaction I turned to look at him. His face was still, his mouth shadowed, his light eyes as unreadable as ever.

"I'm sorry," I said wretchedly, knowing that he was upset even though there was no indication of it in his expression. "That was a stupid thing to say. Please forgive me."

He smiled at once, "It was no more than I deserved," he said pleasantly. "It was no business of mine to tell you how to spend your holiday. I'm the one who should apologize."

"No, I—"

"Ah, to hell with apologies and everything else!" he exclaimed in a sudden uncharacteristic burst of impatience, and the next moment without any warning at all I felt his arms slip around my waist and his lips, cool and hard, against my own. "And I'm sorry for that too," he said as he released me a second later, "if you think it requires an apology. Since we're on the subject of apologies it seems appropriate that I should conduct all my apologizing at once. . . . Are you cold?"

"A little," I said, seizing on any excuse which would explain why the color had drained from my face and my body was trembling, "but not much."

"Let's go back into the square and find a taxi."

Twenty minutes later the cab was drawing up outside Gina's apartment house and Garth was telling the driver to wait. He escorted me to the front door, but when I started to thank him for the evening he took out his wallet and extracted a card.

"I enjoyed it as much as you did. Look here's my address and number—if you change your mind about coming to London call me as soon as you arrive and I'll come to meet you. And if you stay on in Paris, I'll call you as soon as I get the chance to fly back here from London."

The card felt smooth and cool beneath my hot fingers as I

stared dizzily down at the address and phone number. I tried to say "thank you" again, but I could not speak.

"Good night, then, Claire."

"Good night, Garth."

He kissed me again very briefly and was gone. I went into the building, shut the door, leaned against it. I heard the elevator arrive at the floor, the doors opening and closing around me, the ascent to my floor, and then I stood unmoving in the darkness of the apartment, as I recalled all that had been left unsaid between us. At last, after a long time, I reached out and switched on the light.

I saw the note almost at once. It was propped against the telephone and Candy-Anna had printed on it the words: CALL WARREN MAYNE WHEN YOU GET IN. URGENT.

I gave a small exclamation. Delving into my purse I found the right scrap of paper and began to dial the numbers with an uncertain, trembling hand.

"My God, Claire," said Warren plaintively. "It's nearly three o'clock in the morning! What's the big idea of calling up at this hour? I'm not a night owl."

I instantly felt guilty at my thoughtlessness. I had lost all track of time and had never even glanced at my watch. "I'm terribly sorry," I said, stricken. "But I've just got in and I saw Candy-Anna's note to say that I was to call at once as you had an urgent message—"

"For Pete's sake, doesn't that featherbrain ever get a message right? No, I've been calling you to find out whether you'd decided to go to England tomorrow. If you remember—" he paused reproachfully "—you said you'd call me this afternoon at the office to let me know one way or the other."

"Oh, my goodness, I quite forgot!" I was stricken anew by my carelessness.

"Yes," said Warren politely. "Am I to take it that you've decided against going?"

"Well . . . no," I said confused. "I decided I would go. I've got a reservation on an Air France flight tomorrow morning. I—I'm so sorry, Warren—I should have let you know—"

He sighed. "I'll call Air France first thing tomorrow morning to see if they have a spare seat—what's your flight number? No, on second thought, it doesn't matter—I'll never be able to get the morning flight. I couldn't leave my office at such short notice. Tell you what I'll do—I'll try and get on an evening flight tomorrow. Which hotel did you plan on checking in to?"

"I haven't the remotest idea," I said weakly, realizing that Warren's companionship in London was now the last thing I wanted but not knowing how to deflect him from his inexorable course.

"Go to the Regent Palace. Or the Strand Palace. They're very good, very central, inexpensive and they cater to Americans, so you'll feel at home." And before I could even begin to explain to him that I would rather be in an English hotel among English people he added: "I'll try the Regent Palace first and if I find you haven't checked in there I'll try the Strand Palace. If you're not at either I'll meet you in the lobby of the Regent Palace at nine on Thursday morning."

"Yes," I agreed meekly, too exhausted to argue.

"Incidentally where the hell were you this evening? I called and called and finally at midnight I got hold of Candy-Anna. I was beginning to think you'd disappeared too. I was getting worried."

There was something vaguely touching about his earnest concern for me.

"I was just out seeing Paris," I said.

"Not alone!" He sounded shocked.

"Of course not," I said dryly. "Well, Warren, I apologize for not calling you back as we'd arranged—"

"But—" he interrupted and then remembered his manners. I could feel his curiosity permeating the wire which linked us, but he had neither the courage nor the effrontery to ask me outright who my escort had been.

"Yes?" I said mildly.

"Nothing. I'll see you tomorrow night, then. Okay?"

"Yes—many thanks, Warren."

"You're welcome," he said classically. "So long now, Claire."

"'Bye."

I replaced the receiver with a sigh of relief and went to bed as quickly as possible. My last thought before I slid into unconsciousness was to wonder what Warren would have said if he had known I had spent the evening with Garth Cooper.

My flight left at ten, but I saw him as soon as I entered the departure lounge. He was standing by the window and reading 'Le Figaro'. The morning sun slanted across the fine bones of his face, and I saw that his expression was still and withdrawn with the effort of concentration. I stopped dead. I was just wondering why on earth it had never occurred to me that we would be on the same flight, when he looked up from the paper as if he knew he was being watched, and our eyes met. I saw him raise his eyebrows in quizzical astonishment, and as I blushed in confusion he smiled his easy charming smile, tossed his newspaper aside as if it no longer had any significance for him, and came casually across the room towards me.

# FIVE

"So you decided to come to London after all!" The last traces of his astonishment had merged into an expression of satisfaction. "I was hoping you'd come. When did you make up your mind?"

"Oh . . . not long ago," I said uncertainly, and felt myself begin to blush at the evasiveness of my answer.

"Did you have any trouble making your reservation?"

"No."

Fortunately at that moment our flight was called and his attention was diverted from me. We filtered out of the departure lounge, and five minutes later were seated in the plane and waiting for the moment when it would taxi away towards the runway for takeoff.

"You're a rather unpredictable person, aren't you?" murmured Garth mildly. "I thought you had quite decided to stay in Paris."

I smiled uncomfortably. "I had second thoughts."

"Really? Or had you planned to come to London all along?"

"I don't know why you should think that."

"It's not important." He smiled at me. "The point is that you're here. Do you like flying?"

"Sometimes I hate it a little less than others."

"This should be a good flight—we've got perfect weather for it."

I tried to look enthusiastic, but I suppose I was not very successful.

He laughed. "Wait and see!"

As it happened he was right and the flight was perfect, so

perfect that I even forgot to feel nervous at the thought of so many thousands of feet of nothingness between me and the ground. We took off smoothly, soaring effortlessly away from Paris towards the west, and the sun shone with a dazzling brightness on the distant land below.

The stewardess was at Garth's elbow. "Something to drink, monsieur?"

"Yes," said Garth, and to me: "This should be a celebration to mark your first visit to England. How about some champagne?"

"Oh!" I said, flabbergasted at the idea of champagne before noon, and thought fleetingly how shocked my parents would have been at anything like this. "Well, it would be nice," I said guiltily. "Delightful, in fact."

Garth turned to the stewardess. "Champagne for two, please."

The plane soared on, and suddenly I could look out of the window and see the coast, the flicker of white as the waves broke against the rugged cliffs of the French coast far below. I was just giving an exclamation of pleasure when the champagne arrived.

"Drink up," said Garth. "We're nearly there."

"But we haven't even crossed the Channel yet!"

"That'll only take five minutes."

It seemed to take even less than that. We had no sooner left the French coast behind when I saw the coast of England approaching.

"Where are the White Cliffs?"

"We're further north than that, I think."

We left the Channel behind. There was a river below us, an enormous estuary. Little patchwork squares of fields surrounded each of the towns we passed, until gradually the area became densely populated and I guessed we were approaching London.

"You see that winding river over there?"

I nodded. "Is that—"

"The Thames. It looks as if we're going to fly over central London."

And then came the most perfect part of all. The plane took

a westward course parallel to the line of the river and I saw
Tower Bridge, the Tower of London, the dome of St. Paul's,
the spires of a thousand churches, the Houses of Parliament,
Westminster Abbey. . . .

"Exactly like the photographs," I said amazed, as if I had
always secretly suspected the camera of lying.

There seemed to be an endless number of bridges over the
river, some plain solid structures, some elaborately gothic and
fanciful. I gazed down at them all with fascination and hardly
even noticed the plane losing height as we flew on over the
west London suburbs towards the airport. When our wheels
touched the ground ten minutes later I was conscious, for the
first time after a flight, of regret that the journey was over.

"That was wonderful!" I said frankly to Garth as we un-
fastened our safety belts. "If all flights were like that I'd look
forward to them more often. And thank you so much for the
champagne."

We had the usual tedious wait at Customs and Immigration,
except that he, with his British passport, was processed
through the official machine more quickly than I was.

"Where do I get a bus to the terminal?" I asked, confused
by the airport mêlée and looking around for an information
sign.

"You don't want to bother with a bus," said Garth. "I never
do. We'll take a taxi. Incidentally, where were you planning
to stay?"

"Warren Mayne suggested the Regent Palace. Or the
Strand Palace. Do you know them?"

"Yes," he said non-committally. "They're both very central.
The Regent Palace is just off Piccadilly Circus."

"That sounds fine."

We found a cab and set off east again. The road was wide
and modern, the countryside around the airport extraordinarily green and lush to my eyes, but presently the countryside ended and the suburbs began. As we approached the city
there were more towering modern buildings and a massive
elevated road which reminded me of the Pulaski Skyway outside New York City.

"It's not how I imagined London to be," I said doubtfully. "Everything's so modern."

"Did you expect the roads to be full of horse-drawn carriages?"

I laughed, glanced around me at the traffic. "So many tiny cars," I said, "and all driving along on the wrong side of the road. There are hardly any big cars at all."

"There's no room for them."

We drew nearer to Central London. There was a wide main street called Cromwell Road bordered with trees and stately houses.

"Are those houses old?"

"No, fairly new. I don't suppose any of them are more than a hundred years old."

London flashed on past the windows of the taxi. Garth was mentioning English names to me, names familiar yet strange. "This is Kensington . . . Knightsbridge. . . . The park on the left is Hyde Park . . . this is Hyde Park Corner . . . Piccadilly . . . Green Park on the right. . . ."

"So many parks," I said astonished. "And how gracious the houses are here."

We reached the tiny Piccadilly Circus and almost at the same time the Hotel Regent Palace. Garth helped the driver with my luggage.

"How about dinner this evening? I can call for you at about six-thirty and we can go somewhere for a drink first . . . and I'll talk to the Jantzens about Gina. All right?"

"Yes . . . thank you. . . ." I was dazed, overcome by the strangeness of the new country.

"You have my office number if you should want to contact me, haven't you? Till tonight, then." He touched my shoulder lightly but did not kiss me. "Au revoir."

"Goodbye—and thank you."

He got into the cab again. I heard him say abruptly to the driver: "Sixty-two Half Moon Street," and he turned and raised his hand briefly to me as the car drew away from the pavement.

I stood watching the car turn towards Piccadilly Circus,

and then, still feeling dazed, I left the street and went very slowly into the hotel.

Fortunately they had a room available on the fifth floor, and after I had unpacked my luggage and redone my makeup I sat down on the bed and placed a call to the apartment in Paris. I had the nagging suspicion that as soon as I had left Paris Gina had returned to it, but my suspicions proved groundless, for no one answered the phone. Candy-Anna was evidently out working and there was no one else there. Having satisfied myself that Gina was still missing I wondered whether to call Scotland Yard again. I remembered that I had phoned from Paris and asked my friend to call me back, but he had probably returned the call while I had been out with Garth the previous evening. I hesitated. Perhaps I should wait till Garth had talked to the Jantzens. I had little enough information to give to Scotland Yard at present, beyond the fact that she had not after all been with Garth when she had phoned me the previous Saturday. But whose word did I have for that? Only Garth's. If I called Scotland Yard again they would begin questioning Garth, prying into his movements. . . .

I would wait, I thought. I would wait until he had talked to the Jantzens. I instinctively shied away from making a move which would involve him in considerable embarrassment and perhaps estrange him from me. Besides, I believed him. I was quite convinced that he was speaking the truth.

Or was I?

I went restlessly over to the window and stared out over Soho. I was still thinking of Garth a moment later when the phone rang and I went back to the bedside to answer it.

"Miss Claire Sullivan?" said the operator in the building. "One moment, please. I have a call from Paris."

For one long moment my heart thudded in relief, and then the next instant I was listening not to Gina, as I had hoped, but to Warren Mayne.

"Claire? Hi, I thought I'd just call and find out if you arrived safely and managed to check in all right. How was the flight?"

"Fine, thanks." It was thoughtful of him to have phoned and I tried to sound cheerful. "I enjoyed it."

"Good. Look, I managed to get a seat on the flight leaving at six this evening so I should be with you around eight-thirty or so."

"I—"

"I checked with the reservation people at your hotel and they have a room for me for tonight. I'll give you a call when I get in."

"Yes, but—"

"Hey, I'll tell you something odd. I called up Garth Cooper's Paris office this morning to find out when he was expected back in Paris, and they told me he'd just left for London! So he was in Paris yesterday and possibly the day before as well."

"Yes."

"You mean you knew?"

"He was on my flight this morning."

"He was?" He sounded blank with astonishment.

"Yes, we traveled over together. He—"

"But how did you know him?"

"What?"

"How did you know him from Adam? How did you get talking to one another?"

"Oh . . . I met him last night, as it happens. I called him to ask about Gina and he stopped by at the apartment."

"He did?" Warren was frankly incredulous. "Why didn't you tell me, for God's sake?"

"When I last spoke to you it was three o'clock in the morning and you weren't in a receptive mood for a long story. Besides, there was no news. Garth said he hadn't seen Gina since lunch on Saturday."

Warren sounded as if he was just about to voice a very rude word indeed, but fortunately he stopped in mid-syllable.

"It might be true," I said impassively. "I'm having dinner with him tonight so I hope to find out more details from him then."

"You're having dinner?" Warren said, amazed. "With him? Tonight?"

"Yes, so I won't be in when you arrive. If I find out anything I'll call your room as soon as I get in."

"But—" He was speechless. Then: "Do you think that's wise? Hell, I don't want you disappearing too! Can't you change it to drinks at nine? Then I'll be able to join you and see that you're all right—"

I was beginning to believe Warren had been born in the wrong century. He should have been a knight rescuing damsels in distress.

"Please don't worry," I said politely. "I'm quite capable of looking after myself and I don't really believe Mr. Cooper is involved in the white slave traffic. I'll talk to you tonight, Warren—I hope you have a good flight. Thanks for calling."

I managed to get rid of him without sounding too rude, but I sensed that his faith in my level-headedness had suffered a mortal blow. I paused for a moment and felt my own faith waver. Was it possible that sanity had temporarily deserted me and that I had made an appalling mistake by trusting Garth? A shiver edged its way down my spine suddenly. Fumbling in my bag I drew out his card, picked up the receiver and asked the operator to try his office number for me.

I could hear the bell ringing at the other end of the wire. Then: "Cooper-Jantzen—good afternoon," said a girl's voice. "May I help you?"

"Good afternoon," I said. "Could you tell me the nature of your firm's business, please? I'm conducting a survey for purposes of market research."

"We deal in the importing and exporting of china and glass between England and France."

"I see. Thank you."

"Do you wish to speak to Mrs. Jantzen?"

"No, thank you. Is Mr. Cooper there?"

"No, I'm afraid Mr. Cooper's out of the country at present."

"Oh . . . I see. Thank you. Goodbye." I replaced the receiver slowly. Garth had told me the previous evening that urgent business in London prevented him from staying on in Paris, but apparently the business had not been urgent enough to necessitate him calling his office. I wished with annoyance that I had asked the girl when she expected him to return to London, and then wondered if there had been any reason on his part to return without telling his partner. Perhaps, after all, he was not as honest as I had supposed him to be.

Uneasiness, faint and nebulous, shadowed my mind for a moment. I pushed it aside, determined not to let my imagination lead me astray, and, seizing my handbag, I went briskly downstairs and stepped out of the hotel to explore Piccadilly.

I did not walk far since all the strain and exhaustion of the last few days seemed to choose that afternoon to catch up with me, and when I returned to the hotel I spent the remainder of the afternoon resting. At five I got up, bathed and changed; at six-thirty I was just putting the finishing touches to my appearance when the house phone rang. It was Garth, in the lobby. My heart began to beat a fraction quicker. With my mouth dry and my hands unsteady, I left the room a second later and went downstairs to meet him.

"How nice you look!" he said as he came forward towards me. "Not in the least tired. No one would ever have thought you'd spent the morning drinking champagne thirty thousand feet above the English Channel. Did you do anything special this afternoon?"

"No, I just spent the time recovering from the champagne above the Channel! What about you? Did you go to your office?"

"Actually, I didn't let Lilian know I was back until five o'clock this afternoon. I have to admit I wanted some sleep as much as you did so I went straight to my flat. Incidentally, talking of Lilian, I thought you might be interested in meeting both the Jantzens, so I've invited them to have drinks with us at my club before dinner. I hope that's all right with you?"

"Yes—yes, of course. I'd like to meet them. Did you ask Mrs. Jantzen about Gina when you spoke to her?"

"Yes." He opened the door for me and we walked out into the street. Then: "Why didn't you tell me you'd phoned Scotland Yard to investigate Gina's call?"

I caught my breath. I felt my cheeks slowly begin to burn as I wondered how I could have been so stupid not to have foreseen this happening.

"Lilian said they'd had a man around from the Yard as the result of Gina's phone call to you. I presume it was you who suggested that the Yard should investigate."

"Yes," I said reluctantly, too embarrassed to look at him. "It was me."

A cab drew up beside us in response to his raised arm, and as we got inside Garth gave the driver the name of his club.

"What made you think it was a matter for Scotland Yard?" Garth asked pleasantly, as we drove into the vortex of Piccadilly Circus and crowded our way through the traffic around Eros. "What made you get in touch with them?"

After a while I said: "I was worried."

"I should imagine you were," said Garth with amused irony, "if you troubled to phone Scotland Yard from New York."

I was unable to reply.

"What exactly did Gina say during the call?" he said presently. "There must have been rather more to the conversation than you implied."

"It was just that we were cut off," I said in a rush. "And when I traced the call and phoned back there was no reply. I suppose I panicked."

He looked at me oddly as if he suspected I was still keeping part of the truth from him, but made no comment.

"What did the Jantzens say?" I said clumsily, stammering a little. "Did they know anything that would explain the situation?"

"Not really. Lilian was the one who let Gina into the flat but then she had to dash out to meet some friends so she wasn't with her for more than a few minutes. Eric, whom Gina wanted to talk to about show business contacts, was delayed and apparently when he got home Gina had gone. He assumed she hadn't bothered to wait for him and thought no more of it till the police turned up later to investigate. Before they arrived he tried phoning her hotel to apologize for letting her down, but was told she had left that evening."

"Before or after she had been at the Jantzen apartment?" I asked quickly.

"I don't think he bothered to establish that. He called the hotel before the police arrived—before he knew anything was

wrong. At that stage he didn't even know Lilian had let Gina
into the apartment. When the police told him she must have
been there he assumed for some reason that I had let Gina in,
although why he should have thought that I would be with
her I can't imagine. *I* wasn't interested in hearing about his
show business contacts."

"But you have a key to the Jantzen apartment?"

"Yes, I stayed there once and had a key made. I still use it
occasionally to entertain clients. We always do, since it's so
much more spacious than mine. For that matter, Lilian has a
key to my cottage in Surrey as well, since very occasionally we
have clients up for a weekend in the country."

But I was thinking of Gina again. "Which hotel was she
staying at?"

"The Westbury, off Bond Street."

"Then if we could prove she checked out from there after
making her phone call to me it would prove that at least she
was safe after leaving the Jantzen apartment!"

"I'm sure she's safe anyway," said Garth frankly. "To be
honest I think she's gone chasing off after one of the contacts
Eric mentioned at lunch on Saturday. When he appeared to
forget about her on Saturday night I expect she lost patience
with him and decided not to wait around any longer. It would
be just like Gina to race off impulsively with the idea that she
could conquer show business single-handed."

"I thought," I said, "you didn't know Gina very well."

He smiled slightly. "You don't trust me, do you?" He
glanced out of the window. "This is Pall Mall," he said
absently. "At the end here is St. James's Palace. Then we
swing up St. James's Street into Piccadilly again."

I stared out of the window with unseeing eyes.

"You think something happened to her in the Jantzen flat?"
he asked quite suddenly.

I nodded, not looking at him.

"Did she sound frightened?"

"Yes."

"Did she scream? Gasp? Call out?"

"No . . . no, she just hung up in the middle of the call without a word of warning."

"That's odd . . . It seems to me that if, for example, a burglar had entered the flat and accosted her she would have screamed when he arrived on the scene. But if she hung up of her own accord the burglar explanation seems unlikely."

"Yes," I said unsteadily. "I guess so."

"Actually there's not much that could have happened to her. Why should the Jantzens wish her any harm? They barely knew her. There was no reason why she should have been frightened of them."

"No . . ."

"Presumably the police will already have established what time she left the Westbury, so we can get in touch with them this evening, if you like, to find out the exact details and to report that she's still missing."

"And if she checked out after she made the phone call and not before—"

"We'll know nothing happened to her at the Jantzen flat." He hesitated slightly. "You're sure," he said, "you're quite sure she hadn't had too much to drink? I hardly like to ask such a question but it's the only simple explanation I can think of."

"No, I'm sure she hadn't," I said at once. "And if that was all that was wrong, she'd be back in Paris by now."

"That's true."

We turned off Piccadilly into a complicated network of short streets.

"This is Mayfair," said Garth as we passed rows of elegant houses and a few exclusive-looking shops. "We're almost at my club."

The taxi made a right turn and drew up outside a stately townhouse with marble pillars flanking the front door.

"Here we are." He got out first and helped me to the pavement beside him before he paid the driver. As the cab drove off again we went into the house and moved through a series of lobbies, past a magnificent staircase with wrought iron banisters, and eventually into a small intimate bar which faced onto a patio.

"They don't seem to be here yet," said Garth, glancing around at the occupants of the room. "Shall we sit outside or will it be too cool for you?"

"No, I'd prefer to be outside."

He escorted me to a table shaded with a multicolored umbrella and as we sat down a waiter came over to take our order.

"A Tom Collins?" I said doubtfully.

The waiter gave a supercilious smile.

"Try a gin and tonic," said Garth, and as I acquiesced gratefully he added to the waiter: "And a dry martini, please."

As the waiter disappeared into the bar a man and a woman passed him on their way out to the patio. Garth saw them a second after I did, and raised his hand in greeting.

"We couldn't find you!" the woman called. "What are you doing hiding under that ridiculous umbrella?"

"Didn't you read in the paper that it's been the hottest July afternoon for thirty years?"

They laughed, and as they came over towards us I was conscious of a stab of surprise, for they were not as I had expected them to be. I think I had anticipated a sophisticated, polished couple, the wife glamorously efficient, the husband glamorously artistic. But there was little glamor. Lilian Jantzen was plump and blonde and plainly but not outstandingly well dressed; she wore a navy blue linen suit with conventional but unflattering white accessories. She reminded me of a housewife who, having received an unexpected invitation out, snatched the first available outfit from her wardrobe and dressed absent-mindedly while planning the next day's shopping list. The result was passable but lacking in impact. Eric Jantzen was also fair and plump, and had a jovial smile which instantly reminded me of the more obvious breed of American salesman. I reflected with amusement how ironic it was that Garth, who at least looked as if he *could* have artistic talent, was the salesman while Jantzen, who looked like a salesman, was in fact the artist.

Garth introduced us. There was much smiling and shaking hands and then we all sat down again. The waiter returned with our drinks and took the Jantzens' order; I noticed that it was Lilian Jantzen, not Eric, who did the ordering, and that she ordered without consulting her husband.

"How nice," said Lilian absently, glancing around the patio. "This place has improved, Garth." She began to peel off her gloves. "Well, welcome to England, Miss Sullivan! I'm sorry to hear that you've had all this worry about your sister."

"We were both sorry," said her husband. He made it sound like a correction. "Both of us. We don't understand what could have happened. We thought—"

"Have you spoken to Scotland Yard again?" said Lilian to me without waiting for him to finish. "Have they any more news?"

"No," I said. "I thought I would check with them later."

"I'm quite sure nothing serious can have happened to her," she said reassuringly. "She struck me as being a very capable sort of girl who knew exactly where she was going."

"Yes," I said doubtfully, not certain whether I could recognize Gina from this description. "I mean, do you think so?"

"Oh yes!" She was placid, confident. She smiled at me warmly and her eyes lost their vague, abstracted expression, as if she were perpetually thinking of something else more important, and mellowed to a softer, kinder shade of blue. It occurred to me that twenty years ago she would have been a pretty woman. "Gina was alert—intelligent—ambitious. How can one be a successful model otherwise? I personally think she must have flown off to Rome to meet Dino di Lasci, that film producer Eric knows. Eric mentioned him to her at lunch last Saturday and Gina probably got it into her head then and there to go to Rome as soon as possible."

"Then why did she go to your apartment at all on Saturday evening?" I said hesitantly. "If there was no need for her to go—"

"Eric was going to discuss the situation with her in detail, but unfortunately he got delayed and I suppose she lost patience and left. She would still have been in time to catch the night flight to Rome, I should imagine."

Garth said, toying idly with the stem of his glass: "But why the long distance phone call, Lilian? Why call America?"

Eric Jantzen shrugged. "She was young and excited—why not?" I noticed for the first time that he spoke with a faint foreign accent which I could not identify. "She wanted her sister to come to Europe to share in the good times she was having."

"My dear Eric," said Garth, "Claire didn't call in Scotland Yard because Gina was bubbling over with *joie de vivre*."

Jantzen succeeded in looking perplexed. His round, rather comical face puckered between the eyebrows. "Perhaps a burglar tried to break and enter—she became frightened—"

"A burglar?" Garth interrupted. "Don't you mean a kidnapper? It seems that the only item which is missing since the phone call is Gina herself."

"You're full of destructive criticism, Garth," said Lilian lightly, but she did not sound annoyed. She looked at him with those mild warm blue eyes and smiled a mild warm smile, but he did not see her. He was still fingering the stem of his glass and watching the liquid nudge the sliver of lemon peel towards the rim.

"Cigarette, Miss Sullivan?" said Eric Jantzen to me suddenly.

"I don't smoke, thank you."

"Lilian?"

"No, thank you, dear." She gave an identical smile but spoke more absent-mindedly as if to reproach him for distracting her. She glanced back at Garth: "Have you any constructive suggestions instead of destructive criticisms?"

"None that I can really believe in." He accepted a cigarette from Eric Jantzen and fumbled in his pocket for a light.

"Ah, that's just it!" said Jantzen, laughing jovially as if Garth had made a witty remark. "One resorts to the preposterous—visitors from space, perhaps. Or ghosts. Or—"

"Please, dear." Lilian's voice was so extraordinarily placid that I had to look at her to see how annoyed she was. "It's hardly a joking matter."

Jantzen subsided like a pricked balloon.

The waiter chose that moment to arrive with their drinks and presently we had drunk a perfunctory toast and were sipping sociably at our glasses.

"She didn't give you any hint of what she might be planning, I suppose, Garth?" said Eric Jantzen presently as if eager to prove he could discuss the situation with complete seriousness. "She didn't confide in you?"

Lilian was unimpressed. She was just turning to me and opening her mouth to make some remark when Garth said: "Should she have done?"

"I thought you and she were—" He stopped, glanced sunnily around the table and then began to look dismayed as he realized the observation was going to be hard to finish. "She seemed to—admire you?" he suggested tentatively. "Hadn't you been seeing her in Paris? I thought—"

"Really, dear," said Lilian, "there's no need to make Bohemian observations to remind us you're an artist." She stifled a yawn. "It was perfectly obvious that Gina was in love with her career, not Garth."

Jantzen's silence was a more eloquent denial than any words would have been. There was a pause. Then:

"I rather agree with you, Lilian," said Garth idly, "but I suppose we did get on well together on the few occasions when we met. She was bright and amusing and entertaining in her own way." His eyes met mine across the table; the wink he gave me was so quick that afterwards I almost wondered if I had imagined it. "But I prefer a different kind of entertainment."

The muted loudspeaker system which the club used for announcements murmured in the rooms around us and we all started slightly as we heard Garth's name.

"Telephone call for Mr. Garth Cooper . . . Mr. Garth Cooper . . . telephone."

Lilian shed her abstractedness as if it were a redundant article of clothing and was instantly on the alert. "A business call, do you suppose? But no one knows you're back!"

"I phoned Briggs and Douglas from my flat this afternoon over the Rémy contract. Excuse me, please, everyone." He stood up and disappeared quickly indoors just as I remembered that he had told me earlier how he had spent the afternoon sleeping and had not even phoned Lilian until five to announce his arrival.

The Jantzens were looking at one another. Presently Eric Jantzen said speculatively: "Thérèse, perhaps?"

"Probably."

They were silent. About five seconds drifted away, floating upwards into nothingness with the steadiness of the smoke from Eric's cigarette. Then:

"Who is Thérèse?" I said hesitantly at last.

"Thérèse?" said Lilian, vaguely surprised. "He didn't tell you? She is—was—his fiancée. Such a tiresome woman! I was so glad when he finally extricated himself from the engagement a month ago."

# SIX

For a moment I forgot my surroundings, forgot the patio with the gay umbrellas, forgot the Jantzens who were so pleasantly relaxed yet so subtly on edge with each other. I was back in Paris again, talking to Garth of Warren and Gina, and Garth was saying: "I always feel sorry for anyone with a difficult ex-fiancé." Possibilities and answers began to flash confusingly through my mind; if Gina had somehow met Thérèse, if Thérèse had thrown a scene or threatened trouble, it was conceivable that Gina might have become distraught and run away. I said quickly, not even waiting to allow the ideas to crystalize into theories in my mind: "If they're no longer engaged then why is Thérèse calling him? Are they still on friendly terms?"

"My dear," said Lilian in a voice fraught with implications, "friendly is hardly the word to describe the curious attitude Thérèse had towards Garth. She still hasn't accepted the broken engagement and simply refuses to be reasonable—or even dignified—about the situation. She seems to think that by storming around creating passionate scenes and being fanatically jealous, he'll finally give in and agree to go through with the wedding." She made a neat, fastidious gesture of distaste. "So unnecessary! But then what can you expect of the French? With them nothing is ordinary or restrained; everything is *La Grande Passion*."

"Does she live in Paris?"

"No, she lives in London and works for the French Embassy. I must say, I'm disappointed in her behavior—even the

French could surely be expected to be more sensible about a broken love affair! Goodness me, it happens every day!"

Eric Jantzen said to his scotch on the rocks: "She was *in love* with the man."

"Heavens, dear, I hardly think *love* gives one the excuse to act in such an uncivilized manner!" She spoke with a detached incredulity as if love were a trivial illness to be dispelled by two aspirin and a ten-minute nap. "No, I was disappointed in Thérèse. She was a mature, attractive woman—very soignée. In some ways she would have been exactly right for Garth, although, mark you, I suspected from the beginning that she would be too possessive to tolerate the little light-headed flirtations he indulges in from time to time—"

There was a chill in the air suddenly. I felt cold, desolate.

"When one's engaged," said Eric Jantzen, "one is expected to flirt with one's fiancée, not with other women."

"Good gracious, dear, you talk as if Garth were an absolute Casanova! You know as well as I do that he's equally charming to every woman he meets—why, I'm certain Miss Sullivan will bear me out on that!—but he seldom really *intends* to be flirtatious. It's the women who read flirtatiousness into his attentions! And since Thérèse is pathologically jealous she would be bound to consider every small attention as a sign that he was conducting, or trying to conduct, an illicit affair."

"I don't suppose Thérèse was any more jealous than another woman would have been in the same circumstances."

"I disagree," said Lilian shortly. "She was totally unreasonable. It was a good thing they called off the engagement. If they'd married I'm sure Garth would have found her quite impossible to live with."

Eric Jantzen was eloquently silent again. Driven by a compulsion to shatter that silence, I said hurriedly: "Did Gina meet Thérèse?"

The question seemed to surprise them; they both looked at me sharply before looking at one another.

"She didn't mention it," said Lilian doubtfully. "I wouldn't have thought it was very likely. No, she couldn't have. If Thérèse met Gina with Garth there would have been a big scene and Garth would have mentioned it to us later. But he said nothing."

"I—I was thinking that if there had been some sort of scene— in your apartment—if Thérèse had found Gina there with Garth—"

"But why should Thérèse go to our apartment?" said Eric Jantzen, brow puckered again. "There was no reason why she should."

"She might have followed Garth there," said Lilian. "Garth might have arrived after I left Gina alone in the flat."

"But Garth said he wasn't there!"

"Perhaps there *was* a scene and he didn't mention it." She looked thoughtfully at her glass of sherry. "Perhaps there was an unpleasant scene, so unpleasant that he had to take Thérèse away. Then Gina, who was distraught and shocked, made the phone call. And replaced the receiver when Garth returned." She looked across at me, ignoring her husband. "Do you think that makes sense?"

"It makes better sense than any other theory I've heard so far," I said hesitantly. "But why didn't Garth mention any of this to us? And why didn't Gina call me back later to explain what had happened? And where's Gina now?"

Lilian shrugged. "Perhaps we're wrong." She glanced towards the French windows which led from the bar to the patio. "Here he comes . . . Garth, did Gina meet Thérèse last weekend?"

Garth stopped so abruptly that he might have been jerked to a halt by an unseen hand. His face became closed, remote, his expression betraying nothing.

"Do we have to talk about Thérèse, Lilian?" It was the first time I had ever heard him angry. "Is it really necessary?"

"No, dear," said Lilian vaguely in exactly the same tone of voice as she used to her husband. "Not really. I was merely being rude and inquisitive. Was that Douglas on the phone about the Rémy contract? What did he say?"

"No, it wasn't Douglas. It was a personal call from a friend of mine." He sat down quickly at the table and took several swallows of his drink before glancing at his watch. "We must be going, Claire. It's later than I thought it was."

"Oh Garth!" said Lilian, half reproachful, half annoyed. "After only one drink? I haven't even had the chance to ask Miss Sullivan about herself yet!" She smiled at me encouragingly. "You'd like another drink, wouldn't you, Miss Sullivan?"

"Well, as it happens . . ." I searched for an excuse and then decided to tell the truth. "I've had a lot to drink already today, and I'm not really accustomed to liquor, perhaps I'll just settle for the one drink this time. But don't please let me stop you from having another—"

"Maybe some other time, Lilian," said Garth. "Perhaps we can all have dinner together before Claire leaves London. Meanwhile I'm afraid you'll have to excuse us."

Lilian sighed resignedly and made a gesture of disappointment with her plump, neatly manicured hands. "As you wish."

We finished our drinks and went back indoors and through the house to the lobby.

"Well, I'm glad we had a chance to meet, Miss Sullivan," said Eric Jantzen pleasantly as we parted. "Sorry it was so brief. You must be sure and see us again before you leave."

"Thank you—yes, I should like to," I replied.

Lilian said: "How long do you intend to stay?"

"I—I'm not sure. Another few days, perhaps."

"Well, I do hope you have good news soon about your sister." She took my hand in hers and squeezed it sympathetically. "Garth, you'll let us know, won't you, if there's any news? I really feel quite concerned, especially as she apparently chose our flat to disappear from. However, I'm sure nothing serious can have happened. Perhaps Eric's right after all, and she flew off to Rome to see di Lasci." But she sounded doubtful, as if Eric was so seldom right that this possibility was most unlikely.

The doorman flagged two cabs; Garth and I got into the first, and, looking back over my shoulder, I saw the Jantzens about to get into the second. Eric Jantzen paused to wave a brief farewell in our direction.

"He seems pleasant enough," I said, raising my hand automatically in response. "But doesn't Lilian give him rather a hard time?"

"They've always been like that, ever since I've known them," said Garth. "I suppose they're both used to it by now." He turned to face me, and his nearness suddenly seemed overwhelming. "I'm sorry," he said, "for rushing you away like that. It was simply that—" He stopped.

There was a silence.

"Yes?" I said nervously.

His light eyes were hard and angry. "I wanted to be alone with you," he said abruptly. "I wanted you to hear about Thérèse from me, not from the Jantzens."

After a moment I said, "Lilian didn't mean to be indiscreet. She was just wondering if—"

"If Gina and Thérèse had ever met. I didn't answer her question, did I? Well, I'll answer it now. Yes, they did meet. They met last weekend when Gina came to London and there was the most appalling and distasteful scene you could conceivably imagine."

"Gina and I traveled from Paris to London together last Friday evening, as you know," he said as the taxi moved into Berkeley Square. "Lilian knew our arrival time, and, I suppose in the course of casual conversation, mentioned it to Eric, who for reasons best known to himself told Thérèse when she called to ask if he knew when I was returning to London. Thérèse went to the airport to meet me in her car, and found me with Gina. Naturally she thought the worst. She wanted to believe there was some other woman. It would have given her a concrete reason to explain why our engagement collapsed—she couldn't bring herself to believe that the fault was hers, not mine. Or perhaps it would be more accurate to say that she couldn't believe that the fault was ours—that we were incompatible. If she could have believed I had found someone else, she could have blamed me for everything and exonerated herself. So, you see, she wanted to believe the worst of Gina.

"I needn't trouble you with the sordid details of the scene at the airport. It's enough to say that merely to end the scene I put Gina in a taxi to her hotel and took a separate taxi to my flat. I half expected Thérèse to follow me to resume the quarrel but I was expecting too much even of Thérèse. She called me up instead. I told her the truth—that there was nothing between Gina and me, and even if there was it was certainly no longer her business—and hung up without waiting for her to finish."

We crossed New Bond Street and raced eastwards to the perimeter of Mayfair.

"And you saw Thérèse on Saturday?" I said tentatively at last. "With Gina?"

"No," he said. "Gina never saw Thérèse on Saturday and I haven't heard a word from Thérèse since then. She hasn't even called me. Perhaps she's at last beginning to see reason." He took out his cigarette case and then changed his mind and replaced it in his pocket. We reached Regent Street and crossed it into Soho. "On Saturday," he said, "before I took Gina to lunch with the Jantzens, I apologized for the scene, but Gina was very good about it and we agreed to consider it forgotten. Then we had lunch with the Jantzens and went our separate ways."

"I see."

He said wryly to me as an afterthought: "Now you can understand why I sympathized with Gina when her ex-fiancé made such a clumsy attempt to win her back in Paris last week."

"Yes—yes, of course."

"Thérèse and I had been engaged three months, but I soon realized we had made a mistake. We just weren't suited. It became extremely awkward."

I was not sure of what to say. In the end I said nothing, and as the silence lengthened he asked: "Did Lilian mention what happened?"

"About Thérèse? Yes, she said Thérèse was rather unreasonable—and a little jealous—"

"So she did tell you." He seemed more irritated than angry now; his eyes had an opaque, introspective expression. "Yes, Thérèse became convinced that there was something between Lilian and me. It was quite absurd because Lilian and I are business friends only and it's been that way ever since we first met. But Thérèse saw it differently. It so happened that after Thérèse and I became engaged Lilian and I had to be in Paris together for an exhibition and conference. It never even occurred to me that Thérèse would begin to be jealous of Lilian —of all people—but she worked herself into such a state of jealousy that she flew to Paris after us and found that we were both staying at my Paris *pied-à-terre*.

"I suppose that was rather foolish of us, since such a situation is open to misconstruction, but we had done it so often before that we thought nothing of it. I put up a folding cot in the office and Lilian had the sofa bed in the living room; it was economical and convenient, especially in the early days, when every penny counted with us. However, Thérèse immediately thought the situation could have only one possible meaning. I explained a dozen times that Lilian is a dedicated career woman and simply not interested in anything except her work, but I don't think Thérèse ever really believed me. After that things became steadily more impossible between us, until in the end I decided that there was nothing to do except call the whole thing off. Unfortunately I then discovered that Thérèse was so obviously enjoying her jealousy that she couldn't bear the idea of breaking up. It was all a little difficult."

The understatement might have made me smile in other circumstances but at that point I was too busy feeling guilty; I debated whether to tell him that he had misunderstood me and that the Jantzens had not mentioned Thérèse's suspicions of Lilian. Before I could make up my mind we arrived at the restaurant and the opportunity to speak was gone.

The restaurant was large and dignified and, despite the numbers dining, extremely quiet. After we had ordered I said impulsively: "It's very kind of you to keep taking me out to dinner like this, especially when you must have such a lot on your mind."

He looked surprised. "Do I seem to have so much on my mind?"

"Well, Thérèse—"

"She may be on the Jantzens' minds, but she's certainly not on mine." He smiled. "You're the one who has all the worries, not me, although I must confess I'm beginning to share your concern about Gina."

"I'm surprised you're not more worried about her than you are," I couldn't help saying. "I would have thought—"

"Listen," he said, interrupting, "I don't know what Gina told you in her letters but as far as I was concerned she was a delightful relief after Thérèse's melodramatics, a pleasant interlude to take away the bitterness Thérèse had left behind. I wasn't seriously interested in Gina and I'd be surprised if she was seriously interested in me."

"Why take such trouble to persuade me?"

"Because I can recognize skepticism a mile off." Our glances met for a split second of tension across the table and then he laughed carelessly, picked up his napkin and shook it out into a wide square. "And besides," he said, amused, "I'm anxious to prove to you that I'm not a mere philanderer to be regarded with extreme distrust."

My cheeks burned. "Have I given you the impression that that's what I think?"

But he refused to be serious. "Don't sound as if you have a guilty conscience!" He turned and signaled the wine waiter. Then, to me: "Will you have some wine with your roast beef?"

"No, thank you."

"No? Are you sure? Not even a glass?"

But I was adamant. The meal continued but the atmosphere was less relaxed than it had been the previous evening, and after the meal we did not linger over our coffee.

"Why don't we go to Scotland Yard?" said Garth suddenly. "I can see you're too worried about Gina to enjoy yourself. We'll go and see your friend—what was his name?—and report that she's still missing. And at the same time we can find out when she checked out of the hotel on Saturday."

Relief crept over me; I looked across at him thankfully, grateful for his understanding. "Would you mind? I'm sorry to be such bad company this evening, but—"

"Nonsense! And don't bother to apologize for anything—I can see now that I've been inconsiderate. We'll take a taxi to the Yard and get this straightened out without any more delay. Are you ready?"

I was. We left the restaurant and went out once more into the long, light, summer evening as dusk was beginning to fall.

Presently we were in a taxi sweeping along the Embankment beside the river to Big Ben, Westminster and Scotland Yard.

Afterwards I felt better, even though Detective Inspector Fowles had been unable to help much except to go over the details of Gina's disappearance and to promise that further inquiries would be made. We also found out that Gina had checked out of her hotel *after* making the phone call to New York, and that she had checked out alone, unescorted, and apparently of her own free will.

"So she was all right when she left the Jantzen apartment," I said with relief. "But then why did she make the phone call? And why did she hang up as if she was interrupted?"

But there were no answers to these questions, only theories and suppositions. After thanking Fowles we left the Yard and made our way by taxi down Whitehall back to my hotel.

"I don't understand it," I said to Garth. "I just don't understand. Can she really have gone on to Rome, as the Jantzens suggested, to meet this Italian film producer? Why didn't she call me back to say everything was all right? Unless she had a memory lapse I can't believe she'd carry on exactly as if nothing had happened."

"Well, it's in the hands of the police now," Garth said. "If they can't trace her no one can. They'll find her."

He asked me if I wanted some coffee before returning to the hotel, and partly because I was dreading the moment when I would be on my own again without him, partly because I wanted to make amends for my preoccupied behavior at dinner, I agreed. We went to the London Hilton on Park Lane and had coffee on the second floor in the large, spacious lounge. The coffee, which was served American style, was reassuring and delicious. I began to feel better.

"I can't thank you enough for coming with me to the police tonight," I said to Garth. "I was dreading that visit but it all went off very well. I feel much happier now."

He smiled, shrugged his help away as if it were nothing. We began to talk of other things, and soon the time slipped away again until it was after midnight. I think he realized before I did that I was tired; we left the Hilton, found a cab and were driven off around the edge of Hyde Park Corner into Piccadilly just as my eyelids began to feel heavy and my head was starting to ache from weariness.

But I was happy.

He smiled at me in the darkness. "One day," he said, "when that tiresome girl Gina has stopped appearing and disappearing like the Cheshire Cat, you and I are going to go out again in London and have an evening like the one we had last night in Paris."

Everything blurred, tilted, melted into darkness as I closed my eyes. I could feel the material of his jacket straining across his back as he tightened his grip on me; his cheek grazed my own, his mouth was hard, the kiss smoothly painful in its intensity. I pushed him away dizzily, overcome by emotions which I could not even begin to cope with, but he was already relaxing his grip and withdrawing of his own accord.

We were silent. There was nothing to say. It was not as if this had been yet another casual kiss in the moonlight on the steps of the Sacré-Coeur. Now we were no longer casual. I felt committed, involved. Defensive barriers had become impotent, useless structures, shells behind which it was impossible to shelter any longer. There were no barriers any more and yet we were still apart, separate from one another, he with his thoughts, I with mine. And my thoughts said to me: Is he really honest? Is he really telling the truth? And instinct, untrammeled by the logic of the defensive barriers, in spite of everything persistently told me he was not.

I looked at him. His face was shadowed, silent, remote from me.

"What are you thinking?" I said suddenly and on an impulse reached out to take his hand in mine as if I could dispel my suspicions by touching him. His fingers, long and strong, interlocked themselves with mine. His mouth smiled at me faintly but left his eyes withdrawn, their expression unreadable.

"Why," he said, "I was thinking how odd it is that we've known each other less than forty-eight hours. I feel as if I've known you a very long time."

The taxi halted outside the hotel and he got out to escort

me into the lobby. "I'll be in touch with you tomorrow," he said. "I can't manage lunch, I'm afraid, but perhaps I could see you later."

We kissed, parted; when I looked back at him I saw he was looking back at me too. And suddenly I forgot all my doubts and all my worries and remembered only that soon I would see him again.

I was awakened shrilly at eight by the ring of the telephone bell at my bedside. Half asleep I scooped off the receiver and pulled it on to the pillow beside me.

"Claire?" said Warren Mayne, sounding impossibly brisk and bright. "Hi, it's me. What's new? I tried to get you last night but didn't have any luck."

I made an enormous effort. "Maybe we could talk things over at breakfast? I can't think clearly at the moment."

"Breakfast? Sure. I'll meet you downstairs at nine."

When we met an hour later he was still bright and brisk and so obviously full of energy that I felt tired merely to look at him. "So what happened?" he demanded, starting to fire questions at me as we sat down to breakfast and I glanced at the menu. "Did you get anything more out of Cooper? Is there any other news?"

Over orange juice, cereal, toast and marmalade I told him about the Jantzens, my visit to Scotland Yard with Garth, and the news that Gina was alive and well after leaving the Jantzen apartment last Saturday. I also mentioned the Jantzens' suggestion that she might have flown to Rome to see an Italian film producer.

"Well, we can check that easily enough," said Warren at once. "What's his name?"

"Dino di Lasci."

"We'll call him up and ask him if he's seen Gina."

His energy must have rubbed off on me; by the time we left the dining room I had recovered myself and was willing to share his determination to follow every possible lead. We spent the next hour in his room while he put through a call to Italy and finally succeeded in speaking to di Lasci's secretary.

She said she had never heard of a Miss Gina Sullivan, an American model from Paris.

"Could you check with your boss?"

She apparently gave an unsatisfactory reply.

"It's serious," said Warren. "This is the CIA. We have reason
to believe Miss Sullivan was murdered."

I was disturbed by this gross distortion but Warren never
turned a hair. "She's going to ask di Lasci right now," he said,
pleased, to me. "I *thought* that would get results."

But it was all for nothing. Di Lasci came on the wire and
said he had neither heard of nor seen Gina and that he was
unable to help us.

Warren then called London airport and checked the flight
lists to Rome the previous Saturday evening. There was no
indication that Gina had ever made a reservation.

"I should have done that first," he said disgusted, "instead
of wasting money on a call to Rome. Still, there's no harm in
being thorough, I guess. Who shall we call up now? Who
should we talk to? I'd like to speak to the Jantzens, but maybe
I wouldn't learn any more from them than you learned yesterday."

"Probably not."

He thought for a moment. Then, suddenly: "You know who
I'd like to talk to? Cooper's ex-fiancée Thérèse. It strikes me
she's the only possibility we've got to explain Gina's behavior.
If Thérèse came to the Jantzen apartment and created a
scene—"

We argued about it for some time. I was extremely reluctant
to meddle with Thérèse, but I had to admit that Warren's idea
was reasonable enough.

"I can't see that it would do any harm to talk to her," War-
ren insisted. "She should be glad to meet me and find out that
I want to get Gina away from Cooper as much as she does.
You needn't come if you'd prefer not to, but—"

"Oh, I'll come with you," I said hastily. "But where does she
live? I don't even know her last name."

"Call Eric Jantzen—he was pretty friendly, wasn't he? Call
him and ask him for Thérèse's second name. Then we can find
her address in the directory."

"But what excuse am I to give?"

"Just tell him the truth—that you want to check with Thérèse to make sure she hasn't seen Gina since Gina disappeared."

Feeling nervous and ill at ease I dialed the number of the Jantzen apartment and found Eric at home. He was co-operative, appearing perfectly satisfied with my explanation. Thérèse's surname, he told me, was Mariôt. Carried away by his helpfulness he also gave me her address and phone number.

"Great," said Warren, as I replaced the receiver. "Let's go."

"Without calling her?"

"She might put us off with some excuse. Let's take a cab and go over and see her in person."

I followed reluctantly in his wake.

It was about eleven o'clock by that time. The day was gray and overcast but there was no rain and it was comfortably warm. Piccadilly Circus looked sad in the morning light, after its multicolored splendors of the previous evening, and a crowd of tourists mingled with the down-and-outs who sat on the steps beneath Eros. We found a cab, and Warren, treating the cockney driver as if he spoke a foreign language, showed him the piece of paper on which he had written Thérèse's address.

We set off westwards again, our taxi nudging its way through the heavy traffic, and within twenty minutes were in Knightsbridge. At South Kensington Underground the taxi turned down the Old Brompton Road and finally made a left turn into a gracious square flanked by large white houses.

"Thirty-seven," yelled the driver through the glass partition and halted the cab abruptly.

We got out; Warren paid him slowly as if he were translating shillings and pence into dollars each time he pulled a coin from his pocket.

"Well, come on," said Warren, as the cab drove off again. "Let's see if she's here." He mounted the steps to the front door and examined the three bells on one side of the porch. Thérèse's name was printed on the top one. Warren pressed the knob, held it in position for a second and waited.

There was no reply.

"We should have called first," I said.

Warren didn't answer. He was busy rattling the door handle, but without success. I was just about to suggest that we go away and make no further to break into the building, when a voice behind us said: "Want any 'elp, dears?"

We spun around guiltily. Facing us was an exceedingly fat woman with very false teeth which she now displayed generously in a smile. "'Oo are you wanting? If it's the French lady, she's gorn. Ain't seen 'er all week."

We were too taken aback to ask her who she was. She did not look as if she were the type of person who would live at that address but obviously she seemed well acquainted with the house.

"Is that right?" said Warren, stalling, and added clumsily: "Would you be the maid?"

"Maid!" She looked at him as if he were an anachronism from the last century. "Gawd 'strufe, no, dear. I come in and does for Mrs. Cheese in flat B three times a week and cooks the evening meal on alternate Sats." She pointed to the three doorbells. "Mrs. Cheese lives below the French lady."

I realized the language barrier had put out invisible fingers to confuse us. Warren had correctly guessed her rôle but had called it by the wrong name; this was one of the famous London charwomen, not an American maid.

"As it happens we did want to see Miss Mariôt," I said to her with a smile. "Do you know how long she'll be away?"

"Couldn't say, dear, I'm sure. 'Ere, are you American? I thought you was. I know all about America. We watch telly and see it on the films. Skyscrapers and big cars and men with guns. My ole man says it'll be like that 'ere before long."

Warren was evidently torn between correcting her innocent impression of American life and finding out more about Thérèse. As he hesitated I said: "When did you last see Miss Mariôt? I mean, was it a long time ago, or—"

"No, last Saturday." She leaned her massive figure against the railing and settled down to enjoy herself. "It was one of my alternate Sats for Mrs. Cheese so there I was getting the dinner, all 'appy as a lark and singin' under my breath, and the sun was shining (makes a change, that does!) so I flings

open the window and leans out to sniff the fresh air." She
paused meaningfully. Feeling something was required of us we
both nodded. "And suddenly, my Gawd, there she was—shouting and screaming something awful—"

"Miss Mariôt?" Warren asked.

"Course it was! 'Oo do you think I mean—my Mrs. Cheese?
Mrs. Cheese don't carry on like that. Such a carry-on it was,
I could 'ardly believe me ears. Well, there she was a-ranting
and a-raving and making a to-do and she shouts out: 'I'll ruin
you both!' she says all nasty-like, 'you and Lily both of you.'
No, I'm telling a fib. It wasn't Lily she said. It was something
else like it."

"Lilian."

"That's it! You know 'er? Lilian. Anyway, Miss Whatsit, the
French lady, went on ranting about Lilian, and then 'er fiancé,
a very nice gentleman called Mr. Cooper, said—"

"It was Mr. Cooper who was with her?"

"Course it was! I knows Mr. Cooper. Poor man, I felt sorry
for 'im all tied up with that foreigner. I used to meet 'im on
the stairs sometimes and twice 'e gives me a lift to the tube in
'is car. A very nice gentleman Mr. Cooper is . . . So where was
I? Oh yes. So there was all breathing in the fresh air, so to
speak, and all this to-do going on over my 'ead, and Mr.
Cooper says: 'Don't be a fool, Terezz,' 'e says, proper narked
'e was, and she shouts out something else and slams the door
and I 'ears 'er footsteps pounding downstairs past my Mrs.
Cheese's door and then the front door slams and she's gorn.
And I ain't seen 'er since. Nor 'as Mrs. Cheese. Mrs. Cheese
was saying to me only yesterday that she wished Miss Whatsit
had cancelled 'er order of the French newspaper while she was
away as it keeps being delivered and cluttering up the 'all
downstairs. But it's plain to see what 'appened. She broke it
off with 'er fiancé over this Lilian—whoever *she* is (and mark
you I wouldn't blame that Mr. Cooper for taking up with someone else)—and then she went away to recover. No one thinks
at times like those to cancel the morning paper. I told Mrs.
Cheese so and Mrs. Cheese agreed."

We nodded, mesmerized into agreeing with Mrs. Cheese.
I was trying to remember whether Garth had said he had not

seen Thérèse since Friday night at the airport, but as far as I could recall he had merely said that Gina had not seen Thérèse since then. He hadn't mentioned himself.

"When was this?" I said unsteadily. "Saturday?"

"Saturday, it was. That's right. About six o'clock in the evening. I was all set to peel the potatoes."

And Gina had called me at nine-thirty, London time, that same night.

"Well, thank you very much, ma'am," said Warren politely. "You've been most helpful, and we're grateful to you. I guess we'll have to get in touch with Miss Mariôt in some other way."

"Good luck to you, I'm sure," said our informant agreeably and heaved herself up the steps to the front door. "I must be on my way to Mrs. Cheese. I 'opes you enjoy the rest of your 'oliday in England."

We chorused our thanks and began to walk away along one side of the square towards the Old Brompton Road.

"Should I have tipped her?" Warren asked, worried.

"Absolutely not."

"You think so? Maybe you're right. I wouldn't have known how much to tip anyway." He sighed, ran his fingers through his hair. "Boy, what a break! We sure were lucky meeting her like that. What did you make of it all? It certainly looks as if Gina wasn't the only one to disappear that evening, doesn't it? I'm convinced that Cooper's at the bottom of all this—hell, he was involved with both women and—if we can believe the maid—with his partner as well. Looks as if he was two-timing everyone on a grand scale."

I said levelly: "I'm quite certain he isn't having an affair with Lilian."

"Why?"

"Well, for one thing because he's on good terms with Eric."

"Maybe Eric doesn't know."

"After ten years?"

We walked on for a few moments. Then: "According to Garth," I said with studied indifference, "he was trying to avoid any romance with all three women, not to involve himself with them. He had broken his engagement to Thérèse. He was apparently unconcerned by the idea of Gina flying off to

Rome to see a film producer. And there's no proof that he's ever had more than a business relationship with Lilian. He was trying to get away from Thérèse and Gina, not closer to them."

"Let's face it," said Warren ironically, "he succeeded. He got away from them so successfully that now no one can find them."

I didn't answer. I was feeling chilled, frozen with an ice cold pang of dread.

Presently Warren said: "Don't tell me you're hooked on him as well."

I still didn't answer.

"Wow!" Warren hooted. "He sure must have a way with women! I must study his technique the next time I see him."

"Oh, for God's sake, Warren!"

We reached the Old Brompton Road. "Okay," said Warren not unkindly. "You think Cooper's innocent and I think he's guilty. So what's the next step? Let's go back to the hotel and see if you have any messages from Scotland Yard."

Back at the hotel I found not a message from Scotland Yard, but a note to say that Eric Jantzen had called and could I call him back at his apartment.

I did not want to make the call with Warren breathing down my neck so I went to my room and said I would speak to him as soon as I had talked to Eric. Then, sitting on my bed, I dialed the Jantzen number and waited for Eric to answer the phone.

He sounded pleased that I had returned his call so promptly. "Have you heard any news of Gina?" he said. "Did you contact the police again?"

I told him how Garth and I had visited Scotland Yard the previous evening and he listened with interest. Then: "Look," he said. "Are you doing anything for lunch? Our flat is only a short bus ride from your hotel—could I come over and meet you?"

I managed to conceal my surprise. "Thank you very much," I said. "That would be very nice."

"Good! I'll be over in about twenty minutes, then."

I hung up and then spoke to Warren on the house phone to tell him what had happened. He was as surprised as I was but agreed that it was possible I might discover something new. We arranged that I should give him a call later, on my return, and afterwards I had a few minutes in which to relax before I went downstairs to the lobby to meet Eric Jantzen.

He was already waiting for me. "There's a good little restaurant just off the Haymarket," he said. "It's not far. Hardly worth a cab. Would you mind walking, or—"

I said I wouldn't mind so we set off. He talked fluently enough as we traversed Piccadilly Circus and turned into the Haymarket amidst the lunch hour crowds, but I had the feeling he was making an effort. After we had exhausted the subject of the weather and the traffic problem in big cities we reached the restaurant, which was small and neat and obviously inexpensive, and went inside.

By this time I had formed the impression that he did not like to spend money. It occurred to me vaguely to wonder what his financial position was. Artists were notoriously poverty-stricken. I thought of his rich, clever wife and wondered why he tolerated her thinly disguised apathy towards him.

"Where did you first meet your wife?" I inquired over the minestrone. "Was it in England?"

"Ah, so you can tell I'm not English! I shall never lose the accent, it seems. No, Lilian and I met in Switzerland. I come from Altdorf, which is the little village near Lake Lucerne where our national hero William Tell was born. I was a young struggling artist who earned a living painting pretty empty little commercial pictures of the beautiful scenery. Lilian was a sympathetic tourist."

It seemed that Lilian felt compelled to help men less fortunately placed than herself. "I see," I said tentatively, not really understanding.

"We had a lightning romance and married two weeks later in Geneva." He smiled, shrugged his shoulders. "Lilian's family didn't approve, but we didn't care." His large, sad face lit up unexpectedly. "We were young—in love. Those were happy times. I liked London and settled down quickly. Soon I was painting as I had always wanted to paint, and not painting what other people wanted. Lilian was most—" he paused for the right word "—inspiring."

And rich even then, I thought. She must have supported them both from the beginning.

"Lilian," said Eric Jantzen, "is a very wonderful, very talented woman. She believed in me. She had faith. In the end when I had my small share of success, I always said it was due to her because she gave me encouragement and help when I most needed it."

I tried to picture Lilian in the rôle of the devoted, inspiring wife, absorbed in her husband's work. The effort strained my imagination. I couldn't really see Lilian absorbed in any work except her own.

"She must know a great deal about china and glass," I said presently.

"Yes, she knows much more than Garth. Garth's a mere businessman." He dabbed his mouth delicately with his napkin and reached for his glass of water. "But he likes to think himself an authority on glass."

"Tell me, Eric," I said, looking at him with what I hoped was an honest appealing expression. "What is *your* opinion of Garth Cooper? You probably realize that I barely know him, but my sister evidently thought highly of him so I'm anxious to discover what kind of man he really is. I hesitate to ask you, but you've known him some time and you're obviously a person of mature judgement, so I know I can believe what you say."

As I had intended him to be, he was flattered although he tried to disguise his gratification. His face puckered between the eyebrows as he prepared to give his mature judgement.

"Of course," he said at last, "he's always been more Lilian's friend than mine."

I waited. Presently he added good-humoredly, as if it were all a joke: "Why, he's a salesman! And a good salesman: An excellent, successful salesman! He has a saleable product and he sells it in the cleverest possible way."

"China and glass?"

"A mere sideline!" He was still amused, still speaking lightly to mask his seriousness. "Garth's talent is in selling himself—not literally, of course! But he knows how to appeal to people, how to charm them, how to make them like him. He has

a talent for playing the rôle which the English would describe
as 'the nice chap'. But beneath the nice chap façade he's a
hard, tough, able businessman. He doesn't deceive me. He may
deceive others but he doesn't deceive me."

"He doesn't sound like the right man for Gina," I said with
a worried expression. "I hope she's not in love with him."

"She was attracted to him," said Eric. "That's undeniable.
But she was too young for Garth. I know the kind of woman
he likes." He toyed with his soup spoon as if it suddenly held
an irresistible fascination for him. "He likes mature, clever
women, not empty-headed young girls barely out of their
teens." He looked up guiltily. "I'm sorry, I don't mean to slight
your sister, who was charming, but—"

"I understand." I broke a piece off my roll and buttered it.
"You mean Garth preferred women like Thérèse."

"Precisely." He began to eat again. "I like Thérèse," he said
unexpectedly. "Lilian didn't, but then I hardly expected her to.
Thérèse was quick, intelligent and striking—a passionate, intense, exciting woman. If I painted portraits—" He broke off
with a smile. "But I don't! However, if I did, I would have
wanted to paint Thérèse."

My jealousy, ridiculous but unmistakable, made it hard for
me to listen to him saying how attractive Thérèse was. To
change the subject I said with interest: "What sort of pictures
do you paint, Eric? I'm sorry I'm so ignorant of your work—I
believe you're famous here in London."

"Hardly famous!" he said brightening, and began to talk
about himself with a shy, modest enthusiasm which, for some
reason, I found touching. It turned out that he painted abstracts
and had dabbled briefly with surrealism. I said I had seen an
exhibition of Salvador Dali's work at the Huntington Hart-
ford Museum in New York. We talked of art for a while, and
as we talked he lost his air of bogus joviality so that I caught a
glimpse of the person he must have been long ago, when he
first met Lilian—a sensitive, vulnerable young artist dedicated
to his work. I found it impossible to imagine how the prosaic,
businesslike Lilian could ever have understood him.

But perhaps she never had.

"You will tell me if you have any news of Gina, won't you?"

he repeated as we parted in the lobby of my hotel some time later. "Lilian and I are both so anxious to know where she is and if she's all right. You will phone us, won't you?"

"Of course!" I assured him, and thanked him warmly for the lunch before going up to my room. I knew I should call Warren to report on the lunch, but I felt I had had my fill of Warren that morning and when I reached my room I put off the phone call and lay down on my bed instead.

Within ten seconds my mind had fastened itself stubbornly on Garth Cooper.

He had implied the previous evening that Thérèse's suspicions of Lilian had come to a head over three months ago, at the beginning of his engagement. I strained my memory to recall his actual words but was left only with the memory of what he had implied. It occurred to me that Garth was clever at implying facts without saying anything outright. Now on reflection I was certain he had given the impression that Thérèse's jealousy of Lilian was past history, whereas according to the charwoman it was very much a present episode.

And that doesn't make sense, I thought. By last Saturday Thérèse should have been quarreling with him over Gina, not over Lilian. Gina was surely the center of his attentions by that time.

I felt depressed by the possibilities of the situation and by Garth's ambiguous behavior. Above all I began to feel depressed about Gina again, and not merely in regard to her disappearance but in regard to her relationship with Garth. I moved restlessly to the window, stared outside, turned back towards the door once more. Finally on an impulse I picked up my handbag and went downstairs to the street, in an effort to dispel the agony of passive waiting by a burst of action. I had decided to go to Garth's office. Instead of wondering helplessly about his ambiguities I could ask him about them directly instead.

His office was in Knightsbridge. I felt incapable of coping with the Underground system or even the buses at that stage, so I took another extravagant cab and sat back in the shiny leather seat as London slipped past my eyes.

I pictured an imaginary Guide, Philosopher and Friend, the

rôle which I had assumed for so long with Gina. "Dear Claire," my imaginary friend wrote with cold asperity, "you are letting your innate good sense run away from you, I fear. Kindly note the following observations: (1) You should never run after a man—always wait for him to come to you. (2) Never interrupt a man at his office when he might be transacting important business. (3) Disassociate yourself from this man Garth Cooper who is almost certainly not to be trusted. What does it matter whether he implies untrue facts or whether he patently lies about them? The point is that he is probably not presenting an honest picture to you and may have been dishonest about other matters of which you are unaware. (4) Why should you, who seldom have a date at home, believe for one moment that Mr. Cooper is as infatuated with you as you (apparently) are with him? He has clearly been taking a romantic interest in you to blunt the edge of your inquiries into Gina's disappearance. (5) Should you wish to disassociate yourself from Mr. Cooper yet not know how to begin, there is one very simple remedy: don't see him again. (6) Pull yourself together and stop behaving so foolishly. Yours in disappointment . . ."

The cab hurtled into the Hyde Park Underpass and soared up again a moment later into Knightsbridge.

I can't help it, I thought, I love him. I can't help it.

The taxi drew up past Harrods and the driver pointed across the road. "That's the building, Miss. Sorry you're the wrong side but no U-turns allowed here."

"Thank you," I said. I got out, paid the fare and crossed the street. There were office buildings above an exclusive row of shops, most of the windows displaying antiques. Inside the building there was an old-fashioned elevator. A board nearby told me that Garth and Lilian conducted business on the first floor, and after I had realized that the English say first when they mean second I avoided the elevator and walked up the stairs which wound around the shaft. The door marked "Cooper-Jantzen Limited, Importers-Exporters, China and Glass" was directly ahead of me. Suddenly wishing I had not come I walked up to the door and opened it before my nerve could desert me.

Inside was a light, airy, surprisingly modern outer office with thick green wall-to-wall carpeting and restful pale walls. A few feet away from me were two doors leading into rooms which I guessed were the partners' private offices; to my left I caught a glimpse of a file room and to my right was a gleaming desk, an electric typewriter and a very executive secretary with a curtain of jet black hair, blood-red fingernails and cool competent black eyes.

"Good afternoon," I said uneasily. "Is Mr. Cooper in, please?"

"Mr. Cooper is out of the office at the moment." She delicately adjusted a strand of hair. "Have you an appointment?"

"No—no, I haven't."

"I could make one for you." She opened a red leather appointment book. "What name is it, please?"

"Claire Sullivan, but this isn't a business matter. Could I wait for him, or is it unlikely that he'll return soon?"

"No, I expect him back at any minute." She glanced at her watch as if to confirm what she had said, and stood up and moved past me towards the file room. "Would you like to come this way, please?"

Beyond the file room was a tiny waiting room which looked out on Knightsbridge.

"If you'd like to wait here . . ."

"Thank you," I said.

She walked away gracefully, and I sat down and picked up one of the magazines on the table nearby. It was *Punch*. Presently I put it down and picked up *Paris-Match*.

Ten minutes passed. The phone rang twice and I could hear the murmur of the girl's voice as she took the calls. The electric typewriter chattered intermittently, but presently I heard her get up and come through the file room towards me.

"Would you like some coffee?" she inquired from the doorway.

"If you're making some."

"I always make some at three." She sounded bored about it. "Mr. Cooper and Mrs. Jantzen like strong black coffee after long business lunches."

In the file room she picked up a percolator and wandered

into the outer office again. The front door opened, ringing the small bell hooked to the hinge, and slowly shut itself after her.

I was alone.

Standing up in an agony of restlessness I went out into the file room, examined the small photocopying machine, prowled around the file cabinets. In one corner was a closet with its door ajar. I glimpsed a man's raincoat hanging inside, and was just about to turn away when I caught sight of an envelope sticking out of one of the pockets. I wouldn't have looked at it twice if I hadn't noticed that the only word visible to me of the address was written in purple ink.

I thought of the letters then, the notes from Hollywood, the reams from Paris. And all of them written in Gina's favorite shade of purple.

Quickly, smoothly, before I had had time to think twice, I took out the envelope. It was empty. He had evidently either destroyed the letter or put it in a safe place and then stuffed the envelope hurriedly into his raincoat pocket. I studied the postmark. The letter had been mailed in Dorking, Surrey, at three o'clock on Monday afternoon, two days after the phone call to me from the Jantzens' apartment, and there was no doubt at all that the purple-inked handwriting on the envelope belonged to Gina. . . .

# SEVEN

I went on staring at that empty envelope in the silent deserted office. Somewhere far away beyond the windows of the waiting room came the muffled roar of the Knightsbridge traffic; everything close at hand was very still. Suddenly outside the office in the corridor I heard quick footsteps and I just had time to stuff the envelope back in the raincoat pocket before the door of the outer office was pushed open and Garth and Lilian walked in.

"Catherine? Damn it, where is the girl? We employ her to answer the phone, not to spend half the time in the cloakroom making herself look glamorous."

They could not see me. They were still in the adjacent outer office and I was shielded from them by the half open door of the file room.

"There's no need to be so hard on her—she's a very good secretary and the glamor is only put on for your benefit."

"My God, the next thing I know, Thérèse will be calling to accuse me of having an affair with my secretary!"

I had been about to step forward to announce my presence but the mention of Thérèse made me freeze to a halt.

"I must say, Garth, you're in a very bad mood this afternoon! I can't think why you're so upset about Thérèse when you haven't seen her for days—it's *I* who should be upset. Eric seems to have argued himself into believing that my behavior with you is suspect—"

"Oh, Lord!"

"Did you know that Thérèse saw Eric last Friday after you

came back from Paris? He told me last night that there had been some sort of a scene at the airport with Gina."

"Scene! That's a mild word to use to describe such a sordid, embarrassing episode—"

"Why didn't you mention it to me before?" Lilian asked mildly.

"Why should I? Why should I bore you with the unfortunate incidents of my private life?"

"Apparently Thérèse told Eric on Friday, after the scene at the airport, that your interest in Gina was merely a smoke screen to conceal your interest in me."

"Look, I don't give a damn what Thérèse told Eric or what Eric thinks—" Garth's voice had risen in anger.

"Well, I do! I have to live with him!"

"I can't think why you bother! It's so patently obvious that you've nothing but contempt for him that I don't know why you don't leave him."

"I don't want to bore you with the details of my private life any more than you want to bore me with yours," Lilian shot back. "Besides Eric would be heartbroken if we separated."

"And you're being noble and considering his feelings? That doesn't sound like you, Lilian!"

"Listen, Garth." Lilian's voice had assumed the patience of an adult teaching a child to tell time. "The point is that it suits me to go on living with Eric at the moment. Never mind why. It's none of your business. Just take my word for it that I want to go on living with him, and that I was extremely annoyed to discover that Thérèse has apparently been seeing Eric and trying to make him as jealous as she is—"

"For God's sake, Lilian, why blame me? I'm not responsible for Thérèse! If Eric's jealous, ignore him. Let him be jealous! He can't prove anything against you because there's nothing to prove."

"It's very easy to give advice like that, but not nearly so easy to carry it out. I don't want Eric upset. Incidentally, just as a matter of interest, what game are you playing with that girl Gina? Where is she and why are you hiding her?"

"My dear Lilian," said Garth with what sounded like genuine astonishment, "what in heaven's name are you talking about? I haven't the remotest idea where she is, and I'm *not* hiding her. Why should I be? I haven't seen her or heard from her since we all had lunch together on Saturday."

My cheeks burned for him as his lies rang in my ears. Tears, unwanted and inexplicable, pricked behind my eyelids.

Lilian was saying skeptically: "Weren't you having an affair with her?"

"Good heavens, no! Gina's for men of twenty-five and forty-five, not for men in their mid-thirties."

"Gina struck me," Lilian said slowly, "as being for men of all ages. Didn't she at least tell you where she was going after we all parted after our Saturday lunch?"

"No, I excused myself from her and went home to Half Moon Street. I told her I'd phone her later, but in the end I didn't. I was tied up with other matters."

"Thérèse?"

"No, I haven't seen Thérèse since the episode at the airport on Friday night."

Another lie. I thought of Mrs. Cheese's charwoman talking on the steps of the white house on the square. At six o'clock on Saturday evening Garth had been quarreling with Thérèse in her apartment.

"I was dead tired," Garth was saying. "I'd had a busy week in Paris with very little sleep. I rested till about seven and then wandered out into Shepherd's Market, where I had dinner at a small restaurant. I half wondered whether to phone Gina at her hotel, but I didn't. I didn't feel sociable and wanted to be on my own."

"Well . . . the whole business of Gina's disappearance is certainly very odd, that's all I can say. I suppose you had no word from her on Sunday?"

"No, I spent Sunday at the office."

"At the office? Here? On a Sunday? My goodness, you're getting to be as much a slave to your work as I am! I thought you were always the one who told me I should never work on Sundays?"

"I was puzzled over the Rémy contract—last year's, not this. I couldn't quite work out why we paid so much tax on the profits."

"Oh, I can explain all that to you—it's really very simple. Why did you take over the Rémy contract this year anyway? I can't remember why we decided that. It would have been more sensible if I had handled it just as I did last year. Besides, what does it matter about last year's tax? That's all closed now."

"I had a tip that the Inland Revenue were on the warpath again against small businesses like ours. If we get any inspectors coming round I thought I should make quite sure that everything was in order."

"Well, of course it's all in order! You know how careful I always am—"

"Wait, I can hear Catherine coming back. Let's go into your office."

They opened one of the other doors leading off the outer office and moved quickly into the room beyond. Pulling myself together I left the file room and returned to the adjacent waiting room just as the secretary opened the door of the outer office and let it swing shut behind her. The small bell attached to the hinge murmured faintly and was silent.

"Catherine?" called Lilian in the mild gentle voice she had adopted when I had met her the previous evening. "Is there any coffee?"

"I'm just going to make some, Mrs. Jantzen. Mr. Cooper, there's a Miss Claire Sullivan waiting to see you in the conference room."

There was a long moment of absolute silence. I closed my eyes in an agony of embarrassment and prayed that when I opened them again I would be somewhere else. But I wasn't.

"Shall I—" The secretary hesitated.

"That's all right, Catherine. Thank you." He must have moved back into the outer office by that time for his voice was clearly audible. The next moment he was entering the file room and crossing the floor to the waiting room doorway beyond.

"Good afternoon," he said formally, and even before I could reply he had closed the door and we were alone together, just he and I and a thousand doubts in that quiet little room above Knightsbridge.

"This is a pleasant surprise," he said fluently as I found myself incapable of speech, "but I'm sorry you had to choose to call on us when you did. I suppose you were obliged to listen to Lilian and me indulging in some rather undignified bickering on subjects ranging from Lilian's nonexistent extramarital intrigues to the machinations of the Inland Revenue authorities. I apologize if we embarrassed you, but at least I can remember saying nothing I wouldn't have wanted you to hear."

I turned away, not answering, unable to meet his eyes, and stared out over London.

He moved towards me until I sensed he was standing behind my shoulder.

"What's happened?" he said abruptly. "What's the matter?"

My eyes were blind. "Nothing," I said. I did not trust myself to say any more.

"You've heard bad news about Gina?"

I shook my head. As he put a hand on my arm I turned away from him again and groped my way to the door.

"Just a moment," he said sharply. There was a note of uncertainty in his voice. "Just a moment. You must have come here for a reason. What was it you wanted to say?"

I remembered dimly that a long time ago, before I had found out that he must know where Gina was, I had wanted to ask him more about his quarrel with Thérèse on Saturday evening. Now I knew the answer; as far as he was concerned the quarrel was a secret, to be concealed for private reasons. There was nothing I could do, nothing more I could say. My common sense had been correct in telling me I should never have come to his office; it had been a stupid, foolish, misguided step to take.

"I'm sorry," I said with difficulty. "It was wrong of me to come here and bother you. It really wasn't very important anyway. Please excuse me."

After a moment he said: "I don't understand."

I was incapable of speech again. I fumbled with the handle to open the door, but his hand closed on mine and stopped me.

"Please," he said quietly. "Please, Claire. You must tell me what this is all about. What's the matter? Was it something to do with the conversation I had just now with Lilian?"

I thought of the empty envelope in his raincoat pocket.

"No," I said, and found myself looking up into his eyes. He looked puzzled and worried. I was conscious of an overpowering urge to confide in him but I knew I must not. He had lied, not once but several times, and it was now no longer possible to trust him. With an effort so immense that I felt drained of all strength I said: "I think all this worry about Gina is depressing me more than I thought. I came here simply to talk to you and it wasn't until I was here waiting that I realized how selfish I was being in bothering you in your office. But before I could leave you came in with Lilian."

He looked at me steadily. His eyes were very clear. "Well, I'm glad you came," he said at last. "And I'm glad you turned to me when you were depressed. So why don't we sit down and talk about it? Never mind the office. That can wait. If you came here to see me, then why rush away again as soon as I appear?"

I shook my head helplessly. "No—really, Garth—I'd prefer not to talk here—" I broke off, reached out to open the door again.

"Look, Claire—"

"I can't explain—I just don't want to talk—"

"The hell you don't. Well, I do. No matter what you think I want to tell you that ever since we met—"

"I must go. Please—" I tried to open the door.

"—I haven't been able to stop thinking of you—"

"Oh don't, don't, DON'T—" My composure was fast fading.

"But Claire darling—"

I burst into tears.

"Oh God, I'm sorry . . . I don't know what's the matter with me. I've been so clumsy and hamfisted every time we meet—if it hadn't been for this wretched business over Gina—"

"We wouldn't have met at all," I said shakily, raking through the contents of my purse for a handkerchief.

"Here, have mine." He pressed a large white handkerchief between my fingers. I blew my nose, mopped ineffectually at my face, tried to gather together the shattered remnants of my self-control.

"I'm sorry," I said distantly at last. "I'm not myself. Please excuse me if I leave now."

"Let me get you a drink—"

"No, I want to take two aspirin and lie down. I've got a bad headache."

"I'll go down with you and get you a taxi."

"No—"

"I insist."

I was too exhausted to argue anymore. We went out through the file room into the outer office where the secretary regarded us with impenetrable black eyes behind her curtain of black hair. Outside in the street Garth hailed a cab and gave the name of my hotel to the driver, together with a ten shilling note.

"I'll phone you this evening," he said to me. "Perhaps if you're well enough we can have a quiet dinner together somewhere."

"I—don't know—"

"I'll phone you around six. Take care of yourself." He kissed me; I felt his lips brush my forehead as his fingers tightened on my arm, and the tears pricked at my eyes again. " 'Bye."

My lips moved but I could not bring myself to say goodbye. He closed the door, the taxi moved forward into the heavy traffic and I was alone. Leaning back against the leather upholstery, my mind blank with a dozen conflicting emotions, I stared out of the window and felt my cheeks burn once more with bitter, silent useless tears.

When I arrived back at the hotel I found three telephone messages asking me to call Warren when I got back. I tore them up. In the privacy of my room at last I drew the curtains and lay down for about five minutes, but presently I got up again and went over to the mirror to repair my makeup. I felt calmer now. It seemed unlikely that I would cry again during the next few hours. My head ached dully and my eyes felt sore, but otherwise I was conscious of nothing except a numbed apathy. I felt defeated. It was typical, I thought with a detached incredulity, that the one man whom I really fell for would turn out to be a double-faced, plausible liar. I was convinced now that he was having an affair with Gina and that he knew where she was, and for reasons of his own was keeping her hiding-place secret while ostensibly pretending to help me with a hypocritical willingness.

There was no doubt at all that he had been playing a double game. And because I knew he had been playing a double game with me I had found the scene at his office particularly humiliating and shameful. He had summed me up, guessed that his best way of handling me was to adopt a suitably romantic approach and had then played his adopted rôle with great skill. I had been flattered, deceived, clay in his hands. He must have thought me an innocent fool.

The tears were just beginning to prick my eyes again and threaten to ruin my new makeup when the phone rang. I nearly didn't answer it, but then instead seized the opportunity to take my mind off my troubles. "Hello?" I said cautiously into the receiver.

"I was just about to call Scotland Yard to report *your* disappearance," said Warren, aggrieved. "Where the hell have you been? You said you would call me after your lunch with Eric Jantzen, and here it is—nearly four o'clock. I've been worrying myself sick about you."

"I'm sorry," I said. "I was delayed. Do you want to come over to my room? I've got a clue about where Gina may be and I want to talk it over with you."

"You have?" He was agog. "I'll be right over. Hold everything."

The line went dead. I sat on the edge of my bed and held everything, and a minute later he was knocking on the door. I let him in.

"How did you find out?" he demanded excitedly. "What happened? Where is she?"

I suggested he sit down and have a cigarette. "I went to Garth Cooper's office this afternoon," I said without emphasis. "I was suspicious of him. He wasn't there when I arrived but his raincoat was. In the pocket was an empty envelope which had a postmark dated Monday, three days ago. It was addressed to Garth, the handwriting was Gina's and the post-mark said it was posted at Dorking in Surrey."

Warren was so astounded that he dropped his cigarette. There was a great fuss as he snatched it up again and stamped at the carpet. Then: "So Cooper was lying all along! If she wrote to him Monday—"

"He would have got it on Tuesday, or yesterday, Wednesday. He must know where she is."

"Where did you say the postmark was?"

"Dorking, Surrey."

"Surrey's south of here, isn't it? Dorking shouldn't be too far away. Look, I've got a road map of England in my room. Let me just go and get it and we can check and see where this place is."

It turned out to be about twenty-five or thirty miles south of London.

"Looks as if it's a fair sized town," said Warren, pondering over his guidebook. "Why don't we get a train down there to-night and see what we can find out? We must be able to get there by train. It looks as though it should be in the commuter belt."

I hesitated, not certain what to do, my determination dulled by my apathy.

Warren was still browsing over the map. "Dorking . . . Guildford seems to be the nearest other big town. Hey, listen to these names! Abinger Hammer, Shere, Gomshall, Holmbury St. Mary—"

The pain of memory was so intense that I bit my lip.

He looked up. "Something wrong?"

"Garth told me he owned a country cottage at Holmbury St. Mary. He goes down there at weekends."

"So that's it!" cried Warren. "So that's where she is! She's at Cooper's place in Surrey!" He closed the guidebook with a bang and scrambled to his feet. "Okay, let's go."

"Wait a minute," I said. "If Gina's staying in secret at Garth's country cottage she may not thank us for interfering. If she's capable of writing a letter and mailing it, it seems that she's there of her own free will and that apparently she's perfectly well and unharmed."

He stared at me. "What are you suggesting?"

"I think you know what I'm suggesting—you're not stupid. Listen, this is what I think happened . . ." I took a deep breath, summoned my will power, tried to speak in a cool, level disinterested tone of voice. "Gina traveled to London to spend the weekend with Garth, but they were met by an infuriated Thérèse at the airport. There was apparently a scene resulting in Gina and Garth traveling separately into Central London, and naturally after that Garth would be afraid of Thérèse creating further scenes. So he suggested that Gina stay secretly at his cottage in Surrey."

"I don't believe it," said Warren at once. "He's been in London all week—what would be the point of Gina staying down in the country if she had traveled to London specifically to be with him? And why didn't she call Candy-Anna to tell her she wouldn't be returning to Paris for a few days? And anyway, you still haven't explained her call to New York from the Jantzens' apartment on Saturday night."

"Well then, you suggest another explanation which fits the fact that she's probably staying at his cottage in Surrey, unharmed, and of her own free will!"

He looked mutinous. His glance, roving around the room as if for inspiration, alighted on the telephone. "Let's call information and get the number of Cooper's home in Surrey."

"It won't have a phone."

"How do you know?"

"Why would Gina have written if she could have called him up?"

He was silent. "Well, let's give it a try anyway," he said at last. "There's no harm in trying."

"All right," I agreed doubtfully. After ten minutes of talking to various operators in both London and Surrey, he was told the house called Coneyhurst Cottage which belonged to Mr. Garth Cooper in Holmbury St. Mary was listed as having the number Holmbury 626.

"Could you try it for me, please?" said Warren at once.

More waiting followed. Then:

"No reply?" said Warren disappointed. "Thank you. I'll try again later."

"I suppose that's not altogether surprising," I said, trying to cheer him up as he replaced the receiver. "If Gina is hiding at the cottage she wouldn't answer the phone."

"True." He brightened a little. "At least I was right about the place having a phone. Well, what do you say, Claire? How about getting a train down to Dorking this evening, stopping overnight at a hotel there, and then hiring a car tomorrow morning to drive out to Cooper's house?"

I thought of Garth's promise to call later and to invite me to have dinner with him. If I were to speak to him, I thought, I would be weak and accept his invitation. And if I went out to dinner with him I would make matters even harder for myself than they were already. The best course I could possibly take would be to leave town for a day or two.

Warren was just beginning to look surprised by my hesitation when I said abruptly: "Yes, let's leave right away. How do we get there?"

"Let me talk to the people at the desk downstairs and see what they suggest. Then as soon as I get the details straightened out we can pack our bags and check out."

"All right."

After he had gone and I was alone I opened my suitcases and began to put my belongings inside once more. I found it a relief to have something to do, however mundane it was. Just as I was finishing, the phone rang and Warren told me there was a train leaving Waterloo Station soon after seven o'clock.

"We could have a snack here at five-thirty," he suggested, "and then get a cab to Waterloo. The trip takes about forty-five minutes. They've given me the name of a car rental agency in the town and the name of a hotel where we can stay, so now we're all set to go."

After we had had dinner we went to the desk to pay our bills, and I found that there was a phone message for me to say Garth had called. I tore it up and threw it away. Ten minutes later, with our luggage stowed safely into our taxi, we were leaving Piccadilly Circus on our way to Waterloo.

We reached Dorking shortly before eight and took a taxi to the inn which had been recommended to Warren at the hotel desk in London. I think we were both amazed by Dorking. Even Warren, who had never seemed to me to be very aware of his surroundings, was silenced by the wide High Street with its rows of old shops and narrow winding side streets packed with little pubs and antique stores. Our taxi driver informed us that our hotel had been a coaching inn in the old days, and suddenly I remembered a scene in Dickens' "Pickwick Papers" and knew why the name Dorking had seemed familiar.

"Would you believe?" marveled Warren as the taxi turned off the High Street under an ancient arch into the courtyard around which the inn was built. "People *live* here. It wasn't built by Walt Disney. People really *live* here."

And it was there at last that I felt I was in England. London with its vast modern buildings and cosmopolitan atmosphere had vaguely disappointed me, particularly after my brief visit to Paris, but here in Dorking I was no longer disappointed. As I entered my room and looked out of the window towards the large green hill which rose up above the town in the northeast, I had one of those curious, inexplicable moments that made me think I had been in here before. But that was nonsense. No town I knew in New England bore any resemblance to this old market town in Surrey, and none of my ancestors had come from England; my mother's family was Scottish and my father had been an Ulsterman from protestant Northern Ireland. I was a stranger here, and yet in spite of that I felt at home.

We were just in time for dinner; I had yet to get accustomed to the rigidity of English meal times and their inflexible hours. We ate an enormous English meal which seemed to my transatlantic ideas of finance to cost very little money, and afterwards we felt so replete we had to spend an hour in the lounge over our coffee before we could lever ourselves out of our chairs. Finally Warren went off to try to call the cottage again, but he was unsuccessful and in the end we decided to have an early night before driving out to Holmbury the following morning.

I spent an uneasy night. Supposing, I thought, Gina was indeed at the cottage, as it now seemed likely that she was. The scene would have to be handled with great care, and the more

I thought about it the less eager I felt for Warren to be there with me. Warren would charge into the cottage like a bull in a china shop and besiege Gina with questions and demands and accusations. And supposing Gina decided not to come away with us but to remain at the cottage? Warren, who had been living on tenterhooks for longer than I had, might lose his head and do something stupid. I could almost visualize him carrying Gina off by force under the sincere conviction that he was acting for the best. I shuddered. Somehow I must contrive to arrive at the cottage before he did.

The next morning at breakfast I found he had already hired a car and intended to collect it directly after we had finished eating.

"I hate to tell you this," I said apologetically, "but I'm not feeling too well. Could we possibly postpone the trip until this afternoon? I've got a terrible headache."

He looked concerned. "Do you have any aspirin? You'd better go and lie down. Can I get you a doctor?"

"No, no," I said hastily before he could get carried away by consideration. "I'll take two aspirin and lie down and I'll be fine by noon. I'm sorry to postpone the trip, but—"

"That's okay, I understand. Don't worry about it—I'm just sorry you're feeling bad." He thought for a moment. "Maybe I'll drive out there on my own this morning and see if Gina's there."

"Please," I said with great restraint, "please let's wait till this afternoon! I've come over three thousand miles to find Gina and when we do find her I want to be there, not stretched out on a hotel bed."

He looked sheepish. "Sure, I understand. I'm sorry."

I silently heaved a sigh of relief. He decided to explore the town for a while and send some postcards to his friends, and after he had collected the car from the garage he prepared to set off on foot from the hotel.

"You can leave the keys with me," I said. "I don't want you losing them on your travels."

"Good idea," he agreed, completely serious although I had spoken lightly. "I'm always losing things."

He handed over the keys docilely and departed.

As soon as he was out of sight, I slipped out to the car, fitted
the keys in the ignition and examined the controls. When I had
lived at home I had driven a car every day of my adult life
until all my reflexes and reactions were automatic and made
without conscious effort; that was more than three years ago
but I had driven rented cars occasionally since I had been living in New York, and had found that for me driving had become like swimming: once learned the skill is never forgotten.
Driving a car in England would be different, I reasoned, but
not difficult. Presently, after making sure I knew what I was
doing, I started the engine, adjusted the shift and released
the brake. The car trickled forward over the inn's cobbled
courtyard. Soon I was easing my way carefully through the
narrow arch and turning into the High Street. Dimly aware
that I was more nervous than I had anticipated I crept along
behind a green double-decker bus and found myself taking a
right fork at the bottom of the High Street and driving on out
of the town into the quieter residential districts. I stopped at
the first gas station I came to and asked the way to Holmbury
St. Mary. To my surprise I learned that I was on the right road.

"Keep straight on," said a solicitous mechanic. "Through
Westcott, past the Wotton Hatch Hotel. Keep going. Stick on
the main road until you get almost to Abinger Hammer. Then
as soon as you catch a glimpse of watercress beds on the left,
watch out for a left turn. There's a white signboard just before
the clock at Abinger which says 'To Holmbury St. Mary.'
Take that left turn and drive another couple of miles or so and
you'll be right in the village."

I thanked him and drove on. After a small village which I
presumed was Westcott, the road ran deeper into the country,
now and then cutting through sandy soil. I noticed the lush
green of the foliage and glimpsed a range of hills beyond the
fields to the north, but the traffic was much heavier than I
had expected and it was impossible to look at the scenery as
closely as I would have liked.

At last I found the side road past the watercress beds and
turned left to Holmbury St. Mary. The country road was narrow and winding; there was little traffic now and I was able to
take more notice of my surroundings. After passing through a

hamlet where the cottages were so old and pretty that I nearly missed my way as I stared at them, I finally came to a larger village with a green, a church on a hill and some assorted houses and shops.

I stopped beside the nearest passer-by and asked the way to Coneyhurst Cottage. She said she had never heard of it. Discouraged I drove on and stopped at a pub; the pub itself was closed but the landlord was sweeping out the bar.

"Excuse me," I called through the open window. "Can you tell me where Coneyhurst Cottage is?"

He was a tall solid man with a moustache. "Coneyhurst?" He stroked the moustache absently. "Sounds as if it should be up Holmbury Hill. Who lives there?"

"A Mr. Garth Cooper."

"Ah!" He looked pleased. "Yes, I know Mr. Cooper. He often comes here weekends. The cottage is nearly all the way up the hill, an isolated spot with a good view. Take the road to Peaslake up the hill—you'll pass several big houses including Holmbury House itself. Keep following the signs to Peaslake, and just before you get to the top of the hill you'll see the cottage on your left."

I thanked him and returned to my car. The sun came out as I took the road uphill away from the village, and the light slanted through the tall trees with their brilliant green leaves and fell in patterns on the twisting narrow road. Presently the trees ended and the slopes of the hill rose steeply above me on my right. The view to the left was already worth pausing to look at, but I was too near my journey's end now and didn't stop. I passed occasional houses, including the gates bearing the inscription "Holmbury House," and swung uphill even more steeply. There was a fork in the road; I took the turn to Peaslake, as the landlord had instructed me, and ground the shift into a lower gear. I was glad Warren had hired a small Austin. The road was now so narrow that any larger car would have been nerve-wracking to drive.

I was just thinking that sooner or later I must surely reach the summit of the hill when I came upon the cottage. I had expected it to be old and quaint with a thatched roof, but I was disappointed. This was a small house, probably no more than thirty years old, and was perched firmly on the steep hill-side looking out over a panoramic view across the valley below.

Parking the car off the road among the trees I got out and went slowly over to the house. All the windows were closed; there was no sign of life. I found the front door, and after a moment's hesitation rang the bell, but no one answered and presently I moved on around the house and tried the handle of the back door. It was locked. I stood there and wondered what to do. There was a small gardening shed a few yards from the house and for no reason other than curiosity I walked over and opened the door, but there was no one inside—only a few gardening implements and a wheelbarrow. As I turned away the sun went behind a cloud suddenly and a chill breeze swept up from the valley.

I shivered.

The blank sightless windows of the house stared at me, and suddenly, without knowing why, I was frightened. I retreated, moving quickly down the little terraced garden, and on the last terrace beside the hedge which marked the boundary of the grounds I noticed that part of an overgrown, weed-strewn flowerbed had been recently dug and hoed. The damp earth gleamed in the bright morning light.

I stared at it, refusing to recognize it for what it looked like. The patch was about six feet long and three feet wide. Suddenly, hardly aware that I was moving, I was halfway back to the shed. When I reached it I took the spade which was leaning against the wall and went back to the flowerbed at the bottom of the garden.

The spade sank softly into the wet earth and stopped.

I felt horribly cold. Presently I began to shiver again. Then, overcome with an obsession to see all my worst nightmares spring to the most appalling life, I stooped and scraped at the earth until at last I had uncovered a monstrous, distorted, gross object which I only just managed to identify.

It was a human hand.

# EIGHT

After I had finished being sick, I steeled myself to go back to the grave again. There was something I had to find out, something I had to know. When I had finally achieved a state of mind resembling detachment I knelt down on the ground again and bent over the hand, my nose and mouth pressed against my handkerchief. There was a ring on the engagement finger, a brilliant diamond ring which sparkled mockingly in the bright light. I shut my eyes very tightly and then opened them again. It was still there. For several repulsive seconds I thought I would check to see if the ring bore any inscription, but I gave up the idea and retreated from the grave. The engagement ring was proof enough; Thérèse had not wanted to break off the engagement and it was possible she might have continued to wear the ring even after Garth had tried to end matters between them.

The full meaning of my discovery suddenly hit me in an overwhelming wave of shock. Garth's ex-fiancée was buried in the garden of Garth's weekend cottage. And Garth had been one of the last people to see her alive. After she had quarreled with him and stormed out of her apartment, her neighbors had not seen her again.

If the police knew the facts, I thought to myself, they could not help but think Garth was guilty of murder. She was making trouble for him, he had quarreled with her, he was the last person to see her alive . . .

There was ice on my forehead. On reaching the shed I found a tap used for the garden water hose and turned it on. Cold water sluiced out. After washing my hands with a fanati-

cal thoroughness, I dried them on the full skirt of my dress and
went outside again into that cool morning light. Back in the
driver's seat of the car I sat down and started to tremble from
head to toe.

I tried to accept the fact that Garth was a murderer but my
mind balked at such an idea. I was prepared to accept that
Garth had been playing some sort of game where I was concerned but I could not believe that the game included murder.
I tried to think clearly. Where had Thérèse gone after her
quarrel with him last Saturday in her apartment? If he did kill
her, when had it taken place, and where? And why bury the
body in the garden of his own cottage when he could have
chosen a site anywhere on the surrounding hillside?

I could not believe he had killed her. No matter how absurd
and how lunatic my reasoning might be, I could not believe he
was a murderer.

My thoughts, jumbled and confused, went on and on and
on. I wondered if Gina had been in some way involved in the
murder. If Garth were shielding Gina—no, Gina wouldn't have
killed Thérèse. I wondered for the hundredth time where Gina
was and wished with all my heart that I could somehow get in
touch with her, and as I thought of Gina, I thought with a stab
of dread of Warren.

I caught my breath. If Warren came to the cottage and
found the grave in the garden, he would instantly contact the
police. Somehow I had to prevent Warren from following
through with his plan to investigate the cottage that afternoon.

The problem of how I could succeed in deflecting Warren
from an apparently unavoidable course of action filled my
mind as I made my way back to Dorking, but by the time I
had arrived in the courtyard of the inn I was no nearer a solution than I had been when I had left Holmbury St. Mary.
I glanced at my watch. It was eleven-thirty. Praying that I
wouldn't meet Warren on the stairs or in any of the lounges I
slipped into the hotel and hurried upstairs to my room.

With the door tightly closed and bolted behind me, I sat
down on the bed, reached for the phone and asked the operator to put through a call for me to Garth's office in London.

I once read somewhere that a person in love can be con-

sidered to be temporarily unbalanced while the effects of the
malaise lingers in the mind. Certainly if anyone had ever
told me a month previously that I would not report a dead
body to the police as soon as I found it, but would instead
phone the probable murderer to warn him of the danger he
was in, I would have replied indignantly that I would never
be so patently insane.

But I was. To make matters worse I was convinced that I
was doing the only sane thing I could possibly do, since I had
already persuaded myself against all the evidence that Garth
was innocent. I sat waiting tensely in that still quiet bedroom
as my call was connected, and then suddenly Garth's secretary
Catherine had picked up the receiver and was saying in her
cool, studiously polite voice: "Cooper-Jantzen Limited—good
morning, may I help you?"

"Yes," I said rapidly. "Is Mr. Cooper there, please? This is
Miss Sullivan."

"I'm afraid neither Mr. Cooper nor Mrs. Jantzen will be in
the office today. Is there any information I can give you?"

"Do you know where they are?"

"They've arranged to have a business weekend entertaining
French clients at Mr. Cooper's cottage in Surrey. Mrs. Jantzen
went down to the cottage last night to get everything ready
and Mr. Cooper was to go to the airport this afternoon to meet
the clients' plane. It's possible that if you tried his flat you
might just catch him before he leaves—do you have his
number?"

"No—I only have the office number. Could you give it to me,
please? It's very urgent."

"One moment," I heard her flick open an automatic telephone book. "Yes, it's Mayfair—that's MAY—75432."

"Thank you very much indeed." I replaced the receiver and
instantly picked it up again to give the operator the new number. I waited while she dialed and heard the bell ring endlessly at the other end of the wire.

"Sorry," said the operator. "There's no reply."

"Thank you." But I could not believe I would be unable to
contact him. Springing to my feet in a fever of activity I left

my room and went downstairs to the pay phone which I had
noticed earlier outside the lounges.

By a miracle I had the right coins. After skimming through
the instructions, which seemed unnecessarily complicated, I
dialed the series of numbers and waited. The line began to
ring and I thought in a panic: did I dial correctly? And such
was my state of mind that I convinced myself in the space of
three seconds that I had mis-dialed. I hung up, got my money
back and began again.

This time, by some extraordinary miracle, someone picked
up the phone on the first ring.

"Hello?"

I had opened my mouth, drawn breath to speak, but now I
was struck dumb before I could say a word.

For it was not Garth who had answered the phone. It was
Gina. . . .

"Garth?" said Gina, suddenly fearful as I did not reply, and
I realized dimly that I must have stumbled on a prearranged
telephone signal which enabled her to know when it was safe
to answer the phone. "Garth, what is it? What's happened
now?"

"What's happened now," I said shakily, "is that your sister
has finally managed to track you down. Where the *hell* have
you been?" Tears of relief were hot on my cheeks; the room
swam in a dizzy mist of thankfulness.

"Claire! Oh God, where are you? What are you doing?
Claire, I feel so bad about you, so terrible—"

"So you damn well should! I've been worrying myself silly
about you and tying myself in the most impossible knots ever
since you called!"

"I tried to call you back on Monday from Garth's apartment
here but you'd already left New York—you left so *quickly*,
Claire! I never, never thought you'd be on your way to Paris
within two days—"

"What did you think I'd do, for heaven's sake? Dither about
in New York while I wondered all the time if you'd been murdered or raped or kidnapped? Or stand rooted to the floor of
my apartment like the Statue of Liberty while I waited for you
to remember to call back?"

"I didn't forget you, Claire, I did actually try to call you back on Saturday night but your line was busy all the time, and after that I didn't get the chance to call till Monday, and by that time—"

"Why did you call from the Jantzen apartment?"

"I—look, I can't talk on the phone. Garth would be furious if he knew I'd even spoken to you. He said absolutely no one, not even you, must know where I was until Saturday—"

"But look, Gina—you must tell me more! Garth's in trouble. His ex-fiancée—"

"I know."

"But—"

"Please, Claire darling, please—not on the phone. Listen, where are you? At the Regent Palace?"

"Dorking."

"Dorking! But you mustn't stay there! You—you'll be in danger—quick, come back to London. Come back at once. Get the next train to Waterloo. Don't ask questions, darling, just *leave*. Do you understand? Leave right away and come here."

"Yes, but just a minute! Where *is* Garth? I must talk to him. There's so much I—"

"He's on his way by car down to the cottage at Holmbury St. Mary. But Claire, you must come to London at once. Please! You must come!"

"Yes," I said to pacify her. "Yes, I'll get the next train. Don't worry."

"I'll be waiting for you," she said with relief. "And *hurry!*"

"What do you think I've been doing ever since your wretched phone call on Saturday night? All right, I'll hurry—don't worry, and take care of yourself."

"You too, darling. 'Bye now."

"'Bye." I hung up, leaned weakly against the wall and fumbled for my handkerchief. I succeeded in finding the one which Garth had given me the previous afternoon at his office. It occurred to me wryly that I had cried more in the past two days than I had cried during the preceding two years.

When I had recovered myself, I went back upstairs to my room and began to consider what I should do next. I had every intention of joining Gina as soon as possible, but first of all I had to prevent Warren from going out to the cottage to find her, and then I had to try to see Garth to settle matters between us once and for all. But my first task was Warren. Presently I went to his room and knocked on the door, but there was no answer so I assumed he was still out on his walking tour. It seemed that he was making his tour of Dorking in great detail.

I tried again, a quarter of an hour later, and this time I had more success.

"How are you feeling?" he said as he let me into the room. "You don't look too good."

I could hardly have had a better opening. "Well, no, I still don't feel very well," I said listlessly. "Such a nuisance . . . But I've got some wonderful news for you—I've been trying to find you for the past half hour. What do you think happened while you were out? I called Garth's office to see if he had any news of Gina and would you believe it, who should come to the phone but Gina herself! I was so amazed I could hardly believe it! She refused to talk much on the phone, but we arranged to meet at five in the Regent Palace lobby."

"I don't believe it!" said Warren amazed. "She did? But what was she doing at Cooper's office? Where has she been?"

"I told you—she wouldn't talk on the phone! But isn't that marvelous news? I'm going to go on resting here for a couple of hours to get rid of my headache and then we can get a train to London to meet her at five o'clock."

"Why, that's wonderful!" he exclaimed. "Great! Let me call up the station and find out the times of the trains to London—"

"You can go straight on up to London, if you like. But I just want to rest for a little longer—"

"Sure, I understand. I'll wait for you, though, and we can travel up together." He moved over to the phone. "Let me call now and find out the times of the trains."

I thought it unwise to argue with him further for fear of arousing his suspicions. If he decided to wait for me I could always give him the slip, just as I had that morning, and drive off on my own in the car. I heaved a sigh of relief, and as he began to talk into the receiver, I wandered casually over to the dressing table and picked up one or two of the objects which he had left scattered around on the polished surface. There were several postcards of Surrey.

I began to glance at each of them.

"Four forty-five? I see . . . and the one before that?"

His passport lay beside the postcards. I glanced at his photo and saw to my surprise that unlike most passport photographs, it was flattering. He looked young, bold, quick-witted and handsome as he stared defiantly into the camera. I flicked through the pages to the visa section to see which countries he had visited. A trip to Brazil was recorded for the previous year. Then his arrival in Paris and the visit to London.

"Okay . . . fine. Now what time does that reach London? Is it an express?"

I stared. The visits to England and France appeared to be in duplicate.

"Just one stop, did you say?"

I went on staring. Presently I realized that the first stamp of the British Immigration Authorities was dated the previous Saturday and that the second stamp of the French authorities was dated a day later on the Sunday.

*Warren had been in London on the night Gina had made the phone call from the Jantzen apartment. He had been in London on the night Thérèse had disappeared.* Warren had been in London on Saturday and had slipped back to Paris quietly on Sunday, and he had never once mentioned it to me. . . .

"Thank you very much," he said suddenly from behind me. "Goodbye."

He dropped the receiver and I dropped the passport; the noise of the one muffled the sound of the other. Feeling nothing but an amazed, uncomprehending bewilderment I turned towards him with a blank expression. "Is it all right?" I asked naturally. "What train do we get?"

"There's one that leaves at three and I suggest we get that. Why don't I pick you up at two-thirty?"

"Fine. Thanks, Warren," I said automatically, and feeling blank with shock, I left the room and went outside to the quiet corridor beyond.

When I reached my bedroom again I was still incapable

of thinking clearly about my discovery but gradually as I stood by the window of my room and stared out over Dorking my initial shock began to recede. Why had Warren been in London? And why should he have concealed his visit unless he had something to hide? Could he conceivably have had any connection with Thérèse's murder? I spent several minutes thinking of Warren and remembering how I had always dismissed him as a naïve, ingenuous, overgrown adolescent. Apparently I had severely underestimated him. It seemed as if he were not nearly so naïve and frank as he appeared to be.

Another thought occurred to me. Might I not also be mistaken about Warren's single-minded determination to find Gina? I had been amused and touched by the devotion which had made him decide to take a week's absence from his work and fly to London to find her, but supposing his determination concealed a more sinister motive? I thought of Thérèse again, and suddenly I was saying to myself: supposing Warren killed Thérèse and Gina saw him do it. He'd want to find her at all costs once he realized she had witnessed his crime. And perhaps he had not known that she had witnessed the murder until I had arrived in Paris with my tale of Gina's distraught phone call to New York on Saturday night . . .

My thoughts seemed to be racing out of control. I tried to apply a mental brake. There was, I told myself, no reason why Warren should have killed Thérèse. Why *should* he have killed her? As far as I knew, they had never even met.

I began to wander restlessly about the room, and picked up my handbag irresolutely before putting it down again and returning to the window. Perhaps I was being dramatic in assuming Warren wanted to find Gina in order to silence her. Perhaps Thérèse had threatened Gina and Warren had killed her, accidentally or otherwise, in order to protect Gina herself. Then, when I had arrived in Paris and he had discovered from my information that Gina, unknown to him, had witnessed the crime, he had immediately tried to find her to explain the situation. If this theory were correct it would also explain why Gina had not gone to the police, for if Warren had killed Thérèse for her sake, Gina would hardly have wanted to call in the police.

I pulled myself together. I could stay in my room and imagine all kinds of theories, but that would hardly be the most sensible thing to do. The best course I could take would be to find Garth and demand that he tell me the whole truth without half-truths or evasions; since he had been hiding Gina in his London apartment and, before that, at his cottage in Holmbury St. Mary, he must presumably know why and from whom Gina wanted to hide.

My mind was made up. Moving quickly I picked up my handbag again, opened the door cautiously and slipped downstairs to the car, which was parked in the courtyard. The next moment I was in the driver's seat and edging the car out into the High Street as I began my return journey to Holmbury St. Mary.

I was so nervous that at first I took the wrong road out of Dorking and wasted precious minutes crawling through side streets while I tried to get my bearings. Finally, more through luck than judgement, I found myself on the road to Westcott and Abinger Hammer, and after some minutes I was driving past the hotel at Wotton Hatch which I had noticed earlier. It was beginning to rain; by the time I reached the turn to Holmbury St. Mary I had to use the windshield wipers. But the shower passed and as I took the road at last up Holmbury Hill to Garth's cottage, the sun shone palely again and the rain was a mere dark cloud shadowing the road behind me.

I was driving too fast. I had to will myself to slow down. Normally the narrow winding road would have been enough to persuade me to reduce my speed to walking pace but I was so anxious to see Garth and learn the whole truth of the situation that I was forgetting even the most basic rules of highway safety.

Fortunately I met no cars coming down the hill as I went up so I arrived at the cottage without incident. But even before I could park the car I saw that this time I would not be alone at the house; a sleek creamy Jaguar had stolen my parking place, the spokes of the wheels glittering in the sunlight, the hood thrusting gently into the undergrowth which crept up from the ground to meet the bumpers. Someone had ar-

rived before me. I was just assuming that it must be Garth
when it occurred to me that I had never seen his car before.
In London we had always taken cabs everywhere. Supposing
the car belonged to someone else? I hesitated, shivering violently as I remembered the dead hand in the shallow grave,
and then pulling myself together, I let the car roll back a few
yards and parked it off the road below the Jaguar. It must be
Garth who had arrived at the cottage. After all, Gina had
said that he was on his way. I was becoming neurotic, imagining danger where none existed.

I got out of the car and slammed the door shut. Everywhere
around me it was very quiet. On my right the wooded hillside
was still and motionless. Not a breath of wind whispered
through the branches of the trees; a bird sang briefly and
darted into the silent undergrowth. I was alone, part of the
stillness of the landscape as I stopped to listen, and when I
moved forward again I felt the damp twigs crunch beneath
my shoes and my breathing quicken in my throat.

All the windows of the house were still closed; there was
no sign of life. For a long moment I hesitated by the roadside
and then with an effort I stepped off the road and walked
swiftly up the path to the front door. I touched the bell,
waited. The bell seemed to ring far away, a small faint trill of
sound piercing the pall of silence. I went on waiting. I was just
about to ring again when he opened the door.

His face was empty of expression. He looked at me as if he
didn't know me.

"I'm sorry," I said stammering, "but I must talk to you,
Garth."

He said nothing. He was very still, one hand on the latch,
the other a tight fist at his side. As so often happens in moments of great stress I found myself noticing trivial things, that
he was wearing casual clothes, dark slacks, blue shirt and,
oddly, quiet-soled tennis shoes. His hair was untidy, and as I
stood there watching him he smoothed it back with his hand
in the old gesture which I had noticed when I had first seen
him in Paris.

"I can't talk now," he said abruptly. "It'll have to be later."

"But—"

"Go back to London and I'll get in touch with you there."

I shook my head dumbly.

"Look, Claire, I'm sorry, but I can't talk now. I've got guests arriving any minute and I'm not ready for them. You'd better go back to London."

I was stung by his air of polite impatience, his attitude of thinly veiled exasperation. "To London?" I said quickly. "And where shall I wait in London? At the hotel? Or with Gina at your apartment?"

He stared at me. It was impossible to guess what he was thinking. Then: "Whichever you prefer," he said without expression, and began to close the door. "And now if you'll excuse me—I apologize for being so abrupt, but—"

"Don't bother to apologize," I said, infuriated by the fact that he was no longer even pretending to be interested in me, "because I'm not going." My eyes were pricking with the sickness of disillusionment, but my anger overcame my disappointment and wretchedness. I knew now that his interest in me had been assumed from the start to make it harder for me to find Gina, and some perverse, foolish streak of pride made me want to prove to him that he had meant no more to me than I had to him.

"Claire—"

"No," I said, my eyes hot with unshed tears. "No, you're going to listen whether you want to or not! Why did you tell me all those lies? Why did you tell me you hadn't seen Gina since Saturday when all the time you knew where she was? And why did you say you hadn't seen Thérèse since Friday at London airport when you quarreled with her at her apartment on Saturday evening? You lied and lied—"

"Listen," he said, white to the lips, "listen, Claire. Thérèse is dead—"

"Yes!" I cried. "Murdered! And buried over there in *your* garden!"

He opened the door a little wider and I thought he was going to let me into the house to talk to him but he merely moved out on the step beside me.

"I didn't kill her," he said slowly. "You must believe that. I didn't kill her."

"Why should I believe you!" I stormed at him. "You've told me nothing but lies from start to finish—"

"That's not true."

"It *is* true!"

"Oh, for God's sake!" he exclaimed, as if I had touched him on the raw. "Stop shouting accusations at me as if I committed a mortal sin! The only reason I lied—"

"—was to deceive me," I said. "I expected you to be honest with me and instead you—"

"I omitted certain facts—just as you did when you first met me. It was a long time before you told me what Gina had actually said during her phone call to you in New York! If omitting facts makes me a liar, then you're as much of a liar as I am!"

"I—"

"Please," he said. "Go back to London. Go to my flat. See Gina and talk to her. I can't talk to you now."

"I was so worried about Gina!" The unwanted tears now burned my cheeks; I tried to control them but could not. "I was so worried about her . . . and one word from you—*one word* and I wouldn't have had to worry any more."

"There was more involved than you realized," he said abruptly. "A woman was murdered. It was a matter of life and death. All I wanted to do was to keep you out of it—"

"As if you cared!" The harsh words seemed to sear the air between us. I bent my head, turned aside to hide the humiliation of tears. "As if it mattered to you! There's no need to insult me by pretending any further—"

He said, interrupting, his voice hard and angry: "There was no pretense. And no insult. And it mattered more than anything else in the world."

I put my hands over my ears and shook my head as if I could shake his words away. My eyes were dim with pain. I didn't see him move until I felt his arms slip around me and his breath cool against my hot cheek.

"Claire—"

"Let me go!" I twisted away from him. The pain was so excruciating that I could no longer think clearly; my movements were instinctive. I ran from him, stumbling down the path to

the road, and although I would have turned back in a flash
if he had called my name he said nothing and I knew then
that he was relieved to see me go.

I was so upset that I forgot the car. My eyes, blind with
tears, never even saw it as I stumbled past. I went downhill,
down the road without knowing or caring where I was going.
All I was aware of was the blurred brilliant green of the beech
trees overhead and the patterns of light made by the sun as its
shafts pierced the leaves and slanted across the road.

After a while I stopped running and slowed to a walk. My
breath was coming in short gasps and there was an ache in
my side. I stopped, bent double to rid myself of the pain, and
then because it was easier to sit down than to straighten my
back and go on again, I collapsed on the bank by the road. I
sat there for a long time. No one came. Nothing happened.
Occasionally a bird sang and once far away I heard the faint
hum of an airplane.

At last I thought: how absurd to be so upset over a man I
met less than a week ago! How unnecessary! I had behaved
like an infatuated adolescent, imagining myself in the midst
of a whirlwind love affair. The excitement of traveling to
strange countries combined with the strain of Gina's disappearance had made me momentarily lose touch with reality.
However, now I could begin to act like a reasonable, rational
adult once again. I could be critical once more, cool, dispassionate and practical. Love at first sight was for the magazines,
or for people like Gina whose personalities acted as a magnet
to the opposite sex. Fairytale romances were for those with
their heads in the clouds. As for me, I had my feet firmly on
the ground, and fairytales no longer appealed to me.

I stood up. My legs felt weak and unsteady but I set off
walking again. I passed the gates of Holmbury House and
presently found myself on an open stretch of hillside covered
with ferns and heather. Before me, stretching mistily into the
horizon was a sweeping view of fields, trees and the faint out-
line of hills in the distance. The sun shone. The countryside
was beautiful. And because it was so beautiful I felt over-
whelmingly aware of the stark ugliness of my grief. Tears

sprang to my eyes again, and before I could stop myself I was crying, fumbling ineffectually for a handkerchief.

I sat down again by the roadside.

Perhaps it would be better if I admitted I was in love and stopped telling myself I was behaving like an adolescent. I found the handkerchief, blew my nose, pressed a hand to my aching forehead. I felt physically ill. Later, perhaps, I could chalk the entire episode up to experience and resume the comforting dullness of my normal life, but now I found it was impossible for me to be so detached.

The pain of loss was intolerable.

I thought of my lonely little apartment high above Manhattan, the evenings spent alone, the days exhausted trying to teach girls a subject most of them were not interested in learning. My safe, secure, peaceful life! I had never realized before how empty it had been.

I stood up desperately as the present reached out long fingers to taint the past and blur the future. It was as if I had no future, no past, as if my present were as fleeting and yet as horrifying as a nightmare from which there was no escape. I was nothing suddenly. I looked around wildly, praying that I would see someone I could speak to, someone whom I could use to regain my grip on reality and check the disintegration of my world, and as I glanced across the open hillside to the road below I saw a green convertible emerge into view and begin its toil up the road towards me.

I waited.

The car drew nearer. As it approached me I saw it lose speed and the next moment it had halted beside me and the driver was pulling down the window.

"Claire!" exclaimed Eric Jantzen in astonishment. "Well, this is certainly a surprise! What are you doing down here in Surrey?"

Since I had forgotten that Garth and Lilian were entertaining French clients at the cottage that weekend, I was almost as surprised to see him as he was to see me. Just as I was foggily trying to invent a reply he said anxiously: "Is something wrong?"

"No," I said. I couldn't think of anything else to say.

"You've still not heard from Gina?"

"I haven't seen her at all." That much was true.

He shook his head in sympathy. "You look tired," he said kindly. "Everything must be a great strain for you at present. Would you like some coffee, perhaps? Or some tea? I'm just on my way to Garth's cottage, which is very near here, and I'm sure he wouldn't mind if you dropped in for a while. My wife and Garth are entertaining French clients over the weekend, and on those occasions I usually spend the weekend at the cottage too. However, they won't be there yet—they had to go to the airport this morning to meet the plane from Paris.

"They will all drive down here after lunch."

I stared at him blankly. I must have looked mentally deficient. "Oh," I said at last.

This was hardly a sparkling reply, but it seemed to encourage him to reiterate his invitation. "Let me make you some coffee! Please—you look so tired! The cottage isn't far from here, less than a mile—"

I thought in panic: I can't see Garth again. I couldn't possibly face him a second time. And then in confusion: Garth's secretary told me Lilian came down to the cottage last night to prepare everything for the weekend. Garth must have come instead, and Lilian must have gone to the airport to meet the clients. But why doesn't Eric know this? Why does he expect them both to be at the airport?

"Thank you very much," I heard myself say falteringly, "but I don't think I feel like coffee just now." I felt suddenly possessed with a desire to escape, and as soon as the notion crossed my mind I remembered that I had arrived at Garth's house in a car and that there was no escape until I went back to get it. "I—I wonder," I said stammering, "—if you could give me a lift to the cottage? It seems—I mean, I think I've left my car there."

He looked at me first in bewilderment and then sharply in speculation. I sensed he wanted to know why I had been at the cottage and what had happened to reduce me to a state in which I was capable only of producing a series of curious remarks. "Why, of course!" he said with reserve, his eyes watchful. "Jump in!"

He leaned over and opened the door of the passenger seat
for me. As the car moved on up the road he said to me with an
attempt to recapture his air of joviality: "You really should
tell me what's been happening, you know! You don't seem to
be yourself at all. What's been going on at the cottage?"

"Nothing," I said. "I thought Gina might be there but I was
wrong. I walked away from my car down the road wondering
what I should do next. I'm feeling more and more distressed
with every hour that passes."

"Why, yes," he murmured, his eyes on the road. "Yes, I can
understand that. It must be most upsetting."

The car purred on up the hill. We passed the houses, passed
the sign which pointed to Peaslake and moved on along the
twisting road to the cottage.

"Do you have a key?" I said suddenly.

"Oh yes," he said. "We all have a key. Occasionally, if
Garth's abroad, he lends us the cottage for weekends. He and
Lilian do a certain amount of business entertaining here as
well. It's very useful to them."

I was just opening my mouth to tell him that Garth wasn't
at the airport after all when we rounded the last bend and
the cottage came into sight.

I gasped. The words died on my lips.

"What's the matter?" said Eric swiftly. "What is it?"

"I—thought my car had a flat tire," I said faintly. "But that
was a trick of the light. There's nothing wrong."

But I was lying. The shock I had received was not on account of my car, which still stood beneath the trees, but because there was no longer any sign of the creamy white
Jaguar.

Garth had vanished.

"Are you sure you won't stop for coffee?" said Eric again,
parking his car where Garth had left the Jaguar earlier. "It
wouldn't be any trouble at all."

I was too dazed to argue further. I found the idea of coffee
more than welcome, and now that Garth had gone there was
no reason for me to refuse to enter the cottage. "Well, perhaps

I'll change my mind," I said awkwardly. "Thank you very much."

I began to wonder where Garth had gone. If he had returned to Holmbury village he would have passed me on the road. I decided that for some reason or other he had driven on over the hill to Peaslake—perhaps to buy extra food from the shops there. As we walked up to the front door and Eric produced a key I started to feel nervous in case Garth returned from Peaslake before I had finished my coffee and left the cottage.

"Come in," said Eric, opening the door and standing back to allow me to cross the threshold before him.

There was no hall. The front door opened into a long, light living room with picture windows which faced the view across the valley below. There was a staircase to my right, and on the left were two other doors which I guessed led into the kitchen and dining room.

"Nice, isn't it?" said Eric genially from behind me. He spoke with the satisfaction of an owner, not a mere guest. "It's very restful here after London."

The room was filled with antiques. I noticed the Regency chairs and couch, the long carved oak chest along one wall, the grandfather clock by the stairs.

"It *is* nice," I said absently. "What a pity the house is modern and not an old-fashioned cottage to go with the old-fashioned furniture."

"You say that because you're American," he said. "We Europeans have no fond illusions about little old-fashioned cottages with damp in the walls and woodworm in the roof and icy drafts from ill-fitting windows in the winter." He waved a hand vaguely towards the couch. "Sit down—make yourself at home. I'll get the coffee."

I sat down while he disappeared into the kitchen, but presently I stood up again and wandered over to the door next to the kitchen. As I had guessed earlier, it led into a dining room. There was a china closet full of beautiful English china, and opposite it a corner cupboard filled with the most elegant glasses I had ever seen. Unable to resist the temptation I opened the cabinet and took out a glass. The stem was so slender that I thought it would break in my hands, and the rim of the glass was as thin as paper. An engraved design ran lightly round the delicate edge. Putting the glass back hastily before such fragile beauty could splinter into fragments in my hands, I closed the cupboard door and wandered back into the living room.

"Eric, is there a bathroom on this floor?"

"No," he called. "It's upstairs. Second door on the left."

I moved slowly up the stairs. I was thinking of Garth again, wondering what he was doing, when he would be back. I began to hurry automatically. I must not stay in the house more than ten minutes. Then I must leave, drive away in the car, never see the cottage again . . .

I reached the landing and found I could no longer remember Eric's directions to the bathroom. All the doors were closed. I stared at them absently for a moment. Second door on the right? No, he had said the left. The second door? The third door on the left? I wandered down the tiny passage, opened the door, and walked straight into a closet containing a bundle of old clothes. Checking an exclamation of annoyance I was just turning away when I realized that the bundle of old clothes on the floor was not quite that.

I stopped, looked again . . .

My scalp prickled. Horror made the breath freeze in my throat. For one long moment I stood stock still staring down at that dreadful heap on the floor, and then rapidly, hardly aware of what I was doing, I bent down, pulled aside the old coat on top of the pile and found myself inches from a woman's face distorted by violent death. At first I didn't recognize her, and then . . .

It was Lilian Jantzen.

# NINE

It seemed that I stood there motionless for a long time with my mind paralyzed by fright, and then slowly, mechanically I closed the door and leaned against it. I wanted to move, but as in all the most appalling nightmares, the paralysis of shock made movement impossible. After a hiatus which may have lasted no longer than thirty seconds but which seemed to last at least thirty minutes, I managed to step across the passage and blunder into the room opposite. I found myself in the bedroom and facing a picture window much like the one in the living room directly below me. It was now raining outside. Snarls of water spat against the enormous windowpane and trickled impotently down the glass to the sill.

It was very quiet.

I thought: whoever killed Lilian killed Thérèse as well, and who else could have killed them other than Garth or Eric; Warren might just conceivably have killed Thérèse but he couldn't have killed Lilian. Lilian must have been killed either last night, if she really did come down to the cottage then to prepare for the weekend, or else earlier this morning, and Warren has been with me since yesterday evening . . . or did he slip out last night after I had gone to bed? But no, that was before we hired the car, and without transportation how could he have made his way out here? So either Garth or Eric killed Lilian. And either Garth or Eric killed Thérèse.

I was so stupefied with the enormity of the realization that for a moment my mind refused to go further. I kept saying to myself: either Garth or Eric killed Lilian; either Garth or Eric killed Thérèse, and yet the simple question: which one? was something my mind refused to phrase. But suddenly I remembered something. If Gina was staying at Garth's flat she could give him an alibi for the previous evening. He could not have killed Lilian this morning since the house had been empty on my first visit and the body was too stiff to allow for the possibility that Garth had killed her on his arrival less than two hours ago . . .

I had to speak to Gina. If she could tell me that Garth had spent the previous evening with her I would know for certain that he was innocent.

There was a phone extension next to the bed. After fumbling dizzily in my purse for the number I picked up the receiver with shaking fingers and dialed O for the operator.

The line purred three times. Then: "Operator," said a pleasant voice into my ear.

"I wonder if you can help me," I said in a low rapid voice. "I'm trying to get through to a London number—Mayfair 75432. Could you try it for me, please?"

"Mayfair 75432? One moment." The line clicked and she was gone.

I waited. And waited.

"Trying to connect you," said the voice.

I went on waiting. My heart was bumping painfully against my lungs. My palms were so damp that the receiver slipped and almost fell from my fingers.

"Trying to connect you," said the voice again.

It was not until then that I remembered the code Gina and Garth had established with telephone calls.

"I'm sorry," said the operator kindly, "but there's no reply."

"Wait," I said unevenly. "Please ring twice, then hang up, then ring again. Please."

In Britain perhaps they are more accustomed to eccentrics than they are in America. I could just imagine the smart retort I would have received from a New York operator if I had made the same request.

"One moment, please," said the voice placidly, and I heard her begin to dial again.

Maybe my request had provided her with an interesting variation in routine. I heard the bell ring twice at the other end of the wire, then a silence. Finally the bell began to ring again, but Gina hardly waited for it to ring once. There was a click as she picked up the receiver.

"Hello?"

"Go ahead, caller—"

"Gina, it's me. Listen, I can't talk. Just tell me one thing. Where was Garth last night?"

"Garth?" said Gina puzzled. "Last night? Why, he was here! He bought some groceries and I fixed him dinner. He was tired and went to bed early. Why?"

"Get off the line," I said rapidly. "Call the police. Lilian Jantzen's been murdered and her body is hidden in Garth's cottage. Get the police at once."

I heard her gasp. "I'll call them right away," she said and hung up.

I listened to the empty line for a second longer, too mesmerized by my knowledge even to replace the receiver in its cradle. Garth was innocent. And downstairs, alone with me in the house—

From somewhere far away on the dead line I heard a low stealthy click.

I froze.

Eric Jantzen had been listening in downstairs on the living room phone.

The receiver fell out of my hands and clattered on to the table. I could not breathe, speak or move. And then as I stood there in a paralysis of panic I heard his soft measured footsteps coming slowly up the stairs towards me.

I managed to move. I crossed the room, my feet making no noise on the thick carpet, and opened the door. He was at the top of the stairs. When I came out into the passage he stopped. We faced each other.

I thought: if I could edge towards the bathroom, I could lock myself in . . .

But he moved forward towards me and I stepped back into the bedroom.

"Rather rash of you, wasn't it?" he said, still determined to sound jovial. His little eyes, narrow above his fleshy cheeks, were empty of expression. He moved like an automaton, steadily, with precision.

I backed away until I was against the picture window and could retreat no more.

He stopped. "The police will arrest Garth," he said. "You must realize that. All the evidence points towards Garth."

"Yes," I said. Garth must come back soon from his expedition to Peaslake. I had an advantage in that I knew Garth was nearby while Eric thought he was still in London. If I could keep Eric talking until Garth arrived—

"But you don't believe Garth killed Lilian, do you?" he said. "That's why you phoned your sister. She was able to give him an alibi."

I said, playing for time, "The alibi was for last night. He could have killed her this morning."

"And the police will find out she wasn't killed this morning," he said. "I killed her last night, here at the cottage."

There was a silence. After a while I managed to say: "I don't understand."

"I was justified in killing her," he said as if this explained everything. "It was no more than she deserved. She was a murderess."

I stared at him. He found a handkerchief, mopped his face, and I saw for the first time that he was profoundly moved.

"She killed Thérèse," he said. "My wife killed another woman. My wife. Lilian. She was a cheat and a fraud and a murderess."

He was crying openly now. As I watched him with mingled horror and pity, he twisted his handkerchief in his hands. Presently when he was able to speak again he said: "Lilian said it was an accident that Thérèse died, but I don't think it was. I think she meant to kill her. Thérèse knew vital—damaging facts—"

"About Lilian."

"About Lilian. Lilian had swindled Garth out of ten thousand pounds last year by pretending the company owed more to the Inland Revenue than it actually did. Lilian did the books, filed the tax returns; two years ago she had got into debt by trying to expand the business still further, handling contracts which were a little too big to handle. Money was lost, and the profits were low that year. But she had expected the profits to be higher and she had already spent her share . . . she needed money, and as time passed the need for money became pressing. So she cheated. She took money which should have been split between herself and Garth. She could have taken out a loan—borrowed the money—something—but no, she had to cheat. 'If I borrowed there would be so much money wasted in interest,' she said. 'Money that could be put into the business.' She was quite ruthless where the business was concerned. She wouldn't listen to reason. 'Garth will never know,' she said. 'He always leaves the books to me. He'll never find out.' So she took the money and cheated him and laid herself open to blackmail."

After a moment I said: "But how did Thérèse know that Lilian had cheated Garth?"

"I told her," he said simply.

There was a silence. Everything was very still.

"It was like this," he said suddenly. "Thérèse was an ally, a friend. She wanted to break up any attachment existing between Garth and Lilian as much as I did, and she was convinced that an attachment existed. Three months ago she followed them when they went to a conference in Paris—they were both staying at Garth's *pied-à-terre* . . . well, we needn't go into that. Thérèse saw me afterwards and expected me to make some sort of scene with Lilian. She didn't know that Lilian wouldn't have cared if I had. Lilian wanted to leave me. She's had no use for me now for some time."

Tears furrowed his face again, and the rain wept with him, hurling itself against the windowpane.

"But I loved her," he said. "I was prepared to do anything to prevent her from leaving. When Thérèse asked me why I would not fight with Lilian over the episode with Garth in Paris, I told her the truth—that Lilian would have welcomed the chance to be rid of me and that to make a scene would have been pointless. I told Thérèse that the only reason I managed to keep Lilian living under the same roof with me was because I knew she had cheated Garth and I threatened to tell him so unless she stayed with me as my wife."

"What did Thérèse say?"

"Nothing—then. Oh, she probably had a row with Garth but she didn't approach Lilian. That came later." He stopped. "Last Saturday," he said painfully. "Less than a week ago. Last Saturday she stormed into our flat when I was out and Lilian was there alone, and told Lilian that she would make trouble for her unless she left Garth alone. She had had a row with Garth earlier, she said. She told Lilian that Garth was pretending to be interested in a young American girl who had arrived with him the previous evening from Paris, but that she herself wasn't deceived for a moment; Garth's interest in Gina was merely a smokescreen to conceal his interest in Lilian. Thérèse told me the same thing when I had seen her the previous evening; after she had met Garth and Gina at London airport she phoned and asked to see me, and when I met her she told me exactly what was on her mind. And I agreed with her. Gina wasn't Garth's type. I too believed that he was merely using her as a smokescreen.

"I saw Thérèse on Friday night. Early Saturday evening she had a showdown with Garth at her flat and then, still not satisfied, she came to our flat and saw Lilian herself. It was then that she told Lilian that unless she kept her hands off Garth, Thérèse would tell both Garth and the Fraud Squad that Lilian had cheated him out of a considerable sum of money. It was the worst thing she could possibly have said. Lilian lived for her business—it was husband, child, lover, everything to her. She had started it, built it up, nurtured it to success. Where the business was concerned she was fanatical—irrational. She would do anything to protect it. And then along came Thérèse talking of the Fraud Squad, criminal proceedings, the business's reputation smeared beyond repair. . . .

"I don't know what happened next. Lilian said she and Thérèse came to blows and Thérèse accidentally slipped and struck her head and died. But I don't think the death was so accidental as that. I think Lilian deliberately killed her. . . . But there was Thérèse—dead—killed either by accident or design—and in our flat!

"When I came in half an hour afterwards Lilian had dragged the body to the spare bedroom and locked the door. She was more distraught than I had ever seen her look before. She told me what had happened and said I must help her, and it was then suddenly that I saw what I could do; I promised to help her get rid of the body if she would agree to give our marriage a completely new start, never see Garth except at the office and allow me to come with her on all her business trips with him.

"She said she would. She promised. She swore she would do everything I said. So I went out again, to a place I knew down by the river in Pimlico where they sell second-hand trunks and suitcases. Lilian said she must establish an alibi—she rang up a friend, suggested they go to the cinema together. I left her while she was still talking on the phone . . . I had completely forgotten that a few hours before, at lunch, I had invited Gina to call at the flat for a drink that evening. The thought of Gina never even crossed my mind.

"I couldn't find a trunk at that hour—all the shops were shut, even the one I had thought of in Pimlico, and so I decided I would have to use one of Lilian's large suitcases instead. I went back to the flat, and not realizing that Lilian had already left for the cinema, I called out to tell her that I hadn't been able to find a trunk for the body and that we'd have to use a large suitcase. When there was no reply I realized she had left. I set to work at once, found the suitcase, managed to shut the lid with the body inside. Then when everything was ready I took the case out to the car and drove down to Holmbury St. Mary. I thought that if I buried the body in the garden of the cottage no one would come across it, and if the grave was discovered, they would suspect Garth and not us. Garth never bothered with the garden, although sometimes he talked vaguely of hiring a gardener—I thought there was a good chance he wouldn't stroll to the bottom of the garden till the weeds had grown over the grave again.

"When everything was finished at the cottage I went back to London to the flat. Lilian had returned from the cinema and was waiting for me. She said: 'How did you get rid of Gina when you got back from Pimlico?' I didn't know what she meant. And then I remembered that I had told Gina to come by for a drink. 'I let her in,' Lilian said. 'Didn't she wait for you to come back?' And I realized that Gina might have been there when I called out to Lilian to tell her I couldn't find a trunk for the body—she might have been hiding nearby when I had put the body in the suitcase. We talked it over, Lilian and I. It was possible Gina hadn't bothered to wait for me and had left before I returned, but we had to make sure. We tried to find her—and couldn't. She had disappeared. Vanished. There was no trace of her."

"Garth was hiding her," I said shakily. "I found that out today."

"Garth's a clever actor. He had us both convinced he hadn't set eyes on the girl since last Saturday, when we all had lunch together. At least he had me convinced. Lilian . . ." He broke off, staring into nothingness, his mind abstracted and remote from me.

I hardly dared breathe for fear of interrupting his train of thought and reminding him of my existence in the room. I wanted to ask why he had killed Lilian but I let the silence linger on unbroken as the rain swept across the hillside from the valley below.

"The police came later," he said after a while. "We heard then about the hysterical phone call Gina had made to you. The police found nothing at the flat, but we knew then that we had to find Gina somehow. She was dangerous to us. We wondered if she would go to the police but Lilian thought not. The police might have thought Gina and Thérèse had quarreled over Garth and Gina would be a chief suspect if inquiries were made into Thérèse's murder."

I waited, my body aching with tension, and as I watched him he raised his eyes slowly and looked at me. I said quickly, seizing the first subject which came to mind: "I don't understand why Lilian died."

"Because she broke her word," he said. "After all I did for her—after I had disposed of the body and managed to conceal her crime—after all that she broke her promise. She promised she would give up Garth altogether and give our marriage a fresh start, but she didn't mean it. This so-called 'business weekend' here at the cottage was fictitious—there were no clients expected to arrive in London on the Friday morning

plane. I had a hunch she was lying to me and I called Rémy
International in France to check whether the two men were
due in England this weekend. I was told that they weren't. As
soon as I found this out last night I drove down here to the
cottage—Lilian had arrived here earlier, supposedly to prepare
everything for the visitors. When I got here she pretended to
be astonished—she denied everything—said I was out of my
mind. . . ." He stopped. Then: "Out of my mind," he repeated, as if amazed by his own choice of phrase. "She said I
was out of my mind . . . I told her I knew very well she had
merely planned a weekend with Garth, but she wouldn't admit it. She went on lying—on and on. . . . And then suddenly
there were no more lies, only silence. It was a terrible blank
silence. Afterwards I was so upset that I panicked and rushed
away back to London—I only stopped long enough to push
the body in the cupboard and then I drove and drove all along
those twisting country roads. It was all so dark and still and
silent. . . .

"This morning I managed to pull myself together. I knew I
must drive down again to the cottage and bury the body. I
must pretend to be normal, act as though nothing had happened. That was why when I stopped to talk to you I invited
you here for coffee—I was so anxious to appear normal, as if
nothing was wrong. But why did *you* come down here? Why
were you so shaken? I seemed to sense you suspected me.
When you made the excuse to go upstairs I thought: supposing
she wanted the excuse to search the house? And you were gone
such a long time. . . . Then I heard the faint ring the phone
makes whenever the extension in the bedroom is used, and I
knew what must have happened."

"I wanted to ask my sister where Garth was last night."

"But why should she have known? Where was Garth hiding
her anyway?"

"In his apartment," I said.

He stared at me. "She had been with him in his apartment
all this week?"

In a flash I saw how I could catch him off balance. "Why do
you think Gina came to London with him from Paris?" I said.
"Gina was infatuated with him. You were wrong in suspecting

your wife was involved. It was Gina, not Lilian who was infatuated."

He went on staring at me. "But this business weekend which proved to be non-existent—"

"Rémy International must have misinformed you. Garth's secretary confirmed the appointment when I spoke to her earlier today."

After a long silence he whispered: "I don't believe it."

"Well, you didn't believe Lilian," I said, "so there's no reason why you should believe me. But I think Lilian was telling the truth. Besides, I don't think Garth would have been interested in an illicit weekend with her. He had other fish to fry."

"I don't believe it," he repeated. "I don't believe it." He was very white. I saw him begin to tremble as he half turned away from me, and then he was struck dumb as he began to realize what I was suggesting . . . he had killed his wife for an infidelity which had existed only in his imagination.

I moved. I darted across the room, tried to push past him into the passage beyond, but he caught me by the wrist, jerked me back into the room. I struggled wildly but he was much too strong for me, and although I screamed and screamed for help no one came.

I was powerless, frantic with terror. I tried to scream again in one last desperate burst of strength but his fingers closed around my throat and the scream died on my lips. The room tilted, swirled before my eyes, and as the blood started to sing in my ears I knew dimly that all was lost and that there was nothing more I could do.

# TEN

The pressure eased very suddenly. There was a roaring in my ears but gradually that too ceased. I found I could see again. I was on the floor, the carpet grazing my knuckles, and as I struggled to my feet I saw Eric was standing a few feet away from me, his eyes staring at the doorway.

I turned my head slowly, frowning at the pain, my mind clouded with shock, my whole being numbed with incomprehension, and found myself looking at a black, ugly automatic. The automatic was held by a strong firm hand and looked as if it were comfortably at home there.

"Are you all right, Claire?" It was Garth's voice.

It was too painful to nod and my own voice seemed to have disappeared. I managed to stand up but immediately sat down again on the edge of the bed.

"Did he hurt you?"

"Well, of course he hurt me!" Shock made me unreasonably angry. "Where the hell were you? Why did you go away? I was nearly killed!"

"Whose idea was it for you to come back here?" he asked mildly. "Not mine! God Almighty, you almost *were* murdered!" He swung back to Eric. "We'll go downstairs. You can lead the way. Clasp your hands behind your head. I don't want to have any accidents in transit."

Eric moved blindly out into the passage.

"Come on, Claire."

"Don't you order me about!" I stormed. And then, stammering: "I—I'm sorry—I'm not myself—"

"I understand." He waited for me by the doorway, his eyes

still watching the other man, but when I reached him, he took my hand in his and held it for a moment. "All right, Eric. Move on."

It was then I saw that the door of the adjacent room was open and what looked like a portable tape recorder playing silently just beyond the threshold.

"Switch that off, would you, Claire? Just pull the plug out of the wall but don't touch the machine."

I mechanically did as I was told. My mind refused even to try to reconstruct what had happened, but I was dimly aware that Garth must have somehow managed to record most, if not all, of my conversation with Eric in the bedroom. We went downstairs.

"Stand right there, Eric, and don't move. You can put your hands down. Claire, I'd advise you to have a shot of brandy. There's a bottle under the sideboard over there and a glass in the dining room."

He went to the phone, the gun still in his right hand, and removed the receiver with his left. Putting down the receiver on the table he began to dial, still using his left hand.

He dialed nine-nine-nine.

"Police, please." He saw me still standing motionless by the dining room door. "Please, Claire—get the brandy and sit down! You look—hello? Police? My name is Cooper and I'm speaking from Coneyhurst Cottage on Holmbury Hill—it's the last cottage before Peaslake on the Holmbury-Peaslake road. Could you come over here at once, please? A woman's been murdered."

I went into the dining room in a daze and tried to find a glass which I wouldn't be afraid of breaking but all the glasses were the fragile collector's items which I had noticed earlier; my fingers were still so unsteady that I was convinced I would drop any glass I touched, so at last in despair I went to the kitchen and took a cup from the cupboard.

Garth had just hung up when I emerged into the living room once more with the cup in my hand. "Good God, you can't drink Courvoisier out of a teacup!"

"It's a receptacle, isn't it?" I said doggedly. "What can prevent me drinking out of it if I want to?"

It showed the measure of our shock that we were so ready to argue over trivialities.

Eric said he wanted to sit down.

"All right. Take that chair over there."

"I'd like a drink too," he added.

Garth motioned me to pour one for him. Then he said harshly: "How can you be so calm, Eric? If I hadn't been in the house you would have killed Claire, too."

"No . . . no, it was just that I—I suddenly saw—realized—"

"That I wasn't and never had been interested in having an affair with your cold, clever, crooked wife? That you had killed her for nothing?"

Eric said stumbling: "It was such a shock . . . I was overcome . . . I wanted to kill her for telling me, showing me the truth—"

"If you had had an ounce of sense you'd never have listened to Thérèse. Good God, you could have had your wife and good luck to you! Couldn't you guess I could hardly wait to get enough capital behind me to work my way out of the partnership? Did you ever really think I was the kind of man who enjoyed answering to a woman and being told by her what to do the whole damned time? Lilian was still the boss, you know, even though we were officially partners. It was she who had picked me out from the obscure ranks of all the salesmen in London and selected me to work for her—and, my God, she never let me forget it! I was grateful to her and glad of the opportunities she gave me but I got pretty damned tired of playing second fiddle day in, day out, year after year—"

"Then why did you stay with her?"

"I very nearly didn't! We had our quarrels and disagreements, but I knew I could never make so much money so quickly elsewhere and I wanted more than anything else to amass capital, be independent. But unlike you I don't expect my wife to support me while I indulge in unprofitable speculation. When I marry we'll live on my money, not on my wife's."

"Lilian understood—"

"She understood nothing but the business! And cared for nothing but the business! And you know that as well as I do.

Just because you had the misfortune to be in love with her, don't make the mistake of assuming she also knew what love meant. Maybe she did once, long ago, when you first knew her, but certainly I never once caught a glimpse of understanding in her. She wasn't interested in love! She didn't care—not for you, not for anyone. She was narrow-minded and cold and utterly selfish. If you hadn't been so unbalanced as to try to strangle Claire just now I'd feel you were justified in murdering Lilian, and I wouldn't be aiming this gun at you at all."

"I didn't mean to harm Claire—I was overwhelmed—dazed—"

"You did mean to harm her. You put your hands deliberately round her throat and equally deliberately tried to throttle her into unconsciousness."

"I didn't know what I was doing—"

"Tell that to the police, not to me. I might become 'overwhelmed' and 'dazed' too and feel an uncontrollable urge to pull the trigger."

There was heavy silence. At last Garth said to me: "How are you feeling now?"

"Better." I gripped the cup tightly but my fingers were still trembling. "Where did you go after I left here?"

"Nowhere. I drove the car up to the top of the hill and hid it in the bushes. Then I walked back and prepared to set up my tape recorder. I'd found Lilian dead when I arrived earlier, but since I was still expecting Eric to turn up I went ahead with my plans to tape a confession. Unfortunately I set the machine up in the living room, which was no use at all when you both moved upstairs to the bedroom. I was forced to come out of the cupboard under the stairs where I'd been hiding and follow you upstairs, tape recorder and all. Fortunately it was reasonably portable.

"I'd been working towards it all week. Eric was right in believing that the business weekend was a fiction, but wrong in assuming Lilian knew it was fictitious. She didn't know. I planned to have a showdown with both the Jantzens, since I believed they were both involved in Thérèse's murder, so I invented the visit of the representatives of Rémy International and paved the way for luring both of them here to the cottage

where Thérèse was buried. I reasoned they would be more
likely to be trapped into an admission out here in a remote
spot, with Thérèse's grave only a few yards away at the end
of the garden."

"No wonder you were so anxious to get rid of me this
morning!"

"Yes, I'd just found Lilian's body and was trying to work
out what I should do next; for all I knew Eric would arrive
any minute—I'm sorry if I was too abrupt but I was worried in
case things went wrong. I'd taken a gamble in not going to the
police. When I heard that Thérèse was dead and that Eric had
taken the body out of the flat to dispose of it, I knew immediately that when the body was found I'd be the number one.
And if the police believed that Gina and I were involved with
one another, Gina would be suspect number two. Thérèse was
jealous, quite capable of initiating disastrous scenes; it was
Gina and I who would immediately come under suspicion if
she were killed, not the Jantzens, who had no such obvious
motive for murdering her. I had a key to the Jantzen apartment and no alibi for Saturday night—to the police that would
all add up to motive, means, and opportunity for committing
the crime. The same applied to Gina—she was actually there
on the scene of the murder, and her presence could be proved
by the phone call she made to New York and your report of
the call to Scotland Yard."

"What did Gina do after she had phoned me that evening?
And why did she hang up so suddenly?"

"She thought she heard the front door opening, but it was a
false alarm—a noise from the flat below. By the time she
realized this she'd already replaced the receiver and cut off
the call. She pulled herself together and saw she had to get
out of the flat at once—she told me she'd panicked as soon as
Eric left with the body, and made the call to you without even
pausing to think what she was doing."

"Yes," I said shakily. "That sounds like Gina."

"However, after cutting herself off from you she left the flat,
found the nearest callbox and dialed my number. I was the
only other person she knew in London. I told her to come over
to my flat at once, and she did. We reasoned that the Jantzens

would work out that she had seen too much, so I decided she must lie low and communicate with nobody. Early the next morning I drove her down here, as I knew the Jantzens intended to be in town all week."

Eric said unexpectedly: "But we checked the cottage! On Monday I drove down here—"

"Gina had left by then—fortunately. Later on Sunday evening she discovered Thérèse's body, just as Claire did this morning. This so unnerved her that she immediately called a taxi and left for Dorking, where she put up at a hotel. She tried to contact me but by that time I'd left for Paris—I had to go for unavoidable business reasons, and besides I was anxious to act normally, as if nothing had happened. Gina nearly wrote to me in Paris but remembered I was returning to London on Wednesday morning and that a letter to Paris might miss me. So she wrote to my home address in London in order that, as soon as I reached home, I would know where she was and where I could contact her. When I heard what had happened I told her to come to my flat in London. I didn't think it was safe for her to stay anywhere else. On my return I began to set the scene for a showdown at the cottage; I knew by then where Thérèse's body was and I thought I could see a way to establish our innocence and prove the Jantzens' guilt."

"How did you find Lilian's body this morning?" I asked.

"I was puzzled because she wasn't here to meet me—we had arranged that she was to come down here last night to get the place ready, and when I arrived I intended to tell her that Rémy International had postponed the visit at the last minute, and to suggest she and Eric have lunch here with me before driving back to town. As soon as Eric arrived I was going to launch into my counsel for the prosecution act for the benefit of the tape recorder. Having planned everything so carefully it gave me a shock to find Lilian wasn't here when I arrived. On an impulse I decided to search the house, and a couple of minutes later I opened the door of the cupboard upstairs and found her."

In the armchair by the fireplace Eric moved. I started nervously, but for nothing. He had merely leaned forward and buried his face in his hands, as if the mention of Lilian's name and the manner of her death were sufficient to remove him from us, a human being cut off and isolated by grief and despair.

I wondered how long the police would take to arrive. Surely by now they must be well on their way! My fingers fidgeted endlessly with the cup in my hands and as I glanced at Eric again I saw him start and look up abruptly.

"What's that noise?"

Garth didn't move. "What noise?"

"I thought I heard a noise in the kitchen—"

"Stay where you are!" Garth had the gun trained on him. His back was to the kitchen door. "You needn't think you can fool me with that kind of trick."

But I was taut once more with nervousness, every muscle in my body aching with tension. I turned to face the kitchen door, the cup slipping in my clammy hands, and to my horror I saw the handle begin to turn.

I screamed.

Garth swung round but he wasn't quick enough. The door was already wide open.

"All right, Cooper," said a cool, tough voice I barely recognized. "Put down that gun."

I stared incredulously, unable to believe what I saw, and found myself face to face with Warren Mayne.

It all happened so quickly that now as I look back I find it hard to recall the scene in any clear detail. I remember crying out something to Warren; I remember Garth, caught off balance, lowering his gun for a moment—and then in a flash, Eric was upon him and they were fighting for the weapon.

Warren shouted something, but neither of them paid him any attention.

"Help him—separate them—" I scarcely knew what I was saying. I darted forward, but before I could reach Garth, Warren said sharply: "Keep back, Claire. Cooper, drop that gun, or I'll—"

"No—no—" My voice rang high-pitched and terrified in my ears.

Garth slipped on the carpet, fell sideways against the table.

The gun jerked out of his hand, spun in the air and thudded dully upon the carpet six inches from Eric's right hand.

For the last time that day, I heard myself scream.

"Right," said Warren busily, moving in as Eric seized the gun. "Now then—"

There was a deafening explosion as Eric pulled the trigger. I smelt acrid smoke, glimpsed the horrified expression on Warren's face, and then just before I fainted I saw the gun fall from Eric's hand and the blood run from his mouth as he lay dying.

# ELEVEN

When I regained consciousness the room was full of police-men and Eric's body was covered with a sheet so that I could no longer see his face. Warren, white and stupefied, was saying helplessly to no one in particular: "But I don't understand. I thought . . ." But he could not even bring himself to say what he had thought. My head ached, my mouth was dry, and some-one was holding me in his arms as if I were a fragile piece of bone china. I stirred, turned fuzzily towards him. I was lying on the Regency couch and my head was propped against his chest.

"Here," he said, "drink this."

Brandy burned my throat again. My brain stirred and I felt more capable of physical movement. A police inspector, seeing that I was conscious, came over and asked me kindly how I felt.

"Almost all right, thank you," I said with an effort. "Good. We'll take a statement from you just as soon as possible and then someone can drive you back home. Now, who did the suicide weapon belong to? Was it yours, Mr. Cooper?"

"Yes, it was."

"May I see your license for it, please? Just a formality, you understand."

"Yes." He rose to his feet, placed some cushions gently under my head and stooped to see that I was comfortable. Our glances met. I smiled shakily, and felt better.

"Now, young man," the inspector was saying paternally to Warren. "I noted you were carrying a gun too. Do you have a license?"

"Well . . . no," said Warren confused. "It's not an English gun. I bought it in Paris. I'm an American citizen."

"Dear me," said the inspector mildly. "Quite an international history. Thank you, Mr. Cooper," he added, glancing at Garth's license and giving it back to him. "Now I think we'll take a few statements. Supposing we start with you, Miss Sullivan —if you're well enough, of course."

I said I was. We went into the dining room and the inspector and I sat down at the table, while a sergeant sat on a chair in the corner with a pencil and notebook. Under the inspector's direction I told my story from start to finish, beginning with Gina's phone call to me the previous Saturday. The inspector listened and nodded sympathetically, for all the world as if he were a family doctor chatting with an old friend who sought advice. In the corner, the sergeant's pencil whispered steadily across the pages of his notebook.

At last, when I had finished and there was nothing left to tell, the inspector thanked me and said he would have one of his men drive me back to the hotel in Dorking.

"I—I'd rather wait for Mr. Cooper," I said awkwardly. "Is it all right if I stay here?"

"Mr. Cooper may be rather a long time, so I wouldn't advise you to wait. If I were you I'd go back to the hotel and rest for a while. Maybe you'd like Mr. Mayne to drive you back? I doubt if we need keep him long."

I had insufficient strength for an argument so I gave in meekly.

"And you'll keep in touch with us, please, if you don't mind," said the inspector cosily. "We'll want you to sign your statement when it's been typed and you've had a chance to read it over."

"Yes," I said. "Yes, of course."

In the living room, someone was taking photographs of the body. More police appeared to have arrived. The house was overflowing with dark blue uniforms. The inspector asked Warren to step into the dining room and as he obeyed uneasily, I looked around for Garth but there was no sign of him. Wandering into the kitchen I looked out of the window and saw him with three policemen at the bottom of the garden by Thérèse's grave.

I sat down on the couch again to wait. After about ten minutes Garth came back into the living room and moved swiftly across the room towards me.

"Is everything all right? Is someone going to drive you back to Dorking?" He glanced with distaste at the body still waiting for the ambulance, as if it were wrong for me to be in the same room as such a macabre object. "I'd drive you back myself but I can't leave till I've given a statement to the police."

"I think Warren will drive me back. The inspector offered to get one of his men to chauffeur us but I said I'd wait." Because I wanted to talk to you, I might have added, but there was no time; Warren chose that moment to emerge from the dining room. He looked older, graver and more careworn than I had ever seen him look before.

"I want to apologize," he said, walking right up to Garth and planting himself on the carpet before him. "I just don't know how to say it. If Jantzen hadn't turned that gun on himself—"

"Quite," said Garth, embarrassed by this naked display of emotion, even though the display was made with obvious sincerity. "But he did. Forget it—it's all over now."

"Yes, but if I hadn't been such a fool and messed everything up—"

"Could you take Claire back to Dorking, please? She's had a tough day and I don't think she should be here a moment longer." He turned towards me; there was an expression in his eyes which made my heart turn over. "I'll be in touch with you."

"Yes—all right, Garth."

"And don't dare jump on the night flight to America."

"No, Garth."

"If you do, I'll be following you on the morning plane."

I could not speak, but managed to smile. There were tears in my eyes. Everything seemed to shine and glitter hazily in the dim artificial light from the ceiling above us.

"Mr. Cooper?" said the inspector's voice politely from behind us. "Perhaps we could take your statement now, sir."

"Yes," said Garth. "Yes, of course."

"Come on, Claire." Warren's hand was on my arm. "Let's get away from here."

I followed him slowly out of the cottage. It was late afternoon, but still raining so hard that it was already twilight. The rain felt cool and refreshing against my cheek.

Warren led the way over to a small blue car which was unfamiliar to me.

"But this isn't the car I came in," I said stupidly.

"No, we'll have the car agency people pick up that one later. This is the car I hired to drive out here after you." He helped me get in, shut the door and went around to the other side to slide into the driver's seat.

"But I told you I'd spoken to Gina in Garth's office," I said, memory returning. "You were all set to go to London. Why didn't you go?"

"I figured you weren't being quite on the level with me." He switched on the engine. "You were acting too oddly and looked too shook up. After you'd left me to go to rest in your room, I called Garth's office to check to see if Gina had been there, and the secretary thought I was some kind of nut. So I went to your room and got no answer when I knocked on the door. That was when I got convinced you hadn't been on the level with me. When I went out into the courtyard and found the car gone it didn't take much brainwork to figure you'd gone off somewhere on your own, and where else would you go but to the cottage? After a bit of difficulty I managed to hire another car and come right on here after you. I couldn't think what you were playing at but I thought it wouldn't do any harm to find out."

"I should have trusted you," I said ashamed. "But the evidence was all against Garth and somehow I wanted to prove to myself that he was innocent before I told you what I'd discovered." I began to tell him how I had found Thérèse's body in its shallow grave, returned much shaken to Dorking, and tried to telephone Garth only to have my call answered by Gina herself. "She told me to join her at once in London," I said. "But I was too stupid to follow her advice. I felt I had to try and see Garth at the cottage and find out what was going on."

"I can't imagine why you were so convinced Garth was innocent," said Warren, interested. "Was that feminine intuition, would you say?"

"Yes," I said wryly. "I guess you could call it that."

We were freewheeling gently down the narrow twisting road and had just passed the spot where I had met Eric earlier. I glanced out across the beautiful view again, but the rain made the landscape misty and the light was too obscure to enable me to see far. "He seems to like you," Warren ventured delicately, after a pause.

"Yes," I admitted.

"I guess he wouldn't have said that bit about following you to America if he'd been interested in Gina."

"I guess not." So that was his point!

"Maybe there never was anything much between him and Gina. Maybe I just read too much into their relationship. Maybe it was all pretty casual after all."

"Maybe."

This seemed to cheer him up. His new, older, more careworn expression lasted until we reached the junction with the main road at Abinger Hammer, and then he hummed gently under his breath all the way to Dorking.

The mist and early darkness made the town look mysterious and ghostly and very old. Not even the twentieth-century traffic could detract from West Street's antiquity, the ancient houses, the little pub built centuries ago, the glimpse of cobbled side streets. We reached the High Street, crawled past modern shops and returned to antiquity as we drove under the arch of the inn and into the courtyard beyond.

"Let's see if we can get something to eat," Warren said. "We're too early for dinner but maybe they have tea."

"I'd like some coffee."

We entered the hotel and wandered through the lounge towards the reception desk. Someone was checking in, someone tall and willowy with familiar blonde hair straying from underneath a preposterous hat. She wore an incredibly ugly

coat, macabre stockings and flat-heeled shoes, and still managed to look beautiful.

Parisian perfume wafted delicately across the lobby towards
us.

Warren and I simultaneously opened our mouths, but she
turned before we could speak and smiled her radiant, dazzling
smile as she caught sight of us.

"Darlings!" she exclaimed tremulously. "How utterly wonderful to see you both again! I'm *so* sorry you've had such trouble finding me . . ."

"You won't believe it," said Gina, "but none of this would
have happened if I hadn't been so inquisitive. You remember
Miss Stick, our old Sunday school teacher back home? She
always used to tell Mother that my curiosity would be my undoing, and she was so right. It was."

It was an hour later. After our confused, disjointed reunion
in the lobby of the hotel, and my discovery that when the inspector had been interviewing me Garth had called Gina to
tell her it was safe for her to come out of hiding, we had spent
some time talking in one of the lounges before I had excused
myself to go upstairs to my room. Gina had followed me ten
minutes later and was now reclining gracefully on the end of
my bed while I, propped up against the pillows, had slipped
back into my rôle of guide, philosopher and friend.

"You mean," I said dryly, "that your curiosity was the sole
reason for your so-called undoing?"

"The sole reason," said Gina with conviction. "Honestly.
You see, there I was—in the Jantzen apartment on Saturday
night and waiting for Eric to arrive to have a drink with me as
he'd promised, and to tell me all about Dino di Lasci and the
Italian film scene and all the rest of it, and Lilian had just excused herself and rushed off somewhere, and there I was—all
alone with nothing to do except to wonder what Garth's relationship with Lilian was (and you must admit, darling, it
was rather *peculiar* to think of a man like Garth working with
a woman on an earnest businesslike plane, especially as Lilian
was rather attractive in a cosy maternal sort of way) and—"
She lost her way in the labyrinthine sentence, drew a breath

and started again. "So I thought I'd just have a tiny peep around the apartment. Not a big snoop or anything, but just a little peep—"

"What were you expecting to find?" I said with interest. "Love letters, half burned in the grate? Compromising photographs?"

"Well, not *exactly* . . . I'm not really sure what I expected to find, but I just thought it might be interesting and I had nothing else to do—"

"So you went and looked around and while you were out of sight Eric opened the front door and called out to Lilian that he hadn't been able to get a trunk for the body."

"So you know already," said Gina disappointed. "Yes, I guess you would by now. But darling, can you imagine! I was in the master bedroom, and after he said that, I couldn't even move, let alone speak. And then I thought he was going to come into the bedroom! I hid behind the door and watched through the crack, and he opened the door of the room opposite which must have been some kind of spare room and then I saw it—the body, I mean—and of course I recognized it at once because Thérèse had made an awful scene at the airport when Garth and I had arrived the night before. Well, naturally I was just stiff with fright. I couldn't do anything except watch. He got a suitcase out of the closet and—no, I can't even talk about it. It was so awful. Finally after hours and hours—minutes really, I guess—he went out with the suitcase and I was alone again. Then I kind of went mad. I wanted to scream and couldn't. I nearly ran out of the apartment and then I thought that if he came back for something he'd forgotten we'd meet in the elevator, so I forced myself to stay in the apartment for a few minutes. But I was so terrified I felt I had to talk to someone—anyone—but preferably—"

"Me," I said.

"But Claire, you're always so marvelously cool and sane and well balanced—"

"So well balanced I shut my eyes and dived right in to share all the fun."

"Well, of course I was horrified when I tried to call you back later and found I couldn't get through. As I told you on the phone, I called back twice later on Saturday night from Garth's apartment and the line was busy each time—"

"I was calling Scotland Yard and having your call traced."

"I meant to call again on Sunday but Garth drove me down to the cottage to hide and I found the grave in the garden—heavens! I was in such a state after that that I couldn't even make a phone call. Finally on Monday I tried again—and got no reply—"

"I was en route to Paris by then."

"Then Garth said he'd found you in Paris! Honestly, Claire, I could have wept. When I thought of all that money you must have spent—on a wild goose chase! And all because I'd been so selfish and dragged you in without even *thinking*—"

"All's well that ends well," I said mundanely. "At least I had a trip to Europe."

"I don't think all's well that ends well at all," Gina objected. "You won't be able to buy your little red car—"

I remembered vaguely that at one time the idea of possessing a car had seemed important.

"—I missed several important modeling dates. Warren has probably lost his job by taking off without proper permission to come and look for me. . . . By the way, wasn't it sweet of him to go to all that trouble? There's something terribly *comforting* about Warren. When he says he'll move heaven and earth you know he probably will—you know he's not just saying it to sound impressive. When I saw him with you in the lobby I felt a lump in my throat. After all, it's marvelous to know someone cares *that* much."

"Hm," I said.

"And you know, Claire, to be absolutely honest and frank with you and to tell the complete truth—"

"Please do."

"I was a little disappointed in Garth. He was *so* glamorous in Paris! Yet when I was forced to share his apartment with him I found I was bored. Isn't that terrible? But it was true. I thought it would be so romantic to have him hiding me and to be forced to live at close quarters with him for a few days, but the odd thing was that he seemed to lose all interest in romance. Of course, I realize he had a lot on his mind, but . . .

well, never mind. But even when he was at home and resting he just liked to read and listen to Beethoven quartets or something. There wasn't even a television. I did my best not to be a nuisance—I fixed him meals and cleaned every room until it looked like something out of an advertisement, but . . . well, nothing happened. I'm sure if it had been Warren—"

"Yes," I said. "Warren's much more suitable for you."

"You told me all along I should marry him, didn't you?"

"I do remember mentioning it now and then—"

"I think I will. I feel after all this that I just want to settle down and be an ordinary housewife and have six children."

"Wait till that feeling's passed," I couldn't help saying anxiously, "and then see if you still want to marry him. After all—"

There was a knock on the door. Gina swept across the room to answer it.

"Warren!"

"Gina!"

They faced each other starry-eyed. I swung my legs off the bed and went over to study the view from the window. Outside it was dark and still raining and the town lights were blurred as I stared out into the night.

"By the way, Warren," I said suddenly without turning to face him. "Why didn't you tell me you'd been in England last weekend?"

"Last weekend?" echoed Gina. "In England? Were you, Warren?"

I glanced round. He was looking sheepish. "How did you find out?"

"I saw the stamps in your passport. Why didn't you tell me you'd been in London?"

"I," he blushed. "I guess I acted stupidly. I was worried about Gina . . . and I didn't trust Garth. I followed them to London and then tried to do some amateur investigation of Garth's background. When I found out he had a fiancée and that no one seemed to know if she was still engaged to him or not, I called up Thérèse and arranged to meet her on Saturday evening. She didn't show up—since she was already dead by then—and after that I figured maybe I was making a fool of myself and it would be best if I went back to Paris. I got cold

feet, I guess. I didn't mention it to you because—well, I'd behaved stupidly, and—"

"I don't think it was stupid at all!" said Gina indignantly.
"I think it was just wonderful of you to be concerned over me!
When I think of all that trouble you went to—"

They gazed at each other in dizzy admiration, as if neither
could believe the fairytale slice of good fortune which had
befallen them. I began to feel distinctly '*de trop*'.

"Well," I began. "Now that that's all explained—"

The telephone rang. Gina, being nearest, picked up the receiver. "Hello? Oh, hel*lo!* Is everything—yes, thank you. Yes.
Who? *Claire?* Yes, she's right here. Just a moment." She turned
to me in surprise. "It's Garth," she said, and added mystified:
"He says he wants to speak to you. Do you suppose it's about
some new development?"

"No," I said. "This development has been going on for at
least four days." And I crossed the room towards the waiting
telephone.

"I should have let Gina speak to you on the phone when
you arrived in London," Garth said to me. "You had every
right to be angry with me for not being honest with you and
admitting I knew where she was, but the situation was so extraordinary and so dangerous that I was reluctant to involve
you. It seemed to me that the less you knew the better. If you
knew nothing I reasoned that you couldn't be a danger either
to yourself or to us. But I was wrong."

It was Saturday night, exactly a week since I had been sitting in my Manhattan apartment and trying to trace Gina's
call from Europe. Garth had taken me to dine at a penthouse
restaurant, and far below us, spread out in a panorama which
seemed to stretch into infinity, lay the lights of London, the
complex arteries of an enormous city pulsing with a life-force
two thousand years old.

"Have you forgiven me yet for not being quite honest with
you?"

"You were honest about the things that mattered. That's
all that counts." I was feeling too starry-eyed to take issue.

"But you didn't believe me! Why were you so convinced I preferred Gina to you?"

"Was I?" How could I explain that I assumed every attractive man preferred Gina to me?

"Yes, you were! Now you're the one who's not being quite honest! You thought all along that my feeling for you was assumed and couldn't possibly be genuine—"

"Well, it all happened so suddenly! And you *had* been dating Gina!"

"A few casual evenings out in Paris to take my mind off Thérèse—"

"And you did travel to London with her!" Once I got started it was hard to let up—my schoolteacher logic, I guess.

"Thanks to careful engineering on her part—"

"And she ended up by living in your apartment, cooking your meals—"

"Let's say she tried to cook. I hope Warren's handy in the kitchen, otherwise they'll both starve. Incidentally, how's your cooking?"

Far below us the lights of London pricked the darkness with dazzling brilliance. A passing waiter paused long enough to refill our champagne glasses from the bottle in the ice bucket.

"Well," I said, "I do a very very classic soft-boiled egg."

"Really? Just right for breakfast." He raised his glass to me with a smile and his light eyes were no longer unreadable. "To your classic boiled eggs!" he said lightly. "And to the first opportunity I have to sample one!"

We were married three months later.